GARRY DOUGLAS KILWORTH  the son of an RAF sergeant and from King's College London in American Literature. Later he served 15 years in the RAF himself. More recently he was with the British Army in Hong Kong (1988–91), where he wrote for *The South China Morning Post*. He now divides his time between Suffolk and Spain, writing full time. He has won many awards for both his children's and adult's novels.

Other novels by Garry Douglas Kilworth

Fancy Jack Crossman Novels:

The Winter Soldiers

The Devil's Own

Soldiers in the Mist

Other fiction:

Highlander

Witchwater Country

In The Hollow of The Deep-Sea Wave

Spiral Winds

House of Tribes

A Midsummer's Nightmare

The Navigator Kings trilogy

THE VALLEY OF DEATH

SERGEANT JACK CROSSMAN AND
THE BATTLE OF BALACLAVA

Garry Douglas Kilworth

ROBINSON
London

Constable & Robinson Ltd
3 The Lanchesters
162 Fulham Palace Road
London W6 9ER
www.constablerobinson.com

First published by HarperCollins*Publishers* 1998

This paperback edition published by Robinson,
an imprint of Constable & Robinson Ltd, 2002

A copy of the British Library Cataloguing in
Publication Data is available from the British Library

ISBN 1–84119–525–1

Printed and bound in the EU

10 9 8 7 6 5 4 3 2 1

*This second Crossman novel
is for my friend John Brosnan,
who said he enjoyed
the first one.*

Author's Note

Although many prime sources have been used for the research behind this novel, secondary sources have also been invaluable. I wish to acknowledge a debt of gratitude to the following works, authors and publishers:

The Russian Army of the Crimean War 1854–56, Robert H. G. Thomas and Richard Scollins, Osprey Military.

The British Army on Campaign 2 The Crimea 1854–56, Michael Barthorp and Pierre Turner, Osprey Military.

Uniforms and Weapons of the Crimean War, Robert Wilkinson-Latham, B. T. Batsford Ltd.

Battles of the Crimean War, W. Baring Pemberton, B. T. Batsford Ltd. (A wonderful volume!)

The Crimean Campaign with the Connaught Rangers 1854–56, Lieutenant-Colonel N. Steevens, Griffth and Farren.

Rifle Green in the Crimea, George Caldwell and Robert Cooper, Bugle Horne Publications.

The Crimean War, Denis Judd, Granada Publishing Ltd.

1854–1856 Crimea (The War with Russia from Contemporary Photographs), Lawrence James, Hayes Kennedy Ltd.

Heroes of the Crimea, Michael Barthorp, Blandford.

The Thin Red Line, John Selby, Hamish Hamilton.

George Lawson – Surgeon in the Crimea, edited letters explained by Victor Bonham-Carter, Constable and Co. Ltd.

Once again I should also like to thank David Cliff and the Crimean War Research Society, Major John Spiers (Retired) and David Greenwood, all of whom have aided and abetted me in some way or another in the writing of this novel.

The following are the names of real people who appear in this series:

Brigadier-General Buller
Marshal St Arnaud
Brigadier-General Pennefather
General Lord Raglan
Lieutenant-General Sir George Brown
Captain Nolan
Lieutenant-Colonel Shirley
Lord Clanrickarde
Prince Menshikoff
John Gorrie, inventor
William Cullen, inventor
Brigadier-General Lord Cardigan
William Howard Russell, *The Times* correspondent
Samuel Morse, inventor
Major-General Lord Lucan
Lieutenant-General Sir George De Lacy Evans
Major-General Sir Richard England
Lieutenant-General Sir George Cathcart
Lieutenant-General HRH The Duke of Cambridge
General Canrobert (Bob-Can't)
Dr James (Miranda) Barry
Mary Seacole, West Indian nurse
Prince Napoleon Joseph Bonaparte (Plon-Plon)
Carol Szathmari, photographer
G.S. MacLennan, bagpipe music composer
Brigadier-General Sir Colin Campbell
Brigadier-General Codrington
Colonel Troche
General Kvetzenski
General Gorchakov
General Kiriakov
General Bosquet
General Bouat
Captain Enisherloff

Colonel Lacy Yea
Lieutenant-Colonel Egerton
(Ensign?) Coney
General Airey
Brigadier-General Bentinck
Colonel Hood
Colonel Upton
Dasha Alexandrovna, Russian heroine
Henri Giffard, inventor
Lieutenant-Colonel Franz Edward Ivanovitch Todleben
Sir John Burgoyne, Raglan's Chief Engineer
Staff Assistant-Surgeon George Lawson
Captain Patrick Ferguson
Mrs Rogers
Florence Nightingale
Admiral Korniloff
Admiral Lyons
Admiral Dundas
Colonel Ainslie
Lord George Paget
Captain Maude
Captain Brandling
Brigadier-General Sir James Scarlett
Lieutenant Elliot
Colonel Dalrymple White
Colonel Griffith
Captain Ewart
Lieutenant Calthorpe
Captain Morris
Mr Upton
Captain Goodlake and his sharpshooters
Major Champion
Midshipman Hewett
Lieutenant Conolly
Sergeant Owens
John Broughton, boxing champion

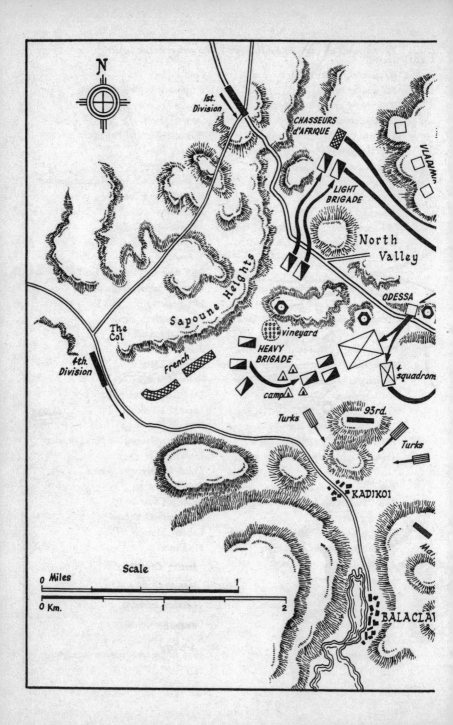

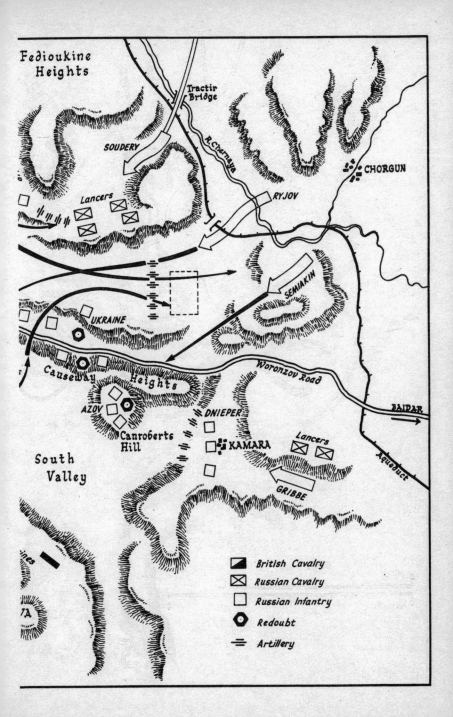

1

Sergeant Jack Crossman lay asleep on the bare boards of an upper-storey room in a hovel north of Balaclava. Normally he shared the room with Major Lovelace, his superior in matters of espionage and sabotage. Tonight Lovelace was out in the field, doing some dirty business alone. Crossman had just returned from a mission, or 'fox hunt' as it was known to insiders, and was resting before the next one.

A deep blue shadow slid on to the sill of the small, glassless window. The shape was almost invisible against the dark moonless sky behind him, though the stars were obliterated by his form as he crouched in the cavity, getting his eyes used to the darkness in the room. Once he could see, the figure dropped silently to the floor. Slowly he lifted his carbine, aiming at the sergeant.

As the man was squeezing the trigger a breeze from the window rustled the loose fabric of his *tchekman* tunic.

Crossman woke with a start to the smell of horse sweat and red cabbage. Seeing the dark figure, perhaps some phantom manifested from his dream, he cried out in supernatural fear. Luckily a soldier's rough instinct also made him roll quickly sideways.

The musket exploded, sounding like a cannon in the

confines of the room. A ball ripped into the floorboards where Crossman had lain and acrid blue smoke filled the air. The intruder dropped his smoking carbine and drew a sword. Crossman's personal revolver was wrapped in his greatcoat, which was being used as a pillow, but he found the handle of his German hunting knife on his belt. He whipped the knife from its sheath and plunged the blade into the man's boot, through his foot, pinning it to the floorboards.

No scream came from the wounded man's lips. Instead he snarled and slashed with his sabre at the sergeant on the floor, taking a piece of dark hair from the Ranger's head. The starlight glittered on the curved blade as the intruder took a second slash at Crossman, who rolled towards the window out of reach. His assailant was still nailed to the floor by the sturdy blade of the German hunting knife.

'Wynter, Peterson, Devlin!' yelled Crossman, calling for the men sleeping on the ground floor. ''Ware intruders!'

The soldiers below would have already been wakened by the shot a few seconds earlier and he did not want one of them running up the stone staircase to be stabbed at the top by this night assassin.

Having warned his men, the tall, lean sergeant leaped from the window, landing in the thick mud below. It was his intention to rush round the front, arm himself, and then go upstairs for the intruder. However, when he rolled on the ground a shot whined by his head and buried itself in the mud with a *plut*. A second figure came out of the darkness, rushing towards him, a drawn sabre in one hand and a pistol in the other.

Out here in the starlight, Crossman could see a little better. The intruders were wearing blue uniforms.

'Bloody Cossacks,' he said, aggrieved.

As the man dashed towards him, Crossman kicked out with both feet at the attacker's legs. The Cossack fell in the mud but tenaciously retained his grip on his weapons. Crossman got to his feet and despite the sucking mud managed to run round the corner. He hit something soft, which turned out to be the flank of a horse. There were two mounts being held by a third Cossack, ready for a quick retreat.

The Cossack holding the horses had been startled. His left hand was full of reins and his right held his own horse in check. He could not reach for his weapons without letting go of the jostling horses, which he was not inclined to do.

The struck mount whinnied and kicked, objecting to being butted in the stomach by a fleeing man. Crossman reached up and felt around the saddle, hoping to find a carbine. He found something, but it was not a weapon as such. It was thin and pliable. A whip, such as Don Cossacks carried.

There came a series of explosions from the house and something fell out of the window, landing in the mud below as a dead weight. This was the first Cossack, Crossman guessed, discovered by his men. The second came round the corner, shouting something to the man holding the horses. He whirled his sabre about his head, ready to strike at Crossman.

Crossman licked out with the whip, lashing the man across the face, keeping him at a distance. Red weals appeared on the Cossack's cheeks and brow. They began to bleed into his eyes, so that he had difficulty in seeing. Giving up on killing the sergeant, the Cossack sheathed his sword and tried to mount his horse, yelling something at his compatriot.

Out of the night came three rapid shots. The Cossack holding the horses immediately fell between the mounts. The horses now bolted, dragging the half-mounted second Cossack along the ground and slamming him into the side of a building. He climbed to his feet, staggered a few yards, and was then shot through the head by Peterson, who had come running out of the hovel into the muddy street.

Silence followed, the air smelling of gunpowder.

'Lord Almighty,' said Crossman, aware that only a very few minutes ago he had been fast asleep. 'I feel sick . . .'

'Did he get you at all, Sergeant?' cried Corporal Devlin. 'Are you hit?'

'No, no. I think I lost one of the curls my mother loved so much, but not my head, thank God. Thank you, Peterson, for getting the last one. Who shot the man in the saddle? Sounded like a revolver.'

'I did,' said a voice behind them, and Major Lovelace stepped out of the shadows, looking like a Mongolian horse breeder in a ragged fur cap, a civilian sheepskin coat, and baggy Turkish trousers. 'It's a good job I came back when I did.'

The horses, having plunged off into the night, were to be seen no more. From their tents and bivouacs, soldiers were calling, asking what was the matter. Devlin yelled out that all was now well. The incident had passed. There was no longer any cause for alarm.

Lovelace said, 'You sure you're all right, Sergeant?'

'Yes, thank you. I was fast asleep when the first one came into my room. I thought it was the devil, come for me.'

Peterson, at his elbow, murmured, 'Thought it was Skuggs, more like, come to take his revenge.'

Crossman glared. The slight but grim-looking Lance Corporal Peterson was a woman in disguise. This fact was unknown to everyone but Sergeant Crossman, who had caught her washing at a rain barrel one morning. There were more than a few such women on campaign in the Crimea. Some had cut their hair short and joined to be with their husbands, some were camp-followers who had taken to wearing the uniforms of dead soldiers and some, like Peterson, wanted simply to take part in the excitement of a war. She wanted to do the things men did, at the same time receiving pay for it. Back in England Peterson might have been a destitute female. Out here she was Lance Corporal Peterson, crackshot with a rifle. It was mainly because of her prowess with a weapon that Crossman kept her gender a secret and retained her in his *peloton*.

Now she waited behind for an answer once the others had gone inside the hovel. Crossman did not like the fact that she was so close to being right. It was true the sergeant had engineered the death of Skuggs, a soldier who had murdered one of his comrades during the Battle of the Alma in order to protect himself. Crossman had all but witnessed the murder carried out by Skuggs but had no proof. Skuggs knew that and had attempted to kill the sergeant on more than one occasion.

Peterson had been present at Skuggs' 'execution'.

'Skuggs is dead,' said Crossman. 'You know that, Peterson.'

'I believe in ghosts, Sergeant. Don't you? Murdered men – why they never rest after death until they've got their revenge.'

Her eyes did not leave his face. She knew nothing of Skuggs' crimes. Crossman had not enlightened her.

Crossman said, 'Skuggs was shot down by a company of Russian riflemen.'

'And we know who sent him to them, don't we, Sergeant?'

'You know nothing, Peterson – nothing at all – and you're not going to know. It's for your own protection. If I have nightmares, it's not because I'm feeling guilty about anything to do with Skuggs' death.'

She shook her head in disbelief, but let the matter drop, following the others inside the hovel.

One of the men now lit a lamp. Wynter and Devlin were ordered to put the three bodies in the woodshed, ready for collection in the morning. They found the first one under the first-floor window, crumpled in the mud where he had taken three Minié rounds in the chest. Wynter and Devlin both claimed to have hit him first as he was climbing back out of the window, a perfect target.

'I don't doubt you'll be getting a few more of these visits,' said Lovelace, untying his boots. 'Those Cossacks are from the company you and your men ambushed on the Fedioukine Hills two days ago. It's my guess they know who you are – the fact that you're a special group detached from the 88th Connaught Rangers. You'll have to watch your back more closely.'

'You think they know me personally?' asked Crossman, raising his eyebrows. 'How could that be?'

Major Lovelace shrugged. 'A spy in our camp? One of the Greeks or Tartars. They can do it too, you know. You killed quite a few of those Cossacks. They're not a forgiving bunch. They'll want your hide very badly after such a humiliation.'

Peterson was watching Major Lovelace in frustration as he struggled with his second boot, trying unsuccessfully to remove it from a fatigue-swollen, sweaty foot.

'Shall I send for your batman, sir?' she suggested.

'No, damn it, I can take off my own boots, sir. I've just been into Sebastopol and back, through the Russian sentries and sailors working on the defences. I can certainly undress myself.'

But despite his protestations, it did not look like it. Finally Peterson could stand it no longer and though she detested the upper class and their frail efforts to care for themselves, she straddled his leg and tugged off the muddy, stubborn boot.

'Thank you, Peterson.'

Major Lovelace then proceeded to remove the sheepskins, until he stood in only his shirt.

'You'll have to excuse me,' he said. 'Those damn sheepskins are full of lice. I couldn't bear them a moment longer. Hand me those trousers lying on the back of that chair over there, will you, Peterson, there's a good chap.'

Peterson, flaming red, did as she was asked, much to the amusement of Crossman.

Once Lovelace was dressed, Crossman proceeded to question him further on his earlier work.

'Now, sir, these Cossacks. You say they're out looking for me?'

'Those were Cossack assassins. They usually work in threes. Didn't you know they're sending out these troikas after you? They know what you did at the farmhouse in the north, where you ambushed them before, and on your other fox hunts. They seem to think you've got it in for them.'

6

'Troika? That's a three-horse Russian carriage.'

'It's their name for a triad of assassins – the carriage is implicit – it's an invisible hearse. So far as they're concerned, it's Sergeant Crossman's *peloton* against the Cossacks, and they're determined to get you.'

'But,' protested Crossman, 'it's simply bad luck that we run into Cossacks all the time. Damn it, they're all over the place, like cockroaches. You can't take a breath of fresh air without running into Cossacks. What am I supposed to do, wave at them and send them on their jolly way?'

Lovelace shrugged and poured himself a glass of wine.

'I'm just warning you, that's all. They're after me too. There's a price on both our heads.'

Wynter and Devlin were now back in the room.

Wynter said, 'And on our'n, surely? We must 'ave got a price on us too? It an't fair if we've not.'

Crossman could not believe his ears.

'Good God, Wynter, why would you want troikas coming after you? Don't you understand it means fighting the war on two fronts? It's all right to meet the enemy face to face, but when they're hunting you down in packs in the middle of the night, well that's plain victimization. If you want to be assassinated, I'm sure one of your fellow soldiers would do it for you – I've heard them threaten often enough to do so.'

Wynter looked round at his 'fellow soldiers' in a shocked and angry fashion. 'Who? Who wants to turn me off?'

'Just about everyone,' growled Devlin, 'when you've got a snoring fit on you.'

'That's enough,' said Crossman. 'All of you get some sleep – you'll need it.'

Grumbling at each other, the men went back to their beds on the floor of the hovel. Crossman and Lovelace remained at the small rickety table in the centre of the room. Major Lovelace turned the lamp down low. He offered Crossman a glass of wine and the sergeant took it. They sipped in silence, each lost in his own contemplations.

The men were just beginning to recover from the flank march down through the Crimea to Balaclava harbour in the south. Having won the first battle at the River Alma against the Russians, the British, French and Turkish allies, numbering some 36,000 men, had set out too late to turn the Russian retreat south into a rout from which they could not recover. French insistence that they go back for the knapsacks their soldiers had left on the ground before the battle, and their Commander-in-Chief, Marshal St Arnaud's, illness, had prevented following up their victory. Now the Russian army had escaped to the east and were probably preparing for another attack on the allied forces.

The southern harbour city of Sebastopol, on the west coast of the Crimea, was the prime target of the allies and they had marched south to take it. However, St Arnaud argued they should not attack the north of the city, but skirt round it and attack the underbelly from the south. He was supported in this by Sir John Burgoyne, the chief engineer of the British force.

Lord Raglan, Commander-in-Chief of the British army, allowed himself to be persuaded to fall in once more with French plans. It was a fact he could not do without the French, for his army was not powerful enough to take on the Russians alone. The British had lost over two thousand men at the Battle of the Alma: three hundred or so left dead on the battlefield, and many dying of wounds later. Injured survivors were shipped across the Black Sea to Scutari Barracks Hospital outside Constantinople.

Raglan's grumbles – for he still favoured attacking the north of Sebastopol while the Royal Navy pounded the south from the sea – filtered down to the troops. The regimental officers and soldiers of the line felt a little frustrated. Most thought a quick attack on the north would finish the war, but General Canrobert, now in command of the French as they reached the city, agreed with the dying Marshal St Arnaud's strategy.

Even as the British were settling in and around the southern harbour of Balaclava, which they had taken with only a few rounds of mortar, Raglan was still pressing for an immediate attack. Burgoyne and the French now argued that Sebastopol's defences should be levelled before an attack took place on the south. The British forces had to spread themselves thinly between Sebastopol and Balaclava, a distance of approximately six miles.

Meanwhile Prince Menshikoff's Russian army had gathered itself together and now lurked somewhere in the eastern hills.

Most of the British officers, and indeed many among the ranks, felt a chance had been missed and that the war looked like being a protracted business because of it. The Christmas of 1854 was approaching and though some still cared whether the Russians took over the Turkish Empire, many thought they were on a hiding to nothing. They wanted to be home with their loved ones when the New Year was celebrated.

Thus the siege had begun. While the Russians daily applied their feverish brains and hands to the task of reinforcing Sebastopol's defences, the allies dug themselves in and failed to make an early assault. They simply watched the fortifications getting stronger and higher, the rank and file growing restless with frustration at this lack of initiative by their commanders. A short war would have been in everyone's best interest, even that of the losers, whoever they might be.

Now, while Crossman and Lovelace drank their wine in silence the dawn began to penetrate the hovel, entering with grey fingers through cracks in the door and through the glassless windows. Crossman made some coffee by roasting the beans in a frying pan, then placing them in a six-inch shell casing and grinding them with a cannonball. It was not good coffee, but it helped to clear the head before the start of the day.

'Well done, Crossman,' said Lovelace, 'you make the best of a bad job.'

'I feel like your fag,' Crossman replied wryly. 'Making you toast and tea of a Sunday afternoon.'

The two men had both been to Harrow before fortune took them in different directions. Crossman, whose real name was Alexander Kirk, remembered the more senior Lovelace, but the other man had only Crossman's word for it that he had been at the famous school. Older boys rarely remember younger ones, who look to those above as heroes or bullies, and, either way, recall their elders well.

'If you are, you made yourself so. You have never told me why you chose to join the ranks under an assumed name – oh, don't look at me like that, I've made a few enquiries and there was no Crossman at Harrow, ever. Why did you not purchase yourself a commission? Could you not afford it?'

Crossman turned away, trying to keep the bitterness out of his voice and not succeeding. 'I had some trouble with my father.'

'Ah, I see – the old man wouldn't put up the money for a commission, eh?' murmured Lovelace, coming to a natural but false conclusion.

But Crossman's father was Major Kirk of the 93rd Sutherland Highlanders, and Crossman's older brother, James, served in the same regiment as a lieutenant. He, Crossman, could have joined his brother with a commission purchased for him by his father, but he hated the old man, who had been an utter bully to his wife and sons. When Crossman found out he was illegitimate, the son of a maid whom his father had seduced and then had committed to the workhouse where she subsequently died, he left home and joined the ranks under an assumed name.

A sudden banging on the door saved Crossman replying.

'Enter!' cried Lovelace.

A company sergeant from the 44th Foot opened the door and peered inside.

'Major Lovelace, sir?' he called.

'What is it, man?'

'You're to report to General Buller, sir.'

Lovelace raised his eyebrows, knowing there was more to come. He had just left Brigadier-General Buller, the commander of the Light Division's 2nd Brigade. Something must have happened rather unexpectedly for him to be called back to see the general so soon after reporting.

The company sergeant continued, 'Marshal St Arnaud died of his illness in the night. General Canrobert is meeting with General Raglan at this moment.'

Lovelace sighed. 'Thank you, Sergeant. I'm on my way.' He turned to Crossman. 'So the old boy has rattled his last breath and we have Bob-Can't permanently in the saddle. Sad. Arnaud was a grand warrior. One of the old school, of course, not like you and me, Sergeant. We're the sharp new men under Buller's command. Lord Raglan doesn't like us. He thinks we're "skulkers".'

'Maybe he's right. Maybe battles should be fought in an honourable fashion, with no skulduggery.'

Lovelace pulled on his boots. 'You think there's no honour in spying and sabotage? I think it's part and parcel of war, Sergeant. I would rather sneak around a bit in the dark, find out a few facts, and thus prevent several regiments from marching into slaughter, than just throw them against an unknown force and hope for the best. Wouldn't you?'

'Isn't it *fate* when a man dies in battle?'

'No, Sergeant, it isn't. When a man stumbles into a previously undiscovered cave and a ten-million-year-old stalactite falls from the ceiling and kills him stone-dead – *that*'s fate, my dear fellow. When a man dies on the battlefield, that's lack of knowledge and planning. Now, hand me that sword, there's a good chap.'

Crossman had to agree that Lord Raglan seemed to have no plan whatsoever before the Battle of the Alma. He had marched his troops to the top of the heights, then marched the remnants down again, without any real understanding of what they were up against or how they were to defeat the enemy. Only the fortitude and initiative of the men in the field had won the day for the British and their allies.

Planning.

The whole war was a shambles as far as planning was concerned. Many of the men were wearing threadbare uniforms with holes, some were shirtless, some were even bootless. Any tents the soldiers had were so old they were rotting at the seams. Now that the British held the harbour of Balaclava it was expected that supplies would come from England, but there were appalling delays due to masses of paperwork and red tape.

Not a blanket could be ordered without the request going through seven independent departments for approval back in England. Even when something arrived in the Crimea, a certificate was needed to allow it to be unpacked, which often did not accompany the goods and so had to be sent for back to England.

The ambulance wagons so desperately needed on the battlefield of the Alma had been off-loaded at Varna and were still not in the Crimea. Surgeons had very little equipment, even lacking candles so they could not work after darkness fell. It was an appalling mess.

Crossman had seen severed limbs tossed carelessly away by surgeons after the Alma. Because of the lack of wagons the dead were dragged by their heels to open pits and thrown unceremoniously in. Wounded men were left out all night on the slopes, pleading for water. This is how the men who had fought at the Alma, heroes every one, had been treated.

The lack of organization and the insensitivity of the high command made Crossman grit his teeth in anger as he entered the downstairs room.

'Stop grinding your jaw, whoever that is,' growled Wynter from under his blanket. 'There's people tryin' to sleep.'

'Time you were up in any case,' snapped Crossman. 'Come on, you lot – up, up, up. The dawn's been with us for some time now. I'm expecting orders for a fox hunt today. I want you men ready, willing and very able.'

The two men and the woman rose, grumbling to themselves, but it was tiredness and discomfort that caused their low spirits, not the prospect of dangers ahead.

2

Once again there was a hammering on the door of the hovel and this time it was the major's batman who was the caller.

'What is it?' asked Crossman. 'Do you want Major Lovelace?'

'No, Sergeant,' grinned the soldier. 'It's you.'

'Well, out with it, man.'

'It's the Connaught Rangers, Sergeant,' said the soldier cheerfully. 'There's a brawl. Your regiment's Grenadier Company was sent down from Careenage Ravine to forage for wood, but they got to the orchard at the same time as some Scotchmen. They're still fightin' now, out by the orchard wall. Some kiltie made a remark about the 88th's colours still being encased after our bash at the Alma River and an Irishman hit him. That started it goin', and it went on from there. There's hell to pay.'

The men with fearful oaths, from Counties Mayo, Galway, Clare and Sligo, raised in Connaught by Lord Clanrickarde, were at it again!

'The damn colours *were* still encased after the battle,' grumbled Crossman. What's that got to do with anything?'

'He said it like an insult, Sergeant, like you was ashamed to show which regiment you was from. And that's the way the Irish took it.'

14

'They damn well would. And I suppose that's good reason to give a man a facer. It would be the Scots, of course. They enjoy a fight as much as men from my regiment. Why am I sent for? Aren't there other people there to sort it out? Where's the company sergeant-major?'

'He's there,' grinned the corporal, who seemed to be enjoying himself. 'It's him what sent me for you.'

Mystified, Sergeant Crossman hastily made his appearance as smart as possible and then accompanied the corporal to the orchard, where there were still men in trousers punching men in kilts, and vice versa, with NCOs trying to part them and catching blows themselves. The company sergeant-major was standing nearby, watching and fuming, holding a private by the collar so that the man's toes hardly touched the ground.

'Sarn-Major?' said Crossman. 'You sent for me?'

The big, barrel-chested Irish sergeant-major's eyes glowed with a strange light as he beheld Crossman. There is nothing so terrifying in the army as a sergeant-major in a cold fury. Such creatures have power emanating from them surpassing even that of God. The mind dwells on the summary stripping of rank . . . swift justice on the wheel – and even hanging does not seem to be out of the question. Crossman quailed inside.

'Ah, 'tis the wayward sergeant, come to see us, is it? Where have you been, my fine rooster? Canoodling with your officer friends, is that it?'

Crossman came to attention before the company sergeant-major.

'I came as quickly as I could – but I have no idea why I've been called.'

The sergeant-major jerked the soldier he was holding by the collar like an angler shaking a freshly caught fish.

The man had a bloody nose, a visibly swelling ear, and a piece of yellow facing had been torn from his red coatee. He looked a sorry mess.

'You don't, eh? Well, you see this piece of rag I'm holding here, with some useless lump of lard inside it? This belongs to you, Sergeant. I believe they call it Private Clancy in moments of enlightenment. You know who Private Clancy is, Sergeant?'

'My new man,' sighed Crossman.

'Ex-actly. And do you know why I'm just a little displeased with this slug in uniform?'

'It's my guess, Sarn-Major, that Clancy started the fight.'

'Be-Jesus, you're a bright man, to be sure, Sergeant. No wonder the officers in the staff tents love you. It's your fine brain they're after, I'm certain of that, for your common sense is nowhere to be seen. Get this snail's shit out of my sight quickly, before I nail him to the nearest apple tree and make a martyr of him before my battered troops.'

'Yes, Sarn-Major.'

Clancy was released. He quickly grabbed his forage cap from the ground. Crossman took his sleeve and led him away.

Clancy was a handsome young man with a dark complexion and thick black hair. He was probably not more than nineteen. Something about his bearing and demeanour told Crossman he was born and bred in the city. Most of the men in the Army of the East had been recruited from the countryside, from farms and villages, but the odd one from the city was there too.

'It wasn't my fault,' said Clancy, in a strange accent. He sniffed the blood running from his nose back up his nostrils where, miraculously it seemed to Crossman, it stayed. Then he tenderly felt a split lip before finishing his statement. 'That Scotchman shouldn't have remarked on the colours. They were just forgot, that's all. It wasn't a purposeful thing, to keep them cased. I hate Scotchmen.'

'It's *Scotsmen* – and I'm one myself, Clancy.'

The dark man gave Crossman a sidelong glance.

'Well, I didn't mean *posh* Scotch – *Scotsmen*. I meant them Glasgow soldiers. You can't even understand what they're saying, half the time. They've got mouths full of marbles.'

16

'You seem to have understood that one all right.'

'He made it plain with his laugh,' growled Clancy, recalling the incident. 'I *had* to hit him, Sergeant. None of the other lads would have spoken to me again if I hadn't. You understand that?' His next remark was a little mournful in tone. 'They don't speak to me much anyway.'

'Is it because you're a gypsy?' asked Crossman, with a little sidelong glance.

'I'm no gypsy,' cried Clancy indignantly. 'I was brought up in Dublin, I was. I'm Anglo-Indian. My father was an Irish merchant who married a lady when he was in India. I've had an education, Sergeant. I can read and write.'

There was just something in the tone of this man's speech which caused Crossman to question him.

'Your father, a merchant, married an Indian lady?'

The young man hung his head a little. 'I suppose he wasn't exactly a merchant – he was a merchant's clerk. And they weren't really married – but, when my mother died,' he added with fierce pride, his head coming up again, 'my father took me back to Ireland with him and sent me to school.'

'You're hardly *Anglo*-Indian then, are you? More like Irish-Indian. There's a mixture to conjure with. What was your mother? Afghan? Sikh?'

'Just a lady from Bombay. An untouchable, my father told me. She expired of a lung disease some time before he was sent back to Ireland.'

'A very fine lady, I'm sure,' said Crossman. 'One's mother is always fine. My own was – in a sense – an untouchable. One of the English untouchables . . .' He stopped there, realizing he had already said too much.

Crossman said, 'Now that you're with my little *peloton*, you'll behave yourself, is that clear?'

'*Peloton?* What's that?'

'It's French for "little ball" – it's what Major Lovelace calls our small band. Lance Corporal Wynter and the other soldiers

17

are not as familiar with French as they might be – they pronounce it "platoon". That's by the by, Clancy. You will behave yourself, understood?'

'Yes, Sergeant.' He took another quick look at Crossman as they walked along. 'You're – you're the one they call Fancy Jack, aren't you? The gentleman in the ranks.'

Crossman halted and Clancy halted with him.

'I'm the one they call Sergeant Crossman of the 88th Foot, Connaught Rangers – and don't you ever forget it.'

'Yes, Sergeant,' replied Clancy in a small voice. 'I won't forget.'

When they reached the hovel Crossman went in before Clancy and announced to the others that they had a new man, a private, who would be part of the team. Clancy came in then, smiling shyly. The others stared at him for a moment. Then, predictably, Wynter spoke.

'A bloody Fuzzy-Wuzzy! What are they sendin' us black men for? An't we got enough trouble without havin' to babysit smoothy-faced Anglo-Banglos?'

The smile immediately left Clancy's face and he stepped forward ready to strike Wynter a blow.

'Clancy,' cried Crossman, 'remember what I told you! Wynter, if you want to keep that stripe you'd better learn to watch your tongue. I won't have that kind of talk amongst my men, is that clear? You raggedy-arsed country boy, what makes you so superior to this man? The colour of your skin? I've just seen Clancy here fell three Glaswegians with one blow. He may look bookish, but he's a brute underneath. He's half-Indian. His uncle was a Thug, which means he'll cut your balls off while you sleep if you mess with him too much. I've seen it done. These men don't draw their blades without letting blood. Be very careful of Clancy, Wynter.'

'Yeah?' said Wynter, in a failing voice.

Major Lovelace came through the door at this moment, having heard the exchange from just outside.

'Yes, Wynter. The sergeant's right. The Thugs are a secret

society in India — assassins born and bred. They also use the garrotte to deadly effect — which is why I requested young Clancy here. He's a past master at throttling men, awake or asleep, it makes no difference to him.'

Wynter's eyes were round and wary and he went back to his corner of the room to study this knife-wielding strangler from a distance. Clancy quietly thanked Crossman for playing up his role in the fight with the Scots, and the sergeant noted his modesty, for he knew that what he and Lovelace had claimed for the young man was otherwise true.

'Leave it for the moment,' he said. 'Accept a little respect for nothing — you can earn it later.'

'Thank you, Sergeant.'

Crossman went to the door of the hovel to smoke his chibouque, his long Turkish pipe, which helped to calm his nerves despite the harsh nature of the Tartar tobacco. He fell into contemplations on a range of subjects from natural history to engineering. Crossman had a lively mind when it came to science, though he was the first to admit his enthusiasm could be boring to others.

He and his American friend, Rupert Jarrard, the war correspondent for the *New York Banner*, often fell into discussions over the latest inventions and discoveries, be they farm implements or new medicines. Jarrard, an ex-frontiersman, took men as he found them, whether they were sergeants or colonels. There was nothing of the snob in him and he often sought Crossman's company.

Of course, Rupert Jarrard was forever looking for a good story, and he knew there to be a peach of a tale somewhere inside Crossman's family history. There had to be a pocketful of secrets in the trousers of a gentleman joining the rank and file of a rough Irish regiment like the Connaught Rangers. However, there was genuine friendship between the two men and Jarrard hadn't pressed unwanted questions.

Rupert was up at the front today, watching Sebastopol from a distance as the enemy built their defences, making barbettes, constructing earthworks with soil packed in gabions and baskets, right before the very eyes of the allies.

Everyone on the allied side was screaming for an assault on the city – everyone but the top generals – and the frustrations amongst the regimental officers and their men were growing daily. It seemed madness to give the Russians so much time to prepare for an attack, but the French would not make an assault without a bombardment first, and for some reason they claimed they were not yet in any position to use their guns. Along with the battle casualties the British army had been severely depleted by disease, and Raglan felt his troops could not make an attack alone.

Crossman sighed. The whole war was faltering. The allies could have struck fatal blows on several occasions over the past few days, but had failed to do so. It was madness.

Suddenly he almost choked on the smoke from his chibouque, and quickly ducked inside the doorway.

Past the hovel ran the mud road down to Balaclava, which had been churned to a quagmire by the *araba* carts, wagons, batteries of field artillery, cavalry and other traffic using it. The British had again come off badly in their choice of ground. They were now on the right, a position of honour relinquished by the stronger force, the French, but it was a bad one, stretching Raglan's thin lines and plaguing him with long supply routes from the harbour to his troops.

Down this long boggy track came a young woman on horseback, riding sidesaddle and wearing a charcoal-grey dress. On her head was a pretty riding hat tied with a white chiffon scarf. She was the wife of Captain Durham, a quartermaster, and her name Crossman knew to be Lavinia Alice. She rode her bay well, using the whip only to tap the beast's flank when its hooves slipped in the mud.

She sat tall and confident in the saddle, exchanged sunny smiles with those subalterns and generals who passed her on the road, and looked for all the world as if she were hacking in St James's Park of a Sunday afternoon. It was said she had something of a reputation, had many followers, and was fond of a bloody battle. To get to the Crimea, which had been forbidden to 'ladies', she had to disguise herself as a common soldier's wife. Lord Cardigan had invited her to stay on his yacht and had loaned her the horse.

'Why are you duckin' out of sight?' asked Wynter, peering over Crossman's shoulder. What's out there?'

'None of your business,' said Crossman testily. 'You look to cleaning your weapon.'

Wynter shook his head thoughtfully. 'It's that woman, an't it? Mrs Durham, the Vulture . . .'

'You keep a civil tongue in your head,' snapped Crossman. 'If an officer catches you talking of a lady like that, you'll have your back skinned on the wheel.'

'Sorry, Sergeant, I'm sure,' replied Wynter, not at all contrite. 'I'm just repeating gossip. You know what they say about her. Anyway, what's interestin' is that you seem scared of her seeing you. Why would that be, I wonder?'

'It's not her,' lied Crossman. 'It's the corporal, walking the other way. I owe him money, if you must know. A gambling debt.'

'You owe gambling money? I don't believe it. All right, I an't going to say nothing about her. I just think it's interestin', that's all. I mean, I know why some young lieutenants might well need to duck down behind doorways when the Vulture comes along – but a sergeant in the 88th Foot? Now that's something to think about.'

At that moment Crossman was saved by the appearance of Lieutenant Dalton-James, who strode up to the doorway. The lieutenant peered within the hovel. He curled his bottom lip in distaste of the interior.

'Ten-shun!' cried Crossman, 'Officer in the room.'

Dalton-James, of the 2nd Rifle Brigade, stepped inside. He was dressed in one of his immaculate green uniforms, which appeared black in the dimness of the hovel. Since arriving at Balaclava Dalton-James had acquired his travelling trunks, full of such necessary kit as a silver egg timer and an ebony walking stick with a bone goosehead handle – and his gentleman's wardrobe, of course. The whole had come by sea from Constantinople and Crossman could not help but wonder what important cargo had been left behind in Turkey to make room for the lieutenant's fripperies.

Still looking around him Dalton-James remarked, 'You have yourself some fine quarters here, Sergeant. There are men up on the line who are still bivouacking in the open.'

'We're extremely lucky, sir.'

'I should say so, even though the place smells like a pigsty.'

'That would be Major Lovelace's socks,' muttered Wynter. 'He's left 'em out for an airing.'

Normally the wrath of Dalton-James would have fallen on Wynter for this insubordinate remark, except that the lieutenant had been so taken aback to learn his senior officer was a member of the household he actually lost his colour.

'Major Lovelace? Here?'

'Not here at the moment,' Crossman said, 'but he keeps a room above as his emergency billet.'

'Oh,' replied Dalton-James, still a little ruffled. 'That remark I made referred only to *this* room, you understand. I want no tattle-tales running to Major Lovelace with elaborate stories.'

'Wouldn't dream of it, sir,' said Crossman, suppressing a smile. 'Did you wish to speak with me?'

'Yes, yes. A fox hunt, Sergeant. Gather round the table, you rabble.'

Crossman and his men learnt that they were to go out into the hills to intercept a caravan on its way from Sebastopol to St Petersburg.

'A cargo arrived by ship in Sebastopol from the Americas,' explained Dalton-James, 'just prior to the arrival of our fleet. This was a shipment of arms which we understand the Russians are keen to get to St Petersburg. They cannot transport it by sea now, since the port is blockaded, so they're

trying to convey the consignment overland to Yalta by caravan. You must find this caravan. If you can convey the goods
it carries back here, then by all means do so, but if there's any
chance they will get back into enemy hands, destroy them.'

'What are these *goods*?' asked Crossman.

'Rifles,' replied Dalton-James. 'Fifty of them. Ferguson
rifles. On no account are they to reach St Petersburg. These
are breech-loaders which have fallen into Russian hands. If
they get them to St Petersburg they'll copy the design and be
turning out weapons superior to those we ourselves use.'

'Oh?' said Peterson, who thought her Minié rifle was better
than any other weapon in the world.

'It's called irony, Peterson,' Crossman said to her. 'We make
a breech-loading rifle, the Russians obtain it and use it against
us, while we continue to use our inferior barrel-loaders.' He
turned to Dalton-James. 'Why do we still use barrel-loading
weapons if we've invented a breech-loader?'

'Breech-loaders are expensive weapons,' replied the lieutenant. 'We'll get them one day.'

'How will we recognize these particular rifles?'

'They've 35-inch-long barrels, 15 bore, 8 grooves in the
rifling.'

'I've never heard of a Ferguson,' said Peterson, 'and I know
my rifles.'

Dalton-James said, 'Your job is to follow orders, Corporal,
not to question them.'

'Yes, sir,' muttered Peterson sullenly.

'What about the carriers?' asked Crossman. 'What do we
do with them?'

'Execute them.'

Peterson said, 'Can't we take some of them prisoner, sir,
them that give up? I mean, it's not a battle. It's a bit like
murdering someone in cold blood.'

'This is war, Corporal. There's no room for sentiment. Now
down to details, Sergeant . . .'

An hour later Crossman and his four soldiers, plus Yusuf

Ali, the Bashi-Bazouk irregular fiercely loyal to Crossman, were taken to a spot south of the Woronzoff Road, which ran over the Causeway Heights. Ali had managed to scrounge a mule and cart with its driver, another Bashi-Bazouk, to convey them this far. They had a lot of walking and climbing to do and needed to save their bootleather.

They were a rough-looking bunch.

Lance Corporal Wynter was a surly Essex farm boy, a bit too knowing for his own good, inclined to disobey orders from time to time. Of medium height, he was lean and strong, and good enough in a battle. Corporal Devlin was a married man from County Kildare, much more reliable than Wynter, which was why Crossman had chosen to recommend him for corporal over the others. Then there was Lance Corporal Peterson, square-jawed and slight, a brilliant shot with a rifle. Private Clancy, the new man who had replaced Skuggs, had yet to show Crossman his worth.

With them, but not of them, was the Turk. Yusuf Ali had been described by Wynter as looking like 'a renegade Santa Claus' with his white beard, his multi-coloured waistcoats and pantaloons, and his corpulent appearance. He was, however, all muscle and a walking arsenal, carrying several pistols, a carbine and more knives than the regiment's Officers' Mess cutlery box.

Dalton-James had explained that a caravan of mules had last been seen climbing behind the Fedioukine Hills above the North Valley. Major Lovelace, out on one of his spying missions, had discovered that this was the caravan carrying the Ferguson rifles. Lovelace enjoyed the cloak-and-dagger side of the work, leaving people like Crossman's band to execute the plan.

The soldiers were dressed like the Bashi-Bazouk, in an odd assortment of local apparel, such as the Tartars would wear. They had scrounged and purchased these items from various friends of Yusuf Ali, having learned quickly that a red uniform is not the best mode of dress for guerrillas scouring enemy hills. Crossman himself looked even more fierce than Ali, in a sheepskin jacket, baggy black trousers held up by a blue sash and a ragged turban hiding his black hair.

His men now carried Victoria carbines, obtained for them by Major Lovelace, to replace the unwieldy Miniés. The carbine had a 26-inch-long barrel, as opposed to the 39-inch-long Minié rifle.

Peterson hated the Victoria carbine, pronouncing it a 'pig's snout', but she knew that dragging a rifle through the hills was the greater of two evils.

'It's worse than the Brunswick, this thing,' she said. 'I bet the dragoons hate it too.'

'They detest it,' confirmed Crossman. 'I was talking to a trooper the other day who said George Lovell should be put up against a wall and shot with his own inventions, except that the firing squad would probably miss with them.'

The evening came in over the western hills, splendid in its autumn cloak. Ali found a cave for the group to rest in during the night, but Crossman posted his men up on high points until the darkness fell, hoping for an early sight of the caravan they sought. When nothing was seen, the men were brought down and sentries posted. Crossman sat up with Ali, discussing the possible tracks the caravan might use.

It was cold up in the heights, with a chill wind coming from the north, and when he finally retired Crossman slept fitfully. His half-awake thoughts were of a woman in a charcoal-grey dress. Guilt promenaded through his dreams.

3

They're called *dragoons*, said Clancy to Wynter, 'because they once carried Dragon firearms.'

'Oh, is that so, Mr Clever Dick? So why was the firearms called Dragons?'

'Because they had a picture of a dragon etched on them, that's why,' replied Clancy. 'I thought everyone knew that. It's pretty common knowledge.'

Crossman half-listened to these exchanges between the handsome baby-faced Clancy, and Wynter with his pocked and pitted skin, his turnip complexion, with some amusement. The new man was beginning to find his feet amongst his fellow soldiers. They kept testing him in various ways, as such men will do, to find his weaknesses and his strengths.

Wynter foolishly kept challenging him on points of knowledge, giving the Irish-Indian a clear advantage in every conversation, for Wynter knew very little about anything except staying alive and keeping his money to himself.

'Wynter, Clancy, we need water. Take the water bottles down to the stream at the bottom of the hill and fill them, *if* you please,' ordered Crossman.

'I just come off picquet duty,' cried Wynter.

'And Peterson and Devlin are still on duty, which leaves

you and Clancy,' Crossman snapped. 'Get to it, man, before you feel the toe of my boot.'

Wynter began to collect the water bottles – wooden kegs bound with metal hoops that held half a gallon of fluid – still grumbling like mad.

'What about the Turk?' he muttered. 'Don't he have to do his share?'

'"The Turk" is out scouting the territory ahead so that you and I don't walk into an ambush,' growled Crossman. 'I'm not going to tell you again, Wynter.'

Clancy had gathered his share of the bottles and stood by the entrance to the cave, waiting for Wynter. The pair of them went down the slope together. Crossman could hear Clancy telling Wynter that it was a shame the sergeant always picked on him, for he was in Clancy's opinion, a fine fellow of a man, and willing as well, if left to his own choice.

Wynter would be lapping up this flattery, Crossman knew, and as the sergeant in question he did not mind being the target of Clancy's criticism, if it meant that it bonded the two men together. Sergeants were supposed to be the bogeymen. Crossman would rather his soldiers got on well together than praise him for his fine leadership and qualities of supervision.

Alone in the cave, he began to pack his gear in the leather bag that served as his knapsack. He tightly rolled his sheepskin coat, used as a blanket at night, securing it with a piece of cord. It would be hot on the march through the hills, even at the end of September. Then he lit his chibouque, took out a notebook and pencil, and began to add to his journal, parts of which he reused in letters to the woman he had always known as Mother.

I have never known so many qualities of rain as they have here in the Crimea, he wrote. *You have your thin rain, usually in the early morning and your heavy afternoon rain which falls down directly as if it were poured from buckets. There is a side-swiping rain, which drenches one's front or back, but leaves the other side of the body irritatingly dry. There is a kind of Irish mizzle, visible as drifting clouds of moisture, which fills the whole atmosphere around, soaking one to the very marrow of one's bones, filling one's lungs with every damp breath. There is rain which comes down as hard as nails and soft plopping rain which comes out of a clear sky, each huge drop of which spreads on one's greatcoat like a blob of ink on blotting paper. Sometimes the rain washes and floods over the ground, gushing over it to form wide rivers of muddy water. On other occasions it drums on the hard earth arousing musty odours but nothing more. It can be freezing cold, or warm and insidious. It can come at a moment's notice, or it can grow slowly in volume and pace over a number of hours. The Crimean rain is not to be taken for granted. It insists on being regarded . . .*

As he was writing, a dark shadow filled the entrance to the cave, and he glanced up, instinctively knowing that this was not one of his men returned early. He half expected to see a Cossack standing there, from one of the death squads hunting him down, but though it made the hairs on the back of his neck rise, the figure was not the shape of a man.

A brown bear stood there, regarding him thoughtfully, its massive head swaying to and fro. Even from so far away, Crossman could smell the creature's stinking breath, and he wanted to gag: its teeth must have been as rotten as those in Wynter's head. That did not mean they were unserviceable teeth though, and there was nothing wrong with its claws.

'Jesus,' murmured Crossman, a wave of religion flooding through him for a moment.

It was a large beast, but fortunately for Crossman it could not stand on its hind legs due to the low ceiling at the cave's entrance. It only had to move a few paces inside, however, to find that room. Crossman's hand went inside his shirt, reaching down to his waistband for his Tranter revolver. He wished it were a 24-pound cannon.

The bear lifted its head as if it heard something and growled menacingly in the back of its throat.

'A bear,' moaned Crossman in reply. 'How did you get here?'

He found the handle of his pistol and withdrew the weapon slowly, at the same time raising his legs so that he was tucked into a hollow, a niche, at the back of the cave. The bear moved further in, sniffing loudly. Crossman raised his firearm, aimed at the bear's head, but his hand was shaking so much he did not fire the weapon for fear he might just wound the creature and have to contend with a crazed animal in a small space.

The bear did not come anywhere near him, however, but went straight to Wynter's knapsack, ripping it open with its claws. There it found what it wanted: salt-beef and biscuits. It ate the meat and biscuits very quickly, then moved on to other knapsacks.

Crossman heard voices then. Wynter and Clancy were coming back up the slope, clunking their water bottles, arguing and making one hell of a din. The newly formed alliance against the Ranger sergeant had obviously not lasted very long. Jack Crossman cursed his men for not being alert and straight-thinking. They were supposed to be out on a fox hunt, not at home in some inn's backyard, quarrelling about this and that. Crossman could hear Wynter's whining tone and the deeper voice of Clancy going at each other.

Shut up, damn you, the pair of you, thought Crossman. By God I'll bang your heads together when I get hold of you.

And where were the bloody sentries he'd posted? What was Peterson doing? And Devlin? Hadn't they seen the bear walk past them? Perhaps it had come up the slope from the stream. That would make sense. It had been drinking. Peterson and Devlin might not have noticed a bear moving through the thick shrubs which covered the slopes down to the water. Wynter and Clancy should have seen it though, if they hadn't been so engrossed in winning their arguments.

The bear glanced up on hearing the two men approach the cave entrance, but it was a disinterested look, as if the creature could not care less who came in so long as they did not interrupt its meal.

At the last minute, Crossman shouted, 'Don't come in here – there's a bear.'

He heard the arguments stop immediately, then saw both men peering into the dimness, their carbines at the ready. Wynter saw the bear. His eyes widened, as well they might, at the size of it. The lance corporal raised his weapon to his shoulder, catching a buckle as he did so.

The bear glanced up at the clinking sound but appeared unconcerned.

'Don't shoot,' said Clancy, grabbing Wynter's arm. 'Leave it be!'

'What?' cried Wynter, confused. 'What's to do, man? It's goin' to eat the sergeant if we don't shoot it.'

'The bear's blind,' Clancy said, moving forward. 'And there's the mark of the chain on its neck. Come down, Sergeant. Move slow towards me. Come on, don't worry, I've seen bears like this. Go round the edge.'

Crossman did as he was urged, Clancy sounding as if he knew what he was talking about. By the time he reached the door, Clancy was standing close to the bear, watching it chomp away on salt-pork and salt-beef, eating the rations the men had humped all the way up into the hills.

'How about saving some of the biscuits,' complained Wynter, 'you knowing so much about bears and such?'

'It might be a tame bear,' said Clancy, 'but I'm not fool enough to take away its food. We'll just have to let it finish.'

He came back out to where Crossman was still trembling a little from the experience.

'You all right, Sergeant?'

'Yes, just a shock that's all. You say this is a tame bear? What, a dancing bear?'

'No, it's not that tame. It's been blinded, Sergeant. Look, its eyes have been taken out. I think it's been used for bear-baiting. They often do that to ones used for bear-baiting – blind them. It's so the dogs stand more chance against it, otherwise it'd kill them too easy.'

'You mean,' said Wynter, 'they sets savage creatures against each other — dogs against this bear? — for sport? I bet that's somethin' to watch, eh? Maybe we could take this bear back with us and earn a bit in the camp.'

Clancy whirled on him. 'That's typical of your kind, Wynter. You don't worry about the poor creature's feelings, do you? All you think about is profit.'

'Bears an't got feelings,' muttered Wynter, but he could see the fury in Clancy's eyes and his tone was half conciliatory. 'Bears are brutish animals, an't they? God didn't give 'em souls and such, I'm sure.'

At that moment there was a hoot from the heights above the cave. Peterson had seen someone coming. Shortly after the hoot came the sound of a shrill whistle. The bear looked up and came to the entrance of the cave, its nose twitching and pointing. The whistle came again and the bear trundled off, down the slope, in the direction of the noise.

'Wynter,' whispered Crossman. 'Follow it. See who it belongs to — but stay hidden. Clancy, gather up the knapsacks in the cave and hide them best as you can. I'm going up to Peterson's lookout point. I'll follow your movements from there, Wynter.'

'Thanks very much, Sergeant,' said Wynter sarcastically, but he did as he was told, following the bear at a distance, keeping well down in the vegetation.

Crossman climbed up a narrow chimney in the cliff face, to find himself in a cleft between two rocks. Peterson was there, her carbine following Wynter's movements through the brush. She pointed, showing Crossman where to look. There, on the path the bear had taken, were three men. Two were Russian soldiers in grey coats. The third was a figure not unlike Yusuf Ali, in baggy civilian clothes. He had a chain on a pole in one hand and some kind of food in the other. There was a whistle in his mouth, which he blew at intervals, at the same time as waving the food in the air, allowing its scent to carry on the breeze.

'Entertainment for the Russian infantry,' muttered Crossman. 'The bear must have got away from them in the night.'

Finally, the bear reached the small group. The trainer threw it the hunk of food. Then as it was eating it, the man looped the chain carefully around the bear's neck. The bear did not seem at all aggressive as it was led away along the pathway that followed the stream eastwards.

Wynter continued to track the small group, following at a good distance, until Peterson and Crossman lost sight of him.

'Well, he may be a pain in the backside,' said Crossman, 'but he knows how to stalk. I'll wait in the cave for his report. Are you all right up here, Peterson?'

'Yes, Sergeant.'

She looked a little drawn, however, and Crossman unwisely enquired further.

'What's the matter, Corporal? Are you ill? You haven't got the cholera? Or dysentery?'

Peterson grimaced. 'Not the cholera, Sergeant, but something just as terrible to a soldier in my position.' She turned and looked at him. 'Women's matters.'

Crossman said, 'Oh,' and coloured up. 'Oh well – I'm sure you'll handle it.'

He left her there, not allowing the images in his head to form anything more vague than the picture of a soldier in discomfort. If he tried to visualize how she would deal with her problems he knew he would start wondering what he was doing harbouring a woman in his *peloton*. It would not do to begin taking such things into consideration when he posted picquets and handed out duties to his band of saboteurs. Best to put it out of his head and let her get on with her own difficulties.

Once back in the cave he began to worry about the Bashi-Bazouk. Had Yusuf Ali run into any Russian patrols? This was, after all, their country, and they would have Tartars amongst them who would know it well.

His fears were confirmed when Wynter returned later in the morning.

'There's fifty or sixty of 'em, Sergeant. Russian infantry. They've made a sort of camp further along, in some fir trees. And they've got Yusuf Ali. He's tied to a tree . . .'

'Damn,' muttered Crossman.

This left him with a dilemma. Peterson and Devlin were at this moment posted on the two best vantage points in the Fedioukine Hills, from where it would be unlikely they would miss sighting the caravan. However, if Crossman were to save Ali he might need all his soldiers. He would have to bring the two picquets down and leave the trails unwatched.

'Damn Ali's hide. He's put me in a spot now.'

'What are we goin' to do then, Sergeant? It could take all of us to get him loose.'

Finally, after much heart-searching, Crossman decided he could not leave Ali to his fate. The Bashi-Bazouk had saved his life on more than one occasion and was, besides, a valuable member of the group. Crossman knew he would be hanged, drawn and quartered on his return, for putting the life of a Turk over the success of the fox hunt, but he simply could not abandon a man who was not only a valuable soldier, but was now a good friend.

'We'll go after Ali,' he said, gathering together his kit. 'From the accounts I was given before leaving Balaclava, the caravan should be around this area today. If it passes while we're otherwise engaged, we'll try to pick up its trail and track it later. Get the picquets down.'

Wynter nodded. 'Lord knows, me and the Turk have got our differences,' he said, 'but you can't leave one of your own to them savages back there.'

The lance corporal went off to fetch Devlin and Peterson, while Crossman found Clancy down by the stream.

'Come on, Clancy, your first bit of action,' said Crossman. 'We're rescuing the Bashi-Bazouk from the Russians.'

'My first bit of action?' Clancy said indignantly. 'I was at the Alma, Sergeant.'

'Begging your pardon, Private – I meant with Sergeant Crossman and his band of misfits. Set to, now. Go help the others break camp. We must be on our way in minutes.'

'Yes, Sergeant.'

The dark-skinned man made his way back up to the cave, leaving Crossman to splash some water on his face by way of performing his ablutions.

'I hope I'm doing the right thing,' he murmured to the bushes and the world in general. 'I don't know whether even Ali would approve of this . . .'

Wynter led the way and the other four followed. During the time they had been a unit the Bashi-Bazouk had taught them how to move silently through rugged countryside. The rotund and flamboyant Turk could pick his way across loose scree without disturbing a single stone. A clumsy beetle made more noise on its feet than Yusuf Ali. Some of this skill, and others, he had managed to pass on to the *peloton*, enabling them to become reasonable scouts and pathfinders, trackers and stalkers.

The days were now cooler and the nights cold, as they were moving into October. In the hills, the light seemed softer and moister. It was preferable to the atmosphere down in their hovel close to Balaclava, where the stink of livestock and human faeces overpowered everything. Up here too, there was no mud to cling to every part of one's boots and clothing. Conditions down there were worsening with each day, since an army on the move can leave its sewage and rubbish behind it, but a static army gradually sinks into a self-made morass.

They picked juicy berries from bushes as they walked, to keep up their strength and to help preserve their water supply. By mid-afternoon they had reached the spot where Wynter had turned back after seeing the Russians. The enemy had struck camp, however, and had taken to the trail again.

For the first time Crossman wondered what on earth a section of sixty-odd Russian infantry were doing, marching through the Fedioukine Hills. Were they going somewhere, or coming from some place? Perhaps they were a larger version of Crossman and his *peloton*. Perhaps they were saboteurs.

Wynter led them on, using the abilities taught him by the Bashi-Bazouk, and finally they picked up the tail end of the Russian file.

They followed until early evening, when the Russians made camp amongst some trees. So confident were the enemy that they posted only two sentries, to the west and south, facing the position of the British and French armies. Obviously they felt they had nothing to fear from the other directions.

While the Russians organized themselves, Crossman and his men took a vantage point in some rocks to the north, looking down on the grove and its occupiers. It was near enough to witness what went on in the enemy camp, yet far enough away to hold quiet discussions on their next move.

Smoke curled out of the trees, drifting up into the evening. The soldiers below clattered and banged, laughing, eating and drinking. Crossman could smell alcohol and knew some of the Russians were becoming intoxicated. The Tartar who owned the bear went off with some soldiers carrying nets and poles with nooses on the end. This group followed the slopes down into the valley below.

Crossman used his spyglass to locate Yusuf Ali, who was tied to a tree in the middle of the encampment. The bear was chained to a stake nearby, docile as a lamb. It was lapping water from a tin dish and shaking its head as if it had ticks in its ears, which amongst its other parasites it probably did. The beast was in poor condition, since its owner obviously did not see to its personal hygiene and the bear, now being blind, could not care for itself as it might have done.

Crossman's group chewed on fragments of salt-pork which the bear had missed on his rampage through their kit.

Before dark had fallen, the bear-handler returned with the soldiers. They had caught some five wild dogs, probably a whole pack. They were small, flea-bitten animals in as poor condition as the bear itself. They barked and snapped at the men and each other, as they were dragged along on the end of noosed poles.

'Here we go,' whispered Wynter. 'You should enjoy this, Clancy – it's what they do in your country, an't it, darkie?'

'My country is Ireland,' growled Clancy, menacingly, 'and don't you forget it, Wynter.'

'Just havin' a bit of fun,' said Wynter, aggrieved. 'I don't mean no harm.'

'Where's the humour in it, Wynter?'

The soldier did not answer but, aware that the eyes of the others were on him, avoided looking up.

In the grove below, things were happening. The bear had been chained high by the neck, so that it now stood on its hind legs and was being prodded by a soldier with a sword. Its naturally quiet nature left it and it began to become enraged, lashing out futilely at the soldier tormenting it. The man laughed, and stabbed and poked, knowing the bear could not see where the sword was going to prick it next. The beast's great claws swished through the air, tearing leaves and branches from the tree to which it was tied. It growled and moaned under this torture, confined by the length of the thick chain.

The Russian soldiers formed a ring, bayonets fixed to their rifles, inside which the dogs were forced forward at blade point, snapping and snarling. The only way out for the dogs was through the bear, who now had a scent of the canines and knew what was to come. It stood high on its hind legs, swiping the air before it, waiting for the pack.

The dogs too, seemed to know what was expected of them. They went at it in twos and threes, leaping up at the bear, biting its arms and chest. Those who did not jump went for the legs, tearing at the poor creature's ankles. Patches of blood began to appear on the bear and its fur began to drip red. The scent of blood made the dogs go insane. They threw themselves at the great beast, the bolder ones going for the throat now, trying to tear out the bear's gullet and so finish it.

'That's disgusting,' whispered Peterson. 'I can't watch this . . .'

The others felt the same but were unable to tear their eyes from the scene, just as a man witnessing a terrible tragedy is powerless to take his eyes from drowning or burning or crushed people, even though the sight is sickening and horror fills his breast.

Pieces of fur flew. Bits of bloody flesh flicked on to the faces of the goading watchers. The crazed eyes of the dogs were white with fear and bloodlust, their jaws slavering and foaming. The bear cried out in its agony and rage, a god of the forest being mercilessly tormented by these canine fiends.

The Russian soldiers, probably some of them of the same mind as the British but unable to go against group pressure, were yelling and screaming now. No doubt bets had been placed on the outcome.

The humans gradually became worse than the animals in their bloodlust and fury, as they urged either dogs or bear to the slaughter. When a dog tore the bear's left ear, there was an insane scream of delight from the spectators. When the bear bit the foot off one of the hounds, another such cry rent the air with horrible banshee notes.

The dogs finally became too incautious, however, thinking they had the bear at bay. First one was slashed from neck to belly, its innards spilling on the ground before the bear, the rank smell of gore drifting up with the evening fire smoke. It lay thrashing and convulsing on the ground as a second dog died with a yelp in its throat. A third had its backbone broken by a massive pair of jaws that wrenched it from the bear's wounded chest. One managed to turn and slip through the ring of bayonets, biting an ankle on the way and causing a soldier to fall to the ground yelling.

One of his confederates ran after the hound and bayoneted it, pinning it struggling to the mossy earth of the spinney floor.

When all the dogs were dead, the bear was still raging and fuming, swiping at nothing. It was covered in blood and flecks of foam. In its blindness the poor creature was full of night-mares which would never go away.

It was at this point Peterson was horrified to see the Russians untie Yusuf Ali and push him forward, towards the frenzied beast. They were going to sacrifice the Bashi-Bazouk to the bear. The lance corporal's heart raced. She snatched up her carbine and aimed it at the beast, intending to kill the creature before its claws ripped open the Turk.

Strong arms pinned her to the earth, not allowing her to use the weapon.

Wynter and Devlin held her down, a hand over her mouth.

'No, Peterson,' whispered Devlin. 'You're endangering the whole of us. We'll be slaughtered if we attack now. We got to wait for the advantage . . .'

'I'll kill you,' cried Peterson, her words muffled by Wyn-ter's big calloused farmhand's palm. 'I'll kill you.'

But no matter how she struggled, they kept her pressed beneath them.

Crossman put his mouth to her ear. 'Calm down, Peterson – Ali would have done the same if it were you.'

Down in the grove, Ali was being prodded towards the bear. When he was almost within reach of the creature's swiping claws he suddenly grabbed the barrel of a rifle. Although the soldier who owned the weapon did not let it go, in a few quick deft movements Ali had freed the bayonet and held it in his hands. The Russian soldiers backed away now, yelling and shouting at him with hoarse voices. Ali ignored them.

He turned and faced the bear with the blade in his right hand.

'By God,' whispered Wynter, in admiration, 'he's goin' to have a go. He's goin' to fight the beast.'

Now that Ali had a chance, they let Peterson up, knowing that she had calmed somewhat. Fearful for the Turk's safety, the group watched in silence as Ali half-circled the bear, looking for an opening.

The Russians were quiet too, witnessing this battle between a great bear and a man. No doubt they believed the outcome would favour the beast. Only the Tartar looked agitated, voicing some opinions to the Russians, as Ali went in swaying and dodging the bear's blows.

The bear obviously did not know what was going on. No doubt it believed that more dogs were going to be unleashed, since the scent of the creatures was still in its nostrils, their bodies lying all around it. Suddenly, the watchers on the hill caught their breaths as Ali rushed inside the bear's arms.

The beast, unable to slash at him with its terrible claws, hugged him close, picking him off his feet. Crossman could imagine what it was like in those powerful forelegs, being slowly crushed to death. He knew Ali did not have long to make a killing blow, if he were to make it at all.

'He's done for,' said Clancy. 'He must be.'

But Ali had kept his arms high, so that the bear gripped him only around his chest, and his limbs were free. With both hands he plunged the point of the bayonet into one of the bear's blind eyesockets, pushing it in and up so that it penetrated the brain. The bear let out a wail of despair. It fell crashing on to its back, releasing the Turk. There it convulsed for a few minutes, the blade still protruding from its skull. Finally it gave out a long sigh pregnant with hopelessness, and died.

One or two of the Russians let out a cheer, but their impetuousness was soon quelled by their comrades.

Another terrible wail went up now, worse than that of the doomed beast. It came from the Tartar, whose living had depended upon sacrificing hapless dogs to the magnificent creature he had blinded with a red-hot poker: the great beast which now lay dead and useless at his feet.

The local man rushed screaming at Ali, tearing at his clothes and clawing at the Turk's face, intent on trying to scratch out his eyes. His fury and despair was enormous, since in a few moments he had been made virtually penniless.

The Bashi-Bazouk was well able to deal with such an attack. He struck the Tartar a blow on the brow with his thick fist and felled the man like a tree. Silence ruled the glade after that, as the Russian soldiers moved to secure the Turk again.

'By God, he's some fighter, that man,' muttered Wynter. 'Don't ever let him hit me, Sergeant.'

Peterson said, 'He did the bear a favour. Someone had to put it out of its misery. Even if we let it go, it would've died of starvation, being blind.'

'I expect you're right, Peterson,' said Crossman. 'But you nearly gave up the whole pack of us away to the enemy. Next time I'll have your skin.'

'Skin? Better'n losing your stripes, eh, Peterson?' said Wynter quietly. 'Better'n being stripped down to a private. I wouldn't want to be a private again like young Clancy here – bein' *nothing* again, so to speak.'

Clancy muttered, 'I may be the only private here, but I'm not nothing – I'm still a gentleman.'

'A *what*?' sniggered Wynter. 'You an't no gentleman.'

'Keep your voices low,' ordered Crossman. 'We may be a long way downwind, but err on the side of caution, if you please, sirs.'

The two men continued to glare at each other, until Clancy spoke again.

'That's because you're an ignorant lance corporal, Wynter,' whispered Clancy. 'If you weren't, you'd know that "private" is an ancient and honourable title, stemming from medieval times. In those days it would have cost you a fortune to become a "private", or man-at-arms. It actually means "private gentleman", if you did but know it.'

'Sergeant?' whined Wynter, calling on an arbitrator.

'He's right, Wynter. Now get some rest before nightfall. You'll need to be alert when we go down to get Ali away from those devils below.'

4

Despite Crossman's orders that his men should get some sleep, Crossman himself was restless. When evening came round he found himself looking up at the stars and speculating on the progress of the war. That he was playing his part he did not doubt. Sometimes, he admitted to himself, he hated being in the ranks. The manners and habits of the common soldier were far removed from his own. He had been raised by patrician parents, had had ingrained in him all the social graces necessary to one of his class. He had abandoned many of these, of course; one could not be too finicky amongst contemporaries the likes of Wynter, Devlin and even Peterson, if one wished to be taken seriously as a senior non-commissioned officer.

Had he been raised a clergyman's, or even a squire's son he had no doubt he would be closer to such men and could have borne it all without the distaste he sometimes felt for people below his station. But he was the son of a laird and had been taught all his childhood that men of the lower classes were for the most part contemptible and there only for the use of the upper class. He knew these thoughts were unworthy, but could not help slipping into them during times when he felt low. They dragged him down and confused his motives.

Then again, there would be circumstances where men of the rank and file would act in a far more noble and intelligent fashion than most aristocrats, and Crossman would be proud to be wearing sergeant's stripes on his arm, rather than being festooned with gold braid and tassles. These contradictions and the complex feelings associated with their origins plagued him when he allowed himself to think of them.

The senior officers, the old men who led them, raised other questions in his mind. Like many, Crossman was not convinced of the necessity of the war or the manner in which it was being fought. There seemed to be no deep forethought or planning in the generals' strategy. Conversations with Rupert Jarrard and Major Lovelace had confirmed his own misgivings about the general staff who were leading them in this campaign. Lord Raglan was too well-meaning, too much the gentleman to be an effective commander-in-chief in modern warfare.

Lord Raglan's idea of war was riddled with schoolboy scruples. One did not spy on the enemy, one did not argue with one's fellow commanders, one played fair with everyone including the foe. Those officers around him who were soldiers first, gentlemen second, like General Buller, secretly did those things which made common sense to the ordinary soldier. To Buller war was not a game, but a necessary evil, victory to be achieved as quickly and as expediently as possible.

Crossman agreed with this view. He was mostly disturbed by the appalling logistics which flourished in Lord Raglan's army. A few days before the fox hunt Major Lovelace had been visited by a friend, Staff Assistant Surgeon Lawson, who used Lovelace's table to write a letter home to his parents. He had left the letter to be collected by one of Lovelace's friends, who was going back to England. The single page had been left folded on the table, there being a shortage of envelopes, and while it was there it uncurled itself and lay open to view. Crossman could not but help read part of it as he sat writing his own missive home.

The letter read: *Dear Mother, Will you be kind enough to send me a map of the Crimea with forts well marked out in Sebastopol? You can obtain them from Wylds in the Strand . . .*

When men had to write home to their mothers to obtain maps of the area in which they were fighting from London shops there was something seriously wrong with the prosecution of the war.

Crossman remained wide awake, thinking of these things while he waited for the right time to go down to try to rescue Yusuf Ali from the Russian camp.

When the camp below was still and only the sentries moved restlessly around on the perimeter of the wood, Crossman woke his dozing men.

'Peterson, you take the south-west corner. Wynter, the north-west. Devlin, south-east. Clancy, north-east. I'm going into the camp to set Ali free and bring him back here. If there's a disturbance, however, I leave it to you to pick your targets and pour fire down into the camp. I know it's dark, but do the best you can. If you hit either Ali or myself, then put it down to bad fortune, not to your own incompetence. I want no guilt left around afterwards—'

'Sergeant,' interrupted Clancy. 'I'm sorry, Sergeant, but I think you should stay here and I should go down there.'

Crossman was a little irritated by the interruption. As well as briefing his men he was psychologically preparing himself for the descent into the enemy camp. It was not a job he relished.

'Why do you say that, Clancy?' he snapped.

'Because I'm good at it.'

Crossman was a little mystified. 'Good at what?'

'At that kind of thing, Sergeant. You remember Major Lovelace told you I was a member of the Thugs at one time? That is why he thought I'd be useful to you.'

'You mean you really *were* a Thug?' said Devlin.

'We didn't call ourselves that, but yes, I was an assassin. I was a member of a secret society, dedicated to ridding India of the British Raj. I was recruited by my Indian schoolteacher and I killed my first man when I was twelve years of age.'

Wynter snarled. 'You killed an Englishman?'

'That was then. I was on a different side.'

'You'd do it again, wouldn't you?' said Wynter, his voice thick with righteousness. 'You're just a murderin' bastard, you are. I knew it from the first time I laid eyes on you. By God, you didn't have me fooled. One of these . . .'

Crossman snapped. 'Quiet, Wynter. Clancy, how do you propose to set Ali free?'

Clancy reached inside his sheepskin coat and pulled out a short piece of thick cord strung with knots.

'I'll throttle the two sentries, then sneak in and untie the Bashi-Bazouk.'

Crossman recalled why Major Lovelace had thought Clancy would make a good replacement for the dead Skuggs. Lovelace had told Crossman that although Clancy had spent some of his time in Ireland, where he received an education of a kind, he had also been back to India. The young man was typical of many who were torn between two nations, his loyalties confused. Because of his connection with Britain he had been recruited by the Thugs, who thought he might be able to get close to their enemies.

Just when the youth was steeped in the dark and bloody mysteries of the Thugs, however, his father's brother – a colour sergeant in the Indian army – sought him out and persuaded him to return to Ireland. At that time Clancy was becoming fearful of discovery after being involved in the murder of three sepoys. He returned to Ireland, where having become restless, he joined the 88th Connaught Rangers as they passed through the village where he was staying with one of his aunts.

Here in the Crimea the enemy was Russia, which did not

place any strain on Clancy's mixed loyalties, and therefore Lovelace considered him to be an asset to any clandestine group out to cause havoc amongst the foe.

'Are you sure you can do it?'

Clancy smiled. 'It's why Major Lovelace recruited me for this platoon. He knew my uncle in India. He knows what happened there.'

'All right, Clancy. Get to it. The rest of you, to your positions. When Clancy and Ali are out of the camp, you'll hear an owl hoot from me. We meet back here. Understood?'

The soldiers slipped off into the night.

'Good luck, Clancy,' Crossman said. 'I hope your talents are all Major Lovelace believes they are.'

'Sergeant,' said the baby-faced Irish-Indian, 'you might even be amazed.'

So Crossman took the north-east corner of the camp instead of Clancy. There he watched as a dark shadow slipped down towards the glowing embers of the fires. Then suddenly it vanished completely. Crossman blinked, wondering if there was something wrong with his vision. Clancy had simply disappeared into the shades of night.

Crossman kept his eyes on the sentry to the west. He waited for what seemed like an extraordinary length of time, wondering whether anything was going to happen. Then, just as his impatience was becoming frayed, he saw the sentry stiffen and drop his rifle to the ground. The man's hands went up to his throat as his head jerked backwards. Then after a few seconds he slid limply to the mossy floor. For a brief moment Crossman saw a dark shape standing over the body, then it was gone, like a wisp of mist into the interlocking shadows again.

A few minutes later there was a tight gargle from beyond the trees, very short, very muffled. Then silence again. Another Russian sentry had gone to his maker. Crossman could not help but feel a chill at the efficiency with which Clancy was doing his job. A shy, boyish individual, who looked as if he should still be at home with his mother, was in fact a cold-blooded killer.

Crossman waited for quite a while after the second sentry had been despatched. Once again he began to grow impatient. He was craning his neck, trying to see what was happening down in the enemy camp, when he felt a tap on his shoulder.

'Wha . . .' he jerked round, to see a smiling Clancy with Yusuf Ali at his elbow.

'You're not paying attention, Sergeant,' said Clancy.

'The hell I'm not,' replied Crossman, ruffled.

He let out an owl hoot and very shortly the rest of his men were back with him.

Yusuf Ali was saying, 'Thank you, Sergeant, for coming back for Ali. I think you should not have come, but I am happy you do so. And this man,' he turned to Clancy, 'he is like myself. I see my young self here. He moves like a snake through the night, then he *strikes*, so quick. Ah, yes. A man of my own kind, Sergeant. He kill without a sound.'

'I heard a sound,' Wynter said. 'I heard some poor bugger gargling a final prayer a few minutes ago.'

Wynter stared across at the enigmatic Clancy, fingering his own throat as he did so, as if he could already feel the garrotte tightening around it.

'I an't going to sleep again, with him near,' added Wynter. 'You can't trust people like that.'

'Clancy is one of us,' said Crossman. 'Whatever he's done in the past is over. He's Buller's man now. You treat him as such, Wynter. I won't tell you again. I'll ask Major Lovelace to send you back to the regiment and you'll be digging trenches before you know it. If that's what you want, just say so, and you can join the rest of the 88th now.'

Wynter was not at all contrite.

'You may be in the trenches yourself, Sergeant,' he said, a nasty tone to his voice. 'You've gone and let that caravan get away, to save the Turk. We'll all be back on the line for this, you wait and see. Buller's men, my backside.'

Crossman had the feeling that Wynter was right. He would be in deep trouble, for the mission was supposed to come first, the lives of the men after. Lovelace was not going to be happy with him, of that he was sure, unless they could somehow find the caravan. It seemed very likely that the caravan would have passed through the Fedioukine Hills by now though.

'I don't like your tone, Wynter, but I have to admit you're probably right,' said Crossman.

Ali stepped forward. 'Not so, Sergeant. There was no caravan. The information of Major Lovelace was wrong. The rifles of which he spoke are near to us now.'

Crossman stared at the Bashi-Bazouk.

'What do you mean?'

'I mean, Sergeant, that some of those Russian soldiers down there are bearing the rifles we seek. I make a good look at one. It is not Minié, or musket, or like any rifle I have seen. They say the bullet goes in breach, not down barrel. A small chamber opens, to drop the bullet in.'

'A breach-loading rifle?' said Crossman, his eyes opening wider.

'Fifty of those soldiers have them. I hear them talking about it. The others have Miniés, also in the same shipment. These they can use. Soon they will wake and find their dead comrades. We must do something quickly. You must make a plan, Sergeant. We need to capture the rifles.'

'A plan,' murmured Crossman, his heart racing in excitement. 'Six men against sixty. It needs to be a magnificent plan to assist us against such odds. I could send Clancy down there to throttle the lot of them, but I fear he would rather enjoy the work too much and my conscience would bother me ever after. I think what is needed here is a game of bluff. I shall go down and tell the Russians they are surrounded by the British army.'

'And what if it doesn't work, Sergeant?' said Devlin.

'Then you pick off prime targets. Go for the officers and the NCOs. Russian soldiers are given even less opportunity to

48

think for themselves than British rank and file. They are drilled to perfection, but are not expected to use their initiative. Get rid of those who give the orders and they'll crumble. They'll fall apart, believe me.'

'You think this plan is a good one?' asked Ali.

'I can't think of a better one.'

Peterson made a funny sound on hearing this, then when everyone turned to look at her, she said, 'That's right, isn't it? We risk our lives to free Ali, only to send the sergeant down amongst the enemy. They'll hang you for killing their sentries – they'll hang you without any further thought.'

'I expect they might, if they call my bluff,' said Crossman, 'but I have to take the risk. Post yourselves in your original positions. Unfortunately for those men down there, we shall have to be ruthless. They need to believe we mean business, but more than that, they need to believe we can carry out any threat I make while I'm down there. Peterson, when I point to one of the Russians, I want you to shoot him dead. I want your best work mind – dead as a doornail. Understand?'

'Yes, Sergeant,' Peterson said. 'I understand.'

'Something you should know, Sergeant,' said Clancy. 'I had to kill another man down there. He was waking up. I left him lying between two of his sleeping comrades.'

'You killed a man in his bed?' Crossman said, the chill returning to ripple down his spine. 'Without waking the two soldiers sleeping next to him?'

'I'm afraid so, Sergeant. It was necessary. He would have roused the whole camp.'

There was a shout from the camp below them and Crossman knew that the bodies of the sentries had been discovered. They would also know they had lost their prisoner and would be wondering if the two events were connected. No doubt they would be thinking the Turk was responsible for these terrible deaths. The anger in the camp would soon rise to feverish pitch and a lynching mood set in. Soon there would be search parties going out, looking for traces of the Bashi-

Bazouk. Crossman did not want this to happen. He wanted all the Russians to remain in the camp until after he had met with them.

Dawn was creeping in now over the hills. Crossman began to descend along the goat track, down to the Russian camp, where cries of alarm were rending the air. Men were rushing to and fro, not knowing what was going on.

A kind of madness sets in when a group of soldiers stir in the morning to find several murdered men amongst them. They wake up and stretch. They look at the morning and think about breakfast. Then they lean over and shake the sleeping man next to them. When that man has not moved they call on him to get up, ask him jokingly if he wants the sergeant-major to bring him breakfast in bed. When he still does not stir, they feel his brow, only to find he is stone cold, with fixed staring eyes. They wonder about this dead man, throttled in his sleep, how close he was to themselves, how no sound was heard nor disturbance felt.

They know it might have been them.

Dead. A mark around his throat like a harlot's red velvet choker. His mouth is wide open. Terror stamped on his features.

The murderer must have stepped between them, picked his victim from amongst them, straddled the living while dispensing death. Eeny-meeny-miney-mo. That one! Settling for this man over the other, arbitrarily. A whim. But it could just as well have been any of them, anyone at all.

There are more nights to come. Many more nights of fitful sleep. Perhaps the assassin will come visiting again, in the early hours, to leave his calling card? These ugly thoughts washed through the Russians' minds.

So, they ran around, like chickens without heads, wishing there was no nightmare amongst them, hoping dead men would jump up and announce it all a jape, praying their commander would call them all together and explain in practical terms that it was not real, but just a test.

Gradually the camp settled down again, fires were lit, coffee was made. The sentries still stared out, their wild eyes darting looks this way and that, peering up into the hills, down on to the plain. But the rest of the men were calmer now, eating breakfast, filling their stomachs.

They talked of the night's events in whispers, occasionally glancing around them as if expecting a visitor, clutching their weapons as close to them as a threatened child might hug a toy.

It was now that Crossman chose to go down amongst them, tell them of their predicament, hoping his story was credible.

A sentry challenged him as he stepped out of the rocks, aiming a rifle at his chest. Since he was dressed in Tartar style he was not immediately recognizable as a soldier, otherwise the sentry might have shot him without question. He held up one hand in a placatory gesture.

'Is there an officer here?' asked Crossman, in German.

He repeated the same phrase in English and French.

A captain duly came out of the trees and confronted him, the rest of the Russian soldiers gathering behind their officer, curious about this newcomer after the night's horrific events. Perhaps this was one of the Turk's rescuers. Perhaps they had a victim here, ready to take the blame for the murders. Maybe they would have satisfaction after all.

'Who are you? What do you want?' asked the officer in French.

He was a small strutting man with a large moustache, probably hated by his soldiers for his arrogance. It would have helped Crossman to know that he was a brutal man too, and would not be missed by a single soldier.

'I come to inform you,' said Crossman, 'that you are surrounded by several hundred Turkish irregulars. Many of them are sharpshooters. I myself am British, attached to their forces, and am sympathetic to your terrible position, but I fear I cannot prevent a slaughter unless you lay down your arms now.'

A Russian lieutenant understood the French and he passed on the words to his peasant soldiers in Russian. A general murmur went around and the Russians began glancing up into the hills with fearful eyes. The captain stared at Crossman and his face twisted into a look of furious disbelief. Clearly Crossman's bluff had not worked on this officer.

'You ignorant pig!'

With these words the captain reached for his revolver and pulled it from its holster, thus saving Crossman the trouble of pointing him out to the sharpshooting Peterson.

The Russian officer was suddenly flung backwards into the mud, a look of surprise on his face. A black hole had appeared on his greatcoat over his heart. Coincidentally, the sound of a shot came drifting down from the hills.

The Tartar who had owned the bear, whose great corpse now lay rotting in the wood, gave out a cry of fear and ran from the place, taking a track which led southwards.

Russian soldiers staggered back from the captain's body, shouting, and pointing at the spot from whence the bullet had come. One soldier raised his rifle to his shoulder and took aim into the general area of the hills. A second shot, this time from Wynter's position, smashed into the side of the soldier's skull and killed him. He fell at the feet of his comrades. This caused more confusion in the Russian ranks.

Crossman raised his hands.

'Lieutenant!' he shouted in French. 'Hold your men! Hold your men before there is a massacre.'

The lieutenant seemed to come to his senses. He barked an order. The order had to be repeated several times before the men became calm again. After the events of the night and this morning's horrible awakening, this new confusing situation was too much for them. They were simple farm hands, most of them peasants from the plains and hills of the Russian Empire. They followed orders without understanding them. It was enough to go to war, into battle, in a land which was as

52

foreign to them as it was to the invading forces, without having to contend with such horrors as night murders and Turkish snipers.

'Lieutenant, tell your men to lay down their arms,' ordered Crossman.

'If we do, we'll be cut down like wheat in a field,' said the lieutenant. 'I will not countenance a slaughter.'

'I give you my word as a gentleman, that there will be no slaughter,' promised Crossman. 'You will be allowed to go on your way. This force of Bashi-Bazouks has been raised for the precise purpose of obtaining those rifles you carry. That's all we want – the arms – nothing else.'

The lieutenant repeated the words in Russian for the benefit of his men, as they were again becoming restless.

The lieutenant's blue eyes stared into Crossman's own.

'Can I trust you, Englishman? I would rather we died with our weapons in our hands than allow you to execute us. You are an officer, sir. You have given me your word as a gentleman. Now give me your word as an officer of Queen Victoria. Tell me she will be for ever damned to the devil's terrible care if you break your oath to me.'

Crossman smiled inwardly at this young man's earnestness.

'May Her Majesty, Queen Victoria go to hell in a chamber pot if I lie to you this day,' said Crossman, anxious to have the deed done. 'There, is that enough?'

The lieutenant, not more than nineteen years of age, nodded, turned to his men and gave an order. The order was repeated by a sergeant and two corporals. Men began to lay all their rifles on the ground, the Miniés too. Crossman told the lieutenant that two or three of his men should gather them up and put them in piles, along with their ammunition pouches. This order too was carried out.

When the rifles had been gathered in, Crossman spoke to the lieutenant again.

'You will go from this place now,' he said. 'Go eastward,

towards your lines. Don't look back. Take your dead with you. You will not be pursued, I guarantee it. Good luck, Lieutenant.'

'Good luck?' snorted the lieutenant. 'I shall be a broken man after this. To go back to my commanding officer without the precious rifles. I'm done for.'

'Blame it on him,' Crossman said, indicating the captain on the ground. 'He's your scapegoat. Dead men have few arguments to offer. Work it out with your non-commissioned officers. They will want to be off the hook too. If you concoct a good story between you, you should be all right.'

'Such as?'

'Such as your captain gave you an order to lay down your arms with his dying breath.'

The lieutenant gave Crossman a wistful smile.

'It could be. *Au revoir*, sir. Perhaps we will meet again on the battlefield. I pray for it.'

'And I pray that the next time we see each other, it will be in a Parisian coffee shop off the rue de Moscow, our countries at peace and our brother officers comrades.'

'No,' said the fiery young man, 'the Lord must give me the chance to kill you first, or there is no justice.'

With that he turned and led his men away towards the east, while Crossman watched him go.

When the Russians had gone the others came down from their positions. Wynter let out a whoop of joy.

'It worked, by golly, it worked. You see how they trailed off, looking so forlorn, eh? We got the rifles. By damn, I thought you was a goner there, Sergeant. I never thought we'd see 'em off. I really didn't.'

'That was a good shot of yours, Wynter. And you, of course, Peterson, though I expect it of my sharpshooter. Well done, both of you. Well done *all* of you.'

Crossman told his men about the conversation that had transpired between himself and the young lieutenant.

Devlin said, smiling, 'You ought to watch it, Sergeant — he'll be looking for you on the battlefield.'

'No he won't,' Crossman said wryly. 'He'll be looking for a gentleman — an officer of Her Majesty, Queen Victoria, not a sergeant.'

Devlin and the others laughed at this.

Their interest then turned to the rifles themselves. Crossman studied one and found it marked 'Ferguson'. Judging by the colour and condition of the stock, it was a very old piece. The rifle had a plug mounted behind the barrel on a vertical axis. When the plug was fully closed it was flush with the top of the barrel. When fully open, the plug was level with the lower edge of the chamber. The bullet which was dropped into the breech was slightly oversized. A rifleman had to tip the rifle forwards to allow the bullet to roll down and touch the rifling. Then the chamber was filled with powder and closed, after which the plug was again raised and the pan primed separately.

It did not take long for expert riflemen like Peterson and Ali to work out the engineering genius behind this weapon. It lay in the fact that the plug had 12 to 14 rapid twist threads to it, so that a three-quarter turn of the trigger guard lever dropped the plug completely. Being breech-loading the rifle could be cleared and cleaned very quickly, and loaded, in the prone position.

'The Brunswick was a bitch of a rifle,' said Wynter. 'The bullet being bigger than the barrel it took all your strength to ram it down. Me right hand was always a mass of calluses, ramming that damn bullet down the barrel of a Brunswick. And try to do it layin' down! Why, it was murder.'

'And even the Minié,' said Peterson, talking of her favourite weapon. 'You always have to expose your head when you're reloading. With this one you can keep your head down all the time.'

It did indeed seem to the group that the Ferguson, old as

it appeared, was a much superior weapon to any the army currently had to offer.

'Clancy,' said Crossman, 'get back up there to a good viewing point. I don't want us to be surprised by anyone. In the meantime, we need to bury these, somewhere where they won't be found by the Russians.'

'I thought we was supposed to take 'em back?' Wynter argued.

Devlin said, 'How can we take them back, you diddle-head? We were expecting a caravan — beasts to carry the weapons — which we have not got. Would you like to carry ten of these back in your arms?'

Wynter, who complained at having to lug *one* carbine over hill and dale, saw his point and said nothing more.

They found a suitable spot well away from the wood, in some soft soil up amongst the rocks, and dug a deep hole with their bayonets. The rifles and ammunition of both types were buried there and one of the rocks marked with a few deep scratches which would appear to the Russians to be made by some wild animal, but was in fact a set of cricket stumps. Since the rifles could not be wrapped in oilcloth, they would soon deteriorate in the earth, but Crossman could see no choice before him.

A hoot came from above and soon Clancy came tumbling down the hillside at a fast rate.

'Cavalry,' he cried. 'Cossacks. Coming down the valley.'

'Bloody Cossacks,' said Crossman. 'Let's move. Come on. The infantry must have run across them and told them where to find us.' He stared at the terrain surrounding them. 'If we climb back up they'll have us cut off from our lines. We'd better go down through the next valley.'

The Bashi-Bazouk led the way, along the track taken by the Tartar who had run from the Russian camp. It was a race over uneven ground. The Rangers finally found a dry water-course, the bed of a braided river, where the going was slow but over which the Cossacks could not ride. As well as pebbles and rocks the size of a man's head there were huge boulders which had tumbled down from the sides of the hills into the wide river plain. These served as cover for the British.

The Cossacks could not ride the group down over ground which was covered in rocks and stones. There was a kind of standoff, with the British moving down the gully in the general direction of Balaclava while the Cossacks were able to keep in touch along the banks of the dry river by riding parallel to their flight. Clearly the cavalry commander believed it was just a matter of time before he caught the runaways, since there was no desperate attempt to clatter over the rocks and stones and risk breaking the legs of the horses. He waved his sabre in the air, the sunlight flashing on the blade, as if to signal his intention to put every man to the sword once they were caught.

'Are we going to get out of this, Sergeant?' cried a breathless Clancy, clambering over huge smooth stones. 'I only joined you lot a few days ago – now it looks like you've done for me.'

'Stop moanin',' Wynter shouted at him. 'Save your breath for running . . .'

A Cossack bullet zinged from a rock, narrowly missing Wynter's head.

'Pity he's such a bad shot,' muttered Clancy. 'He might've earned himself a medal there.'

More shots from Cossack carbines rang amongst the stones of the dry creeks. Crossman's men returned the fire on occasion. Neither side had much success because one group was firing from horseback and the other on the run. Every so often the dry river bed would narrow, allowing both parties to come into closer contact and Crossman's men had to dodge from boulder to boulder, crouching down, firing as swiftly as they could to keep the Cossacks at bay. Wynter and Peterson would hold the flanks while the others funnelled through them, then Ali and Devlin would take over until the other two caught up.

Eventually they came to a bridge. Six or seven Cossack horsemen raced for this structure, hoping to reach it before Crossman and his men, which they did with ease. Crossman's heart sank a little. He expected the Cossacks to dismount and take up a line across the bridge, thus effectively cutting off the British retreat.

'Pick off those breakaways,' he yelled at his men. 'Peterson, Ali . . .'

The *peloton* discharged their weapons at the Cossacks but emptied only one saddle. Fortunately, instead of keeping their heads and dismounting, the front two Cossacks rode on to the bridge. It was plainly only a footbridge and an old one at that, the woodwork rotten in places. Within a few seconds both horses and riders had plunged through the planks and crashed on to the rocks below. The other Cossacks reined their mounts and turned them from the bridge.

Crossman and his men reached the two Cossacks. One was on his feet, drawing his sabre. Ali plunged a dagger into his chest on the run, leaving him to fall with a groan beside his screaming charger. The other was trapped under a struggling beast, which was unable to rise because of a broken leg. They did not bother with him. In the meantime the remainder of the Cossack vanguard had finally dismounted and were climbing along the remains of the bridge. Crossman and Ali were able to pick them off with careful aim, using revolvers. Devlin, Wynter and the others reloaded and discharged their weapons at the rest of the oncoming cavalry, causing them to wheel away from the bridge.

Once the bridge was behind them the river bed widened again and Crossman's men were safe from a direct encounter.

All afternoon and into the evening the two parties travelled like this, with the Cossacks sometimes within range of the carbines, and at others just blue dots on the horizon. Never did the two groups lose sight of each other, so that when darkness came and both had to stop because of danger of injuries, they could see each other's camp fires in the distance.

'No point in not having a fire,' said Crossman, 'since they know where we are anyway and they can't cross that black piece of wilderness without endangering themselves, even without their horses. We might as well be comfortable. They're probably thinking the same.'

Still, he roused his men at first light and urged them to break camp quickly. Before the sun was over the hills they were on their way into the next valley. Unfortunately the Cossacks had risen even earlier and had gone off in half-darkness. Again the game of tag continued throughout the morning, with the Rangers sticking to rough ground and the Cossacks circling them, trailing alongside, using the better paths.

Finally the Rangers came to the gorge which led to the fishing village of Balaclava. Here they had to make a run for it, down the gorge, with the Cossacks now in full pursuit. When the horsemen were in range, the small *peloton* of the 88th turned and fired, unseating two of the riders. There were at least fifty of them. They came on at full gallop.

'Steady lads,' said Crossman, realizing they had to make a stand. 'Take your positions. Pick your man. Don't waste shots – aim for the horses.'

'These damn carbines,' complained Peterson. 'If I had a Minié now I'd take more than one of them with me . . .'

They fired at will, Crossman emptying his revolver into the main wedge of blue horsemen. It seemed as if they were going to be overwhelmed this time. There were too many Cossacks to hold back for ever. Soon they were close enough for the Rangers to see their weathered, creased faces and almond eyes. There was a determined look in those eyes, the eyes of plainsmen who know when they have their quarry cornered. Sabres were unsheathed at the gallop. A rush of wind billowed through blue cloth, Crossman could see rows of even teeth in the wide mouths of the oncoming Cossacks.

'They're laughing, damn them,' he cried. 'They think they've got us at last. Give them all you've got lads. Fire your weapons one more time, then use them as clubs. Take them out of their saddles . . .'

The foremost Cossack rode straight at Crossman, knowing him to be the leader. Crossman had one last round in his Tranter five-shot pistol, an unofficial weapon but one dear to the sergeant's heart. He squeezed the first trigger, bringing the loaded chamber into line with the hammer, then squeezed the second, the firing trigger. The round went through the Cossacks' face just left of his nose, flipping him backwards from his saddle. His wild little charger went careering away, swerving off to the side, its leathers flapping.

Crossman rushed forward and snatched the sabre from the dead man's hand. Then he stood there, waiting as the rest of the troop bore down on him. He swished the sword menacingly, defiantly, ready to do battle with the next man.

The rider came, swept by Crossman, reaching down and slicing with his sabre. Crossman felt it shave by his left shoulder as he was striking out himself. His own sword bit into the cavalryman's boot, cutting through the leather and into the foot as if it were cheese. A yell came from the rider's mouth, but whether it was pain or anger Crossman never learned, for at that moment he noticed something extraordinary.

A woman was riding along a ridge high above them, looking down on the battle scene. She was dressed in riding habit, with a long, flowing chiffon scarf tied around her hat. The wounded Cossack had noticed her too and his eyes followed her for a moment in astonishment. She seemed calm but interested, staring down at them, looking for all the world as if she were hacking in Rotten Row and had come upon a troop of Her Majesty's Guards training in Hyde Park.

Just then Wynter shouted, and there was joy in his voice: 'We're saved! Our lads are coming! Sergeant!'

Crossman did not turn round for fear of being ridden down by the Cossacks. He watched though, as those in front reined their horses, wheeled, and began galloping off to the north.

The injured one joined them. At the same time there was the sound of a fusillade behind his Rangers. Finally, he turned to see the picquets of the 93rd Foot, the redcoated Sutherland Highlanders, firing over their heads from their positions on the sides of the gorge.

Another company of the 93rd came at a run, down the throat of the valley. A troop of Royal Horse Artillery were also approaching at the gallop, bringing up field guns.

Wynter let out a cheer and was joined by the other Rangers.

'Hurrah for the ladies in kilts,' shouted Clancy. 'To the rescue, my Scotchmen friends.'

'A week ago you were punching them on the jaw,' grunted Crossman, still unable to cure his men of their preference for using the incorrect term, *Scotchmen*. 'Now they're your best friends.'

Crossman and his men gathered themselves together and walked towards the 93rd's picquets. Looking as they did like a band of renegade brigands they were challenged and Crossman called out that they were a group of 88th in civilian clothes, coming in to report to Major Lovelace, staff officer to General Buller.

'You're 88th?' cried a Highlander's voice. 'Ah'm no so sure I wouldna prefer to shoot a few Paddies rather than Cossacks.'

There was general laughter from the soldiers around him.

'I'll give him *Paddy*,' growled the cherubic-looking Clancy. 'I'll mash his face for him.'

'Now, now, lad, just a joke, ye ken,' said a sergeant-major, stepping out of a cluster of boulders. 'Don't take it tae heart sae quick, like.'

Crossman grinned and shook his head. 'Well, well, Sarn-Major McIntyre. How do you do, Jock? To the rescue once again, eh? This time you saved me and my lads from a tussle with the Cossacks which we were not likely to win.'

'Sergeant Jack Crossman? Is that you under that rotting beast? What are ye doing inside a mountain goat?'

Crossman laughed, delighted to see his old friend.

'The sheepskin coat? It's what all the best Irish regiments are wearing this autumn. You Highlanders are so far behind the fashion of the day, Jock.'

Jock McIntyre shook his head sadly. 'What a set of rogues. I don't know how you do it, Jack Crossman, I'm sure I don't. Here we are, the best regiment in the British army – the best in the world, in fact – and we get the boring jobs of guarding the passes. Well, on your way, man. I'll be looking for a dram later, by way of reward.'

'And you shall have it, Jock.'

Crossman took his men on down through the gorge, giving the sergeant-major a last wave.

Clancy said, 'Pretty pally with the ladies, aren't we?'

Crossman glowered. 'You keep a civil tongue in your head, sir. If you want to hate someone, try the Cossacks. My advice is to try to get along with everyone, but I doubt you'll take it, lad, because you're of a mind to hate.'

Clancy thus silenced, he turned around to find that a woman on a horse blocked the path. The only way around her was out on the road, which was ankle-deep mud. She sat high on a side-saddle, peering down at him with a strange expression. He knew her name of course. It was Mrs Durham. Mrs Lavinia Durham.

'Alexander?' she said in a shocked voice. 'Is that you? I'd know that voice anywhere, even if the man did look like an Assyrian wolf come down from the hills. That is you, isn't it Alexander Kirk? Speak again. Let me hear your voice.'

'Out of my way, ma'am,' growled Crossman, highly alarmed. 'Out of my way, if you please. You have me confused with another man, I'm sure. I'd be obliged if you would pull your mount aside and let me and my men pass.'

She did so, eventually, but he did not like the look in her eyes and guessed that he had not seen the last of Mrs Durham.

5

When Crossman reached the hovel he found Lovelace inside, waiting for his report.

'Well, Sergeant? No rifles for me?'

'No, sir,' said Crossman, taking off his cap. 'We have them, but they are buried in the hills. There was no caravan. The rifles were being carried by a company of infantry . . .'

Crossman told the story of the fox hunt, while Lovelace listened patiently. Crossman's men were gathered around, listening also, not correcting any details for that would have earned a rebuke from Major Lovelace. Afterwards, he would talk quietly with each of them in turn, knowing the importance of different perspectives, aware that one man might have noticed something another had not. Always gleaning information, piecing together pictures of the enemy's movements, size, regiments.

And the men respected Major Lovelace, were gratified that he should ask their opinion, should seek their view on things. It made them realize they were not unimportant, even as lowly soldiers of a line regiment. The major made them feel they were doing a worthwhile job, work of value. It raised their own confidence, their status in their own eyes, and made them more effective to him in terms of striving and loyalty. They were prepared to give their all simply to please the major, to earn a 'well done', to stand in the light of his favour.

'Tell me about the rifles, sir,' asked Crossman. 'What was their significance?'

'You noticed they were breach-loaders? Well, the rifle was the invention of one Captain Patrick Ferguson of the 71st Highlanders. He commanded the Light Infantry Company of his regiment in the Americas in 1776. There were claims that six aimed shots a minute could be fired from his rifle – four when moving forward at walking pace – and the weapon was extremely accurate up to 500 yards, but would of course shoot much further.

'Unfortunately, Ferguson's company did not prosper, even though the weapon proved itself. I suspect the manufacturing costs were too great for army purchasers. The army lost interest in the project. Ferguson himself was killed at Kings Mountain in 1780, along with his men, and his rifles fell into American hands. They were preserved in a private armoury, and purchased by Russian agents this year.

'The weapons were shipped to Sebastopol and arrived just as the allied armies stepped on shore. The Czar heard about the rifles and ordered them to be sent to St Petersburg, where a company is ready to copy the design to supply Russian troops. It appears that our audacity in invading his country has been responsible for opening the coffers of the Czar to an almost limitless degree. Since we blockaded their port, the Russians decided to send them overland. You have prevented those rifles from becoming standard equipment throughout the Russian army.'

Crossman asked, 'You think if we managed to retrieve the hidden rifles, they could be manufactured for the British army?'

'I doubt it,' Lovelace said, sighing. 'The old problem still holds – the expense. Perhaps even the Russians wouldn't have produced them in any great numbers, but we had to make sure. It's possible of course that now the Russians have an idea

how the breach-loaders work they may still be able to manu-
facture them, but it will take them longer to produce them
without a Ferguson to use as a template. By the time they do
the war will probably be over—'

'They had Miniés too,' interrupted Peterson.

Lovelace nodded. 'Some of the Russian army was supplied
with Miniés after their setback at the Alma. I'm afraid we've
lost our advantage so far as the murderous effect of the Minié
is concerned.'

'They an't got our calibre of soldier, though, have they?'
said Wynter in a burst of patriotic fervour. 'They an't got the
likes of us.'

Lovelace gave Crossman an old-fashioned look and then
said, 'No, quite right, Wynter, the British soldier is unique.'

Wynter seemed satisfied with this reply.

Lieutenant Dalton-James came over later and was briefed by
Crossman and Lovelace.

'You'd better come with me, Sergeant,' said the haughty
Dalton-James, 'and explain to General Buller yourself just why
the fox hunt was only partially successful.'

Dalton-James moderated his criticism only because of the
presence of Major Lovelace. He knew the major would side
with Crossman, having himself experienced rebukes from
Lovelace in the past when he had given the sergeant a dressing-
down. There seemed to be a bond between the major and
sergeant which was not quite the thing. Dalton-James disap-
proved of friendships between commissioned officers and the
ranks. It was bad for morale and bad for discipline. He had no
doubt the major would come to regret this unwise attachment.

When Dalton-James and Crossman arrived outside General
Buller's room, in a small farmhouse, they found him in
conversation with the Commander-in-Chief, Lord Raglan.
They waited in the corridor for the conversation to finish.
General Campbell, commander of the Highland Brigade, was

also present within. The two men outside could not help but overhear the talk.

'We *must* attack now, sir,' Buller was saying. 'Cathcart has pleaded with you and now I am pleading with you.'

General Cathcart had almost demanded an immediate attack on Sebastopol after the dreadful Flank March down from the Alma, through dense foliage in which men lost sight of one another. Such a hazardous march, ending in catching up with the rear of Prince Menshikoff's retreating army at Mackenzie's Farm, the home of a Scottish settler, would only have been justified by a swift storming of the north of the city. In the event all that occurred was a skirmish with Menshikoff's troops and the capture of a baggage train containing, among other things, ladies' lingerie and, to the delight of some of the young officers, *risqué* French novels.

'Canrobert is against it, General Buller.'

'Sir,' said Buller, his voice almost groaning, 'if we do not attack we shall prolong this war beyond what is tolerable. Every day they build their defences higher. We face a terrible winter in this part of the world. Any losses we suffer during an attack on Sebastopol at this moment will be doubled by the winter if we sit and wait.'

Sir Colin Campbell said, 'I'm afraid I have to agree with General Buller here, my lord.'

Lord Raglan's soft and measured tones, his gentle reply, was almost too low for the men outside to hear.

'Gentlemen, I *understand* your fears, but Burgoyne believes we have to wait for the siege train. As you know, we are placing guns all around Sebastopol. Soon we shall be in a position to destroy any defences the Russians may or may not have placed in our path. Our primary task is to bombard Sebastopol and our secondary task is to establish a supply base at Balaclava. This is my decision, gentlemen. Now I bid you good morning.'

Lord Raglan came out of the room with his aide, who had remained silent throughout, and left the house.

After their Commander-in-Chief had gone, Buller said to Campbell, 'We have extended our lines over six miles of hilly ground to encompass Balaclava – how in blazes does he justify that?'

Campbell sighed. 'I don't know – I don't know – but we have our orders and we must carry them through. I'm going to have a word with General Scarlett. Perhaps he can do something to persuade Lord Raglan of the precariousness of our position and the bleak future we face if we delay our attack any longer.'

Once Campbell had gone Dalton-James took Crossman in to see a brooding Buller. The general was slouched in a rickety chair in front of what appeared to be a butcher's table, being made of thick wood, deeply scored and hollowed where presumably it had been scrubbed clean of blood. There was a hand-drawn map on the table, open where the general had been studying it. A crude compass lay by this chart. The general had been usefully employing talented soldiers at drawing maps and making rough compasses, since both were in very short supply.

The general's face brightened on seeing the men before him.

'Well, how did it go?' he asked.

Dalton-James nodded to Crossman, who said, 'Good and bad, sir.'

'You captured the rifles?'

'Yes, sir, but we had to bury them. There were no mules or horses to carry them.'

Buller's face fell for an instant, then it brightened again.

'You know where they are? We'll send your Bashi-Bazouk out with a beast of burden or two. The Turk will bring them back for us. He's a good man – what's his name . . .?'

'Yusuf Ali, General,' supplied Dalton-James, eager to be part of the conversation now that it was clear no row was going to ensue. 'I'll find another Turk to go with him.'

'Right. Well done, Sergeant. See to it, Lieutenant. They

might be useful, those Fergusons. Any ammunition with them?'

'I'd guess at a thousand rounds, sir,' said Crossman.

'Excellent.' General Buller rubbed his hands together. 'At least we're making progress in the little things. If only we could budge His Highness . . .' He stopped as if suddenly realizing the impropriety of making such a remark in the presence of a junior officer and an NCO. 'Well, there we are. Off you go, the pair of you. Well done, again.'

The two men, given their leave, went back to the hovel together, where Dalton-James went into conversation with Major Lovelace over the arrangements to retrieve the rifles.

Crossman went out to find water to wash. He was stripped to his waist and was dipping his head in a rain barrel, when Lavinia Durham came around the corner on her horse. He pretended he had not seen her and waited for her to move on. It seemed, however, he was not going to escape her that easily.

'I am not moving from this place, until you speak with me, Alexander,' she said.

She had that determined look on her face that he knew so well. Crossman sighed and reached for his coatee, having abandoned his sheepskin coat before going to see Buller. She gasped when she saw the stripes on the sleeve.

'Sergeant?' she said, looking down at him. 'Are you not an officer?'

He was concerned that someone would see them and wonder what was going on. There was traffic using the road and at any time one of Crossman's superiors might pass them.

'Lavinia, get down from that horse and speak with me properly, if you please,' Crossman said in an authoritative tone. 'I am not going to converse with you from this disadvantageous position. You already have me up against the wall. Equal footing, if you please, ma'am.'

'Don't speak to me in that tone of voice, Alexander. You have no hold over me now, you know,' she said, tilting her chin a little. 'Bertie is my lord and master now.'

And Bertie is welcome to this side of you, my dear, thought Crossman.

Despite her words the small and shapely Lavinia Durham dismounted and held her horse by the reins as she looked up into the tall man's eyes. He stared at her pretty round face with the little curved nose and big hazel eyes. She had not changed a jot. Still pretty, rather than beautiful, with a permanent slightly cross expression on her face, underlined by a determined mouth. In spite of himself he felt his heart melting.

When she looked up into his eyes from close quarters her expression softened.

'Oh Alex, what happened to us?'

'If you mean in the past, we – we were too young,' he said. 'Much too young.'

Her mouth firmed up again. 'You did not need to go away so suddenly, without a word.'

Old anger flared inside him too. 'I'm afraid I did need to – and you, you could have trusted me. You could have waited.'

Her eyes moistened. 'I still don't understand why you had to go. Will you not explain it to me now? I mean, how is it that you are a man in the ranks? A sergeant? Your father's regiment is but a few paces away. Your brother is with him. Do they not know you are here, Alex? What has happened to you? I deserve an explanation.'

'Yes, you do, but not here, Lavinia. Some other time. I – I have to tell you, however, that I'm enlisted under a false name. The name I am known by is Jack Crossman. It means nothing – it is just a *nom de guerre*. My father and brother have no idea that I'm serving in the ranks and I would prefer it to stay that way, if you please, my dear.'

'I am not your dear.'

Two French officers passed them by, from the Chasseurs d'Afrique regiment, a basketful of frogs between them. They had obviously been out collecting. One of them smiled at Lavinia and saluted the way one salutes a lady.

She wrinkled her nose. 'Do you know they cut the legs off the poor creatures while they are still alive?'

He couldn't resist it, hoping humour might lighten the situation. 'The frogs or the Frenchmen?'

She turned to face him again. 'Both,' she replied. 'I've seen it done to both. Now, sir, are you going to apologize for being so familiar? It's not right, you know, to call me your dear. I belong to another.'

'No, I'm sorry, Mrs Durham. You are a married lady now. I hope you are very happy. I wish it with all my heart. I'm sure – I'm positive – *Bertie* is a marvellous husband. He should be. He should be very proud of having such a wonderful wife.'

She looked away with a sour expression. 'As to that, well, it is convenient. I get to do as I like, for he is an indulgent husband, but I do not know what *happiness* means.' She stared Crossman directly in the eyes. 'You know I have a reputation?'

He shrugged. 'It is none of my business, Lavinia.'

She nodded, the sour expression returning. 'Yes, I have a reputation. They call me the Vulture, do they not? Because I like the blood and gore of battle. Well, I refuse to apologize for my enthusiasm for warfare, but it's not so much the blood, it's the excitement. I need excitement in my life, Alex. I'm that kind of woman. I love the roar and thunder of battle, the shouting and the clash of steel. I love the colour—'

'The colour of blood?'

She shook her head and looked away. 'See, even you do not understand. I thought you might, but I was wrong.' She turned back with a fierce expression. 'But I am not a wanton woman, Alex. That part of the reputation is wrong. I do not have secret liaisons with men. I have many friends, many followers, but no lovers. Do you understand me?'

He was shocked by the intensity of her words and by the force of her aspect.

'If you say so, then I believe you,' he said gently. 'You always spoke the truth, Lavinia. Sometimes it was not the truth people wanted to hear, but you spoke it anyway. If you say you are true to your husband, then I accept your statement without reservation. Not that it matters to me, in any case. I have no claim on the truth from you.'

'It's important to me that you believe me.'

'I do, I do.'

She slapped her quirt against her thigh, making her mount jump a little, jerking the reins in her hand.

'Why do they do that?' she said, almost as if she were speaking to herself. 'Why do they fill their smutty minds with such nasty pictures?'

'Because they are frightened men and need something else to think about but the blood and gore of battle.'

'You would excuse them,' she flashed. 'I think it is because they have minds like dung heaps.'

'Possibly,' he said, smiling a little at the fire in her. 'Lavinia, it has been pleasant speaking with you, but I must go on. I – I have to meet my commanding officer and report,' he lied.

She suddenly thought of something. 'Why were you dressed like a sheep-stealer? And that beard, it looks frightful on you, Alex. You're such a handsome man underneath. You smell like a goat. What is all this?'

He was trapped. If he fobbed her off with some silly story, she would dig elsewhere and come up with the truth. He knew her well. It was dangerous to let her loose with only a fragment of the real picture. She might go running to the wrong parties and questioning the wrong men. It was better he put her straight, here and now, and trust to her secrecy.

'I'm – I shouldn't be telling you this, but I will – I'm working incognito. It's my job to go out and count the enemy battalions. It's not hazardous work, but it has to be done. I'm with the 88th Foot for my normal duties, but Major Lovelace is my real master.'

'I thought Fitzroy didn't like spies?'

'Fitzroy?'

She smiled. 'Lord Raglan to you. He doesn't, you know. He can't abide them. Are you under his orders?'

'No, my commander is one of his generals. Lavinia, you mustn't say a word about this. It could get people into trouble. Not just me, there are many involved.'

'I might keep it to myself, if I'm inclined to.'

'Lavinia, please.'

'Just as I might not go to your father and tell him you're here, dressed as a bandit, smelling like a goat. I might even not tell him you're in the ranks, a sergeant. It all depends, doesn't it?'

She mounted her horse again, leaving him in a torment of suspense.

He took hold of the bridle and held her there for a moment, looking up into her lovely face. Her small riding hat was tipped a little forward, in the style of the times, and there was shadow over her eyes, but still they sparkled. Her riding habit emphasized her shapely figure as she sat high in the saddle, waiting for him to speak. He had once adored her. There were still small embers in his breast. At that moment he wanted to hold her close to him, but she was now forbidden to all except the unremarkable Bertie, with his paunch and hearty laugh.

'Lavinia,' said Crossman, 'I loved you once.'

She stared down into his eyes with a strange expression on her face.

'And you will love me again,' she said ominously, whipping her horse forward, jerking the bridle from his hands.

She trotted, then cantered away, up the path alongside the road, scattering soldiers using the only hard piece of ground in the gorge with the carelessness of a refined lady.

Crossman sighed in hopelessness. Why did things have to suddenly complicate themselves? As if life were not bad enough with Cossack death squads hunting him by night and Lieutenant Dalton-James badgering him by day, he had to run into his only former sweetheart, here on a muddy track in the

Crimea. If God had some plan for him, it was an enmeshed one, full of crisscrossing lines and complex meetings.

He had met Lavinia at an Oxford ball when he was at the university. She was a sparkling jewel then, fresh-faced, innocent, a little too forward (always a little too forward) but not outrageous in her behaviour. They had fallen in love, as young people do, in an instant. Picnics by the Thames had followed. Hunts with her brothers. Riding down to Fordwells village of a Sunday, where a lenient aunt of hers allowed them time together alone. It was a sweet time, a time of pure love and gaiety, of anxiousness, of earnestness.

Then he had gone home, to talk of her to his parents, and had found instead the truth about his birth.

It was all in the past now, all history.

He thought about his joke that had gone wrong, just a few moments ago. She was no longer the innocent, naive girl he had once known. His sweetheart had seen the horrors of war, had witnessed men's brains being splashed over the battlefield. She had seen bodies smashed beyond recognition, broken to pieces with round shot, shattered by grape shot, blasted by shells. Lavinia had watched operations, had probably assisted the surgeons, as limbs were cut from bodies while their owners were still conscious. Had heard them screaming in agony, watched the losing of gouts of blood, seen the soldiers die minutes later.

Nine out of ten amputees died of shock or loss of blood, yet still the surgeons refused to give them chloroform, saying that an operation for an amputation was such a serious thing for a man he ought to be awake to observe it. Such horrors would be distressing he knew, even to the eyes of a seasoned camp follower.

Rupert Jarrard came over later in the day to talk with Crossman. 'Hello, Jack,' he said, finding Crossman sitting outside the hovel smoking his chibouque and reading a magazine about the latest inventions of the day. 'Back from another hunt?'

Jarrard was not so much in evidence since they had moved to Balaclava, wanting to be up at the front line when he was working, and in the French encampment when he was not. He had found a pretty, unmarried *cantinière*, who seemed besotted with such exotic creatures as American correspondents. Jarrard, in turn, found French women irresistible, so the match was good.

Crossman looked up and smiled. 'I might say the same of you, Rupert. You stink of French perfume.'

Jarrard waved a hand. 'Oh, as to that, well – I think I might be in love, Jack.'

A snort escaped Crossman's nostrils. 'I think you would fall for any woman who says, *"Oui, oui, monsieur."* '

'And what about you? You have your French lady, what's her name? Lisette?'

'A gentleman does not use the first name of his friend's betrothed, Rupert, even if she is far away in Paris.'

'Ah, but I'm no gentleman, Jack. I'm an American pioneer turned newspaperman. You won't find much of the gentleman in those two. And there was another before her, wasn't there? That Irish girl with the dark eyes? I think it was the Irishness in her that attracted you, rather than the woman herself.'

'You mean the widow, Mrs Rachael McLoughlin? She is now Mrs Corporal O'Clarey.'

'Ah, she married the flute player.'

'Yes. A camp-follower can't stay single for very long, unless she starts selling her favours to the soldiery. She must marry to survive, Rupert, and Rachael O'Clarey is a good woman, with a beautiful disposition.'

Rupert nodded, staring into the middle distance as if he could see her there. 'I understand the attraction, Jack. When I saw her standing on the battlefield at the Alma, her shawl around her shoulders as dusk fell on the dying and the dead, she was like some ethereal being, some lovely faerie from an Irish tale. She held me in thrall too.

'But you can't compete with musicians, Jack. The girls only have to hear the plaintive, haunting tunes from a flute and it melts their souls. It's not fair competition.'

Crossman nodded, taking a puff of his chibouque. 'That's true enough. They should put the flute players in the front battalions, so they're facing the worst of the fire. But, Rupert, enough of the fair sex – have you seen the latest piece of science?' Crossman's voice rose in excitement as he prodded the magazine in his hand with the stem of his chibouque. Women were all very well as a subject for a slow, thoughtful conversation, but for real enthusiasm one needed inventions, quirks of science, new mechanical contrivances.

'Straite's arc lamp, which, if you remember me telling you, is an improved version of Sir Humphrey Davy's safety lamp, has been perfected by yet another Englishman, a Mr W. Petrie. What do you think about that then?'

Jarrard took the magazine and, looking at it, said, 'Sounds like an exclusive club for Englishmen.' He read on a little, turning over the page, and then smiled.

'Ah, but see here, on page 7. The first mechanical dishwasher has been developed in the United States. Now there's pause for thought.'

Crossman scowled. *'Dishwasher?'* he said scornfully. 'What good is that to the world? Why, there are plenty of maids to wash dishes. Would you take work away from those below stairs, Rupert?'

'In my country, Jack, we hope to dispense with servants altogether, and replace them with machines. In America every man is a king and mechanical devices his slaves. A dishwasher is a marvellous tool. It removes the drudgery for ordinary women in the kitchen. Women of ordinary families are entitled to some free time too, Jack.'

Crossman shook his head, this being far too democratic for his way of thinking.

Their conversation went along these lines for a while, arguing the different merits of one invention over another, and the superiority of their national inventors. Inevitably, however, the dialogue got around to the war. Both men felt it was not going well for the allies.

Rupert said despairingly, 'The men are still in rags, Jack. It's October and still no new clothing has arrived. There are soldiers with bare feet, their uniforms in tatters. What is the army thinking of? I've seen doors being torn off hovels to be used as operating tables for the surgeons. You are one of the richest countries in the world. What is all this?'

'Poor – no, *terrible* logistics, Rupert. The system seems to have become totally unwieldy. We came here ill-equipped, and for the most part, untrained. I told you previously, the British army is administered by *seven* different departments, all independent of one another. We have commitments all over the world. Is it any wonder the war is going badly?'

'Yet you won the Battle of the Alma.'

'Due, as you know, only to the courage and resourcefulness of the ordinary common soldier and his regimental officers.'

Jarrard nodded, making mental notes for his next article, which would arrive much too late in his newspaper's columns for any effective action to be taken.

The two men talked on, into the evening, fond of their meetings with one another. When it was time to go, Jarrard bid his friend goodnight, and made his way on a borrowed horse towards the French lines.

Crossman stayed outside, the gnats and midges not so bothersome after the light had gone completely. His thoughts turned naturally to Mrs Durham. He found himself comparing her with Lisette Fleury, now in Paris. There was a growing feeling in his breast for Lisette, who had come to him one night on their Crimean farm, hungry for love. The two women seemed to have much in common on the surface, but then when he considered it carefully, were really quite different.

76

When Crossman had come to the Crimea the last thing on his mind was women. There was too much anger in his life to allow softer thoughts inside. It was true he had been attracted to the Irish widow, her big brown eyes and lost expression had aroused the protector in him, but that had not been love. Then Lisette had – had what? – had happened. Accidentally, almost. At the farm where she had hidden Crossman and his men from the Cossacks. Now he had been confronted with an older love, one from his past, and his feelings were confused.

He sighed and tapped the bowl of his chibouque on his boot heel, emptying it of cold ashes.

Not a mile or two from where Crossman was sitting contemplating the complications of his life, two eager young men were sharing a camp fire. They were cousins, not much more than boys, who had each joined different regiments of the cavalry. Private Feltam was in the 17th Lancers and Rough-rider Eggerton in the 6th Inniskilling Dragoons. Both were proud of their regiments, but mutual respect did not allow each the freedom to express it in front of the other, as most troopers of rival cavalry regiments might do.

'We have not seen much action yet, cousin,' grumbled Feltam. 'I am almost ashamed to write home.'

'It'll come, it'll come,' replied the more phlegmatic Eggerton, stirring the flames with a stick. 'Not our fault Lord Raglan sees fit to hold us back.'

'Still and all,' Feltam said peevishly, 'you'd think we'd be given our chance, wouldn't you?'

Nearby, their horses were snuffling and snorting quietly, rivals too in this competitive world of the soldier.

Eggerton, thicker set than his cousin, with a ruddy farmer's-boy complexion, shrugged his shoulders.

'We'll be given our chance, you mark my words. The war has only just started. All those foot regiments digging themselves in around Sebastopol! They're not there for nothing. Once you get into a siege, it can take for ever. There'll be plenty for the cavalry to do in time.'

Feltam nodded. A thought had just come to him. It was not the first time he had considered such things, but it was the first time he had had a chance to mention it to his cousin.

'Listen, cousin – I – I want you to do something for me. I'll give you a letter, to take to my mum – you know – if anything happens . . .'

Eggerton sighed. 'You always was one for thinking on the bad side of things. We'll be all right. We'll look after one another. I won't let them Ruskies do nothing to stop me and my cousin from getting home.'

'Yes,' replied Feltam, brightening. 'The important thing is to get some action. I couldn't go home without some action under my belt. How would I face my father and brothers?'

'It'll come,' answered his cousin, smiling at Feltam's eagerness and anxieties. 'It'll come sooner than you think . . .'

6

Private Linthorne, of the 7th Foot, Royal Fusiliers, had been seriously wounded in the chest at the Battle of the Alma, and had spent most of his subsequent days in the *Kangaroo*, a so-called hospital ship with none of the facilities of such a vessel. There were hundreds of disabled men on board and not a bedpan between them. They either staggered to somewhere to do their toilet, or fouled their bedspace. In the whole ship there were two surgeons, and five orderlies to dispense food and water. The walking wounded, of which there were few, spent wearisome hours at the duty.

Men died by the day, the hour, the minute.

It distressed Private Linthorne beyond endurance that he had to defecate in his trousers. There was no change of dress, no bedlinen, only his uniform and a piece of canvas sail to act as a sheet. The canvas was so rough it chaffed him and rubbed him raw when he tossed and turned in his pain. He spent much of his time in a pool of seawater, which leaked in through the hull and kept him soaked to the skin.

The ship rolled and dipped, adding seasickness to other maladies. There was the stench of gangrene in the atmosphere below decks, the danger of disease from those who had infectious illnesses, and the filth of the beds found its way into open wounds, ensuring blood poisoning and festering.

The overworked surgeons fell asleep on their feet, as they laboured at removing limbs and ministering to the shattered, broken men who had taken the heights of Alma against all odds. Men who had walked into the mouths of cannons to save their friends, their officers, their country from humiliation. Men who had rallied and shouted, 'Come on, lads! Come on!' while their battalion was being cut to pieces by canister and grape shot. Men who now lay in pools of piss and shit, crying to God for water, for their mothers, for death to come quickly.

These were the heroes of the Alma, now brought to the most ugly of circumstances by lack of supplies. This was how the brave died, locked in a stinking hell, lacking attention and the meanest, the most basic of facilities. Logistics was killing them like flies. For want of a chamber pot a soldier would never see his home again. For want of a blanket he died in the night. For want of a bandage he bled to death. There were no pots, no blankets, no bandages. Only the rough boards of the ship, a torn strip of canvas for the lucky ones, a harassed sailor or marine with the all-too-infrequent drink of water.

When the ship arrived at Scutari, most of the men were already dead. Some had clung on to life though, and Private Linthorne was among them. He had some hopes of seeing a bed, with real blankets, perhaps even sheets. He had some hopes of a change of shirt. He had some hopes of having his chest wound cleaned and dressings to plug the ever-widening hole.

Some hopes.

He was allowed to keep his strip of canvas, but there was nothing else but the floor of the barracks. Rats ran in and out at whim. The place was rife with fleas. There was no lighting, no warmth, no basic necessities. Linthorne was crowded in a corridor with others who lay on dirty, rotten boards crawling with cockroaches and swimming with diarrhoea.

There were bedpans.

A dozen of them to share between hundreds.

The toilets, so-called, were blocked and overflowing, reaching in rivulets between men's bedspaces.

Patients were set in lines, to make it easier for the orderlies to feed and water them. The food was foul and hardly fit for the rats, and was often left laying in the filth which washed over the floor. There was no change of shirt, nor means of washing the dirty ones.

Provisions stood piled high on the docks, but were awaiting certificates from London for permission to open them. The Purveyor would let no one near cases or boxes which had no certificate. These stores were 'extra' in his opinion, as every soldier was required to bring with him into the hospital such items as were needed by that man. It was no fault of the Purveyor if a man had his legs shot away and had to be carried unconscious to the ship, his belongings left with the regiment. Rules were not flexible items in the Purveyor's world.

Unknown to Linthorne, in England a lady of genteel birth, a Miss Nightingale from an extremely well-to-do family, was enlisting support for her plan to bring nurses to Scutari. Miss Nightingale was not a sweet, delicate young person with refined senses, but a tough and determined woman driven by a zeal which enabled her to ride roughshod over weak and strong men alike. Men who stood in the way of her goal. She could have stayed in her family home in Derbyshire and enjoyed a pleasant existence, occasionally visiting the second home in the New Forest, or going to the family's Mayfair rooms for the London season, with its balls, parties and visits to the theatre.

Instead Miss Nightingale rolled up her sleeves, sought out those who could be most useful to her, including Queen Victoria, and set about tackling the business of bringing order into the chaos of the British Army Medical Department. She went at it like a small hurricane, driving through obstacles if it were quicker than going round them, gathering her nurses about her.

81

Unfortunately, for men like Linthorne, she would arrive at Scutari too late.

Before he had left the battlefield Corporal Matthew Cooper had asked Private Linthorne to 'Hang on. If you can only hang on, they'll get you to home again, Harry. A hero's welcome, you'll get, back in our village, eh? Just hang on.'

Private Linthorne, on reaching the innermost sanctum of Hell, could hang on no longer.

During his first night at Scutari Barracks Hospital, Harry Linthorne, a farm labourer's son, quietly died.

One of the advantages of living in the hovel at the south end of Kadikoi village was the interesting traffic which passed while one sat outside of an evening watching the world go by. Crossman's men had all gone to the Turkish canteen. They had been told to go there, rather than to the nearer canteen belonging to the 93rd, because Crossman knew there would be trouble if they went to a Scottish regiment. Someone would say something fairly innocuous but a brawl would ensue.

Crossman was dressed in his coatee and Oxfords, the buttons of his jacket undone around his throat to prevent the stiff collar chafing his neck. He sat quietly watching the bullock carts, horsemen and pedestrians struggling through the mire that had once been a road, up from and down to the Balaclava harbour, which was now bristling with ships.

The entrance to the natural harbour was quite narrow, while the high rocky sides protected any vessels in its deep waters. The remains of a Genoese fort stood above the harbour in the form of a tower and ramparts. It was an ideal haven for anchorage. Crossman had visited the much larger harbour in Kamiesch Bay, which the French held, but this had very little protection from high winds, the land around being flat.

However, the French were, as usual, much better organized

than the British, having arranged neat streets and shops, thereby achieving more than a light touch of civilization.

It was upsetting to Crossman that the ships in Balaclava harbour were full of needed stores, which were not being unloaded. There were plenty of empty buildings around the harbour which might have been used for warehousing, but the Purveyor, in a wisdom difficult to comprehend, continued to secrete those provisions in the recesses of ships without labels or means of identification. If a regiment required soap the messenger was faced with a vast array of vessels and had no knowledge even on which ship this cargo lay, let alone which part of the hold, under which canvas, at the bottom of which other cargo, in tight nooks and crannies almost impossible to get to without a sailor's knowledge.

The much needed soap might lie under coils of rope, boxes of nails, packets of flour, bales of socks, all themselves needed at some time or another and just as difficult to find.

Crossman's contemplations were broken by a greeting.

'Good evening to you, Sergeant.'

It was the sturdy figure of *The Times'* correspondent William Russell in his peaked cap, greatcoat and boots. There was mud splattered up his legs but he seemed not to care. He was on his way up to the lines, probably to join some young officers in their tent, where he would drink their brandy, sing their songs with them, smoke their cigars, and then inveigle information from them for his next scathing article on the inadequacies of the British command in the Crimea.

'Good evening, sir,' said Crossman. 'A fine evening.'

'If you mean there is no rain,' called Russell jovially, 'then I agree with you. The Crimea has more rainy days than Ireland, I swear, and that's no mean accomplishment.'

Then with a final wave of his hand, Russell struggled on through the quagmire. It was said that his articles and other news of the privations of the soldier on the front were stirring the conscience of the nation back in Britain. The word around the camps was that a lady named Florence Nightingale was recruiting volunteer nurses and had promised to use her own money to transport them and medical provisions to Scutari, to care for the sick and wounded there.

It was true that there were many women, mostly wives, like Mary Seacole and the redoubtable Mrs Rogers – wife of a trooper – who cared for the sick and wounded night and day. But this Florence Nightingale was a *lady*, with the power of a good family behind her, and was thus able to do something about the system rather than just deal with an immediate need.

Following Russell a short time later came the mounted Lord Cardigan, up from his yacht on which he had Raglan's permission to sleep of nights. He sat high in the saddle, staring straight ahead, a haughty expression on his face. He would no more have deemed to say 'Good evening' to a sergeant of the Connaught Rangers, than speak to one of the flea-bitten mongrels that trailed wearily up and down the harbour road. Ever seeking and finding affronts to a gentleman of his rank and status, there seemed to simmer within him a total distaste for the world.

Crossman stood to attention as the brigadier-general passed by, and thought he saw Cardigan's eyes flicker over his person, but could not have been certain. He was discomforted by this because Cardigan was a good friend of his father. They were both men of the same stamp: unintelligent, self-absorbed, full of self-importance and pride, utterly courageous.

Crossman felt a stab of unease in case he had been recognized by a man who had visited his father's house several times, but soon quelled it. He knew he looked very different now from that callow beardless youth who had dined with Lord Cardigan. And he was in the uniform of a foot soldier, a sergeant. It was very unlikely even his brother would know him.

Darkness came, lit by many camp fires. Crossman was now ever wary of a Cossack death squad finding his dwelling, and kept his Tranter loaded and stuck in the waistband of his Oxfords.

He went inside to make some soup. As he was stirring the gruel a sharp knock on the door make him jump.

'Who is it?' he called.

'Message for Sergeant Crossman.'

He went to the door, expecting a soldier with a note from Dalton-James, informing him of a new fox hunt. Instead there was a sailor standing there. Crossman was handed a missive of pink paper sealed with wax. The fellow, a small weaselly man with bad teeth, looked away as Crossman broke open the seal and read the letter. It told him to meet Mrs Durham on the quay at Balaclava harbour 'or suffer the consequences of exposure'.

'Thank you. There will be no reply,' said Crossman, quietly.

'Suit yerself,' said the sailor, sauntering away into the night.

Crossman sighed. What was he to do? If he ignored the note Lavinia might well go to his father and inform that powerful man of his presence in the Crimea. Or perhaps she intended to reveal his real name to Major Lovelace or one of his superiors? Who knew what the scorned woman would do? Yet, if he obeyed the command, for such it was, he might end up in deeper trouble than simply hiding his identity. She would have him at her beck and call, a slave to her caprices.

He decided to ignore it. Lavinia could not have changed that much since the time they were in love. She used threats but rarely carried them out. It was not in her nature to hurt those she liked. She was a complex creature. Eager for life experience she could be devious when necessary to get at and do the things she wanted, yet she was intensely loyal and would not oppress a friend. She loved the sound and fury of battle, yet she could be tender and solicitous. She appeared to be a wild, free spirit, yet she had married a rather dull, heavy anchor of a man, whose very status and personality chained her.

As these thoughts swirled through Crossman's mind, Lieutenant Dalton-James arrived. Crossman stood to attention and saluted. Dalton-James accepted his obeisance with a haughty air.

'I have a fox hunt for you, Sergeant. You leave almost at once.'

'Thank God,' murmured Crossman, much to the puzzlement of the officer. 'Thank God for that.'

'You might decide you will not like it as much as you think you will,' Dalton-James said, tripping over his tongue a little. 'This is not one of your rip-roaring adventures, Sergeant. This is a little more basic.'

'Tell me, sir.'

'You realize that despite the fact that the siege of Sebastopol is under way, it is not terribly effective. There are roads in and out which our thinly stretched lines have been unable to seal. Prince Menshikoff left a garrison of some eighteen thousand men in Sebastopol, mostly sailors. This has since increased to around twenty-five thousand. Almost ten thousand of those working on the defences, however, are prisoners – forced labour. Political prisoners, criminals and foreign citizens.

'It will be your job to go into Sebastopol and rouse these prisoners to rebellion. Get them to attack their guards and destroy the defences if possible, if not at least help them defect to our side. Any questions?'

'Do I do this alone?'

'I do not think it wise for you to take your whole *peloton* with you. One or two more men working together are more effective in such situations. There will be others in there: Turks, some French, a few Austrians serving with the French, but your role will be crucial. You must do all you can to cause disruption and confusion. You may take one more soldier with you, in case you need a messenger. Choose your man.'

Crossman thought about it for a moment and then said, 'I'll take Wynter.'

Dalton-James's eyebrows shot up.

'Wynter? You don't like Wynter. I thought Peterson was your favourite?'

Crossman said, 'I have no favourites, sir. Peterson is indeed a brilliant shot, but this kind of thing would worry – him. He is not made for the clandestine work. Wynter has been in prison back in England – several times, I'll warrant. He will fit in very well. He'll be up to all the dodges. No, Wynter will make the ideal companion on this one.'

The lieutenant shrugged. 'Very well – I said it was your choice and I will not go back on that. You leave at midnight. Where are your men?'

'At the Turkish canteen, if they obeyed my orders.'

'Which were?'

'Not to go anywhere near the Scottish canteen.'

The lieutenant nodded. 'Very wise. You show improvement, Sergeant.' He moved in closer and spoke with a quieter voice. 'We all know you're a gentleman, don't we, Sergeant? One day I will find out your secret. Major Lovelace keeps you protected, for his own devices, but Major Lovelace leads a dangerous life. One day he will not return from one of his own fox hunts, and then we – that is, you and I – will have a more serious talk on this subject.'

Crossman stared straight ahead. 'As you wish, sir.'

'Indeed, Sergeant, as I wish. Now I suggest you go and fetch Wynter and apprise him of his duties.'

With that Lieutenant Dalton-James, smart as a pin in his rifle green, left the hovel.

'May your liver rot in your gut,' muttered Crossman, furious at having to put up with being humiliated like a common street gamin. 'May your eyes be damned in your skull.' Then, becoming a little more inventive, 'May Mrs Lavinia Durham discover she loves you and may her ardour exhaust you beyond endurance.'

It occurred to Crossman then that Dalton-James was actually one of Lavinia's followers – one of those young subalterns and lieutenants who hovered around her like moths around a bright flame, desperate for female company, for a quick smile, for a light touch on the sleeve by a pretty gloved hand.

'I'll fix you, Mr Dalton-James,' said Crossman, with the wicked thrill of schoolboy malice. 'I'll fix your limber, one of these miserable days.'

He left the hovel once again, lamp in hand, to search the damp night for his *peloton*. Finding the Turkish canteen, he sought out his men amongst the Bashi-Bazouks, Turkish infantry and some French Zouaves who preferred the bawdier Turkish canteen to their own. There was a woman as sturdy as the bear Yusuf Ali had killed, dancing near-naked for the delight of the raggedly-dressed Bashi-Bazouks and the Zouaves.

Young infantrymen, dark-skinned from a life under a harsh sun out in the open, stared dropped-mouthed at everything going on around them. These boys had been recruited from farms and outlying districts of the Turkish Empire, as well as from Istanbul shops. They were as much awed by the hard-drinking Zouaves, the belly dancer and the gambling, as any farm boy back in England would have been by some famous London brothel. This was sophisticated life for them. They would remember it for their grandchildren, up in the hills of nowhere.

Crossman found his men, clustered around a carpet seller who was trying to get Devlin to part with his money.

'Go on Devlin,' Wynter was urging. 'Knock him down lower. Show him how an Irish can haggle.'

'You cuta-my-troat,' said the carpet seller. 'You starva-my-chillen. I give you good price. I lose money for you, because I like you, Englishman.'

'Irish, damn you. I'm Irish,' said Devlin, 'and I'll give you a shillin' and not a penny more.'

The carpet seller, who looked as if he had just come out of some backyard desert, shook his head sadly. He rolled up his wares and tied them with a filthy piece of cord. Then he humped it on to his right shoulder.

He started to walk away, then turned at the last minute.

'Two-shillin' – here, you take. Two-shillin'. I must eat tonight.'

Devlin, now feeling ashamed of himself for having led the carpet seller on, flipped a coin his way.

'Here, I don't want your damn carpet – there's a shiny silver thrupence for you, to buy some grog.'

The carpet seller looked at the coin in the dust at his feet and curled his lip. Then he marched on, carrying his tube of heavy carpets as if they were feathers. Crossman shook his head at Devlin.

Devlin said, 'Sergeant? Well, I gave him the coin.'

'He has his pride too, Devlin. Never mind, pick up the money and let's go. I want you all back at the house, before Wynter and I leave on a fox hunt. If I don't find something for you to do, Lieutenant Parker will be down and have you working with the sappers and pioneers, digging trenches.'

The Rangers exchanged glances.

'What's this?' said Wynter, obviously not sure whether to be pleased or annoyed. 'Just you an' me, Sergeant?'

'Yes, Lance Corporal Wynter, just you and me. Now let's get moving.'

The others trailed after Crossman, who set a quick pace back to the hovel.

'So what's all this, Sergeant? Just you an' me? Don't knows as I like that,' Wynter whined as they followed him inside.

'Don't knows as you've got much choice,' Crossman said, copying Wynter's accent and tone. 'You'll do as you're told, or go back to the regiment. You and I, Wynter, will be going into Sebastopol. We're to become prisoners of the Czar. Once we are incarcerated, we shall rouse the other prisoners to revolt and, if need be, die in the ensuing riot. Any questions?'

Wynter made a face. 'You asked for me, din't you!'

'Yes I did. You're the only ex-convict amongst the group. You'll be there to teach me how to act like a criminal.'

'Me, a blagger?' cried Wynter in a hurt tone.

'You know damn well you were. I need your expertise, blagger. We have to get arrested first, then survive amongst the convicts. You'll know how to do both.'

'Oh, I will, will I? And what happens when they find out we're Englishmen? They'll shoot us.'

'Only you,' murmured Crossman, silkily. He was enjoying himself enormously at Wynter's expense. 'You see, I speak German and French, so I'll pretend to be one or the other. You, I'm afraid, will be shot dead once they discover who and what you are, and there will be nothing we can do about it.'

'And won't we be sad?' said Peterson, cheerily. 'We'll all hang our heads in sorrow.'

'Eh?' cried Wynter, looking at the ring of smiling faces around him. 'Eh? Oh yes, don't worry about poor old Wynter, he'll just be shot. That's rich, that is. That's all the thanks you get in this man's army. You're ready to lay down your life for your country and they just laugh at you.'

And they did, quite heartily, much to Wynter's further consternation.

7

At the last moment Crossman had decided to take Ali with him. It seemed sensible, since the Turk could converse in one or two of the local languages. In any case once Ali had found out about the fox hunt he was hard to reject, insisting that Crossman take him too. The three men were unarmed, since as prisoners they might be searched at any time. Crossman had decided it was better they went without weapons.

They were dressed as seamen, with rough, bleached clothes and cotton caps. On their feet they wore canvas sandals made from sailcloth. If they were questioned they were to say they were Icelanders whose Norwegian ship had set sail without warning, due to fears of an immediate allied attack, leaving several men on shore. Lieutenant Dalton-James had chosen Iceland as their country of origin because it was less than likely that there would be other Icelanders around to challenge the lie.

'I don't speak any of the lingo,' Wynter had muttered while they were being briefed. 'How am I s'posed to seem real? They'll take me off somewhere an' shoot me soon as look at me, sir.'

'Just babble,' an irritated Dalton-James had suggested. 'Who's going to know what you're saying?' The lieutenant did not like having his schemes questioned. 'Leave it to the sergeant to tell your interrogators in broken English how you came to be there.'

Once they were ready a map of the city was produced – perhaps the same one the young surgeon had requested his mother buy at Wylds of London? – and under candlelight the three men attempted to memorize and absorb the layout of the place. They had been into Sebastopol before, to rescue some 93rd soldiers who had been captured and incarcerated there. However, they wanted to familiarize themselves with every corner. Major Lovelace also briefed them on what he knew of the city, its weak points and its strong areas, naming major buildings and the purposes for which they were currently being used. By the time they set out, Crossman thought himself as well briefed as he could be in the circumstances, but he knew success relied on a huge element of luck.

The three men reached the Woronzoff Road and began walking towards Sebastopol. It was the middle of the night and they encountered no other persons on the road. There were small encampments some way off it, but whether they were Russians or the allied armies, Crossman did not know.

Opposite the village of Chorgun they crossed low ground to the banks of the River Chernaya, and followed the river's narrow gleaming path towards Sebastopol where this waterway flowed out into the harbour.

As they were scrambling along, Ali said suddenly, 'The man who bring the Cossacks – I kill him yesterday.'

'You found him? I'm amazed. You're sure it was the right man?'

'A Greek. Yes, he do it for money. I cut his throat while he sleep. He feel nothing.'

'What man?' asked Wynter. 'What's all this?'

Crossman explained. 'You remember the death squad? They

92

didn't find me by accident and I doubt a Cossack would know me if he saw me. There are plenty of tall, dark, handsome sergeants in the Connaught Rangers . . .'

Wynter snorted.

'. . . and someone had to lead the bloody Cossacks to me and point out my whereabouts. Ali has found that man and despatched him.'

Wynter said, 'Ali would kill Greeks just for fun.'

That aspect did worry Crossman. The age-old antipathy, nursed since the times of the Battle of Marathon, Thermopylae and Alexander the Great, was in the blood of almost every Turk and Greek. They killed each other on the flimsiest of excuses.

'You sure it was the right man, Ali?' asked Crossman. 'You're certain?'

'I watch him, I follow him, he go to more Cossacks in the night. I only kill him when I see him take more money. I kill two Cossacks also.'

Crossman was relieved. 'You caught them all together and killed all three?'

'Four Cossacks. Two get away.'

'That's all I need to know, Ali. I'm sorry I doubted your integrity. Wynter, you heard what he said.'

'I'm impressed,' sniffed the lance corporal.

They reached the outskirts of Sebastopol without encountering any problems. Ali led them through some dark ruins until they were inside the city. It was remarkably easy, but then it was a well-known fact that Sebastopol was not sealed, from either side. Both armies were stretched. Prince Menshikoff hoped to alter this balance with an attack from the interior, but when that would happen was anyone's guess.

They found the doorway of a large house and slept in the portico. It was cold but their sheepskins kept the worst of the night airs from making them too uncomfortable. Crossman could not help but think of the men on the other side of the city walls, trying to sleep in trenches half-filled with water, clad only in the threadbare uniforms they had been wearing when they left England over a year ago. He felt he was lucky, despite the nature of his task.

In the morning the three men were woken by the house owner, who demanded to know what they were doing on his property. They left without answering, throwing sulky glances over their shoulders in the manner of gypsies who believed that all property-owning was a plot to keep them from living the life they were destined to follow.

They stalked through the town. As soon as it was light, gangs of workers appeared. Within a short time there was massive, feverish activity everywhere: digging gun emplacements; dragging large guns up from ships in the docks; carrying fascines and gabions to bolster the perimeter defences; building new walls and pulling down old ones. It seemed that the citizens of Sebastopol were determined to keep the enemy out of their city at all costs. They had, after all, been repelling invaders since the days when ancient Panticapaeum landowners on what was then the Cimmerian Bosporus fought off Scythian raiders with the help of their serfs and landworkers.

'Let's casually survey the town first,' said Crossman. 'We need to gather as much information as possible, before submitting ourselves.'

Wynter said, 'How about some food? I've eaten what I brought in me pockets.'

'Why, Wynter, we're expecting you to steal some for all of us. Give it one or two hours more, though. You might not be as good at blagging as you think you are.'

They continued to reconnoitre the town, keeping out of the way of officers who looked as if they might ask them why they were not on some work party or other. Their prior-learned knowledge of the streets and roads allowed them to keep to alleys where they were unlikely to meet Russian soldiery.

Ali pointed out the prisoners, being brought up from the jail under guard. They looked a weak, half-starved set of creatures. Crossman had little hopes of finding any captured

94

British soldiers here. Most of them had been taken along with Menshikoff's army, into the interior.

Crossman discovered, as no doubt Major Lovelace had found out on his clandestine visits, that the strongest points among the outer defences of Sebastopol were the Malakov and the Redan, both of which would have to be taken before the town would fall. They wandered over the Mamelon and the Karalbelnaya suburbs, including the magnificently engineered dockyards, which it was the intention of the allied armies to demolish in order to remove any threat from a future Russian navy in the Black Sea, the door of which led to the Mediterranean.

At around ten o'clock, Wynter went on a thieving exercise, leaving Crossman and Ali tucked amongst some large mooring buoys, which were stacked on the dockside. Since the harbour was now blocked with scuttled ships, there was little activity around the wharfs. Wynter came back with bread and meat.

'Well done, Wynter,' said Crossman. 'But what about the wine?'

Wynter's sly face broke into a grin and with a flourish he produced a bottle from inside his coat.

'I knew you'd say that,' he exclaimed triumphantly, 'so I made sure I got some.'

Sergeant Crossman nodded and inspected the bottle.

'But, Wynter,' he said, in a tone of disappointment. 'This is a Chardonnay. One needs a nice full Claret to wash down such fulsome meat. Either go out and steal a bottle of red, or change the meat for green fish, if you please.'

'You know what you can do, Sergeant.'

'Yes, I suppose I do,' Crossman said. 'Eat and drink, or go without.'

'Exactly.'

The Bashi-Bazouk said nothing, well used to this kind of banter between British soldiers, and finding it neither amusing nor boring. It was simply conversation to keep up the spirits, and he let it go over his head.

When they had finished their meal they went to where

they knew the prisoners were working, on the outskirts of the city. Huge blocks of stone were being cannibalized from both ruined and complete buildings, to make walls around the perimeter. Trenches were being dug. Stanchions were being driven into the ground to form the backbones for fences. Bags of sand and mortar, rocks and debris were piled high to form barricades from behind which the citizens could fight.

While the Turk distracted the guard, the two British soldiers slipped in amongst the convicts and began labouring with them. One or two of the men and women looked askance at Crossman and Wynter, but then shrugged and carried on working. Crossman had decided it was best to keep Ali on the outside, with the two of them inside, in case something went wrong.

They worked for the whole day, under a benign sun, carrying rocks and stones, buckets of earth, and other materials, building a dyke around the city. It was back-breaking work, punctuated from time to time with alarmingly close shots from the picquets on the other side.

'I'm not so sure I wouldn't rather be in the trenches with the 88th right at this minute, Sergeant.' complained Wynter. 'I should've gone for that, instead.'

'Perhaps you should have,' agreed Crossman. 'I'm almost of that mind myself.'

A bullet, probably from a Minié, whined close to Wynter's shoulder, making him jump back.

'I bet that was one of Parker's sharpshooters,' growled Wynter, staring in the direction of the British army. 'He knows we're over here and he's got all the best shots in the regiment looking for us. He 'ates me, that man does.'

'Lieutenant Parker hates everyone, Wynter, so there's no call to feel special. He hates his commander, his men, and especially his mother and grandmother. You are quite a long way down his hate list, so get on with your labours before we attract attention to ourselves.'

The guards were not over-zealous, being mostly naval

ratings put to the work. They lounged around, smoking pipes, talking with one another, sometimes chatting with the prisoners. From the tone of the conversations the prisoners themselves seemed quite keen on the defences, since they believed they would be marched away *en masse* by their captors and shot if the British, French and Turks ever entered Sebastopol.

The whole atmosphere was remarkably relaxed. Occasionally an enemy ship was sighted out beyond the harbour and work would pause for a moment while the convicts discussed its intentions.

'One day they're going to start blasting us,' said a Pole to his companion in German. 'Then all hell will be let loose.'

There was a general murmur of agreement amongst the prisoners and guards, as the words were passed on in different languages, and then work began again with renewed vigour.

In the evening a copper sun melted into the sea and the prisoners were marched back to the jails. Wynter and Crossman found themselves sleeping amongst flea-infested men crowded into a courtyard. Crossman gave a blessing that they were at least out under the stars, chilling as it might be, and not packed into some hellhole of a dungeon.

The facilities were of course wanting, in that there was one bucket between seventy men, but the British soldiers made sure they were in the far corner, away from its stink as it overflowed from too much use.

In the morning they were given some maggoty slop which they were told was food. Crossman ate his without a blink, but Wynter refused to touch it. Another prisoner took it from him and ate it, maggots and all. Once again they were marched out to the perimeter of the city and set to work. Some time in the morning a priest came and blessed such defences as had been raised over the past week.

There were also visits from officials from time to time, come to inspect what they themselves had designed. Admiral Korniloff himself dropped by with a retinue of Russian naval officers trailing behind him. He praised the efforts of the convicts, saying there would be a review of their cases once the war was over, with a general amnesty certain.

This speech was greeted with cheers from the workers.

Crossman saw that he had a difficult task ahead if he were going to rouse the prisoners to rebellion.

He probed his fellow convicts with gentle questions during their rest periods. They were made up of dozens of different nationalities: Greeks, Poles, Ukrainians, Germans, Dutch and many others. He spoke mostly in German, but sometimes in French. No one seemed suspicious of him, and why should they? He was a prisoner like themselves, caught in the pincers of a war between several nations, all of which regarded individuals as expendable items in their endeavours to win.

Wynter worked only on those who spoke some English, keeping to Dalton-James's story that he was an Icelander, at the same time praying he did not meet one of his own 'countrymen'.

Ali came to see them one night, re-establishing contact. He was able to slip in and out almost at will, for what could not be done without the guards knowing, could certainly be effected with a well-placed coin. He enquired about progress and said that he had a hideout for them if there were any problems once the riots were started.

'It is in the north of the town, on the edge – a small hut of a goatherd – with grass top.'

'A surfed roof? Tell me exactly where.'

Ali drew a map on the ground, giving Crossman and Wynter some landmarks to know the hut by. Later, he went back out into the town, returning with a quantity of food, which they shared with other prisoners, thus making themselves popular quite swiftly.

Soon they had befriended one or two small groups amongst their fellow convicts, who quickly came to trust them and hold them in high regard.

Progress, thought Crossman, though he was anxious that these new friendships need be tested quite so soon.

8

After a week, Crossman and Wynter had worked hard at gaining the confidence of a disgruntled hard core of the convicts. Now Crossman, for Wynter was inhibited by his lack of language, started spreading discontent and hinted at rebellion. He felt he was doing rather well, having received murmurs of agreement from many of his fellow prisoners.

However, one morning while he was labouring at helping to defend Sebastopol against the external forces of evil – an ironic touch which tickled some strange sense of humour in him – he looked up to see Colonel Todleben, the chief engineer of the city's defences, standing talking to one of the overseers. Crossman looked away again quickly, as Todleben glanced across at him, still talking with his man.

Crossman felt a wave of apprehension go through him and, hoping he had not been recognized, he dared not look up again. He had fought Todleben in a duel recently – the result of an aborted attempt to assassinate the brilliant engineer – which had left the sergeant wounded. The pair had battled it out with swords in a marquee not very far from where he was working now and Crossman had lost. Although later pursued through the city, the wounded sergeant had been allowed to leave the tent alive due to a prior agreement.

Whether Crossman's face had left an impression on the colonel's mind was not something the sergeant wanted to put to the test.

Just at that moment there came about one of those incidents which can either seal a man's fate or leave him full of regret for the rest of his life. In front of the spot where the sergeant was labouring was an unstable wall of a building, now standing alone, devoid of supports. When a nearby cannon went off, firing at the British lines, it caused a judder and a tremor to run through the ground. This was enough to topple the wall, which leant down towards several workers. They scrambled out of the way – all except one man, who had his head down, bent to his task of clearing rubble.

Crossman and others, including Todleben, shouted at the fellow. He looked up, but he seemed transfixed by the teetering edifice above him. Crossman was left with an agonizing choice, but it was not in his nature to hesitate. He ran forward instinctively, grabbed the man by his collar, and hauled him backwards out of the path of the falling wall. The brickwork crashed to the ground, heavy lumps flying, spinning away from the masonry, but the man was safe. He clutched Crossman's arms by way of thanking him, unable to speak after his near escape from death. The dust billowed, then began to settle.

Crossman felt an ominous tap on his shoulder.

He turned to look into the face of Colonel Todleben.

'I thought I knew you,' said the colonel in German, as Crossman's heart sank. 'It's the sergeant, isn't it? So, what are you doing here, sir? Pulling down our defences from the inside, eh? Destroying us from within?'

Wynter, on one side of Crossman, melted into the crowd of convicts around him. Out of the corner of his eye Crossman saw them close ranks around his lance corporal, and he knew that at least one of them was safe.

Staring into the colonel's eyes, he said, 'I'm – I'm a

prisoner, sir. Captured by your Cossacks and sent here to assist the – the convicts.'

Colonel Todleben smiled and shrugged, the disbelief evident in his features. Then, turning to two of the marines accompanying him, he ordered, 'Take this man into custody. Bring him to the attention of Major Zinski.'

He then said to Crossman: 'I'm afraid you're out of my hands from now on. I'm colonel of engineers, not of captured spies. I'm sorry. We duelled and you fought honorably – for that I wish you well.' He paused before adding with a frown, 'That was a very brave thing you did just a moment ago. You must have known it would bring you to my attention. Why did you risk it?'

Crossman smiled wryly. 'I could not help myself.'

Todleben shook his head sadly. 'I believe that. Unfortunately you make a poor espionage agent, Sergeant . . .?'

'Crossman.'

'Yes, Crossman. A man in your job needs to be cold-blooded, ruthless. Lives should be expendable to spies. Never mind. It is in your nature. Good luck.'

'Listen . . .' cried Crossman, but he felt a bayonet prodding him in the neck, and promptly closed his mouth.

He was taken to a large building which he guessed was Todleben's headquarters, and placed in a cell below ground level. There was dirty straw on the floor, but no furniture of any kind. It was damp and cold. There were no windows. He was left to his own thoughts most of the time, with interruptions only by the two brutish guards, who seemed to enter his cell at whim to maltreat him.

An hour later he stood before Major Zinski. The major was a thickset man, big-boned and heavy-jawed. Everything about him was oversized, from his huge hands to his massive head with its short bristly haircut. The eyes in that head were humourless. They stared at Crossman as if he were a beetle that had scuttled out from behind a wainscot. In short, Major Zinski had the look of a policeman.

Crossman had been roughly treated by the two marines. He presented himself sporting a black eye and a split lip. The major asked him how he had acquired them.

'No serious matter,' said Crossman. 'It seems your men cannot keep their hands to themselves.'

Zinski spoke sharply to the two marines in Russian, so that they stiffened and stared ahead with worried eyes, but Crossman wondered whether they had indeed been reprimanded. Had they been his men he would have dismissed them and brought in another two guards, but these men were allowed to remain.

'Now, Sergeant, we'll start with your name.'

'Sergeant Jack Crossman.'

'And which regiment? Are you a pioneer, or a sapper?'

'Neither of those, but my regiment must remain my own business, Major.'

The major looked sharply at Crossman, and the sergeant sensed a movement in the men on either side of him. He fully expected to feel a rifle butt come smashing down on his foot, but nothing like that happened. After a short period of silence, Zinski sighed.

'What are you doing here, Sergeant?' asked the major. 'You were never captured by the Cossacks and I'm absolutely certain you are not a deserter to the Russian side. Why are you helping to build our defences? You're over here on one of your furtive activities. Why do you come here to fill baskets with bricks and soil and plug our walls, eh?'

'All right,' replied Crossman, as if confessing, 'you've found me out, Major. You see, I'm a volunteer soldier. I joined the army because I love fighting and I get paid extra for fighting in a war overseas. Promotion comes quickly on the battlefield, so war is what soldiers like me want the most.'

Crossman leaned casually on the desk.

'Now, if the defences of Sebastopol fall too quickly, it'll all be over, won't it? So I thought, during my time off picquet duty, when other men are writing their letters home and resting, I would come over here and help build up the city's defences, so that when the allies attack, the city will hold out longer. You see what I'm up to? I want to perpetuate the war, keep it going, and that way I'll rise swiftly through the ranks.'

The major raised his eyebrows and yawned.

'An ingenious plan, Sergeant, and worthy of a good story-teller. I'm sending you back to your cell now. These men won't beat you again, but you will receive no food or water. When you're ready to talk to me, simply mention my name to the guards and they will bring you to me.'

He *was* beaten again, when the guards changed. It seemed it was part of the ritual of all the guards to knock their prisoners about. When Zinski asked to see him again, a day later, and noticed that he had fresh marks on his face, the major spoke sharply to his new jailers. However, these two men were replaced shortly afterwards with a fresh couple, and the whole process began all over again.

Crossman could not decide whether it was a system defined by the senior officers, or normal practice amongst the guards, which was only curbed individually.

Time in the cell passed very slowly for Crossman. All he had to do with himself was concentrate on his terrible thirst. The hunger was not so bad, but the thirst drove him crazy. He tried licking the damp stones on the cell floors and walls, but this seemed to make his parched state even worse. He found it better to sip beads of water from the bricks through a piece of hollow straw, keeping his expectations low.

Nightmares began to invade his head, which now throbbed and hammered with pain as he became dehydrated. He tried befriending the marines, attempted to wheedle water out of them, but they would not budge. He tried thinking of other things, anything but drinking, but images flew into his mind of waterfalls, bottles of beer, lakes and streams, cool refreshing rain. They tormented him, awake or asleep, and he realized he would become a husk and die if he did not soon receive a sufficient quantity of liquid in his body.

The third time he came up in front of Major Zinski was after three days of no food or water. Crossman was weak and giddy, and desperate. He felt a wreck and he knew he looked it too. Major Zinski shook his head sadly.

'You are very stubborn, Sergeant. All you have to do is tell me what you're doing here. If you don't, I shall be forced to have you placed in front of a firing squad and shot to death as a spy. Or hanged from a flagpole. I would not like to do that. Execution is such a humiliating death.'

'I cannot – I mean I can't tell you why I'm here,' said Crossman in a low husky voice. 'I was told to come, then I would be contacted later. I – I think they wanted me to mine your main magazine – blow it up – destroy your ammunition stores. But that's just a guess, you understand. I have no real knowledge of my task, not until I'm contacted.'

'Who was supposed to contact you?'

'A Hungarian fellow. I don't know his name.'

'Why were you working with the convicts?'

Crossman shrugged. 'It seemed a good place to hide myself, amongst prisoners.'

Zinski leaned forward and played with a pen.

'They say you worked very hard – you were one of the best men they had on the work party.'

Again Crossman shrugged. 'We're taught in my country that if a job's worth doing, it's worth doing well. I can do no other than give my best, to whatever cause.'

'There was no other reason?'

'What other reason could there be?'

'I don't know, Sergeant, I'm sure. I find you as devious as a monkey. You say things, but I can't believe them.'

The major then spoke to one of the guards, who reached for a jug of water and a glass, and then poured a drink, offering it to Crossman. The sergeant took it and sipped it slowly, but before he had taken very much, the glass was knocked out of his hands and shattered on the stone floor. A few more words were spoken to the guards, who stared straight ahead.

'Clumsy fellow,' murmured the major, turning again to address Crossman. 'Now, you were saying . . .?'

'All right, I give in,' said Crossman, sinking to his knees. 'I planted explosives in the walls as I was working. I had my pockets full of gunpowder, you see, and I packed it in with the fascines and gabions. Subtle, eh?'

He looked up and stared into Zinski's eyes.

'Even when I tell the truth you choose not to believe it – so why don't you just have me shot here and now? I'm fed up with all this. Just get it over with.'

An order was snapped and one of the guards took a pistol from his pocket and pressed it to Crossman's temple.

'Goodbye, Sergeant,' said Major Zinski. 'It is a sad end for a man of your character.'

Tears sprang to Crossman's eyes involuntarily.

'Goodbye,' he croaked.

Nothing happened for a very long time. Crossman could feel the muzzle of the pistol against his forehead. It began as a ring of cold steel, but his body heat warmed it, and after a while he could only feel its pressure on his skin. Finally, he gave out a long sigh and fainted.

When he woke, he was being held on his feet by the two marines, but the pistol had been removed from his head.

Zinski said, 'You may have another drink of water now.'

'No thank you,' whispered Crossman, hoarsely.

'Drink it. It will not be dashed from your lips. Don't be a fool now.'

Crossman took the water and drank it, the cool liquid hurting his parched, raw throat as it went down. He wisely refrained from taking too much, since his stomach had shrunk over the three days. Sugared plums were then offered to him from a bowl on the desk and he took them and ate them noisily, with the guards looking at him with blank expressions on their faces.

Major Zinski spoke. 'You were not told which magazine you were intended to destroy?'

'I'm not even sure that was my mission. I simply believe it might be. I suppose it would be your largest magazine. Or perhaps more than one? I'm not certain.'

'All right, I believe you. A quantity of foreign explosives was discovered by the Star Fort magazine last night, ready to be detonated. It was successfully dismantled and made safe. I think one of your compatriots must have been sent over to do the job you were supposed to do, but he too failed.'

Lovelace, thought Crossman. So the major's fox hunt had been foiled too. They were both failures.

'Ah, I see by your expression that I've touched a truth nerve,' smiled Zinski. 'Good, I'm glad not to have to execute you. You will be returned to your cell to await transportation out of here. I'm sending you to Russia, isn't that nice?'

He was taken away again. This time there were no beatings. Food and drink were brought to him. The food was not particularly appetizing but it was adequate. The water was gratefully received and cherished. To a thirsty man a bottle of water is a treasure. He cuddled it to his breast, drinking it slowly, in small quantities. It tasted better than any wine his father had offered him, and his father was a lover of good wines, a gourmet with an excellent palate.

One day not long afterwards, the guards came to him and roughed him up again, before dragging him before Major Zinski. The major was furious. He was pacing up and down in his office, slapping his thigh with his gloves. He rounded on Crossman as soon as the sergeant was pulled through the doorway and presented to him.

'A riot, amongst the convicts. Do you know how much damage they've done? Set us back ten days. *Ten days*. I expect you're pleased. I suppose you know nothing about this? You are innocent of any involvement? Tell me your lies.'

Well done, Wynter and Ali, thought Crossman – but only ten days? – he was not as pleased as Zinski expected him to be. Obviously from Zinski's reaction a ten-day setback was a disaster to the Russians, but to Crossman it seemed only a minor achievement.

'Did any get away, over to the other side?' asked Crossman.

'Some.' Zinski suddenly seemed distracted, perhaps his great mind working on how to pursue repairs quickly. 'Naturally one or two go every day, just as we get the occasional man from your side. There are always malcontents. Today, however, we lost several dozen convicts. They went over the wall – braved fire from both sides.'

Crossman's spirits plummeted.

'Only a few dozen? Out of thousands?'

Zinski smiled grimly. 'My marines and sailors shot some of them, of course. But it was not the mass exodus you seem to have hoped for. Most of the prisoners know that freedom is just around the corner for them here. Why would they risk that?'

Crossman conceded, 'It was very clever of you to offer an amnesty. However, you didn't tell them it would only be for those who survive the massacre to come, when the allies open up with their artillery, and our ships' guns blast you from the seaward side. Do they realize a storm of iron and lead is coming their way soon? Have you told them?' asked Crossman.

'They know they're putting up defences against *something*.'

'Yes, but it will be a holocaust that visits them when the siege guns begin raining death on this town.'

Zinski shrugged and ran his fingers through his hair.

'Never mind, we will work that much harder to repair the damage you have wreaked.'

'I still have not said I was to blame.'

'But you were.'

Sergeant Crossman nodded, seeing no gain in continuing to deny it. 'In part, yes.'

'There are others, then?' growled Zinski.

'Were. They will have gone now.'

'Leaving you?'

'Of course – I am expendable,' said Crossman. 'We all are – except perhaps men like Colonel Todleben – engineering geniuses.'

Zinski snorted. 'Engineers?'

'Colonel Todleben is much needed by your people, but I am considered only a slight loss to mine. One or two will be sorry, others will be mightily pleased. A week from now and I shall not be missed.'

'How very sad,' said the major. 'So much damage too. We can unspike the guns, of course, but they burned and looted, destroyed tools, pulled down walls – killed several of my marines – for which you will be held responsible.

'It's a mess out there. Once I straighten it up, I'll come back and deal with you properly. You will have to be hanged, of course – there's nothing I can do about that now. There are others who will want to witness your execution: Admiral Korniloff for one. In the meantime, you will be whipped.'

He barked an order at one of the guards, who took a quick, pale glance at Crossman.

'*Da*,' said the man.

Crossman was taken to the cellar and there chained to the wall at a height which allowed him to touch the floor with just the tips of his toes. Then the shirt was torn from his back exposing bare skin. He knew then he was in for a beating and gritted his teeth. The next moment he heard a swish and felt the excruciating pain of a whip on his back. Water sprang to his eyes but he was determined to make no sound.

From the sound of the weapon he guessed it was a flail rather than a single-strand whip. He felt it cut into his skin and tear the flesh from his ribs and backbone. After twenty strokes it was no longer possible to remain quiet and he let out a groan. He was hanging by his arms now, all the weight on the joints. Now he wondered whether he would get through this flogging alive. Each stroke of the flail sent a jolt of agony through him until he felt he could stand it no longer.

'Stop now,' he ordered them in his authoritative sergeant's voice. 'Stop this instant.'

But of course they took no notice. In fact he heard one of the men laugh very nervously as he spoke in undertones to his companion. The flogging continued, during which time Crossman passed out once or twice, only to be revived by an extra hard lash of the whip. Such strokes had every nerve in his body at screaming point. He wondered how much pain a man could stand before death safely enfolded him in its soft black cloak.

The flogging with the horsehair Tartar's whip went on until he passed out for the duration.

Afterwards one of the sailors who helped with the flogging was sick. His vomit stank the room, but no doubt he had finally blanched at the sight of white bone through raw flesh. The other one rubbed ointment in Crossman's wounds, and placed a large towel-sized lint over his back.

Crossman lay down on his dirty straw and all but died that night, having received over eighty lashes.

9

While Crossman was undergoing incarceration, Wynter was busy fomenting discontent amongst the convicts. He had decided that for once – and it was a sobering thought – the responsibility for a mission was now wholly on his shoulders. Wynter did not count the Turk, Yusuf Ali, for Ali was not British and therefore would only ever be a helper.

Wynter's prejudices were born out of an age when the British ruled much of the world and even a poor farm boy from a tiny village in Essex considered himself superior to all foreigners, especially those with skins which were dark by nature.

So, Wynter believed himself to be the commanding officer now and it was up to him to complete the mission.

'I wish the sergeant had told me more about what was to be done,' he complained to himself.

But if he lived in an age when the Englishman was king, he was also in an era where communication between superior officers and their subordinates was scant. Soldiers of Wynter's rank simply did as they were told, with no explanations given, nor any expected. Crossman was more democratic than most senior NCOs and officers, whose autocracy was their power.

'We got to start a riot. Cause a bit of havoc,' he reminded himself. 'An't going to be easy.'

He began to foster closer relationships with the men who spoke English. With these prisoners he dropped the pretence of being anything but English. Wynter was fond of barefist fighting and began a competition amongst the convicts. He found matched pairs and they fought during their rest hours, the guards betting along with the convicts on the outcome. Sometimes Wynter fought too, but for the most part he encouraged bouts between others. This activity increased his status amongst the hardened convicts, who welcomed any distraction from their work.

When they were sitting quietly of a late evening, after a poor meal of thin soup and hardtack, Wynter would inform his companions that life was much sweeter in the camps outside Sebastopol. He told them they would be treated with great respect if they went over to the other side. He said the pay in the British army was very good, that the food was excellent and that they would be welcomed with open arms.

'You can't beat it,' he told them. 'I'm a lifer meself – wouldn't have no other work.'

Unlike Crossman, who stuck fairly closely to the truth, not promising much which he could not deliver, Wynter was prepared to lie through his teeth to get what he wanted. He was a much more natural undercover agent than Crossman, in that he was prepared to do anything to achieve his end, even if he compromised his honour and integrity. The fact was, Wynter did this kind of thing as a normal course of behaviour in his life. It was part of the survival kit of a man who was trying to escape absolute poverty.

'For every man who gets to the British lines,' he told his fellow workers, 'there'll be a reward in sterling. Twenty English pounds for every deserter to the British side. You'll be treated like heroes. We've got every convenience over there – good food, wine, warm clothes, transport. You won't want for nothing, I can promise you that. You'll be rich men when this war's over. I can give it to you reliably that any man who comes out of Sebastopol with me, will be first at the loot when we go back in again. That's Wynter's promise.'

'You have much wine over there?' asked a man with a squint. 'What about rum and brandy?'

'We've got the lot,' confided Wynter. 'We've got rum coming out of our ears. Why, the navy ships get flagons of it every day. And brandy too.' He gave a little laugh. 'Most of our sailor boys are drunk half the time. We're much too generous with our booze, we are, in the British army.'

'What about my wife and children?' asked one man. 'They will be here in Sebastopol.'

'Married men get extra rations,' said Wynter. 'I'll have a word with the quartermaster myself. You can send in food by our secret couriers. I mean,' he laughed, 'how did you think *I* got here?'

Once this had been translated for the other convicts there was general laughter amongst them. Yes, how did the Englishman come to be among them? Why, they came and went as they pleased, these people. They were having the laugh of Admiral Korniloff and his sailors.

'All it takes,' Wynter explained, 'is one good riot.'

Ali came to him one night, to question his methods.

'What you do?' asked Ali. 'I hear things.'

'You let me be,' said Wynter, who was actually terrified of the Bashi-Bazouk, having seen Ali do things that would make a murderer blanch. 'I'm doin' good work here, Ali.'

'We get the sergeant back. We rescue the sergeant.'

'I'm willing to do that,' Wynter agreed. 'O' course I am – but you tell me how we do it. He's stuck in that blamed big building with guards all over the place. We'd never get him out alive and you know it. Best wait for an opportunity to arise, then we'll have him away. At the minute we've got to do what he wants us to do – get the riots started.'

The Bashi-Bazouk was not thoroughly convinced by Wynter's show of concern for his sergeant, but he allowed himself

112

to be persuaded not to go crashing into the place where Crossman was being held. It was true the building was well guarded and it would almost be a suicide mission to get him out by force. They would, as Wynter had said, need to wait for a better time.

'I stay with you now,' Ali told Wynter. 'We make the riot together.'

'Aw, I was doin' good without you, Ali.'

'I stay.'

'Well, I'm in charge then,' protested the lance corporal, desperately. 'I outrank you.'

'No. Ali in charge.'

'We'll both be equal then, because I an't doin' what no Turk tells me to do, and that's flat. I'm a lance corporal. That means somethin' in the British army, see – and Lord Raglan is in charge of the whole show, so that makes anyone who's in the British army in charge.'

'Not Raglan. General Canrobert is in charge of whole army. It is the French who says to go or not to go.'

'Blast the damn French,' expostulated Wynter. 'Didn't we beat them at Waterloo? We're the lads who've licked 'em time and time again. You don't follow orders from someone you've pasted in a fight. We're equal, you and me, and that's flat.'

Ali finally seemed to accept that Wynter was not going to be told what to do 'by a blamed Turk' and the Bashi-Bazouk decided he would get things done a roundabout way, rather than confront Wynter head on.

So, the pair of them worked together, and finally they set a date for the revolt of the convicts.

The day arrived and, when he thought the moment for which he had planned so long was right, Wynter suddenly turned on one of the lax guards and wrenched his musket from his hands. Firing it in the air, he cried, 'Let's take 'em lads!' The convicts rose up – though not as one man, unfortunately – and attacked

113

their guards. Soon, those who were taking part in the riot, which was about a quarter of the total number of convicts, were running through the streets and along the defences, smashing everything.

Some of them headed towards a huge warehouse where the flour was stored that was used to make the bread for the whole of Sebastopol. Ali had hidden a quantity of explosives and they retrieved this and used it to blow the warehouse to smithereens, sending up a monstrous grey cloud of powder to hover above the city.

Wynter and some other men began to tear down the defences they themselves had erected, slashing at fascine and gabion baskets with captured swords, cutting them open and letting the rocks and earth spill out so that the earthworks collapsed. Fires were started all along the outer perimeter of the city, and this spread to some of the buildings within the town itself. In this way the garrison was kept busy fire-fighting, as well as trying to quell the riot.

Officers were barking superfluous or useless orders, counter-manding each other, causing more chaos by their inept actions. The truth was the Russians had not expected the rebellion, since promises of later freedom had been made to the convicts which the authorities thought would ensure their loyalty. No one was prepared for the riot.

Those convicts not taking part in the revolt stood to one side, neither helping nor hindering the rioters. It was not their business to stop their fellow convicts from destroying the city.

Gradually, however, the garrison mobilized itself. Wynter found himself in a street with a mob. At the end of the street was a line of marines aiming their rifles. He had just time to drop to the ground when the first volley ripped into the rioters, killing many of them where they stood. A second volley cut down several more. Thereafter, a ragged fusillade picked off those trying to run into side alleys, or climb through windows of nearby buildings.

Wynter crawled slowly across the street towards an alley,

using the dead bodies around him as shields. Fortunately for him there were still enough of the convicts in a panic and on their feet to provide easy targets for the marines. He managed to reach the alley and run along it to the end.

On the other side he met a squad of armed sailors, trotting at a quick pace up another street, their muskets at the ready. Wynter threw his hands in the air, crying, 'Not me. I haven't done nothin'. It was them in the next road down.'

A trembling sailor immediately detached himself from his fellows and made as if to bayonet Wynter in the stomach, shouting something at him in Russian. The lance corporal could see that the sailor was scared and had reacted out of fear.

Wynter grabbed the end of the musket, struggled with the weapon, successfully turning the blade away from himself.

'Hey, listen to me. I an't one of them rioters. I'm one of the good ones.'

By this time the rest of the man's squad was almost at the end of the street. The sailor glanced towards his departing comrades, realizing he was being left behind. He yelled to a friend, who halted and turned. Then he tried to kick Wynter in the genitals, several times, anxious now just to free himself of this ragged man with his strange tongue.

Wynter grimaced as a boot caught him on the thigh.

'Here, I've had enough of this,' he told the sailor.

Pulling the man towards him, Wynter struck him on the jaw with his fist, sending the sailor reeling against a wall. Another two punches and the man slid down the wall to rest in a sitting position on the ground. Wynter picked up his musket and faced the man's comrade, who was now running to his assistance.

'Don't try it, lad,' warned Wynter, but the sailor came on, his eyes fixed on Wynter's face.

Wynter raised the musket and pulled the trigger, hoping the weapon was loaded and ready to shoot.

A puff of flame went up, but the musket failed to discharge.

'Damn me and my luck,' whined Wynter. 'A blamed misfire.'

The sailor was only a few yards away now and he raised his musket to fire at Wynter. Sailors were not natural users of rifles, since they did not normally employ them in the course of their work, as did marines or soldiers. This one obviously wanted to be close enough to be sure to hit his target.

Wynter launched his weapon as a spear. It went through the air like an assegai. The bayonet struck the sailor in the abdomen and the poor man dropped his musket immediately, clutching at this object which had penetrated his bowels. He went a sickly green colour and sank to his knees with a groan on his lips. He looked up once at Wynter, a hurt expression on his face, as if the Englishman had played a schoolboy trick on him. Then he managed to wrench the weapon from his abdomen and simply remained kneeling on the ground, his hands covering his wound, staring at the flagstone in front of him.

'I'm sorry about that,' said Wynter, appalled at the horrible wound he had delivered. 'It an't the same as on a battlefield, with the roar of the guns in your ears, is it?'

Seeing he could do nothing for the man, Wynter raced away, back down the street, towards the edge of the city.

The rioters were now being cut down by the garrison and some of them were going over the dykes and walls, towards the British and French lines. Picquets there, not knowing what was going on inside Sebastopol, thought they were under attack and began firing on the escaping convicts. Some got through, however, and blurted out in broken English that they were deserting to the other side. The word went up along the line that the Russians' convicts were defecting.

Wynter made his way over the wall and began a zig-zagging run away from the harbour, northwards towards the Inkerman ruins. He had some idea in his head now that if he kept going, he could be out of this war for ever. He could steal a horse and ride out of the battle area. Or indeed, walk from it. In the north there were many farms and vineyards where he might find work. He was a farmer's boy after all, and had skills to offer. They were not all Tartars who owned the farms. He would find a place which suited him and be out of this bloody mess.

But the argument with himself was brief. He knew in his heart of hearts that he would not be happy on some foreign farm. And though he had few qualms about leaving Crossman back there in some dungeon, it seemed to him that there were only the two alternatives: run away, or go and get Crossman. If he returned to his lines without the sergeant, he knew he would be sent back to the regiment, to do ordinary duties.

And though he did not feel he owed the sergeant anything, he acknowledged a kind of bond between them now. They had been through things together, like two poachers out on some Essex country estate, sharing the experience of being chased by gamekeepers and laughing at it over a drink at the inn. They were not exactly brothers-in-arms – he could never have a close love for an aristocrat – but they were now certainly cousins of a kind. Wynter found it strange to realize that he would be a little upset to have to leave the sergeant there, rotting in that jail. It was a new feeling to him, this worrying over another man.

He retraced his steps and once again entered the city. A sort of calm had fallen over the place now. The rest of the day Wynter spent in a broken-down shack at the edge of the docks, then in the evening he went looking for Yusuf Ali where he knew he would find him waiting.

Indeed, he found the Turk in the very street where he expected him to be. There the two men got together and discussed how they were going to release the sergeant. Wynter felt peculiarly noble, standing with Ali, talking about their next move like two veteran enemy agents. A maturity had fallen on his shoulders from the sky and he liked the wearing of it.

10

Jack Crossman had lain for some days, he knew not how many, hovering between life and death, at the end of which a gloating Major Zinski came to tell him the riots had failed to bring down the walls of Sebastopol.

The whipping Crossman had received, on top of the privations they had put him through – the beatings and the starvings – had almost completely broken his resistance. His spirit was almost shattered and his will to live all but drained from him.

His dreams were fitful and demons predominated, proliferating in hallucinations which visited him night and day. The guards had all but ceased to feed him now, since he had been condemned to death, for why waste precious food on a man who is to die anyway, especially during a siege? They did give him water. And they had ceased to torture him, which was blissful relief. His body was racked with pain, his will was almost gone, but it was his mind which saved him from slipping into the dark kingdom.

In his head, to keep himself from going, he constructed marvellous inventions, machines which would astonish the world with their innovative creativity.

This exercise ensured there was still the remains of a fire

in Sergeant Crossman, still a glowing ember, when they came to fetch him to hang him one cold morning in October 1854.

Using what little Russian he had learnt from Yusuf Ali, he asked the guards for the date.

'What is the number of this day?' he asked awkwardly. 'I want to know the date if I am to die.'

After many shrugs and blank looks, they finally understood what he wanted and enlightenment shone in their eyes.

'Seventeen October,' he was told.

He nodded gravely as he shuffled unsteadily between the pair of them, the chains on his wrists and ankles hobbling him. Crossman saw himself in a full-length mirror in the hallway, which the soldiers used to primp themselves before going into Major Zinski's office to face their superior. He was horrified to see an emaciated creature with a grey-fringed beard and wearing rags. There were sores on his skin, blemishes and black bruises showing through the dirt and grime. His lips had bursting pustules on them, while the nose was raw and veined. He stared at his image with dull, listless eyes buried in a bearded face full of hollows.

'You poor soul,' he croaked ironically.

They then led him out into a courtyard where a rough gallows had been erected. He halted on the steps going down to the yard and looked around him. Where were the rest of the officials? There were only the two guards and a sailor in a bloody, leather apron standing on the gallows, testing the rope.

'I'm to be hanged by a ship's butcher,' he said, 'while Zinski and Korniloff have breakfast in some white room, on white tables, with white tablecloths.'

Having lived in the dirt for so long he was now, among other things, obsessed with cleanliness, and jealous of those who could have it while he could not.

He stood on top of the steps, ready to walk down and put himself into the hands of a ship's butcher who had been chosen to execute him simply because that man was used to slaughtering domestic animals.

Before Crossman was able to descend, all hell broke loose.

The world was suddenly full of thunderous noise, of bangs and explosions, of zinging, whizzing sounds. First they came from the direction of the sea, then from all around the city, and finally from the interior. Out in the streets, beyond the courtyard wall, people were running and shouting. A building that loomed above the wall suddenly crumbled on one corner, part of its masonry collapsing. There were bright flashes in the sky, and the ground shook and rocked.

'The bombardment,' grinned Crossman, talking to himself. 'The bombardment has started. That's where they are, Zinski, Todleben and Korniloff. That's why Zinski's ordered me to the gallows today. The flags have been raised. They knew the bombardment was about to begin.'

Round shot began landing everywhere now, and shells from the seaward side of the town were bursting, one landing on the building roof above their heads.

The guards nervously pushed Crossman forwards, urging him to shuffle towards the waiting butcher, who was staring up at the sky, as if expecting a package of meat to be delivered from that direction.

Crossman stepped forward, a few inches at a time.

He could see red flags on the poles. All around Sebastopol red flags had been hoisted to signal the beginning of the bombardment. In the bastions and batteries, guns were being brought to bear on allied positions; were being fired, dropping their shot into enemy salients, inside distant trenches. Embrasures disappeared in clouds of thick smoke and fumes, to reappear moments later, revealing again the black round mouths of guns. Earthworks were struck and erupted in showers of soil and grit. Buildings were blown apart.

All around Sebastopol warships from the British and French fleets were pounding the harbour and forts, and were being attacked in return.

In the streets around the Place du Théâtre, where the first enemy shot had fallen, sailors and soldiers, and the convicts alongside whom Crossman had worked, were running in panic through the streets, buildings shattering before their eyes. Above them the heavens were convulsing, filled with puffs of black smoke and the flashings of flying pieces of jagged metal. They could hear the deadly whine of shrapnel and the singing hail of musket balls from bursting cylinder shot. In their nostrils, in their eyes, were the pungent, acrid fumes from their own artillery, returning the storm of allied shot in kind.

The din was terrible, both from the screaming of the wounded, the groans of the dying, and the cannonade itself.

Crossman shuffled slowly through all this noise and confusion towards the gallows where he was to hang.

Suddenly, there was a tremendous explosion directly in front of him. The gallows disintegrated before his eyes, catapulting the hapless ship's butcher high in the air like a rag doll, to land somewhere in the far corner of the courtyard. The marine on the right side of Crossman vanished.

Crossman was thrown on his back.

A massive hole had suddenly appeared in the courtyard wall, behind where the gallows had stood. Crossman could see a cannon there, on the other side, smoke coming from its barrel.

One of his guards had been carried off by the shot which had first smashed through the gallows. He saw the other one unsling his musket from his shoulder, but the marine was shot dead before he could aim his weapon. Then two dark figures, silhouettes, came running through the blue haze which clouded the hole in the wall. The smoke and dust were so thick they could have been a brace of those demons which had been haunting Crossman in his cell.

One of them hoisted Crossman on to a strong back. The other made sure the guards were dead. Then the sergeant felt himself being carried, through the havoc in the streets, where shells and shot were still landing. It was not an unusual sight,

121

here and now during the bombardment, to see two men running, one of them with a third man slung over his shoulder. There were wounded everywhere, being transported by whatever means, to a place where they could be tended.

The two men ran into a cobbled square and were passing a wooden horse trough when a shell landed in it. Unfortunately the horse trough was dry and the fuse continued to burn, but a Russian sailor ran and threw himself on it, pulling out the fuse and thus rendering it harmless. The sailor had saved all their lives. They did not stop to thank him.

All the while they were running they stepped over and around dead bodies, which littered the squares and streets and alleys.

Finally, they had to stop for a rest. Crossman was unshouldered and put in a sitting position. He found that the person who was carrying him was Yusuf Ali, while Wynter had been running alongside. He had never been so glad to see the faces of friends in his life. For a moment the thunder of the artillery was forgotten.

Wynter kneeled down beside Crossman and looked into his face.

'Damn me, Sergeant, you're in a bad way, an't you?' The dirty face of the lance corporal grinned. 'Still, we got you out in time, didn't we? You was just about to be turned off by that hangman, wasn't you? Where did he go to, by the way, after we fired the gun at the wall?'

Crossman croaked, 'You blew him to hell.'

'Did we, by golly?' said Wynter. 'Flipped him off his perch, did we? That must have been his brains splattered on the side of the building. Well, there's a show for you.'

Wynter lit up a clay pipe he had extracted from his pocket, probably to calm his nerves.

'Me and Ali had to wait until the bombardment started,' he said, leaning his back against a wall. 'Another gun goin' off amongst all the whizz-bangs of a cannonade didn't make no difference. The Turk shot the other guard when we came

122

through the hole in the wall.' Wynter grinned again. 'Lucky our cannonball didn't hit you instead of a guard, Sergeant, or we'd be carrying a mess of blood and cartilage through the streets.'

Crossman said, hoarsely, 'Where did you get the gun?'

'That blamed cannon? Why Ali pinched it an hour ago from the docks right under their noses. It was stood by the quayside, with the rest of a battery, hitched to a horse. He took the horse, limber, the lot. Just jumped on its back then rode off with it hell for leather, waving a thank-you-very-much-sir.'

Wynter paused for effect, enjoying his own story.

'When he got back to the wall, I was waitin' for him. We'd planned it like that, you see. They've been shifting guns here there an' everywhere for the last week or so. We had our eye on a little cannon. We wanted one small enough to run off with and big enough for the job, so to speak.'

'You're bloody geniuses,' Crossman said, cracking a smile. 'You're lifesavers.'

'And don't you forget it, Sergeant,' said Wynter, waving a finger in his face. 'I'll make sure you don't forget this one — providing we get back, that is.'

He knocked out his pipe when Ali tapped him on the shoulder.

'We go,' said the Bashi-Bazouk, impassively. 'Come, Sergeant, on my back.'

'Get these damn chains off me,' complained Crossman.

'All in good time, Sergeant,' Wynter said, helping Ali up with his cargo. 'Just wait a bit, till we got somethin' to get 'em off with.'

'You steal a damn great cannon,' grumbled Crossman, suffering the indignity of being thrown and draped over Ali's shoulders once again, 'but you couldn't get a hammer and chisel?'

'We didn't know you was chained. We found out where you was and that they were goin' to hang you today, but the codger Ali bribed to give us the information didn't say nothing about you being shackled.'

They moved through the streets once again. There were still bodies all over the place. The noise and danger had not abated one bit. Round shot and shells still rained remorselessly down on the city and were being thrown up again in reply. The air remained full of heavy metal which took hundreds of lives that day, especially in Sebastopol itself.

Yusuf Ali and Wynter carried the sergeant between them to the edge of town, where they had a hideout down an old disused drain. It was cold and musty underground, but they were relatively safe from both the bombardment and the Russians. Ali went out again straight away. He returned with some tools, food and water. While removing Crossman's shackles he told him that Admiral Korniloff had been killed in the barrage.

'They cry,' he said. 'He was good leader to them.'

'I suppose he was,' said Crossman, 'though I find it difficult to feel sorry. It was he who ordered my hanging, through Major Zinski.'

'You have to hang,' Ali said practically. 'To Russian people you are one bad spy.'

'That's true enough. The Cossack regiments would be toasting Korniloff had the victory been theirs. What about you, Wynter? You did a good job with the revolt after I left. Zinski and Todleben were disgusted with the convicts' rebellion.'

Wynter grinned. 'We burned a big magazine of flour. They didn't like that one bit, the Russians. Lots of other damage too. It went down well, though not many of us got over the defences and into allied lines.'

'You said *us*,' murmured Crossman, feeling weary. 'Did you go and come back again?'

'I sort of half went and then decided I couldn't leave you and Ali here.'

'Very noble of you, Wynter. Are you sure you didn't think

about deserting? You could have got clean away. They would have thought you were dead. You could have been out of this war and in some comfortable place.'

Wynter's eyes turned a little cold. 'I thought about it, Sergeant, I won't deny it. I thought about doin' it, going off and finding some farm or other. I'm good at farming. But I changed me mind in the end. I dunno why.' He grinned. 'One of life's myst'ries, I suppose. I mean, why would I want to risk me life for *you*, a bloody gentleman's son who gives me what for all the time? Damn that, eh? But I did, and there's no accounting for it. No accounting at all.'

'Lance Corporal Wynter, I do believe you've got streaks of honour and loyalty in you. I'm amazed.'

Wynter grinned again. 'If it's them I've got, I'm bloody well amazed meself, Sergeant, you can be sure of that.'

11

Ali and Wynter managed to find their way through the Russian lines and into high country on the other side. They were pondering on how they were going to get the sick Sergeant Crossman back to the hovel where he could be nursed. Crossman was against being delivered into the regimental surgeon's hands.

'He'll have me in some damn field hospital, or on a boat going to Scutari. They'll kill me in there, that's for certain. Just get me to the house. I'll mend in good time.'

He was too weak to walk, and Ali was about to go off and steal an *araba* to carry him in, but by a lucky stroke a squadron of 17th Lancers met up with them.

'Who are you, sirs?' cried a Light Brigade captain. 'Make yourselves known to me.'

'We're 88th Foot, Connaught Rangers,' cried Wynter. 'Got a sergeant here who's in a bad way.'

The captain was astonished that the ragamuffins facing him were infantry from his own army. He looked suspiciously at the Turk and queried if he too was 88th Foot. Wynter told him he was seconded to the Connaught Rangers as a scout, but was in fact a Bashi-Bazouk.

'Are you telling me the truth, sir?'

'Yes, indeed, Captain,' said Wynter. 'You can arrest us if you like and we'll sort it all out later, but this here man has got to have medical treatment. Can you lend us a nag?'

A kind of rippling went through the troop, a clattering and jangling of stirrups and scabbards, as the riders shuddered and mounts shied at this horrifying idea.

'Loan you a – a horse?' cried the captain. Then he stared down at Crossman, who was bent over double, hardly able to keep upright even in a sitting position. He wheeled his mount and cried, 'Private Feltam, if you please. Take the sergeant to the hospital on your horse.'

'Yes, sir,' said the trooper, dismounting.

Crossman was lifted carefully up on to the charger and then Feltam got up behind him. Most awkward was the lance, which was handed up to Feltam after the pair were settled. The nine-foot ash pole sporting its red and white shalloon pennon was then attached to the lancer's upper arm by a lanyard, with the shoe of the lance in a leather socket near the stirrup, leaving both of the rider's hands free.

They rode off, leaving Wynter, Ali and the squadron of 17th behind them, with Feltam holding Crossman on with one arm and using the reins with the other.

'You all right, Sergeant?' asked the private. 'You look a bit banged up. You feeling well?'

'As well as can be expected, thank you,' replied Crossman in a weak voice, 'but I beg you will take me to Kadikoi village, where I have my quarters. I have no desire to die in a filthy hospital with some surgeon hovering over me, a bloody knife in one hand and my liver in the other.'

'You don't sound like no sergeant. You sound like an officer,' said Feltam.

'That is the cross I have to bear.'

Feltam appeared to digest this piece of information without further comment.

However, he did say later on, 'My cross is that we haven't

seen no action yet – not proper action. We get ribbed by you infantry fellows all the time. Insults and all that.'

The horse plodded patiently on, taking ground rough and smooth with equal footing.

'Yes, you've been rather left out of it, you cavalry. Well, perhaps you're being saved for some dramatic endeavour? Who knows what is in Lord Raglan's mind? I must admit he seems to be treating his cavalry like some delicate treasure, to be cosseted and kept, but not to be used. I'm sure Lords Cardigan and Lucan feel the same way you do.'

'Lord Look-On!' snorted Feltam. 'We're a blooming laughing stock, we are. Even the Cossacks and Russian hussars have the laugh of us, having done more than we have.'

'How is the bombardment going?' asked Crossman, to change the subject. 'Have we made an assault yet?'

'There's another blooming thing. We could have charged right in there when we first came down. They had no defences to speak of. We've sort of left them to build their walls, bring up their guns, and now we've got something to knock down we can't seem to do it. The French magazine blew up on Mount Rudolph just after the barrage started. That meant we was on our own from then on, the French guns having packed it in.'

Crossman learned that after the French magazine blew up, the Russians attacked Mount Rudolph with a small force, to put the French guns out of action. The Chasseurs de Vincennes charged the Russians and routed them before they could do any damage. Feltam spoke of this charge wistfully, as if he wished he were French and able to take part in the action.

The British navy had not fared well in the battle with the forts. The screw-ship *Agamemnon*, with Admiral Lyons on board, had steamed into the fight only to be holed in several places by the Russian guns. The *London* and *Sanspareil* were almost blasted out of the water, while the *Bellerophon* burst into flames. Over 300 sailors were killed in the battle and when Admiral Dundas signalled the end of the attack to his fleet, the Russians were virtually unscathed.

Crossman told Feltam about the shell which had landed in the horse trough and the bravery of the man who had leaped on it and drawn its fuse before it exploded.

'Ah, that's because I hear tell they get awarded the Cross of St George if they do that.'

Crossman shrugged. 'Why would a man want a medal that much?'

'Because I also hear tell that having the Cross of St George stops them from going on the wheel.'

'You mean, if it's awarded to a soldier or sailor it exempts the man from corporal punishment?'

Feltam nodded. 'So's I hear tell.'

'Well, what Wynter would do for one of those crosses!' said the sergeant to himself. 'Then I would have nothing to use to threaten the man.'

Finally, after a long and dusty journey at a very slow pace, they reached the village of Kadikoi. Feltam was not too happy at taking the sergeant to a hovel, especially when there was a hospital just near to the house. Crossman told him he would take full responsibility for his own death, should that occur as a result of not receiving proper medical attention.

'That's all right,' said the worried Private Feltam, 'but you'll be dead, and not able to vouch for me.'

'True, true. I'll think of some way of leaving a message.'

When Peterson, Devlin and Clancy came out of the hovel to answer Feltam's halloo, they discovered a very sick sergeant of the Connaught Rangers. They carried him inside and up the stairs to his old room. There they laid him on a bed of straw and blankets. Peterson made some soup. Clancy made a fire in the room. Devlin went off somewhere to fetch help.

Mary Seacole, the Scots-West Indian woman who had done much nursing in the Crimea, was now running a small shop called The British Hotel, and could not come to nurse one man. Mrs Rogers might have come, except that she was up on the front line, tending to the wounded there. After a few enquiries, Devlin did find someone, and returned to the house.

Crossman was laying back on his bed of straw. He had been given a drink and some soup and was now feeling much less like dying. When Devlin came to him he was able to show some interest in his potential carer.

'Who have you found?' asked Crossman in a weak tone.

'Why, Sergeant, one of the wives. She asked to be the one to come to you. She seemed distressed by your condition. So much so, I might have thought she had some personal interest in you, Sergeant, if I did not think such assumptions improper.'

Hope sprang eternal to Crossman's breast.

'Is it – is it Mrs O'Clarey, the corporal flute-player's wife? She who used to be Mrs McLoughlin? Is it she who is anxious about my condition?'

Devlin looked mystified. 'Why no – 'twas a lady.'

Crossman half sat up in bed in alarm.

'A *lady*? You don't mean Mrs Durham?'

At that moment the female in question appeared in the doorway and removed her hat, taking out the pins and sticking them back in the crown so that she would know where to find them.

'You see,' she said, 'I told you so, Corporal. He wanted no other but myself to minister to him in his illness.' She then turned to Crossman and looked genuinely distressed. 'Oh, Alexander, how pale you look – how thin! Are you so bad, my dear? You look close to death. I must build you up again.'

Corporal Devlin's eyes were almost popping out of his head at this speech.

Crossman said, 'You – you have me confused with another.'

Her face registered mock surprise. 'Of course I do. I did not mean *Alexander* at all, I meant *Sergeant Crossman*. And I did not mean, *my dear* in that sense. I mean, *my dear sir*. Now,' she leaned down and began to tuck in the blanket so that he was bound like a swaddling child, 'we must minister.'

'Devlin,' cried Crossman in panic, 'get this lady out of here – get her out, I say.'

Lavinia Durham raised her eyebrows. 'Corporal, you will do no such thing, or my husband, who is a captain, will have you flogged for insubordination. Leave us now.'

Devlin stared agog at his sergeant, then once more at Mrs Durham, then left the room.

Lavinia found the rickety chair that was the only other piece of furniture in the room. She sat on it, commenting that she would have to get a table, a jug and a glass, and some other things for the room, if she were to stay there until he got well.

'Don't you have some battle to gawk at?' moaned Crossman.

'Don't be uncharitable, Alex. You know perfectly well that a siege is not as exciting as a proper battle, with hussars riding by in glorious colour, and French Zouaves, and Bashi-Bazouks. I dislike artillery exchanges where there is no movement going on – no exciting charges by the cavalry, or infantry rushing up hills – and so prefer to be here with you. If there is blood to be seen, it is in this room.'

'What about your husband, Lavinia? He'll be monstrously angry when he hears you're tending to my every need. Think of your husband, my dear.'

'Now, there, you are calling me *my dear* again. I can do it to you, because I was the one who was jilted, but you must not do it to me – it is most improper, Alex. It robs me of all my dignity as an abandoned woman. How can I be strong and forgiving if you insist on being so familiar?'

Crossman groaned.

'You left me without a word of explanation,' continued the lady, matter-of-factly. 'We had an understanding, too, I'm sure you'll grant me that. You called me a *nonpareil* at one time, if you remember, and compared me to a summer's day.'

'All I did was read you a Shakespeare sonnet.'

'In some circles that is enough to justify ordering the wedding gown, my dear. Still, maybe I had a lucky escape, for your behaviour is quite strange – even a little mad. You come from a long line of officers, yet here you are hiding in the ranks. I could never have married a man who had so little regard for his lineage. How would it be if I were the wife of a sergeant? And perhaps,' she gave a little shudder, 'had we married you might still have thought of enlisting in the ranks, to prove some point of honour, or for a wager, or whatever the reason is for your being in that horribly rough uniform.'

'Perhaps.'

'My dear, it would be too ghastly for words, now wouldn't it? Can you see me socializing with the likes of a Mrs Private Baggins or a Mrs Corporal Boggins? No, Alexander, it would not do. It would simply not do. You must see that I had no choice but to marry a Bertie of some description after you left me. And though Bertie's family might be in trade, they are respectable. Bertie and I understand each other. I have his money and the status and freedom an unmarried woman would never be allowed. In return, he doesn't need to be loved. He needs a beautiful, well-bred wife to show the world.'

'And you are beautiful?'

'Of course I am – you've told me so yourself. No cause for false modesty. I have the body of a Greek goddess and the mind of a Tudor queen. Loveliness and cunning. It's a fascinating combination, Alexander, and it keeps me in male company. Men like an enchantress, a *femme fatale*.'

Crossman gave up. He could never fence words with Lavinia Durham. She always had the better of him, like a swordsman who is at the top of his skill and knows he cannot be beaten. Her confidence overwhelmed him. He wondered what her husband would say when he knew that she was nursing a sick sergeant in the Connaught Rangers. He would have an apoplexy.

Later, while she was working with her needle in the lamp

light, she said in a quiet tone, 'You actually had a lucky escape, Alexander.'

He knew that she meant she was hell to live with – a wilful woman, a hoyden in her maidenhood and not much better now, though she could get away with more being a married lady – and that he would have lamented a betrothal to her.

'This way,' she added, biting the thread to part it, then turning the full force of her hazel eyes on his, 'your autumn years will not be full of regret.'

What an extraordinary woman she was, he thought, more perceptive than he had previously given her credit for.

Major Lovelace looked in later that night to see how Crossman was getting along.

'Congratulations, Sergeant, on your fox hunt. I hear you did rather well in the end.'

'Wynter did, and Ali. I was rather out of it, sir. All I managed to do was get myself in this state.'

Lovelace shook his head. 'You were the commander in the field. If it had gone disastrously wrong, you would have taken the blame, whether it was your fault personally or not. In which case you should not balk at taking credit for a mission which helped the allied cause. It was a small setback for the Russians, I'll grant you, but we had other things going on at the time. Each small effort amounts to a greater whole.'

'I would be grateful if you would thank Ali and Wynter for their part.'

'I shall do so, Sergeant.'

Mrs Durham, sitting doing some embroidery in the lamp light by the table she had had delivered, looked up and spoke.

'Listen to these two men, speaking to one another as if they come from a different class. You both know you are from the same station. Probably Sergeant Crossman would outrank you, in civilian life, Major Lovelace. Does that not seem strange to you?'

'Ma'am,' replied Lovelace, 'everything seems strange to me

at the moment, especially your presence in this room. However, I want the sergeant to recover and I know that the best person to help him do that is a caring female. My men are so heavy-handed they would probably kill him inadvertently in his delicate condition. But I must confess, I wonder at the propriety of this arrangement. I hope I do not have some irate captain hammering on my door demanding satisfaction.'

'If you mean my husband, sir, his satisfaction comes from other things. He is happy to have a wife who is a lady and who will call him husband and give him some status in life. Captain Durham is not from a very good family, sir. His father was in trade. This might mean little to you or I, but it means a lot to Captain Durham, who feels he has the smirch of coal dust on his brow and is continually anxious that it remains hidden under his wife's lace and velvet.'

Lovelace frowned. 'I feel sorry for the man, if he is that anxious to join with aristocratic society. I have a sergeant here who is just as eager to rid himself of it.'

Mrs Durham smiled politely. 'Well, there you have two different opinions, one from either end of the scale. Each man has what the other desires. I once knew a man who loved mountain climbing, but confessed that whenever he was up on some high peak he desired to be at home by his fire, with his dog, his wife and his slippers. Yet, when he was thus, he wished to be up a mountain again, in the blizzards and snowy wastes.'

Lovelace could not but help admire this woman, whose intellect was more than moderate.

'To what would you ascribe these changing moods, ma'am, in this mountain climber friend?'

She looked up from her embroidery and smiled.

'Why, sir, to the fickleness of man! What else? You are never satisfied. Name me something you wish for, but have not yet got.'

'I want us to win this war, by God,' said Lovelace, determinedly.

'But having won it would not be enough. You would then want to win another. It is as I say, there is no satisfaction to be had in you men. With women it is different. We are satisfied even to take second best, if that is all that is available. Ask Sergeant Crossman if this is not so.'

Crossman gave Lovelace a bleak look, which told the major everything he wanted to know.

'I'll look in on you again soon,' said the major, leaving his side. 'You're in good hands.'

12

Private Feltam did not leave the hovel straight away, but stayed to talk with Peterson, Clancy and Devlin in the downstairs room. He took off his tall *czapka* from his head and placed it carefully on a stool by the door. The infantry soldiers were fascinated by the skull and crossbones badge with the words 'Or Glory' underneath. There were lions' heads fittings in brass to hold the chin-chains on either side. All in all, it was a most intriguingly designed piece of headgear.

Peterson made him some broth, envying him his uniform, while at the instigation of the others the trooper talked of his experiences in the war so far.

'We haven't seen much action in the Crimea,' he confessed. 'We've chased a few Cossacks and we've been chased by 'em, down and up at different places. I really wish we could have a go. I really do. I'd like to think of us having a go.'

Peterson felt sorry for the lancer, who seemed genuinely distressed that the cavalry were not pulling their weight on the Crimean peninsula.

'You had a bit of a go at Varna though,' she said. 'I heard something about it.'

Feltam shook his head gloomily. 'Not as such. You mean the "sore-back reconnaissance", don't you? Lord Cardigan rode us up to the River Danube and back. Over two hundred miles looking for Russians, but they'd already gone. We had to shoot five of the horses which dropped from fatigue on the trail. One of them was mine. I finished the journey in a cart. The other mounts – well, over seventy horses – were unfit for duty after the ride. Some of 'em died later. A lucky one stumbled just as we come into Varna and it had to be shot there and then – right in front of that lady upstairs with the sergeant.'

'Lucky, you say?' queried Devlin.

'Well, we was only allowed to shoot horses with glanders or broken legs. The poor beast would have died anyway, from its labours. Breaking its shin-bone like that, we was able to put it out of its misery, see. Mrs Durham, she started to cause a fuss over the horses, but Lord Cardigan gave her one of his looks and she soon quietened down.'

Feltam took another sip of his broth to wet his throat.

Clancy said, 'But you did have a go at the Russians near MacKenzie's Farm, I remember – when we were on the flank march down to this here Balaclava?'

Feltam's face lit up a little. 'Oh, you mean when we went after 'em but then Lord Raglan called us back? If he hadn't took us off them, we'd have been in a fight all right. We chased 'em away, good enough. There's proof of it in the supply wagons we captured.'

Feltam leaned forward conspiratorially and the heads of the others went down to meet his.

'You should have seen some of the booty we took from them wagons,' he said in a whisper. 'Not the sort of thing you could take to church on Sunday.' He nodded and winked.

If the others were intrigued, Peterson was on the edge of her seat with curiosity.

'What sort of things, trooper?' she asked. 'Tell us.'

'Well, there was some wigs of hair, some brandy and lots of women's underclothes.' He chuckled. 'We changed the frillies for the pennons on our lances, just as a joke you understand, and waved 'em around a bit. Till Lord Cardigan caused a bother and told us to take 'em off.'

The other two men present laughed uproariously.

'What a lark,' said Clancy. 'Fancy using a lady's petticoats for a flag!'

Peterson said with a scowl, 'I don't see what's so funny about that.'

Devlin looked at her in surprise and she turned away and stared at the wall for a moment.

'Is that all of it?' asked Clancy. 'Just the women's undergarments?'

'Not at all,' smirked Feltam. 'There was these books in French, with pictures. The pictures,' he paused dramatically, to take a quick sip of broth, 'was of *naked* women.'

Clancy looked as if his skin were tingling. 'Naked women? With no clothes on?'

Feltam nodded. 'You could see everything. And men were doing things with them. You know. We laughed to see them pictures. Some of the officers knew how to read French. When we was camped by the river, they read some out to each other, with us listening. You wouldn't like to repeat *them* stories to your parish priest. I don't mind telling you I went all hot. You should have heard the one about the butler who hid in a bedroom cupboard and watched the master and one of his chambermaids frolic on the settee.'

'I should like to read that one,' said Clancy, eagerly. 'I could get someone to work out the French. Have you got one of those books on you?

'No, they was took from us by the officers. One or two of the troopers tore out a picture, but I didn't get anything. I can look at one when I want to. I just ask.'

'I should like to see one,' said Clancy, wistfully.

Peterson snorted. 'I don't see what you want to look at rude pictures for, Private Clancy – or read rude stories. You ought to be ashamed of yourself.'

'Well I'm not, so there,' replied Clancy, with some fire. 'I would wish to see them and that's that.'

Thereafter, Peterson refused to look at Clancy, and if he looked her way she scowled at the wall.

When the twilight came, Private Feltam said he ought to be getting back to where the lancers were camped. His horse was getting restless outside, whinnying and scraping the ground with its right foreleg. He put on his magnificent *czapka* and bid them farewell, before mounting and riding off away from Kadikoi, up towards the Light Brigade camp near a vineyard about a mile north of the village.

The darkness crept in over the shadowed hills, purpling the road before the trooper's horse. Though it was October there were still many birds to be seen, especially hawks hovering over the short grasses of the valley. A fox, burnished bronze, ran across Feltam's path, chasing unseen prey. A little while later a primrose moon came up, casting its pale light.

Feltam did not appreciate the beauty of the evening though. He was in a troubled frame of mind after speaking with those infantry fellows. Normally he felt quite superior to foot soldiers. He was one of the élite. Cavalry. And Light Brigade, at that. Dashing heroes, the Light Brigade. They were dressed in splendid attire, which flashed in the sun. Ladies swooned at the sight of them.

Yet he could not help but think those 88th Foot, those Connaught Rangers back there, had seen more glory than he had so far. And they themselves admitted they fought in a square at the Alma, and were not up in the thick of it. Yet they were quietly haughty. They had not said anything, had not bragged about being in action, yet there was a confidence in them which Private Feltam felt was decidedly superior to his own.

'It's a damned shame,' he kept saying to himself. 'They ought to use the cavalry. They ought to have used us at the Alma. They ought to have let us charge into Sebastopol. They ought to let us have a *go*. We are the boys for that. We just need our chance.'

And as he was thus engaged with himself, in deep thought punctuated with some conversation, Private Feltam's *chance* came to him out of the hills.

He could not believe his eyes. There were four figures coming down a gentle escarpment, heading for Kadikoi in the quickening darkness. One of them looked like a scarecrow on a nag, with his ragged civilian clothes. He seemed to be leading the others, who were definitely Don Cossacks.

Where were they going so late in the evening, deep inside territory where they might easily meet up with British troops? They seemed to have their eyes fixed on Kadikoi, where Feltam had left the sick sergeant. What would they be wanting to do in Kadikoi village, full of men who were their enemies?

Suddenly one of the three Cossacks saw Feltam and spoke to his compatriots. They reined their mounts and sat staring at him in the gloaming.

Private Feltam was at first at a loss as to what to do. He might have called for assistance, had it been likely there was anyone within earshot. But looking round he saw he was a long way from Kadikoi, whose one or two lamp lights he could see twinkling in the distance, and certainly nowhere near the Heavy or Light Brigade camps. He was on his own.

Clearly the Cossacks expected him to ride off, for they waited patiently for him to clear their path.

Suddenly, the excitement welled up inside Feltam. He felt his heart drumming in his chest. Here was his chance, by heaven! Here was the action he had craved. Did he dare to attack three Don Cossacks on his own?

By God, yes, he did dare.

Unslinging his lance from his shoulder he took up the charging stance. He drew out his percussion pistol and held it and the reins awkwardly in his left hand. Then he made a 'Tra-la-tra-la' sound, copying the trumpeter's call for the charge, and spurred his mount forwards with his blood racing in his veins and his lips numb with fright.

Seeing him coming, they prepared themselves. The civilian calmly lifted a carbine to his shoulder, but before he could fire it Feltam shot him in the face with his pistol, then let the weapon fall to the floor. It was a lucky hit, for Feltam had too much motion to aim properly, but it unsettled the Cossacks to see their guide fall backwards from his saddle and down into the dust beside his fearful horse's hooves.

'Death or glory!' cried Feltam, his lance point aimed at the first Cossack's chest. 'Here's the 17th!'

The point of the lance skidded off the chest of the Cossack, who was turned partly sideways, and entered the hollow of the man's shoulder. It struck bone and broke off, leaving the point buried in the rider. At the same time, one of the remaining two Cossacks drove his lance into Feltam's thigh, close to the groin, and pain shot through the soldier, making him shudder.

The Cossack withdrew the lance, however, satisfied with seeing blood, and whirled around for a second try. The third Cossack could not get into the fray, Feltam already having a Cossack on either side of him. The lancer drew his sword at the same time as the wounded Cossack. Their blades met with a clash, the Cossack's sabre sliding down in a sparking movement to clang against the three-bar hilt of Feltam's sword.

Feltam performed a deft under-movement he had practised many times, dropping the slightly curved blade under the Cossack's sabre, and then thrusting upwards at the man's throat. This caused the Cossack to lean back, avoiding the thrust. Feltam then brought his sword up and then down on the side of the Cossack's head, splitting the skull. The man slid to the ground, his brains spilling on the dark earth.

The second Cossack was coming in again with his lance. Feltam hacked at the pole, chopping it in two, but the broken end still caught him in the chest, knocking him sideways in his saddle. He whirled round, slicing the air with his sword, catching the rump of the Cossack's mount. The horse gave a scream of pain and went charging off into the darkness, the Cossack sawing at its mouth with the bit.

One Cossack remained, just a few yards away. Even in the poor light of the moon Feltam could see he was just a boy, not more than sixteen or seventeen years of age. His eyes were full of terror and his hands shook.

Feltam howled at the boy, his face twisted into a terrible, savage mask.

'Arrggghhh! Come on, you! I'll spill your guts for you, you godless bastard. Come on, come on!'

It was enough for the young man, to be faced with such a roaring, evil presence in the near-darkness. Supernatural fears clouded his brain, to overwhelm his courage. He turned his charger and went after the man on the wounded horse, quickly disappearing in the dusk.

Relieved that he was not going to have to fight further, Feltam cheered. 'Horray! Horray!' he yelled hoarsely. 'The 17th have charged, and won the day.' He was almost feverish with excitement, not even feeling the wound near his groin, the warm blood soaking his grey overalls. A moment later a shot whizzed by his ear. Feltam looked up, alarmed, and saw a silhouette further up the hill.

The Cossack boy had returned and fired his carbine, hoping for a miracle such as the one Feltam had managed earlier, with his shot at the civilian.

It was not to be and the Russian finally vanished from sight again, this time for good.

Feltam rode back to his camp in a rather more sober mood than he had experienced at the end of the fight, prior to the bullet passing near to his head. He reported his action to his lieutenant, who sent some men out after the bodies. Congratulations came from all sides and other privates, NCOs and even the officers looked at him with some envy in their eyes. Roughrider Eggerton was brimming with pride for his cousin.

142

Feltam felt taller but solemn in his victory, as if having done this great thing, he was now an older and wiser man. He wished he could go back to those 88th lads at Kadikoi and tell them of his feat for his regiment's sake, but not for his own. Now that he had done it, he did not feel the need to boast.

When his wound was finally looked at, it was found to be a deep gash, but nothing that would not heal on its own. Some padding and skilful bandaging and Feltam would be ready for duty within a few days. This he felt was another stroke of fortune, or perhaps God's will, for he would be fit for any future action with the lancers. He hoped there would be such action *some*time, though just at this very moment his taste for war had been sated.

13

Wynter was almost impossible to live with now that he had returned from the latest fox hunt triumphant. He lorded it over the others in the *peloton* until they could stand it no longer. Wynter was insufferable with his blustering and swaggering. It was making the others choke on their food and drink. Devlin finally confronted him.

'Wynter, you're forgetting your place around here. I'm the full corporal. I'm in charge. I want no more of your boasting and bragging. Enough is enough, man.'

'You don't seem to realize who you're talkin' to,' Wynter replied pompously. 'Me and Ali, why we're the men for the game. We made a riot all by ourselves and got the job done. Major Lovelace praised us himself.'

Corporal Devlin pushed a fist under Wynter's nose.

'If you don't close that trap of yours, I'm going to take you outside and give you the larruping of your life.'

Now Corporal Devlin was not a particularly big man, although he was bigger than either Peterson or Clancy. Wynter looked at Devlin through narrowed eyes, weighing him up and obviously coming to the conclusion that he could take this Irishman any time he liked.

'Now,' said Wynter, taking off his coatee.

Devlin did likewise, while Peterson hovered round them saying, 'You'll get us all into trouble if you start fighting. Let's try to settle this some other way.'

'Eh?' said Clancy.

The two men in question both looked at Peterson in surprise.

Devlin said, 'What other way is there?'

Peterson looked around the three male faces and realized her views and ideas were those of a woman. Negotiation first and last. Only fishwives with the brains of a dead cod would go out in the street and use physical violence against one another to prove their point. Fishwives and men. Confrontation between men always ended in the same way: battling it out with their fists.

She could not explain to these two blockheads that once it was all over and one of them lay broken-nosed and bloody-mouthed in the dust, with the other swaying over him, just as damaged, that things would still be the same. Nothing will have been proved, except that one man could hit harder than the other, which might have been demonstrated that much easier by punching hessian sacks full of sand. However, she knew she was treading on dangerous ground, so she turned away.

'No other way,' she mumbled. 'You go ahead and knock each other's head off.'

Both men nodded. This was the right answer so far as they were concerned and they went outside.

Wynter threw the first punch, while Devlin was still trying to find suitable ground. He hit the corporal a clout on the side of the head and sent him reeling. Once Devlin had shaken his head however, and had set his feet firmly on the earth Wynter suddenly found himself getting the hiding of his life. Bold, solid punches came from the Irishman, whose fists seemed to Wynter to be made of hardwood. Wynter kept getting the odd one through the Irishman's guard, but for every strike he achieved he got three in return.

Finally, his arms aching and his face and chest numb from blows, Wynter keeled over and lay on his back.

' 'Nough, Corporal,' he wheezed. 'I'm done.'

Clancy slapped Devlin on the shoulders. 'By gosh, you're some fist-fighter, man. Could you teach me? Could you show me how to fight like that?'

Thereafter Wynter did not mention his great feats of prowess. He might have done, and fought Devlin again, and perhaps won the second time, but there seemed to be some sort of unspoken law that if you lost that one fight it meant you followed the expectations of the winner. Devlin had demanded nothing from the outcome of the fight. Wynter had promised nothing. Yet it was as if a contract had been drawn up and signed between the two and Wynter was adhering to all the clauses.

Shortly after this fight had taken place, Lieutenant Dalton-James, resplendent in his rifle green, came to see Sergeant Crossman on his sickbed. The lieutenant castigated the men for the sloppy way they were keeping their quarters and told them they were lucky to have a roof over their heads.

'There are other men still out in the open,' he said. 'You should be thankful enough for this warm, comfortable billet to keep it in good army order. I expect it to be cleaned up when I come down from seeing Sergeant Crossman.'

'Set to, set to,' said Corporal Devlin, looking at Peterson. 'You heard what the lieutenant said.'

'Why me?' cried Peterson.

'Because you're good at these things,' Wynter mumbled through a thick split lip. 'Look how well you keep your own part of the billet.'

It was true she was the tidiest in the room.

'And you should do the same,' she cried at the other lance corporal.

Dalton-James studied this exchange with disgust.

'Just get it done,' he ordered, 'all of you. Wynter, Devlin, why are your faces in that state? Have you been visiting the Scottish canteen?'

Peterson was all attention at this question.

'No, sir,' mumbled Devlin. 'We had a little boxing match – to keep us fit, you understand.'

Dalton-James nodded slowly, guessing exactly what had gone on. To Peterson's horror the lieutenant did not seem to disapprove altogether. His next statement filled her with a new disgust for officers, who she thought would be superior in intellect to the boneheaded soldiers with whom she had to live.

'Well, next time keep to body blows. I hate to see soldiers walking around with faces like jam scones. Keep the punches low – not *too* low – and wear your man down.'

'Yes, sir,' they chorused, grinning.

Dalton-James, having delivered his homily, went up the stairs to see Crossman. In the far distance, the guns were booming, as they had been since the first day of the bombardment of Sebastopol. The barrage was following its usual pattern: during the day the guns blared at each other and Sebastopol's defences crumbled, then at night they were restored, ready for the onslaught on the next day. It was like the eternal spinning of the planets.

On reaching the room above, the lieutenant was surprised to see a lady in attendance. But when he glanced at Crossman, lying on a straw mattress, he forgot the female immediately. It was the first time Dalton-James had come to the sergeant since Crossman had returned from Sebastopol, and though he knew Crossman was unwell, he had not expected to see him laid so low.

The sergeant looked thin and wasted. His face was hollow and gaunt, and was a frightening grey colour. He was lying on his stomach, his bare back exposed, showing horrible festering wounds. Despite his detestation for the sergeant, Dalton-James was quite shocked by the man's condition and felt sorry for him.

'You don't look too well, Sergeant,' he said, using the usual army understatement. 'But I see you're in good hands.' He nodded towards Mrs Durham. There were not many junior officers who did not know Mrs Durham, at least by sight, and Dalton-James put himself among her particular admirers. 'Good day to you, ma'am. I hope you are well. I see you are performing one of your typically unselfish acts of kindness. The army thanks you.'

'The army can do as it pleases, Lieutenant. I am here because my good friend Sergeant Crossman is unwell. I have come to care for him, not because I am unselfish or kind, but because his recovery is important to me.'

Dalton-James raised his eyebrows and was a little disconcerted by this speech and the tone in which it was delivered.

'I – er – I'm sorry I did not gauge the situation accurately enough. Do forgive me. Sergeant Crossman has at one time been a friend of your family?'

'Was, is, and will always be, Lieutenant. A friend of my family and once, years ago, a *very* good friend to me.'

There was no mistaking the underlying meaning of that statement. Crossman had at one time, undoubtedly before he joined the army, offered for her hand. Or at least, had been expected to. Yes, that was it. Crossman had given her cause to think he would come up to the mark, but had failed to follow through with his proposal. Perhaps that was why he was in the army, hiding himself under an assumed name in the ranks, to escape the scandal or the wrath of her family?

That meant there must have been a huge rift between them. She had obviously suffered unrequited love from a man who gave every indication of coming up to scratch, but for reasons of his own (which Dalton-James had no doubt were selfish) had not.

Yet she still wished to care for him? Dalton-James knew

many women who would have gladly placed a knife between the shoulder blades of such men. Yet here she was, still good friends with a blackguard who, even if promises had been made, was now unable to make those promises good. She was indeed a truly noble person, a lady of great quality, a *nonpareil*.

'Madam, I have nothing but admiration for you,' Dalton-James said in a tone which revealed how deeply affected he was by her self-sacrifice and dignity. 'You shame us all.'

Crossman snorted in disbelief at this remark.

'And you, sir,' said the lieutenant, turning on him with a frown, 'must give me an explanation. I realize you are unwell, but I must have some answers. The breach-loaders were found where you had buried then, but I have to inform you that one of the Ferguson rifles is missing.'

'One?' whispered Crossman, hoarsely. 'Why, anything could have happened to it. We did not count them. We merely took away from the Russian infantry what they had. Perhaps they disposed of one somehow?'

'Or perhaps they kept one hidden from you and are now copying the design in St Petersburg?'

Crossman shook his head.

'We searched them all thoroughly. No Russian soldier carried arms out of that valley. We even took the officer's pistol. Are – are you sure the count is accurate?'

'Sergeant Crossman, I am able to do simple arithmetic,' said the lieutenant, pompously.

'I'm sure you are, sir – but were the figures you received in the first place accurate? Some informer must have given us the information. Was his information totally correct?'

Dalton-James had not thought of this. He took it that when he had been told fifty rifles by his superiors, it was fifty, and not forty-nine. This was something he would have to mull over before taking any further action. He prepared to leave, glancing towards the Madonna at her embroidery, who seemed to him to be forever in a state of grace.

'Ma'am? I take my leave.'

'As you wish, Lieutenant. My compliments to the colonel of your regiment, who is a personal friend of my father.'

'Indeed, ma'am. I shall convey them with all speed.' He paused, then turned again to stare down at Crossman. 'Oh, by the way, Sergeant, I see no reason for your men to lounge away their lives here waiting for you to recover. I intend to contact Lieutenant Parker of the Connaught Rangers and have him return them to their normal duties until you are well.'

'Sir?'

'Have you any objection to that? They seem to be doing little except playing at cards and having fist fights among themselves. Worthy enough occupations for a soldier who needs respite from the activity of war, but for idle men these are pastimes which encourage indolence.'

Crossman could think of nothing to say, except the fact that his men would be mightily unhappy at the thought of digging trenches. Still, if they were doing nothing but gambling and fighting, they would be better off in the trenches. He nodded his head, briefly, and then lay it down to sleep.

14

Since it was going all day and every day the distant booming of the guns became, like surf falling on a tropical shore is to islanders, a sound which was no longer consciously regarded by the residents of Kadikoi village. The war had settled into stalemate. Men were dying on either side, violently and of the ever-present diseases, but with no gain to anyone except heaven and hell. The wounded were put on the death ships which carried them across the Black Sea to Scutari Barracks Hospital, many of them arriving as corpses.

The surgeons were kept busy, cutting off limbs and pronouncing soldiers dead. They were sad men, some still sensitive, but most having lost their empathy in the constant flow of blood and gore.

Purveyors were busy protecting their precious mounds of stores from the avaricious troops. The more goods and equipment a purveyor held, the greater his power. Without them he was nothing and so he clung on to them as long as possible.

Generals made plans and discarded them. Colonels worried over their regiments, captains over their companies. Private soldiers and NCOs in the line regiments were either bored or terrified, depending on their current circumstances. The cavalry in their dashing uniforms, astride their dashing chargers, were busy patrolling the countryside, desperate for a chance to clash swords with the enemy. Engineers – sappers and miners – were busy digging holes and filling them in again.

Crossman lay idle.

He was at last able to sit up in bed, though still very weak. There was an animal quietly gnawing at him from within and he fought against its demands to be fed. To divert himself he picked up his chibouque, filled it, lit it with a lucifer, and then much to the annoyance of Mrs Durham, began to smoke it.

'The smoke from that chimney is foul,' she declared.

'I'm sorry,' he replied, 'but we gentlemen have no place to which we may retire for our brandy and cigars after dinner. You should be pleased. It keeps the insects away.'

'I would rather use my perfume to do that,' she replied. 'They seem to be repelled by this particular sort.'

He shrugged but continued to smoke his pipe. It was unsatisfying. He needed something else. Suddenly the feeling was intense. A kind of jolt, a powerful streak of yearning ran through his body and was impossible to ignore. Shaking violently, he tapped out his pipe bowl on the floor, the red-hot ashes tumbling on to the boards and smouldering there. He poured some water from a mug on to the tiny fire. Then he cleared his throat to try to gain control of the treble he knew would sound in his voice when he spoke again.

'Lavinia, I'm – I'm in pain again.'

She looked at him through the blue haze of smoke and shook her head in a definite fashion.

'No, Alexander, you are not in pain.'

But the craving was growing in intensity, so that it was impossible to ignore. He was caught in an obsession, and helpless to control it. His mind had one thought and that was to satisfy the urgent need which his body signalled to his brain. Though he was actually disgusted with himself, he continued to plead with her.

'Lavinia, what would you ask of me?'

'How I would have loved to have heard those words at some other time, but the answer is still no, Alexander. We have to wean you off the laudanum. You are becoming too dependent, like some ancient dowager with the gout, except that it matters in your case because dowagers are old and have little left to look forward to, but you are young and have a life ahead of you. You may have some at precisely ten of the clock and no sooner.'

'You are beyond everything, Mrs Durham,' he gasped, hating her at this moment. 'I should like to strangle you.'

'My dear Alex, you have wanted to throttle me so many times in our lives. I do believe I bear the ghostly marks of your fingers on my neck. Fortunately, you are too weak at the moment, despite the fact that you are mending tolerably well. Perhaps you will hate me less once the craving for the opium wears off. Did you know that poor little Chinamen are dying of too much opium and all because we British want to trade for porcelain and rhubarb?'

'I'm not interested in blasted Chinamen or their rhubarb,' snarled Crossman. 'I need my laudanum.'

'No you do not. You only think you do. I gave you the laudanum to ease your pain. Is it my fault that at one time you have indulged in opium?'

He turned his face to the wall. 'I didn't indulge,' he said. 'It was necessary to me at the time.'

'You became an addict.'

'I wish I had never told you. The circumstances – look, Lavinia, I broke it before, I will break it again.'

'You certainly will. I intend for you to break it now. You will wait until ten o'clock.'

'Blast and damn you.'

'Yes, Alex, blast and damn me. There, I have sworn an oath. Does that shock you? I think it shocks *me*.'

'Nothing shocks you, Lavinia.'

At that moment there was a shadow in the doorway and Crossman looked up, expecting to see Lovelace. Instead it was a harrowed-looking Rupert Jarrard. He seemed a little embarrassed by the exchange he had heard and turned to go.

'Rupert!' cried Crossman, desperate for some distraction. 'Do come in. Please, come in. Don't leave me with this harridan.'

It was Jarrard's turn to be shocked.

'Jack, how can you be so insulting to this lady? As I understand it, she has cared for you night and day. You should be eternally grateful.'

Crossman said hollowly, 'That shows how much you know about it all. She is torturing me, Rupert. She delights in cruelly tormenting me. It is revenge for imagined past wrongs. She has me at her mercy and is inflicting pain and misery upon me in my helpless condition. She is a harpy.'

Jarrard looked at Mrs Durham, who said, 'I won't let him have his opium.'

Jarrard nodded grimly. Stepping into the room he said to Crossman, 'Jack, you must get a hold of yourself. Mrs Durham is only doing what we all know is best.'

'A conspiracy,' groaned Crossman. 'You all hate me.'

'Don't be childish. Look, I've come to talk to you for a while.'

'Your French paramour is on duty, I suppose?' replied Crossman, waspishly.

'Now that's not fair, Jack, I've been very busy. There's a lot going on at the front. If you weren't so selfish you'd stop and think that men are dying out there.'

Crossman stared at his friend and suddenly felt remorse for his bad behaviour.

He groaned. 'I'm sorry. Talk to me, Rupert. Take my mind off – things.'

Jarrard sat down after removing his Navy Colt and placing it carefully on the table. Then they talked about engineering, about the latest inventions, about discoveries in medicine, about farming, about anything and everything to do with 'science'.

Jarrard pronounced it ridiculous that an Englishman was expected to wear special clothes to go bicycling, or fell-walking, or digging for fossils. Mrs Durham intervened here and heatedly disagreed with the American. They argued about the subject, with Crossman merely listening in.

'Of course it's essential that a man is correctly dressed and wears the appropriate clothes for the pursuit he is undertaking,' she said. 'How otherwise are standards to be kept? A man will be coming down to dinner in his gardening jacket otherwise, and then where would we be?'

'My father eats his dinner in the same clothes that he wears to work,' said Jarrard through his teeth. 'You people are desperate snobs, if you ask me—'

'Not at all, Rupert,' interrupted Crossman. 'It is simply a matter of good breeding. Etiquette to the British is as important as freedom to an American. If we had a Declaration of Independence – quite unnecessary of course because we have never been *dependent* – it might say, "We hold these truths to be self-evident, that all men are created equal, that they are endowed by their Creator with certain inalienable Rights, that among these are Life, Liberty and the pursuit of Happiness." But it would also record, "Additional to these is the expectation that all men will respect that it is their duty to appear dressed correctly for dinner, no matter what their class, country or creed."'

Jarrard laughed.

Mrs Durham said, 'You are so stupid sometimes, Sergeant Crossman.'

Crossman was grateful she kept his secret in front of others – apart from that slip in front of Devlin, which he hoped she had covered – only calling him 'Alexander' when they were alone together.

'I know, Mrs Durham. It will be the death of me.'

At that moment another man entered the room, dressed in the colourful costume of a Bashi-Bazouk, with a floppy Santa Claus hat, various shirts and waistcoats of ethnic design piled one on the other, baggy pantaloons, leggings and soiled boots. He had with him a sun-darkened woman wearing flowing cottons covered by an open goathair robe. Her breasts were bare to view and thrusting through a long smock which was undone to the waist and trailed ties. It was a natural state for one of her tribe. She smiled shyly at the men and Mrs Durham. Jarrard came to attention and nodded curtly but politely.

'Ali!' cried Crossman, delighted at another distraction as the opium pangs gnawed at his insides. 'What have we here?'

The Bashi-Bazouk came forward with a half-dozen quail in his right hand. His female companion stayed in the shadows by the doorway.

'I bring these,' he said. 'For the woman to cook.'

'A Turk bearing gifts,' Crossman said, shaking his head. 'Do you think we should accept them, Rupert?' He smiled at Ali. 'Of course we do. A little joke. Thank you my friend, the *woman* will be delighted to cook them.'

'You see what I mean?' said Mrs Durham, her hands fluttering. 'Falling standards. No doubt this Turkish gentleman here wears these same gaudy garments at dinner and he is teaching our young men to do the same.'

'Our young men have but one uniform,' said Crossman, 'and that is what they stand up in. They eat, sleep and kill in the same clothes. That is not their fault. Now, *woman*, be so good as to pluck these birds and put them in a boiling pot of water.'

Mrs Durham took the quail with a little laugh. She had enjoyed the banter, not believing half of what she had been arguing for herself. Lord Cardigan had an extensive wardrobe here in the Crimea, but most of the officers had only a single threadbare uniform, and many lived and died in the same conditions as the private soldiers, suffering the same privations. It was a new, enlightening experience for them, and they came to value the character of their men to a much deeper degree than ever before.

'I shall do my best with them,' she remarked. 'Though I

156

don't believe I have plucked a bird before in my life. You must show me what to do, Mr Jarrard. I understand from Sergeant Crossman you have been a frontiersman, a pathfinder such as one might read about in one of Mr James Fenimore Cooper's *Leather-stocking Tales*.'

'I travelled the Oregon trail, ma'am,' admitted the correspondent, 'and am considered a pioneer amongst my friends and acquaintances.'

'Then you will know how to pluck a turkey, which I'm sure is much the same as a quail only a larger task.'

Jarrard picked up his Colt and the pair of them left the room, going below where there were the rudiments of a kitchen. The Tartar woman remained by the doorway. Ali stayed with Crossman, staring at the sergeant, presumably trying to gauge whether he was getting better. Crossman was disconcerted to notice that Mrs Durham had taken the bottle of laudanum with her, so he could not ask Ali to give him some. He wondered if he could persuade Ali to get some for him from somewhere and bring it to him later.

'You are an excellent shot, Ali,' he said to the rotund but hard-looking man standing by his side. 'I still don't know how you manage to shoot a quail with a large-bore rifle and not blast it to pieces.'

'I am good shot,' smiled Ali, agreeing.

Suddenly Crossman stared at the rifle in the Bashi-Bazouk's hand, recognizing it first by the leaf back-sight, then noticing other familiar features.

'Ali?' he said. 'That's a Ferguson rifle, damn you.'

Ali glanced down at his weapon as if it had just appeared in his hands by magic. He shrugged.

'Damn you, man,' cried Crossman. 'You kept one of the breach-loaders. Don't you know I'm suspected of allowing that weapon to fall into Russian hands? That, or worse. Dalton-James will have me hanged for it.'

Ali shrugged again. 'I kill bear for this gun,' he said 'It is mine by right.'

'I don't think so.'

'Yes, I think so,' Ali proclaimed in a definite tone. 'It is mine.'

Crossman sighed and lay back, then laughed. 'Oh, keep the damn thing, but don't let Lieutenant Dalton-James see you with it. Thank you for the birds, Ali. You are an excellent man as well as a good shot. You can come to my dinner table dressed as you like, whenever you like. Do you understand?'

Ali grinned. 'No,' he said.

'Well, it doesn't matter. How have you managed to get ammunition for the Ferguson?'

'I make it.'

Crossman had forgotten about the resourcefulness of poor Eastern peoples. To make ammunition for this rifle Ali would have created his own mould for the bullets. In fact, he had probably improved upon the weapon since it had been in his hands.

Ali stayed for a while, talking awkwardly with Crossman, then signalled to his companion that they should leave. She smiled once at Crossman. On seeing her bared breasts he felt a stirring in his loins. By the time Mrs Durham came back up to him, the laudanum cravings were on him again. He desperately needed a distraction. There seemed to him to be one on offer, of which so far he had declined to take advantage.

'Lavinia,' he said huskily. 'I'm cold.'

She raised her eyebrows. 'You want another blanket?'

'No.'

She stared hard at him and then smiled.

'Oh, I see,' she said, and began to undress.

When they were making love, just a few minutes later, she said to him in a faraway voice, 'I never thought you would, Alexander. You're such a prig, you know.'

'I know,' he sighed above her, as her body warmed his, 'it's such a bore.'

15

The dawn had still not yet arrived, but he and Mrs Durham were up and dressed, ready for the new day.

'Am I really a prig?' he asked her.

'Yes, you are sometimes, Alex. A prig and a prude. Other people don't welcome self-righteous condemnation from their peers. Ladies especially like a little bit of wickedness in a man. Not too much, though. Just enough to make them feel wicked themselves for fostering the relationship.'

Crossman shook his head. 'Very strange,' he said. 'But I have taken advantage of another man's wife. I should be disgusted with myself.'

The lady snorted. 'Bertie is my husband in name only. He – I shouldn't be telling you this – he does not make love to me, Alex, at least not often. Once every half-year perhaps. There's nothing physically wrong with him. He's just one of those men who have muted desires.'

'He's still your husband,' Crossman pointed out. 'And I should not have—'

'We – we should not have – and yes, or course we should have. We were in love once, you know.'

'That doesn't give us the right to deceive your husband,

nor do I want to discuss your married life. I think this conversation has gone as far as I want it to go.'

'But it was you who raised the subject in the first place.'

Suddenly there were explosions outside, mounting in volume. Crossman peered out of the small window through which the Cossack had come to kill him not long ago. He could see nothing, however, since it was still very dark.

'That's not the guns around Sebastopol,' he said. 'Those are much closer. That's coming from the other side of the gorge.'

'Are they our guns, do you think?' asked Mrs Durham, in a perfectly calm voice.

'I would say they are in our redoubts.'

'Is it a battle?'

The sound of 'Boots and Saddle' came to them now, from the cavalry brigades in the north-west.

Crossman said, 'Today is the anniversary of the Battle of Agincourt. If it is an attack I hope the French are not feeling too peeved with us. We shall all need to pull together.'

He could see the flashes of the guns now, on the distant ridge. They were like ephemeral stars, there and gone. Rifle fire now sounded and distant drums and trumpets mingled with the closer sound of the bagpipes. These were all soon drowned by the noise of the guns on a rise in the South Valley just below the Causeway Heights which the allies called Canrobert's Hill.

'The Turks have opened fire.' Crossman said. 'That must mean the Russian army is close.'

At that moment there was a commotion outside and someone came bounding up the stairs. Crossman, sitting in a chair, was astonished to see Jock McIntyre, the sergeant-major from the 93rd Sutherland Highlanders, in the doorway. McIntyre peered into the room, getting his eyes used to the gloom, then saw Crossman in the chair.

'Jack Crossman,' he said. 'Are ye well?'

'I have not been,' said Crossman. 'But I'm close to being fit again.'

'Quick, man, we need ye,' said the sergeant-major. 'They're getting all the invalids from the hospitals. The Russians are coming across the valley with their cavalry. There's only us to stop them.'

'Us?'

'The 93rd Foot. Sir Colin Campbell has marines further up, but we're all that stands between the Russian army and Balaclava.'

Crossman got to his feet, a little unsteadily, but once he had his Minié in his hand he used it as a crutch.

Mrs Durham cried, 'I must find a horse!' and rushed from the room, her eyes shining.

'Are ye well enough, man?' asked McIntyre. 'What is it?'

'Nothing that a good row won't cure, one way or the other,' said Crossman. 'Let's go to it.'

When they got outside the guns were pounding out regular rhythms. A soldier in a kilt came running up to McIntyre.

'Sir, a rider has just arrived with a message for Colonel Ainslie from Lord Raglan. We're to hold on. The 1st and 4th Divisions are to assist us when they reach us.'

McIntyre huffed. '*If* they reach us in time.'

'What do you mean, Jock?' asked Crossman. 'You sound as if you know something I do not.'

'The 4th are under General Cathcart, ye ken? Sir George is none too happy wi' Lord Raglan, for not immediately attacking Sebastopol after the flank march.'

'Surely he wouldn't disobey an order?' questioned Crossman. 'He's not that stupid.'

'No, but the man has a lot of power. He's next in line for command after Lord Raglan. I wouldna be surprised if he disna stay put for a while to show people how angry he is that Lord Raglan listened to General Brown instead o' him. The 4th will be rarin' to go, of course, seeing as how they didna take part in the big bash at the Alma. It all depends on whether General Cathcart lets them off the leash.'

The two men made their way to where the 93rd Sutherland

Highlanders were stretched in a long line, two deep, across the mouth of the gorge which led to Balaclava harbour. Crossman, aware that he looked ravaged and thin, did not expect to be recognized by either his brother or his father, both totally unaware of his presence in the Crimea, and now close enough to hit with a pebble. Crossman found it strange to be standing in the same line with them, waiting to die under the hooves of Russian horses. Nevertheless he edged away from where his brother stood, wanting still to remain unknown to them. His father, being a major, was on a horse. Major Kirk rarely looked down into the faces of the men and if he did it was a general scanning of the line to see that it was straight.

Crossman placed himself under the command of the two Grenadier Guards subalterns who had gathered together the invalids and extras. There were groups of Turks to the 93rd's left and right, who were already firing at the oncoming Russians, though the enemy were too distant to hit. The regiments' wives were not far away, watching. God help a husband who disgraced himself on the battlefield. God help a wife who saw her husband fall and die. Crossman would rather the women were well out of it, but it was none of his business.

The enemy was coming into the Fedioukine Valley out of the north-east from the direction of the Woronzoff Road. They found the 93rd blocking the mouth of the gorge by Kadikoi village which led to Balaclava harbour.

Brigadier-General Sir Colin Campbell, pacing up and down on his horse in front of the 93rd, was giving his Highlanders some grave advice.

'You must die where you stand, men!' the general was saying. 'There will be no retreat. Hold your ground. Let no Highlander fail in his duty. Wait for my orders. I want no man to charge the enemy without he receives my command to do so.'

Sir Colin would have obedience to his command. His men would not turn and run. Nor would they become overeager, like the Scots Fusilier Guards at the Battle of the Alma. This regiment had surged up the hill without waiting: an act which had infuriated the rest of the Highland Brigade.

The warning about running away was quite unnecessary. No Sutherland Highlander would show his heels before the command to retreat had been sounded. The warning about charging the enemy too soon, however, was required, since they were an eager bunch. Given their heads they would have been hurtling across the plain at that moment, their kilts flying, their mouths screaming Celtic curses at the oncoming Russian army.

Crossman, in the front rank, looked down along the line of red coatees. Over half a thousand bayonets protruded out in front, the rising sun flashing on their wicked-looking steel tips. The white plumes of the Highlanders' black ostrich-feather headgear waved in the morning breezes. There were grim faces below these bonnets, glaring out into the Balaclava plain.

'Steady, my boys,' cried Sir Colin Campbell.

Just then over the hill from the north-east came many of the Turks from the redoubts, having been overwhelmed by the sheer numbers of Russian field artillery. Though the Turks in No. 1 redoubt had fought bravely, they had lost many men and could not hold the Russians any longer. They and the other redoubts had abandoned their guns and were running for their lives. Behind them was an astonishing sight. The Russian cavalry came over the rise in great volume – over thirty-four squadrons of horse.

The enemy cavalry was supported by artillery and some twenty-five battalions of infantry.

There was a sharp intake of breath along the thin red line as the Highlanders saw what they were facing.

A cry came from a group of nearby Turkish infantry, as they loosed one last volley before running back down the gorge towards the ships. This distracted Crossman for a moment. Then some of the Scottish wives began chasing the

Turks, yelling at them to come back and assist in the fight, one of the more sturdy women swinging at the fleeing soldiers with a heavy stick.

'Get back here, ye dowiely cairds!' she screeched. 'Are ye men or rabbits?'

This caused merriment in the ranks, with the woman's husband calling, 'Gie them what for, wifey!' which raised another laugh.

The Turks from the redoubts did not deserve this kind of treatment, though. Their bimbashi leader was wounded and bleeding profusely. They had had enough for one day. The ships in the harbour were their destination, a place of refuge from that mighty force which rode and tramped resolutely towards them.

Crossman could hear the sound of boots pounding the earth now and remembered his remark to Peterson as they were marching towards the Russian-defended Alma heights.

What's the most frightening sound in the world, Peterson?

What, Sergeant?

The sound of 60,000 men marching towards you, while you stand waiting behind your guns. Even if your army is just as strong, or stronger, the stillness makes you feel alone. All you can hear are the boots of the enemy tramping inexorably closer. It is the sound of doom, Peterson. It is the sound of hell on the move. I'd always be an attacker before a defender.

And that was how he felt now. He would have much rather been marching forward, than standing still, waiting for the attack. And though there were only 50,000 boots, there were also 6,000 hooves – and few friendly guns between the enemy and this small line of under a thousand men. His heart was in his throat and he had already forgotten his craving for opium. He believed, like most of the men there, he was about to die.

The Russian cavalry in all its splendour fanned out before them. The Russian intention was plainly to cut and hold the Woronzoff Road, while their cavalry opened up the pass to

164

Balaclava harbour for the onslaught of his troops. Colonel Ainslie now called for calm amongst his men.

In the distance Crossman could see the Light Brigade at the end of the South Valley, the Heavy Brigade nearby but deeper in the valley. Russian round shot was beginning to fall amongst them. Lord George Paget was leading the Light Brigade and he halted his squadrons when they reached the second redoubt. There they waited, still under fire.

Crossman began thinking about the young trooper in the 17th Lancers, Private Feltam, and wondered what the boy would be feeling now. Perhaps he was hoping that today, at least, they would be allowed to charge and show what they were worth.

The Royal Horse Artillery were making movements over the valley as well. Their hessian boots, tucked into their tight trousers, gleamed in the sunlight. Crossman envied them their swashbuckling freedom of activity as C Troop swept by. In the distance, with the Heavy Brigade, who were also moving up the valley, was I Troop, with the wheels of its four 6-pounder guns and two 12-pounder howitzers raising the dust behind the horses. It made Crossman feel leaden-legged and rooted, somehow.

'Look at yon sun,' cried a 93rd soldier somewhere down the line. 'It'll blind the gunners.'

Horizontal rays sliced through the valley now, from the east, which the allied guns had to face.

Up on the Sapoune Ridge at the west end of both the North and South Valleys, which ran parallel with the high Woronzoff Road separating them, were the British staff officers. Lord Raglan was there in prime position, able to look down both valleys. Crossman had no doubt the Commander-in-Chief would be calm and watchful, if not decisive.

There was the sound of a galloping horse from behind the line of infantry and Crossman turned to see Lavinia Durham, skirts and blouse-ribbons flying, come riding up from the harbour on a good horse. She went by the line of men, throwing up a wave, her face shining in excitement. Then she was past them, heading north-west, in grave danger of being caught up in the middle of the battle, but seemingly careless of her life. Crossman shook his head slowly but could not help a smile forming on his lips.

'What a crazy woman,' he murmured to himself. 'She'll be the death of somebody one of these days – probably herself.'

16

Before the eyes of the 93rd, I Troop came under immensely heavy fire both from the enemy guns and from skirmishers who were now trying to pick off the gunners. I Troop's commanding officer, Captain Maude, twice lost his horse from under him. Wounded himself, he mounted a third horse, but Lord Lucan came up and ordered the troop to retreat with their guns. The spectators saw one of the gunners blown out of his saddle by round shot as the troop galloped to an area of safety.

Now about four squadrons of Russian cavalry detached themselves from the main body and came towards the 93rd, their loose metal clinking in the silence. They looked numerous and formidable high up on their mounts. Their intentions were obvious and Crossman could hear many of the Highlanders swallowing hard, steeling themselves for the onslaught.

Facing a cavalry charge when formed in a square was a terrifying enough ordeal, but they had a wide pass to protect and they were strung across it. Each man knew that he was vital, standing between the Russian army and the British ships tied helplessly to the wharfs of Balaclava harbour. If the enemy rode over him then the war might be lost. It is a hard thing to know your body is all that stands between the might of a foreign foe and the destruction of your army.

When he glanced to his left Crossman noticed with surprise that Lieutenant Dalton-James had joined the line with several of his Rifle Brigade. In their rifle green they contrasted darkly with the red coatees of Crossman and the other soldiers along the line.

Not far away Sergeant-Major McIntyre was having to reassure a new young recruit who had joined the regiment only three days before, having been sent out from England with others to replace those who had fallen at the Alma. The boy was voicing concern that he had never before killed a man and was afraid his finger would freeze on the trigger. It was a genuine worry of many men new to the battlefield.

'Just imagine that's Butcher Cumberland's troops, sittin' in them saddles, laddie,' said McIntyre, speaking of the infamous general of the King's army at the Battle of Culloden, 'and yon officer is the Duke o' Cumberland himself. Ye'll soon be blastin' hell out o' them.'

The rattling, jingling horsemen came closer. There is nothing like high danger to ward off the savage clawing of an opium tiger. When you feel you are about to die all else becomes relatively unimportant. The need for laudanum prowled somewhere in Crossman's mind, but it had been pushed back now, into a dark corner, and lurked rather than attacked.

Sir Colin Campbell had a few more words with the battalion. Crossman had already loaded his rifle with ball and powder, had rammed down, and had placed a percussion cap on the nipple. When the order came, he raised his rifle to his shoulder and took aim with the leaf sight. It took great effort, he not being in prime health, but habit helped. The long dark barrel of the weapon pointed at the enemy who seemed to be massed in a great horde of yellow-grey bodies on the backs of their chargers.

He cocked the hammer.

Out of the corner of his eye he saw Mrs Durham, still riding hard, on the far left of the battlefield. She had made it through to a high place from which she could watch the slaughter. Crossman hoped she would not have to witness his own demise, but felt deep down that his time had come.

'Ninety-third! Damn all that eagerness, I'll not have it,' roared Sir Colin, as the regiment showed an inclination to rush out to meet the oncoming cavalry. 'Wait for them! Wait for them!'

A slight movement went down the line after the rebuke as the soldiers tried to shuffle off the tension. Perhaps some of the more educated minds were at that time drawing parallels with the stand of the Spartans at the pass of Thermopylae. There too several hundred had stood firm in the face of a mighty army of thousands. The conclusion was not comforting. The Spartans had held the enemy – for a time – but were eventually overrun and were slaughtered to a man.

The men along the line hardly appeared to be breathing now, they were so still. It was as if someone had told them they were to play statues. The waiting was almost unbearable. Seconds stretched to minutes, a minute seemed an hour. Wait a bit, wait a bit . . .' whispered the man next to Crossman. A quick glance told the sergeant that the solder was simply speaking to himself, keeping his nervousness in check. Each man had his own method of getting through the waiting.

In contrast the Russians thundered noisily closer on their mounts. The legs of their horses gathered speed, until they were at the full gallop. Crossman could sense the excitement amongst the riders, as they came hurtling on, the wind rushing past their faces, any long hair streaming behind them. They were exhilarated, full of the thrill of the charge. Crossman had once owned a hunter, knew the emotions of a flat-out gallop, which must have been twice as strong when armed and charging forwards to kill men rather than foxes. They must have felt invulnerable, mighty, invincible.

The sensation of facing a cavalry charge, standing rooted

to the ground, was the complete opposite. Crossman felt exposed and unprotected, like a straw man standing before an oncoming rush of fire. They loomed high, large and came on fast and furious. It seemed to him that nothing could stop these mounted devils, whose impetus would surely carry them over the whole battalion of Highlanders, crushing bodies beneath their hooves, drumming flesh and blood hard into the earth.

Their sabres drew the level rays of the sun to the honed edges of the blades, which flashed like mirrors. Their weapons were horizontal now: out before them like the barbed stings of giant insects. The whole body of them bristled with sharp weapons. Their horses snorted in the cold air, pumping sprigs of steam through their nostrils, the leather creaking on their backs. A mass of muscle and bone, the horsemen came on like an impressive engine of death, almost as if they were each part of a single body, a great monster with a thousand arms and legs.

'Steady, lads!'

The faces of the enemy were visible now. Crossman picked a man: a hussar riding a dun-coloured Viatka. He could see the rider's eyes staring back at him, as if they had chosen each other in single combat. He was small with a round face below his black headgear, weather-creased, with crow's-feet at the corners of the dilated eyes and mouth. The man's nostrils were flared with excitement, dark and cavernous.

The rider's sword looked threatening and deadly, the point glinting in the sharp morning light.

'Aim!' came the order.

Crossman murmured, 'Bloody hussars.

'FIRE!'

The volley ripped from the long row of rifles. There was a ripple down the line as the Miniés kicked shoulders. Gunsmoke bloomed and was carried away on the breeze.

This first volley hit the oncoming riders like a heavy sea-wave, knocking them back in their saddles. Some riders dropped to the ground. Wounded men spun on the backs of their horses, let weapons fall to the earth, slumped over their mounts. Several dead remained where they sat, held on by their seized legs, their frozen grips.

Some of the riding dead were carried away by their panicking horses, who had immediately felt the change in their masters and knew all control had gone.

Like a sudden strong wind bends wheat, so that volley had bent the horse riders. Like a sudden strong wind carries away chaff, so the instantly killed were carried off. Like a sudden strong wind leaves shocked victims in its path, so the Russian cavalry reeled and sucked in breath.

'FIRE!'

A soldier with a double-barrelled weapon of some foreign design leaned forward over Crossman's shoulder and fired at the same time as the Connaught Rangers sergeant. Crossman's ear rang with the sound of the shot, his cheek was scorched with the flash of the powder. Seeing that Crossman had been burned the man said something quickly in what sounded like Hungarian or Polish, which Crossman took to be an apology of some kind.

The Russian cavalry was checked again by this second volley hitting them like a blizzard of stones. This was even more devastating in its effects than the first. Horses whinnied, fell kicking and screaming to the ground, their hooves flailing and catching the flanks of other horses. Some men shouted guttural curses. Others died with strangled yells, fell under the stamping legs of their comrades' mounts, were trampled into the earth. Chaos ruled as men disentangled themselves, their weapons and tack caught up with that of their neighbours.

Crossman let out a grunt of relief as he loaded his weapon for the third time, mechanically but surely.

'I hate those bastard Russians,' snarled the foreign soldier in satisfaction. Crossman glanced at him and he added, 'I am Polish. They massacre my people.'

The two men shouldered their rifles and took aim for the third time.

This crashing volley was a little ragged and it rippled down the line like a fusillade. Still it did its work and now the Russian cavalry wheeled to the left, as if to try to come round on the flank of the Highlanders. The grenadier company immediately wheeled round as easily as a farmyard gate on oiled hinges, to face the horsemen again. These riflemen now fired volley after volley into the Russian riders.

Crossman quickly became weary as the strength needed to ram down the bullet was sapping him. His weapon was hot from firing and the barrel had subsequently expanded a little, but still it was not an easy task to get the conical ball down the barrel with the ramrod. Lifting it to his shoulder each time was physically exhausting. Anticipating the savage kick when he fired the rifle was mentally exhausting. He was never so glad as to see the Russian cavalry start to retreat. Hussars rode away into the advancing morning, beaten by foot soldiers.

They had had enough. *He* had had enough. A cheer went up from the Highlanders. Bonnets were thrown high into the air. They were rightly exhilarated. Crossman felt a wind of excitement sweep through him. They had survived, with no casualties so far as he could see. The Russian cavalry had been stopped as if it had hit a stone wall. It was a glorious victory – a small one on a large battlefield – but nevertheless an action which he knew would be remembered.

If only it could have been the Rangers, he thought. How proud then, my boys.

But it had been the Highlanders. It was *their* day, and though he would not be especially remembered for it, like most of the invalids, Rifle Brigade and others, he knew he had taken part. It would not be a piece of his regiment's history, would not go on the Rangers' colours, yet *he* had been one of the line. His rifle had kicked, spat lead, blossomed smoke in the face of the enemy. It was his day too, damn it.

Crossman looked along the line to where his father sat on his grey, looking pompously pleased with himself.

'*Not you*,' murmured Crossman to himself, '*the men*.'

His elder brother was there too, his face shining with elation. Crossman felt his heart melt as he regarded James and was glad for him. He felt like shouting 'Three cheers for Lieutenant Kirk!' but refrained. It would not do to raise one man's name over others. They had all taken part, even those on horses, he conceded, though their involvement was not as great. If the worst came to the worst they could ride away. In retreat they would not need to rely on the strength and speed of their own legs. They had not had to look up into the faces of the enemy. They had sat on an equal level with their opponents, staring over the heads of those who had been told to stand or die.

Crossman felt he should slip away now, but the Polish soldier had grasped him by the hand.

'You are a man like me,' said this enthusiastic gentleman, as full of elation as the rest. 'I am from W Battery, Foot Battery, you know? I fight with you British against the hated Russian. I stand with you against the damn hussars.'

'The bloody hussars,' grinned Crossman. 'We lifted their coat-tails, did we not?'

The Pole shook his hand vigorously.

'By God, yes. We made them show their arses. I killed that one out there. I saw him fall. He is as dead as flint. They killed my family in Poland. Now they are paying.'

One or two of the sick men, taken from their hospital beds, now sat on the ground, exhausted. Even they looked happy, though some of them were on their last legs. Crossman hoped they were not too ill, that they would live a little longer and be able to enjoy having survived this action.

'Well done, my Highland boys!' cried Sir Colin Campbell. 'Good shooting.'

'I need a drink of water,' said a Highlander. 'I've a thirst on me now.'

'Ye need a dram, more like,' cried another, 'but yer nae about to get ane.'

Laughter went up where there had been anxiousness and anticipation just a few minutes before.

Crossman detached himself from the Pole and stepped back from the line, to sit on a hummock. From there he could view the rest of the battlefield. There was activity again amongst the Russian cavalry who were now advancing along the valley. Coming up to meet them was the Heavy Brigade. The RHA were also in evidence on the field.

C Troop, under the command of a Captain Brandling, was swinging into action again. Crossman knew the tall, gentlemanly Brandling by sight, having bumped into him when that officer was accompanying Major Lovelace one evening, and now recognized Brandling, even at a distance, by his neat little charger and his frock coat.

The RHA officers wore short jackets with gilt frogging, but Brandling had come to the Crimea as part of the siege train and therefore looked a little incongruous in his long-tailed coat. Sickness amongst the RHA had given him command of C Troop. His particular troop of the RHA had already been shot up several times, but was still in the fighting. Brandling brought C Troop around behind the Heavy Brigade, to its right flank as they were moving forward to engage the Russian cavalry.

'By God they're going to have a go,' said Crossman to Jock McIntyre. 'The Heavies are going in!'

'Lord help them,' replied the sergeant-major. 'They're outnumbered by far. Look, the Scots Greys are out front, wi' the Guards and Royals just behind . . .'

'And the Inniskillings,' added Crossman.

'There's General Scarlett, leading 'em on,' cried Lieutenant James Kirk. 'Go to it, my lads – go to it!'

The 93rd watched and held its breath. They had done their part and were now spectators. They had stopped a full cavalry charge of four squadrons with only a single battalion of foot soldiers and no casualties. It was an astonishing and incredible victory. They had saved Balaclava from being overrun and the many supply ships in its harbour from being destroyed. In their hearts they were thanking God for deliverance and hoping the rest of the battle would go as well for others.

17

There was a kind of suppressed energy in the air, which was translated into movement by the bustle of the cavalrymen and the agitation of their horses. Here and there a wild creature darted from behind the safety of one rock, to the greater safety of another. Up above a hawk hovered, still as a paper bird on a piece of thread, watching the activity below it.

'Into line, left wheel!' came the command. Then, 'Rest easy.'

Men relaxed in their saddles. Horses nodded and shook their heads, made flapping sounds expelling air through loose lips, and found a more comfortable footing with their hooves. The eyes of both men and horses were still alert, however, glancing this way and that, seeking the enemy.

Although there had been many false alarms and the men had been roused unnecessarily more times than they cared to recall, the cavalry somehow sensed that this was their hour, the day on which they would either distinguish themselves, or be humiliated. They were certain it was the former and that future historians would pen their achievements in admiration.

Overhead, a few dark clouds rode lightly across a pale sky. There was a wind gradually growing in strength, coming down the South Valley. There might have been birds to hear, if the guns had not been pounding all around. There might have been the scent of herbs, if such smells had not been overpowered by the gunpowder gases. There might have been horses to admire – bays, chestnuts, greys, piebalds, others – if these creatures had not been encumbered with the trappings of war.

Rough-rider Eggerton, of the 6th Inniskilling Dragoons, known as 'the Skins', cousin of Private Feltam of the Light Brigade's 17th Lancers, was part of the Heavy Brigade led by Brigadier-General Scarlett.

Sir James Scarlett was a large, bluff man in his mid-fifties, genial of manner, held in affection by his troops, and generally liked by his peers. He had no battle experience, but the ADC he had chosen, Lieutenant Elliot, had been on campaign in India. Sir James enjoyed being the commander of the Heavy Brigade and had designed his own helmet to suit that post. Rough-rider Eggerton could think of no better man for command of the Heavies than Sir James.

Eggerton himself was an excellent horseman, his position as rough-rider confirming that, for it was one held by the NCO who assisted the regiment's riding master in his duties. Thus, he in no way felt inferior to his cousin in the dashing 17th Lancers, who rode in a swirl of colour and whose military élan might have been the envy of a lesser man. Rough-rider Eggerton, in his stolid but dependable way, was just as proud of the Inniskillings as Feltam was of his dapper Lancers.

Eggerton suffered the jokes from his cousin about plough boys riding cart horses with a benign smile on his country boy's face, since he had grown up riding cobs and shires and thought no less of them than a master does of his hunter. He was big-boned and muscular enough to hammer his slim cousin into the ground like a fence post had he so wished, but merely ruffled his hair in front of his friends, which was enough to halt Feltam's jests.

At the same time as Crossman was in the 93rd's line, facing the Russian cavalry, the Light and Heavy Brigades were just south of No. 6 redoubt, behind a vineyard. Then General Scarlett gave the order for the Heavy Brigade to lead off around the vineyard and out into the South Valley proper. Right behind General Scarlett were the Scots Greys on their distinctive white horses and Eggerton's squadron of the Inniskillings.

Eggerton gave his cousin Feltam a brief wave.

'We're off,' he called. 'Look to yourself, lad.'

Feltam, who was afraid of attracting attention from his own brigade commander, the feared, bad-tempered General Cardigan, simply nodded.

'I hope to get a chance to prove myself too,' Eggerton had said to him when he had learned of his cousin's exploits with the Cossacks. 'I hope the Heavies get a go.'

'We've both got to get a *proper* go yet,' Feltam had said. 'I mean, I've charged just by myself, but you need to have your fellow troopers with you – a full-blooded charge with the dust around you and your pals all cheering like mad, eh?'

'I'll say,' Eggerton had grinned.

The difference between the Heavy and Light Brigades was in their respective weights and heights. The Heavies had heavier horses, heavier weapons and some said, heavier men. Where the Light Brigade jingled, the Heavies jangled. Where the Lights were magnificent, the Heavies were impressive. The latter's mounts were tall as well as stocky. They did not fly as fast on their hooves, but they got there, and when they did the enemy were usually knocked out of the way like sacks of straw.

Eggerton felt comfortable on his mount, a four-year-old charger of nineteen hands, called Brackish because he liked a touch of salt in his drinking water. Brackish was solid and dependable, did not shy at the guns blazing all around him, was careless of the round shot landing with great thumps on the ground, and could be relied upon to keep his head pointing in the direction indicated by his rider. He was a good battle horse.

Once they were moving off and wheeling around the vineyard, Eggerton could see what was holding General Scarlett's attention: the fight between the Highlanders and the hussars.

'Look at that, will you?' he said to his companion. 'The infantry are always getting first go.'

'Good old 93rd, though,' said Sergeant Kilcrannock, the man to whom Eggerton had spoken. 'They'll lick 'em all right.'

Two seconds later Sergeant Kilcrannock spun round in his saddle, struck by a cannonball. He was left twisted and facing the wrong way on his mount which had halted in its tracks, knowing there was something the matter with its rider.

The sergeant's sword arm was missing. His face registered his bewilderment at finding himself back to front on his horse. 'Rough-rider Eggerton,' he said slowly, 'I think I've been hit, haven't I?'

'Go back,' said the shocked Eggerton, turning Kilcrannock's horse. 'Go back to the camp, Sergeant.'

The sergeant was distressed as his men filed past him, sympathy in their eyes, while he remained in that undignified position on his saddle. His horse had begun to plod in the direction which Eggerton had pointed it, when Kilcrannock was cut down by fire from skirmishers coming down from the Fedioukine Hills. He slipped quietly to the ground, his charger standing by his body, seemingly unperturbed by the whole affair.

Eggerton glanced back and saw what had happened. He shook his head. He felt he should experience some kind of sorrow at that moment, because he and the sergeant had been more than acquaintances, but the battle was beginning to boil around him, and he could feel churnings of fear and excitement in his stomach instead. He turned his attention to the hills and the valley, wondering where General Scarlett was taking the Skins.

At that moment the general was staring at the 93rd, but

Lieutenant Elliot touched his arm and pointed to the high ground on the left, where a horde of Russian hussars and Cossacks were cantering down. The whole slope was a forest of lances. Weapons and metallic pieces of tack glinted in the early weak sunlight. Over two thousand horsemen began to descend like dark phantoms out of the dawn mists upon the leading three hundred of the Heavy Brigade, consisting of the Greys and Eggerton's single squadron of the Inniskillings.

Previously the men had complained to each other of fatigue. Now they had the real enemy before them their tiredness was swept away like darkness at dawn.

Eggerton's heart began beating faster as the order was given to wheel into line to face the enemy.

'By God, we're going in,' he whispered to himself. 'Hard luck, cousin – I'm to be first.'

Lord Lucan came pounding past the Greys on the far side from Eggerton, to have a quick word with General Scarlett.

Colonel Dalrymple White, commanding the Skins, and Colonel Griffith of the Greys, both began to dress their men.

The officers had their backs to the enemy, but the men themselves could see the Russian cavalry floating down upon them, almost certainly to envelope them and smother them with their greater numbers. More than one trooper felt as if they were staring at death drifting down the hillside. These were no mean enemy, but Cossacks who had thundered over the plains of Russia in savage hordes for centuries, putting men, women and children to the sword; and Russian hussars, admired and copied by most other modern armies in the world, including the British.

However, like those of the regiments of foot at the Alma, the colonels of the Greys and the Skins wanted the maximum of impact from the kind of blow a solid, compact squadron gives when it hits the enemy *en bloc*. Despite the gravity of their position, they were going to have their straight line. They knew that though it was a dangerous manoeuvre it was necessary and would serve them well in the end.

To those who were watching from the Sapoune Ridge — the French and British observers — this seemed like sheer madness. It was as if they were witnessing some ceremony in a park. Finally, just as the Russian cavalry was throwing out wings, intending to encircle them, the Skins and Greys were ready.

C Troop of the RHA galloped by, seeking higher ground for their guns. They yelled encouragement to the Heavies, telling them to give the enemy what for. Eggerton's broad farmer's boy face broke into a grin as he thought to himself: There's nothing like a British soldier for pepping up his pals.

Eggerton looked up at the Russians, to see that they had halted for no good reason. Even if all strategy and tactics had fled the minds of their commanders, common sense should have dictated that they hurl themselves down on the Heavy Brigade in their large numbers and annihilate them before they could get themselves into a gallop. Yet here they were, doing quite the reverse.

'Here we go,' said Eggerton to Brachsh. 'Don't let me down, sir, and I'll not let you down.'

'Charge!'

With swords drawn the Greys and Skins went at the enemy, the Inniskilling Dragoons cheering like mad, while the Greys let out their famous moan of delight. The Russians looked startled to see only three hundred men charge towards them, though there were other squadrons behind, not yet formed up, some of them not even around the vineyard yet. The 4th and the 5th Dragoon Guards were to come, and the Royals, and the 2nd squadron of the Inniskillings.

Eggerton saw General Scarlett, fifty-five but still impetuous, strike the wall of Russians fifty yards ahead of the line, to be swallowed up immediately by the enemy. Eggerton could see the general's long sword whirling, hacking, slicing the air. On a tall horse the general was visible above the mêlée. His aide-de-camp, Lieutenant Elliot, was next to the fray. The lieutenant was wearing a cocked hat and this seemed to excite the Russians far more than the general's helmet. An enemy officer could not contain himself and came out to meet Elliot, slashing wildly at the lieutenant with his sword.

Elliot, still at full gallop, was clearly worried about the isolation of General Scarlett and wanted to go to his aid. He cleverly avoided the cut by the Russian officer and drove his own sword point first into the man's breast as he passed. Such was his charger's speed the whole blade went through up to the hilt. Elliot's momentum twisted the officer round in his saddle and lifted him up, then dropped him like a butchered carcass of beef on the ground a few yards from his horse.

The Cossacks and hussars were now making a bizarre sound: the same kind of noise a child makes when blowing through a comb wrapped with tissue paper. It sounded like a million angry insects to Eggerton, and chilled him to the marrow. If before he had thought the Russians were farm boys just like he was, he now looked on them as very strange creatures indeed.

Finally Rough-rider Eggerton was upon the Russians, who fired their carbines into the three hundred. A horse went down next to Eggerton, its legs kicking as it screamed in pain. Hooves struck Brackish in the stomach and he too whinnied shrilly and shied at this pain from an unexpected quarter. Eggerton fought to stay in the saddle as a Russian cavalryman came at him, slicing the air with the honed blade of his *shaska*.

'Come on, old fellow, don't let me down now,' said Eggerton in as gentle and firm a voice as he could muster. He was afraid he was going to be one of the first down and not get a good go at the thing.

The Russian was left-handed and came to his wrong side, so that as well as struggling to calm Brackish, Eggerton was having to reach over his mount to parry blows. Private Grype, who had already despatched one Russian, came to Eggerton's assistance and almost severed the head of the Cossack with a strike to the back of the neck. Then Grype himself was down, his horse wounded in the belly by a lance, one arm and one leg trapped underneath the animal as it thrashed on the ground. Eggerton, now in full control of Brackish, reached down and pulled him free.

Private Shakespear of the Greys came up then and took Grype by the arm and hauled him up on the back of his horse.

Eggerton was now being pressed from all sides, the battle one mass of heaving mounts, all crushed together. Some of the Russians at the back had turned and galloped away, but it hardly relieved the centre of the mass. Eggerton struck out and down time and again, only to see his sword bounce maddeningly off the thick Russian greatcoats. It was no good using his weapon as a sabre unless he could get a good cut at an enemy's head, so he attempted to use the point in the way that Lieutenant Elliot had done, but in fact there was little room for thrusting either. Troopers were closely hemmed in, restricted in their movements, some could not even strike with their swords.

Eggerton felt a burning pain as a lance went through his mouth and out of one cheek, tearing a hole he could put his tongue through. Luckily the Cossack withdrew the lance for a second attempt. The Russian's shako looked formidable, as though it would withstand even a heavy blow. The rough-rider managed to knock the man's headgear to one side and then split his skull twice with the edge of the blade. Brains and blood splattered Eggerton's tunic, covering his hands and face with tiny specks.

Eggerton felt both horrified and exhilarated by his feat. Around him there were screams of wounded and dying men. Troopers struggled to release themselves from the heaving mass of arms, legs and bodies. Horses went down, never to rise again above the thrashing waves of human shoulders and arms. Men disappeared from saddles, lost below the surface of this terrible heaving sea of flesh. It was at that moment that the Royals hit the west wing of the Russian column, driving even more of its members into the struggling throng.

Eggerton whirled his sword about him, creating a space for

himself. Brackish, who also disliked being in the press, kicked out with his back legs, ensuring that no attack would come from the rear. A lancer came at him from the right flank, but Eggerton put his sword between his teeth and found his carbine, shooting the man in the face as he approached. Then, sword in hand, he galloped off to the assistance of a corporal who was besieged by a dozen Russian hussars.

Sword striking at the helmets and shoulders of the hussars, Eggerton managed to put the Russians to flight, though he received a severe wound on the left shoulder. There was also a dent in his helmet, which was now askew on his head. Unfortunately for the British cavalry, they were not wearing greatcoats and their thin coatees did not stop the slashing cuts from the swords of the Russians.

Eggerton began to bleed profusely. He looked about him, wondering whether to leave the field. Then he saw Lieutenant Elliot, who was bleeding from a dozen wounds, still fighting furiously with the Russians. The rough-rider stopped feeling sorry for himself immediately and went back into the fray.

'Damn me, let me get in there,' said a voice by his elbow. 'I an't goin' to miss this one, Albert.'

Eggerton looked on amazed as two butchers from the camp rode by in their shirtsleeves and aprons. They were both wielding swords, but one still had a meat cleaver stuck in his belt. Laying about them, they were like a team of carvers, slicing through hanging joints of meat.

The Russians were experiencing shock waves all around as, moments before the Royals hit them, the 5th Dragoon Guards had smashed into their column from the front. The Cossacks and hussars, unable to retreat, accepted the files, moving sideways to allow this wedge of muscle, bone and flailing steel entry into their mass.

At the same time the 1st Squadron of Inniskillings pitched into their east wing, whose unfortunate cavalrymen had their backs to the Skins' charge and were helpless to do anything to avoid the crush.

Finally, the 4th Dragoon Guards struck the Russian right flank, driving the Cossacks and hussars sideways and inwards with cheers and yells. Many Russians were bowled from the backs of their mounts, to fall under the hooves of their comrades' chargers. Terrified horses were knocked from their feet and rolled over, kicking at the sky with their legs.

Now the struggle was in earnest as the Russians, though still vastly superior in numbers, were being attacked front and sides. The only way out of the confusion was to the rear and many of them were taking that route. They began to fragment and break up, groups of them seeking ground out of the battle area.

The charge of the 4th Dragoon Guards was so successful they forced their way through the thick mass of Russians to break out of the far side, splitting the Russian column in two.

Eggerton was fighting like a madman now, hacking at every Russian who came past him. He vaguely heard the call 'Rally the Inniskillings!' and looked about him for the rallying officer, but could not see him through the thickets of lances. The other regiments were rallying now – the Greys, the Royals, the 4th and 5th – as the Russians broke ranks and scrambled away. While he was turning, searching for his squadron, Eggerton saw a flash of light above his head and instinctively ducked forwards and sideways.

A hussar's sabre came swishing down, grazing his spine, to slice through the back part of the saddle. Brackish lurched on, receiving the blow, though luckily the leather saddle was not quite severed right through. Eggerton swung back and out with his own weapon, catching his assailant in the teeth with the flat of the blade. The Russian let out a peculiar grunt and peeled away, to ride off after his comrades, who were now pouring away from the battleground.

Finding himself without opponents, Eggerton dismounted and inspected the damage to the saddle, discovering to his relief that Brackish had not sustained a cut. He remounted, his bottom balanced awkwardly on the two parts of the saddle.

The wound to his left shoulder was beginning to ache badly. He glanced at it once and then, on seeing a gaping gash and what looked like the whiteness of bone, immediately turned his head again. Pulling a kerchief from his pocket, he pushed it inside the cut to his coat, wedging it there to stanch the blood whose flow had slowed almost to a mere seeping.

I troop of the RHA was now sending shot into the fleeing enemy, assisted by W Battery at Kadikoi.

'Hurrah!' cried Eggerton, on trotting over to his comrades. 'Hurrah! Hurrah!'

They were all cheering and waving their swords in the air, exhilarated to be alive after such an encounter, happy beyond measure to be the victors of such a glorious charge.

'Everything went so splendidly,' said an excited cornet, who now took out his pocket watch and studied it carefully.

'Less than ten minutes,' he gasped, clearly astonished. 'The whole action took only about eight or nine minutes. Can you believe that? It seemed like an hour at least.'

'Time plays funny tricks in a battle,' said an older man, a troop sergeant. 'It slows right down when you're in danger of death. You could drink a quart of ale in between each heartbeat, I swear.'

'Now that's when time gets speedy,' said another man, 'when you're at the canteen, drinking, and expecting to be called out for duty at any time.'

The others laughed.

Eggerton began to feel weak and a little giddy, but he did not want to leave his comrades just yet. He wanted to savour the fruits of their shared victory. It was his first charge at an enemy – indeed the first charge of most men there – and these few moments after the action were to be cherished. He was alive and virtually whole and he was never going to experience the same emotions again.

Looking round him, he saw the men who had fallen, their horses standing over them or wandering aimlessly among the corpses. These men had made the charge but could not enjoy the afterglow of such a feat. They had routed an enemy of superior numbers, yet they were unable to reap the benefits. Eggerton found that infinitely sad. Fancy going through all that and not being able to appreciate it.

His shoulder was seriously stiffening up now. The arm below it was going numb. He felt for the hole in his cheek and stuck the point of his tongue through. That was not so bad. That one was merely interesting and would heal by itself. The shoulder was different. Though the bleeding had stopped the wound needed cauterizing, a painful business in itself.

'Hey, Rough-rider Eggerton!' exclaimed one of the privates, noticing him shivering with the shock. 'You're badly wounded – get you to the doctor, man.'

'Others are wounded too. There are some with worse,' he said, more to cheer himself than to state a fact. 'It won't carry me off, that's certain.'

'It might if you don't get attention,' said the private. 'Go on, get you over there.'

So Eggerton rode off to find the surgeon's tent in the camp ahead. On the way he passed the Light Brigade, who were still standing, waiting for orders to move. For the moment he could not see his cousin, Feltam, but he could sense an impatience amongst the cavalrymen. It then struck Eggerton as odd that the Light Cavalry had not charged the enemy when they were in disarray. It seemed to him sensible that, once the Heavies had broken the ranks of the Russian horsemen, the Lights should have gone in and taken advantage of the situation, preventing the Russians from rallying, routing them for good and all.

'We've got some strange commanders here,' he told himself. 'Even a simple man like me can tell when the going's good for a charge. I bet Feltam's feeling bad about this. He would have wanted to go in, I know. What are them officers thinking of, that they should wait and do nothing?'

It seemed an opportunity missed and Eggerton began to feel terribly angry about the affair. After all, he and his comrades had done the hard work. It needed but a charge by the Lights to complete it all. What a sorry state of affairs. What a waste of a good opening. What a fat chance missed.

18

From her vantage point on a ridge, Mrs Durham was beside herself with excitement, having witnessed the charge of the Heavy Brigade from start to finish.

'Oh well done, Heavies,' she cried rapturously. 'So very well executed, boys.'

Watching the charge had been the most electrifying experience of her life so far. She could not imagine anything would surpass it. Seeing the colourful brigade of eight hundred horsemen in their short red coatees fling themselves at the sombre mass of two to three thousand Russians wearing their sober grey overcoats, had been spectacular. It had been small vivid bands against a large dull horde, and the bright boys in their scarlet coats, with their splendid verve and style had won.

It had been all trumpets, and clashing swords, the cheers of the Skins and the ecstatic moans of the Greys, fences of lances, the zuzzing of the Russians, banging carbines, rattling bridle rings, energetic cries, shouts of despair, and finally the booming of the guns to put a period mark at the end of the conflict.

The Greys had been so easy to distinguish, on their white horses, it was no wonder they received the majority of the adulation and applause from the spectators. But Mrs Durham had seen it all, had been able to follow each squadron as it went into the mêlée. She thought the Inniskillings had fought supremely well; the 4th and 5th Dragoons had surpassed themselves in bravery; the Royals had covered themselves with glory; and the Greys were wonderful, courageous and so, so handsome.

'Bravo!' she cried, clapping her hands together. 'Oh, so very well done, my brave, brave warriors.'

One would have thought from her words and demeanour that she was the commander of the day, had personally ordered the attack, and was experiencing the most pleasant feeling of being both in the right and victorious. They were *her* warriors and hers was the credit for the outcome. One by one they would go to her and pay homage to her generalship, grateful that they were under her leadership, and not that of any other. God forbid they were under the authority of some wishy-washy commander who was more concerned with good manners than winning a war.

Captain Nolan, a young ex-Indian army cavalryman, stood by her and grimaced at her exuberance.

Well, I agree that was a fair show, ma'am, but for the best you have to witness a charge by the finest light cavalry in the world — those men you see down there. What a pity it is that it's led by the Noble Yachtsman. He should have charged, damn the man. He could still do so. Why don't they use the Light Brigade now and turn that retreat into a rout?'

She could see the man was simmering with rage. Captain Nolan, she knew, was passionate about light cavalry. He had written a book about its many advantages over other types of cavalry, and other infantry and artillery. She owned a signed copy, which he had presented to her himself. That the Light Brigade was allowed to go stale was infuriating and brought out the nervous, excited warrior in him.

She stared where he was pointing and saw Lord Cardigan pacing his horse up and down in front of a restless and frustrated Light Brigade. Most of the men had dismounted. Some were smoking their pipes and drinking a little rum. Others looked as if they were on a picnic, biting on hard-boiled eggs and crunching on apples. They seemed lacklustre and in want of something to relieve their idleness.

'I might agree, Captain,' she said, 'if only they were to do something.'

'That is not their fault, ma'am. Lord Raglan sees fit to keep the Light Cavalry in a bandbox. They must await his orders,' seethed the captain.

'When will he let them out?'

'That question, ma'am, can only be answered by Lord Raglan himself.'

The handsome young captain with his neat little moustache attached to his small neat face on his tight neat body, gave her a curt bow, as if to indicate the end of the conversation. He still stood by her side, however, staring out over the valleys below, watching the movements of the battle with a keen eye. While thus engaged, he offered her a cigarello, which she refused, then lighted one for himself.

The Russians appeared to be formed up in a kind of open square now, their troops on both sides of the North Valley. They lined the Causeway Heights on the one side and the edge of the Fedioukine Hills on the other, so that they commanded the whole length of the valley apart from the west end. There were infantry, cavalry and guns on the Fedioukine side and at the east end, and infantry and cavalry on the Causeway Heights side.

Mrs Durham glanced again at the Light Brigade, which was at the eastern end of the South Valley, separated from the North Valley only by the Woronzoff Road. The two valleys ran parallel with each other and met at that point at the termination of the Causeway Heights. The French cavalry in the form of the Chasseurs d'Afrique were on the other side of the road, at the head of the North Valley.

Lord Cardigan still looked unsettled, walking his charger

191

up and down in front of his troops, glaring first at the enemy, then in the direction of Lord Lucan, there not being much difference between the two so far as he was concerned.

'Captain Nolan!' called a staff officer. 'Lord Raglan wishes you to take a message to Lord Lucan.'

'What will they have me do?' he said, blowing out smoke in an irritated manner. 'Shall I be ordered to tell the Light Brigade they must on no account become embroiled in a fight in case they get their cherrybums dirty?'

'Please go, Captain, or you may be in trouble. You have been given an order. I should put out that cigarello if I were you. It may upset the senior officers to see you smoking.'

'I see a number of them with cigars,' said Nolan, but he put out his smoke just the same.

'Captain Nolan!' came the cry again.

Captain Nolan saluted Mrs Durham, saying, 'They obviously need my superior horsemanship. Calthorpe's next on in the rota but he can't ride for a penny, like most of these other staff officers. Such a bore. Excuse me, ma'am.'

She nodded, giving him leave to go, thinking him a rather silly puffed-up man.

'You must do your duty,' she said.

Captain Lewis Edward Nolan, General Airey's ADC, attired in the splendid uniform of the 15th Hussars, mounted his horse and rode off astride his tiger-skin saddle to answer the summons.

Moments later Captain Nolan was slipping and sliding down the steep slope on his mount. He was indeed a superb horseman: Mrs Durham had to give him his due. Horse and rider were as one as they skidded on loose stones to arrive at the bottom of the escarpment as a complete pair. Any other man, she admitted to herself, might have been unhorsed by that slope.

The captain went galloping off towards Lord Lucan waving a piece of paper.

What a fuss he makes of everything, that man, Lavinia Durham thought.

She looked across the South Valley to Kadikoi, where stood the man who had recently made love to her.

Now he was one of the heroes of the battle. She would congratulate him later. The red-coated infantry regiment were still there, ready for any new attack which might come their way. Theirs had been a magnificent stand, the 93rd and their extras, against four squadrons of cavalry.

She knew that normally a battalion formed itself into a square, or at least went four lines deep, when being attacked by cavalry. It was standard practice, in order to prevent being outflanked. But the Sutherland Highlanders had not the time for these niceties and had still routed the enemy.

'Hello, my dear, enjoying the spectacle?'

A rotund little man was approaching her.

It was her husband, Captain Durham, Quartermaster. She was very fond of Bertie too, in her way. He was her provider and her safe harbour from which she could venture out on her little escapades and then return to haven.

'Yes thank you, Bertie. It was good of Lord Cardigan to loan me this horse. He simply flew here.'

'I say, wasn't that a magnificent charge the Greys did down there? Did you see it?'

'Not just the Greys, Bertie,' she admonished. 'There were others there too. The Inniskillings, the Royals and the 4th and 5th Dragoons.'

'Yes, but,' he expostulated, 'they took their lead from the Greys. The Greys went in first you know.'

'And one squadron of Inniskillings.'

'But the Greys, my dear! You saw them. Sir Colin Campbell approached them afterwards. I don't know what he said but he looked full of admiration.'

Mrs Durham stared down at the battlefield again. That silly Captain Nolan was with Lord Lucan, the commander of the Cavalry Division. Lucan was, on paper at least, his brother-in-law, Lord Cardigan's, superior, Cardigan being commander only of the Light Brigade. In truth the two were so haughty neither would take orders from the other, no matter who gave what to whom.

Captain Nolan was gesturing wildly, flinging an arm out to indicate something. Both men were red in the face. She could not imagine that Captain Nolan was insulting an officer as senior as Lord Lucan, a major-general, but it certainly looked like it.

'What are they supposed to be doing, Bertie?' she asked.

'Oh, as I understand it, my dear, they intend the Light Brigade to attack those Russians who are carrying off the guns from our redoubts. You see that little bunch of grey figures over there, hitching up a cannon? And another group there, further along? Shouldn't be too much trouble for our cherubims and their chums,' he added, using the polite form of the nickname for the 11th Hussars.

'Lord Raglan said the cavalry is to attack *immediately*,' repeated Captain Nolan. '*Immediately*.'

'I heard you the first time, Captain,' growled Lord Lucan, looking down the valley now and shaking his head. 'I'm not deaf y'know. Keep a civil tongue in y'head, sir, if you please.'

Lucan read the note which Nolan had given him. It was written in General Airey, the quartermaster general's, almost indecipherable scribble.

Lord Raglan wishes the cavalry to advance rapidly to the front – follow the enemy and try to prevent the enemy carrying away the guns. Troops Horse Artillery may accompany. French cavalry on your left. Immediate.

'That word there,' said Lucan, pointing. 'Is that *sorrow*?'

'*Follow*, my lord. *Follow the enemy*.'

Lord Lucan stared down the South Valley again, seeing a row of cannon at the far end with cavalry massed behind it.

'Those guns?' he said, stroking his chin. 'Those guns, sir?'

'The *Russian* guns,' confirmed Captain Nolan, not looking, full of impatience. We are ordered to charge them now.'

Lucan sighed and shrugged. He rode with Captain Nolan over to Lord Cardigan. Cardigan glared at both men, no love lost between any of them. The general thought Captain Nolan an insufferable popinjay who insulted his name behind his back. Cardigan hated these Indian army people anyway: the fact that Nolan had been in that service was enough to damn him in Cardigan's eyes.

'Well?' Cardigan said peremptorily. 'What now?'

Another heated exchange of words took place. Finally Cardigan raised his eyebrows, looked down the valley, seeing the same formidable array of guns which Lucan had seen. He then barked an order. Men began to mount their horses, throwing away half-eaten biscuits and cups. Captain Nolan rode over to Captain Morris of the 17th Lancers. Morris was Nolan's close friend.

'Are we going?' asked Morris, excitedly.

'At last,' said Nolan, grinning. 'Any chance I could join you, old chap?'

'Help yourself,' Morris replied, grinning back, making a space.

At this moment the Light Brigade was in two lines, with the 13th Light Hussars, the 17th Lancers and the 11th Hussars in the first line. The second line consisted of the 8th Hussars and the 4th Light Dragoons. As Mrs Durham watched, the 11th Hussars moved behind the other two in the front line, making three lines in all, with the 8th and 4th at the rear.

'Well, they can't take their horse artillery with 'em,' said Captain Durham, lighting up his short stubby pipe.

'Why not?' asked his wife.

He pointed with the stem of the pipe. 'See the valley? It's farmland, a lot of it. Most of it has been ploughed and is furrowed. Iron-hard furrows in *this* soil, I'll be bound. You send horses with cannon and limber over that lot and you'll lose 'em for sure. No, the guns won't go.'

'You are clever, Bertie.'

'Not really. Been through the same training as most of those chaps. Simply chose to be a storekeeper, rather than ride my backside bare through storms of bullets, that's all. Not a hero, I'm afraid, my dear.'

'That's all right, Bertie. You aren't built like one. Leave the heroing to men like Captain Morris.'

'Yes, I suppose so,' he said, puffing on his pipe. 'Chaps like Captain Nolan, eh?'

'Oh, *him*,' she said. 'My dear, you're more of a hero than Captain Nolan any day.'

Captain Durham filled his chest with air. 'Am I, m'dear?' he said. 'Nice of you to say so.'

Trumpets were sounding below them now. Things were becoming interesting. There was now to be a second charge of the day. Mrs Durham's excitement rose. Her cheeks started to tingle. Death or Glory. How wonderful it must feel, she thought, to be one of those men down there in the valley, ready to ride hell for leather at the enemy.

'Oh do make a good show,' she breathed. 'Do, do.'

19

'The brigade will advance. First Squadron of the 17th Lancers will direct.'

Private Feltam heard the order with a sharp thrill. The First Squadron of the 17th Lancers! That was him. They were going to charge the enemy at last. He was not quite sure which enemy that might be, but he was glad that his cousin Eggerton was not going to be the only man from their village to have had a go. He, Feltam, was to take part in a charge.

The trumpeter of the 17th Lancers sounded 'Walk, March – Trot'.

Feltam urged his mount forward at a walk, then broke into a trot, careful to keep his place in the line. It would not do to be noticed going ahead or dropping behind. He did not want to disgrace himself now that he was having his chance. To the rear he could hear the bugles for the second and third lines.

Harnesses jingled in the morning air. Slowly the line of trotting horsemen went down the mile-wide valley like a roll of crimson surf, covering only a fifth of its width. Behind this two more gentle combers of red foam. Out in front rode the proud, haughty Brigadier-General Cardigan, last of the Brudenells, his moustaches blowing gently in the breezes.

It seemed the world was holding its breath.

When they had gone about two hundred yards, and the general had not ordered the line to turn either right or left, Feltam knew they were going the length of the valley. They were going to run the gauntlet. Feltam was not sure what was happening, but he had to put his trust in his leaders. There must be infantry to support us somewhere, he thought, looking around him, for it would be suicide to go in without support.

Perhaps the infantry were about to attack the heights on either side and occupy the attention of the troops there? And possibly there was a plan for the Heavy Brigade to ride at the guns on the western side of the valley, to silence them? Who knew what devious tactics were in the minds of the great generals, who must have been more intelligent than Feltam, or why would they have been put in charge of things?

Private Albury, to Feltam's right, said, 'Where the damn hell are we going?'

'We'll see soon enough,' replied Feltam, not happy about the rasping tone of Albury's cursing. 'You just keep a gentle tongue in your throat − you may be going on your final journey in a few minutes, and you don't want to arrive with your lips still twisted on a curse. Think on that.'

'Nothin' wrong with a good oath,' muttered Albury, but he looked a little abashed by Feltam's warning.

They went a few further yards when someone else let out an oath.

'Keep that line, damn you!'

Lord Cardigan was reprimanding someone for being too quick, too eager to charge. By turning his head slightly, Feltam saw who it was. It was the captain who had accompanied Lord Lucan with the message to attack. This officer's impetuosity would cost him dear, if Feltam knew anything about his brigade commander. Lord Cardigan would have the man's ears for bridle rings after the battle was over. Feltam could see that the back of Lord Cardigan's neck was red with anger.

At that very moment a shell burst overhead and the noise made Feltam's head ring. His horse shied a little, but was soon calmed. The 17th's line rippled, as if the shock wave from the explosion had travelled down its length. Lord Cardigan stiffened in his saddle, going poker-straight.

Someone, somewhere was screaming in a high-pitched voice, like a rabbit with a weasel at its throat.

'Jesus, Lord Almighty!' said a startled Albury, looking round. 'What's that?'

'That captain who brought the order,' answered Feltam. 'He's been hit.'

The captain's horse rode across and in front of them with the screaming officer still in the saddle, his sword arm raised but his hand empty of a weapon. He seemed locked in a position which registered defiance, yet his face was twisted with the shock and pain of sudden death. Then he slipped sideways and backwards, to fall heavily on the ground, under the hooves of the oncoming 11th Hussars. Captain Morris looked back at the body, his face stricken with horror.

They were now in a sandstorm of bullets, coming from both sides of the valley. The air seemed to darken with the amount of metal fragments swirling around them. Round shot was falling amongst them, crashing through horses' legs like balls through skittles, toppling the riders. More shells burst on them, filling the air with whining fragments of hot steel. The atmosphere was thick with metal splinters, like deadly insects. It seemed impossible to ride through that storm without being struck by something.

'Good glory,' cried Feltam, numb with sudden fright, 'we'll all be killed for certain.'

But he kept on riding, still at a trot, as did all those who remained in their saddles. Men and horses began to disappear from the line, either swept away by round shot, or struck in some vital part by musket ball or splinter of shell. Others were wounded but kept their place in the line. There were grim white faces all around as, incredibly, the amount of fire

199

began to increase with the guns and rifles in front opening up.

The air sizzled with a hot metal rainstorm.

Feltam's horse, Dagger, was struck twice almost simultaneously, in the neck and flank. Dagger snorted in pain but did not falter in stride. Moments later Feltam experienced a red-hot agonizing pain in his left shoulder.

'I'm hit,' he said to Albury, but it was merely a statement of fact, not an excuse to cut and run. Discipline was immaculate. They had trained for this and Feltam knew what he had to do. He was certainly not going to drop behind now, when they were so close to their goal. How he would regret it later, to be one of those who never made it.

'So am I,' came the response from Albury, and Feltam looked across to see Albury's lance arm hanging uselessly by his side, his weapon dangling from a shattered hand and dragging in the dust, making a snaking mark. 'I an't going back though,' said the wounded man, with a voice full of fury.

Feltam experienced the same rage washing through himself, as he saw men he knew blown from their saddles, or their horses shot from under them. Familiar faces, acquaintances, good friends. They were all going down by the dozen now, in a blizzard of grape shot. Feltam could hear the *pocking* sound of small pieces of metal striking bodies, passing through soft flesh, burying themselves in muscle and bone.

The man on the other side of Feltam was Private Simms. Simms was close enough to touch Feltam and he suddenly reached out and tapped Feltam's shoulder. 'Tagged, old son,' he said, giving Feltam the wistful smile of an infant who has been called in from playing games on the heath. Then letting out a soft sigh he slipped from his saddle, down into the dust.

The Russian infantry, armed with Liege rifles, were using them to good effect from the heights on either side of the mile-wide valley.

The lines of cavalry were well down now, on their way into the mouths of the guns, and still they were trotting, with the rednecked and church-steady Cardigan deliberately keeping the pace down and the lines straight.

But as they drew nearer the cannons the 17th Lancers' fury increased and by ones and bunches they broke into a gallop, the regular drumming of their hooves turning to a sound of thunder. Cardigan glanced behind him at Feltam's line, looking with an annoyed expression at Captain Morris who led it, but if he was not to be swallowed by his own cavalry he had to stay ahead of the horsemen. He too broke into a gallop, charging forward, the wind tearing at his headdress feather.

'Come on, chums,' cried Feltam, yelling to the 11th Hussars, who were about four hundred yards behind. 'Come on, then. Let's get into 'em!'

He was exhilarated now, all pain forgotten. He could see the mouths of the cannons, blaring grape shot. The air was full of metal wasps. But with the wind rushing past his ears, he lowered his lance. It was all blood and fury now! This was the stuff! All he wanted to do was prick one of those bloody gunners with the point of his lance. Right at that moment he hated the beggars, for cutting down his friends like wheat, for standing smugly behind their cannons and destroying the 17th Lancers as if they meant nothing to anyone.

'Up, up, 13th,' came a cry from Feltam's right. 'Don't let those bastards of the 17th get there first!'

Albury cried, 'Don't let 'em catch us, Feltam!'

The enemy was the enemy and there was a job to be done by all, but it would have been disastrous to let the light dragoons draw in front of the lancers. Feltam and Albury had to be there *first*. It was a matter of honour.

Feltam increased Dagger's pace and the wounded animal responded magnificently. Just then Feltam was hit in two more places, in the left elbow and the chest. He knew he had been struck but it was something only at the back of his mind. First and foremost he had to pass through those guns. He could worry about wounds later. He began yelling and cheering as they came up on the Russians, the flank fire from the heights having ceased now for fear they would hit their own troops.

The guns in front blazed for the last time, booming along the line, their flashes like the quick opening and shutting of a row of furnace doors. A wave of hot air riffled through Feltam's uniform, warming his face and hands. Men and horses went down on all sides. There were curses and prayers in the air. Albury cried out, 'The paths of glory – Feltam . . .' and then he was gone. Others went down in the grape shot in packs, falling in heaps of twisted legs and arms.

Feltam's eyes were on those behind the guns, the previously self-satisfied figures behind that row of brass cannon, who were beginning to twitch and run now.

'Yes, yes, you beggars,' he yelled at them, as the gunners finally turned and broke away. 'Thought you were safe! I'll prick you, by damn. I'll puncture your backsides!'

Ignoring his own priggishness about oaths, he let them have a mouthful of curses, he hated them so much at that moment. And he had never felt such triumph as he surged past the first line of guns, his lance directed at the chest of an infantry soldier. The man tossed away his rifle and threw up his arms, but Feltam's lance pieced his heart and rolled him aside.

Then Feltam's neck jerked sideways as he himself was lanced by a Cossack coming in from the side. He swung his own lance round like a staff and struck the rider on the side of the head knocking him off balance in his saddle. A friendly dragoon shot the Cossack in the back, then hacked him off his horse with his sword.

A second Cossack attacked Feltam from the front. Feltam desperately parried the man's lance with his own, but unfortunately drove it down so that it lodged in Dagger's chest. Dagger reared in agony, kicking out with his front hooves and driving off the Cossack's mount. The poor animal now had the broken point of a lance buried in his chest and he was wheezing heavily.

Feltam patted Dagger's head, emotion welling in his breast at the thought of his charger's pain.

'Sorry old boy,' he said. 'We'll get you back now.'

Apart from being severely wounded, Dagger was blown with the ride, and he began to totter a little in his stride.

Captain Morris was rallying the 17th now, and the swords were out, hissing down on the heads of the hated Russian gunners. Morris called to Feltam, but the private's horse was now all in. Dagger sank to his knees with a groan and Feltam had to dismount. Another lancer was walking away from the fight, carrying his saddle, and he said to Feltam, 'You'd best keep your tack, chum. You can come by a horse easy enough.'

Feltam saw Morris and about ten others go charging at some startled Russian cavalry, who in turn tried to force their way back through the massed Russian troops in the rear, to avoid the blood-spattered and furious bands of lancers.

Dagger died with a rattle in his throat, but Feltam could not get the saddle off his back, since the weight of the horse was too much for him to lift and pull it out from under. Two Russian hussars came at him then, one on either side. Feltam drew his sword and whirled it about him, keeping them back long enough to be able to slice one through his boot.

This man rode off with his foot dangling. The other hussar came in close enough for Feltam to jump up at him and drag him from the saddle. The lancer then drove his sword through the man's chest, pinning him to the ground.

Feltam was feeling dizzy now. Surprisingly his multiple wounds were not bothering him that much, but he was losing blood. Looking round he saw Lord Cardigan riding back towards the British lines, still poker-straight in his saddle, looking as if he were hacking in Hyde Park. The general had obviously had enough of things amongst the guns, felt he had done his duty, and was now on the way back. Feltam had some thoughts about leaders staying with their men and actually doing some leading, but these were soon pushed aside by the precariousness of his position. He was still on foot and quite vulnerable.

The dead Russian's charger was standing quietly nearby, the reins draping on the ground. Feltam mounted this horse and brought it under control, before riding towards Sergeant-Major Stannard, who was beset by a group of Cossacks. Stannard looked badly wounded. Feltam waded into the Cossacks, his sword swishing, and grabbed the Sergeant-Major's bridle with his free hand, then led him away at a canter. Fortunately none of the Russians followed.

'You all right, sir?' he cried. 'Can you make it back?'

The sergeant-major's heavy-lidded eyes regarded him.

'Thank you, Feltam. I'll be all right. Let go the bridle. Look to yourself, trooper.'

Feltam did as he was told and the pair of them began to return at a slow pace down the valley. They were well over on the right, facing their own lines. It was certain they would be shot at by the infantry lining that side of the valley, but then Feltam saw the French cavalry, the Chasseurs d'Afrique, coming charging up that side. Feltam could see them in their distinctive red and blue, as the Chasseurs attacked the guns and infantry on the slopes of the Fedioukine Hills.

'Hurrah for the Froggies,' he said. 'Sarn-Major, they've cut us a path back through.'

'Do not be disrespectful to our French allies,' grumbled the sergeant-major. 'They are not what they eat.'

'No, sir,' answered Feltam, cheerfully. 'But they've done us a good turn, anyway. Look at them burn into those Russians. Better late than never, eh?'

The bowed figure of the sergeant-major, racked with pain, agreed with the private.

The Heavy Brigade had also followed the Light Brigade up the valley, but well behind, fatigued as they were by their earlier encounter with the enemy. When Feltam was halfway back down, giddiness overcame him and he passed out in the unfamiliar saddle of the Russian hussar's horse. When he came to he found his cousin Eggerton by his side, leading his horse back to safety. He wondered where Eggerton had come from and his first thought was for the sergeant-major.

Eggerton put him at his ease, saying the sergeant-major was in good hands, also being led back by one of the Heavies.

'You stay in the saddle, boy,' said Eggerton. 'We're not so far from home now. You've been hit bad, eh? What a charge! But it was folly, cousin, sheer folly, for you've all been shot to pieces. I don't know what them generals are thinking of, sending you in there like that. I never heard of nothing so foolish before today.'

'I make you right on that one, cousin,' replied Feltam, still gripped by a wooziness. 'But you're wounded yourself. I can see the pad of blood on your shoulder. Did you follow us in?'

'I got this wound in the Heavies' charge. Don't you worry about me, I'll live. No, we only came part-way for you. Lord Lucan got hit in the leg and several officers killed, so we stopped. I heard Lord Lucan say, "They have sacrificed the Light Brigade, they shall not have the Heavy," and we halted and retired out of range.'

'Good thing too. It *was* sheer folly. I've never heard of a charge being made right into the guns. I could see down the barrels, cousin. It was hell.'

'You did glorious deeds out there,' said Eggerton, 'but I have no envy for you this time.'

20

Only the two spots of colour on her otherwise pale cheeks indicated that Mrs Durham was feeling emotional. Her eyes were fixed on the valley below, where bloody men and horses were staggering back: the remnants of her beautiful Light Brigade. It seemed impossibly tragic. Captain Durham knew what she was thinking. How could such an order have been given without the consequences being obvious?

'My dear,' he said, taking her hand, 'it was a mistake – a terrible mistake.'

'Of course it was a mistake, Bertie,' she said, turning on him and giving vent to her passion. 'Who could have called such a massacre anything else?'

'No, I mean it really was a mistake. The message was misread or something. Lord Raglan is beside himself. He intended that the Light Brigade should attack the Russians carrying away our guns from the redoubts on the Causeway Heights, not that they should charge the guns at the end of the valley. It's all been a ghastly error.'

Her face showed that she now understood.

'But surely Lord Lucan, and Lord Cardigan, could not have misread such a message. If they had been told to attack the Russians on the Causeway Heights, they would have done so.'

'I think the tone was a little more vague than that – and the messenger was so full of zeal he did not take the time to explain it properly – indeed he may have been under a misconception too. I'm inclined to think, though I dislike criticizing my betters, that the missive was poorly phrased. I heard General Airey repeat it to another officer. It sounded something like "The Light Brigade is to advance quickly and stop the enemy carrying away the guns."'

'But that could mean anything on a battlefield with guns all over the place.'

'As I said, my dear, I do not think the communication was of a very high standard.'

She shook her head in bewilderment. 'What do we have these people for, if not to lead competently? They all speak of Wellington, indeed they seem to worship his memory, yet none of them tries to emulate him. Those boys have died for nothing. What happened to Captain Nolan?'

'His body lies down there on the plain. Lord Cardigan rode past without a glance. I think that's Captain Morris kneeling by the corpse now. If I'm not mistaken, Captain Nolan was the first to die, when the shells began falling.'

Mrs Durham said nothing in answer to this information. She simply stared down at the tattered remains of the pride of the British army. She could see Lord Cardigan, sitting on a knoll, wiping his face with a handkerchief. He was staring miserably down into the valley at his precious cherrybummed troopers, the 11th Hussars. He had equipped them, drilled them. They had been his pride and joy.

Even Cardigan must be feeling dastardly, she thought, though she knew from her frequent contact with him that he was a very selfish man.

Lord Lucan was speaking with Lord Raglan, expostulating, waving his hands in the same manner which Pontius Pilate used when shrugging off all responsibility for the crucifixion of Christ. General Airey looked distressed, pacing up and down near the two arguing men. What would they make of it back in England? The Light Brigade, destroyed. How the Russians must have been laughing up their sleeves.

But the Russians seemed to have had enough. The 1st and 4th Divisions, the former under the Duke of Cambridge and the latter under a dilatory General Cathcart, were now in the battle area. The Duke's division had come along the Woronzoff Road to the head of the valley and Cathcart's division had descended the col and now marched along the Causeway Heights round to the redoubts.

'It's all of a piece,' said Mrs Durham, shaking her head, the tears forming slowly in her eyes and then rolling down her cheeks.

'My dear,' said a shocked Captain Durham. He put his arm around her, thus proving that each of them could still surprise the other. 'Please – you will distress me too.'

After the stand of the 93rd Crossman spoke to Lieutenant Dalton-James.

'Sir, if there's going to be some action in the North as well as here in the South Valley, perhaps we could get some men up on the Causeway ridge, between the two. It's a very commanding position.'

Dalton-James stared at the man he so disliked for a good full minute, but here was something which transcended petty feuds. Here was a chance to get some free-handed action. The 93rd had to stay where they were in case of another attack on Balaclava, but Dalton-James with his few riflemen and Crossman and his walking wounded could do some fighting on their own. They were at that moment under no one's direct command.

'What about the redoubts up there?' asked the lieutenant, briskly. 'The Woronzoff Road has been cut and there's Russians all over the Causeway ridge. We'd be going into a hornets' nest.'

'We could go up in skirmishing order,' replied Crossman.

'Follow those goat paths, using the boulders for cover. Even worm our way over the ridge on our bellies. It could be done.'

Dalton-James studied the landscape with a keen eye.

'The rifles,' he murmured. 'We could use the Fergusons. That way we might stand a chance going up on our bellies, Sergeant. One doesn't need to kneel or stand up to reload a Ferguson as one does a Minié.'

'But where are the Fergusons, sir?' asked Crossman. 'Are they close by?'

The lieutenant smiled smugly. 'Follow me,' he said. 'Bring your men with you.'

They were not Crossman's men, but the soldiers who had been in the hospital for minor wounds and illnesses sensed a battle. They heard the order and formed up behind Crossman, who led them after Dalton-James and his riflemen. The lieutenant took them to a house on the edge of Kadikoi village, not far from the place where the 93rd had made their stand. He went in the house with two of his men and emerged with two long crates. These contained fifty (or rather forty-nine, since Ali had stolen one) breech-loading Ferguson rifles and ammunition. These, along with boxes of gunpowder, were issued to the invalids and to his own riflemen.

Crossman quickly showed the men how to load and prime the weapon, demonstrating the sequence of actions twice. They were soldiers. They knew how to use weapons. All but the most dense of them got it the first time round. Soon they were ready to make the jogging run across the South Valley to the ridge. It was just over a mile to the bottom of Causeway Heights.

Dalton-James led the way, full of his own importance, but eager for action. Crossman followed with some of the slower invalids. When they got to the foot of the ridge they suddenly came under heavy fire from above and scattered for the rocks. One of Crossman's men fell with a bullet in the neck. A rifleman was wounded in the thigh. Most, however, were behind a rise and out of the line of fire.

'Where are they, sir?' called Crossman to Dalton-James. 'Can you see them?'

'Canrobert's Hill,' called the lieutenant.

Crossman studied the landscape to his right. Canrobert's Hill, so named by the troops, was a hill which was close enough to the Causeway Heights to be almost part of it. He could see Russian infantrymen up there now, defending a redoubt they had captured earlier from the Turks.

Crossman signalled to his men, pointing.

'How we goin' to get up there, Sergeant?' asked a private with a bandage around his head. 'Can't see a way up.'

Crossman was in a better position than this man to see a dry watercourse snaking up the hill. The rocks on the sides of this channel, deposited by flash floods in the winter, were not the best cover but they would have to do.

Crossman indicated that his men should follow him and began crawling forward on his elbows, lizard-like towards the watercourse. Others followed him. All around there were shots zinging from the rough ground, ricocheting off stones. A tiny piece of flint struck Crossman on the cheek, drawing blood, but he managed to make cover without being hit. He started to return fire with the Ferguson. It was an ideal weapon for this terrain. Load and fire, load and fire, load and fire, with no real exposure of the body.

Once the Rifles and Crossman's men began returning fire, the Russians up on the top of the hill, there in great number, began to shoot down on the skirmishers with merciless if a little wanton fervour. Dalton-James lost two men in reaching the sergeant.

But the Fergusons were taking their toll too. The Russian soldiers had to lean over the brow of the escarpment to aim at the British, during which time it was like shooting ducks at a fairground. A head and shoulders would pop up and half a dozen Fergusons would blaze away. Russian bodies began to roll over the brow, dropping several feet on to the slopes.

Crossman noted that they were wearing the uniform of the Azov Regiment.

'That's the mark, lads,' cried Dalton-James. 'Keep it up. Keep it up.'

Crossman was not satisfied with shooting ducks. It was in his mind to reach the top of the ridge where they could pick off more Russian soldiers by lying with their bodies down the slope, looking over the rim. He began to edge forwards, shuffling prone along the watercourse, the higher banks keeping him hidden from the Russian sharpshooters. Two or three of his men followed him while the others remained with Dalton-James, covering the sergeant's ascent.

The Russians were having to expose themselves from time to time, to ram home ball and powder, but Crossman and his men could stay down flat in the watercourse and reload in safety. Then the Fergusons could be poked between rocks on the bank of the dry stream, the rifleman exposing only part of his head to aim, and with luck another Russian infantryman was killed or wounded.

Splinters of stone flew everywhere as the intensity of the fusillades from above increased. Crossman's eyes were smarting with the dust. Gunpowder smoke from the weapons irritated his nostrils. The pangs of craving for the laudanum were returning accompanied by a raging thirst. At that moment, as he lay in a dust bowl at the bottom of the dry stream bed, Crossman wanted to be anywhere but where he was now. There were too many enemy rifles above him. It was a foul-weather storm of lead they were sending down the slopes. He almost decided to stay where he was until the action was all over. The weariness was such that he just wanted to fall asleep.

The man next to him, a private in the 44th, lifted his head just a little too high. A bullet hit him smack in the forehead. He fell back over Crossman with a last sigh. Crossman rolled the soldier from him. This incident was enough to put more energy into the sergeant's tired bones. Once more he began to tackle the upward climb, only one man left with him now. The pair of them snaked through the dust, the air above them humming with deadly bees. Then came a shout from above.

Clearly the commander of the forces on Canrobert's Hill had had enough of these attackers. He was frustrated by those whose bodies remained hidden while they still managed to reload their weapons. He gave an order to attack. Russian infantrymen began to come down the escarpment from above. Crossman and his last man were about to be overrun.

'Here they come, Sergeant,' cried the soldier, a young corporal. 'Let's make 'em work for it.'

The two of them sprawled on the edge of the watercourse, loading and firing as fast as they could manage, the barrels of their weapons becoming red-hot to the touch. The sound of rapid fire came from below too and Crossman could hear Dalton-James yelling at his men to keep up the fire power. Russians began to tumble as they were hit, the momentum of their descent sending their bodies flying down the slope. One man, wounded but still on his feet, managed to reach Crossman.

The expression on the soldier's face was one of intense determination. His bayonet glinted as its point bore down on Crossman. The sergeant flung himself sideways as he was struck, the point of the bayonet going through the collar of his coatee. There it lodged, the cloth twisted round the blade. The Russian gave himself a firmer footing so he could yank it out. In doing so he fell backwards a pace or two. This gave Crossman the opportunity to recover his balance.

Crossman's Ferguson was not loaded at the time. He went up on one knee and used his rifle like a club, going not for the head, as he might have done if standing, but for the legs. The stock of the Ferguson struck the Russian on his shins, making him scream with agony. Then the man's feet went from under him and he slid headfirst down the slope. Shots were picking holes in the dust all around him, but he made the bottom without being hit again. Wisely he lay still, being now unarmed and virtually helpless.

Crossman continued up the dry watercourse with his last man, the first wave of the enemy having been massacred by the rifles of Dalton-James's men below. Dalton-James began to ascend with his Rifles now, zigzagging amongst the boulders. When Crossman reached the brow of the hill, the lieutenant and his men were about three-quarters of the way to the top. All the opposition seemed to have melted completely away.

Crossman crept below the slight overhang of the lip of the hill. Working his way along he found a spot where he could pull himself over to a gentler slope above. From here he had a view of the plateau on top of the hill.

He discovered that the Russian infantry had dropped back to the redoubt, where the guns were firing on the British cavalry below. They were obviously unsure of how many foe were coming up the hill. Their commander had decided, giving due consideration to the fact that he obviously did not want to put his head over the edge of the overhang to look for himself, to use his discretion and fall back to a safer and more defendable position, and there to await any further attack.

Glancing to his left Crossman had a view of the North Valley. He was astonished to see the ground littered with bodies of men and horses. They were not yellow-grey-coated figures down on that bloody plain, but the bright colours of British regiments. It was a second or two before he realized some awful tragedy had befallen the cavalry.

'Oh my God,' he murmured. 'They've slaughtered Cardigan's cherrybums.'

It looked very bad indeed. The Russian cavalry were at that moment riding down knots of the Light Brigade, who if they were able to fight themselves free, were taking the route back along a valley flanked with Russian infantry. It was like a rabbit shoot down there. Crossman could see small figures dragging saddles, or just themselves, back to the north-west end of the valley. Many were in tatters. Horses lying on their sides, their legs striking air. On the far side the French Chasseurs d'Afrique were battling with Russian lancers.

The guns of the redoubt had now stopped firing. Crossman guessed the Russians had panicked and were busy spiking the cannons, to prevent them falling back into British hands in a useful condition. Crossman wondered if Russian culture knew about irony. They were at that moment beleaguered by only two men! If they had spiked their guns they would be kicking themselves later for panicking so quickly.

A hail of shots whined around Crossman and he looked up to see that the Russians had fired a volley at him.

In the next few moments, as he fired back, Dalton-James crawled up beside him.

'What's the position, Sergeant?'

'There's too many of them, sir. We've given them a good pasting but they're massed around the redoubt itself. I can see one – no, two – of the officers – look . . . good God!'

'What is it?' asked Dalton-James irritably. 'What's the matter, Sergeant?'

Crossman thought he recognized one of the officers. The younger man was an infantry captain, but the older was a staff officer, a major. Crossman watched as the major turned again to look in his direction. Yes! It was the man responsible for torturing Crossman while he was a prisoner in Sebastopol.

'Major Zinski,' murmured Crossman with some satisfaction, as he loaded his Ferguson under cover of the overhang. 'Major bloody Zinski.'

'Look,' cried Dalton-James, pointing down the slope. 'Here come the 4th Division!'

Indeed, a British battery had begun to open fire on the redoubt. The 1st Battalion of the Rifle Brigade were coming up the slope in skirmishing order, with two companies of the 63rd West Sussex Regiment behind them. General Cathcart's

4th Division were winding their way along the far end of the Causeway Heights and recapturing redoubts from No. 6 to No. 3. Some of his men had been detached to storm Canrobert's Hill.

Crossman looked over again towards the North Valley and saw that the French were now on the plain with men of the Guards and Highland Regiments descending from the hills towards the valley floor. The Russians there had fallen back a little, as if awaiting another attack like the charge of the Light Brigade. After such a crazy action, anything was possible.

Thanks to Crossman and Dalton-James the men now coming up the hill met with no resistance. The two companies of the 63rd reached the brow intact and began to engage the Russians around the redoubt. However, it was not long before the Russian infantry received reinforcements from the Woronzoff Road and the British were under pressure to retreat. They still had not enough men to hold the position against a concentrated Russian attack. Finally, as the Russians began to swarm around the redoubt, massing for a charge, a captain of the 63rd gave the order to fall back down the slope.

Crossman, however, wanted one last shot. He popped his head above the lip of the hill and sought his target. For a moment all he could see were grey uniforms. Then he picked out a clutch of men bearing the insignia of commissioned officers. Amongst them stood the grim-faced Major Zinski.

'You don't know it yet,' whispered Crossman to himself, 'but you're a dead man, Major.'

'What are you babbling about?' asked Dalton-James, starting to drop down the slope. 'Come on, man, stop wasting ammunition on a lost cause. I order you to follow me immediately, or you will jeopardize both our lives.'

Crossman ignored the order. He took careful aim. Then he squeezed the trigger.

Just at that moment Major Zinski turned away. He took the bullet in the back of his right shoulder. Crossman saw him jolt forwards. Then the major sagged a little, before being assisted by a lieutenant. He remained on his feet, turning again to look across at where the shot had come from.

'Yes, it's me you bastard!' cried Crossman. 'I hope that hurts! I hope that hurts like hell! I hope it bloody rots and you die slowly, in agony . . .'

He was able to shout no more because Dalton-James had caught hold of his coatee and was dragging him down. The pair of them half ran, half tumbled down the slopes after the retreating British soldiers. A line of 63rd, on reaching the bottom, covered the retreat of those behind, firing up at the Russians as once again they began poking their rifles and heads over the top of the hill. The British made an orderly retreat across the valley to where the 93rd were guarding the gorge.

In the end, although Crossman and Dalton-James had not retaken the redoubt, they knew the Russians had spiked the guns in No. 1 redoubt, which had saved them from being used again on the British regiments scattered in the North and South Valleys. Lives had been lost but many more lives had been saved. It would be some time before the captured guns were back in working order.

The battle was now at an end. The Russians had cut the Woronzoff Road, which would seriously hamper British supply lines. They also remained in control of No. 2 and No. 1 redoubts. There they stayed, advancing no further. The British for their part had gained some small advantage in that they had saved Balaclava harbour and safeguarded the most direct route to Sebastopol. The 4th Division went back to their lines outside Sebastopol, some six miles distant. Crossman and what remained of his ragged invalid army arrived in triumph at the hospital, where they regaled friends and acquaintances with the story of their feats. Later one of Dalton-James's sergeants came and collected the Fergusons, taking them away.

Dalton-James made his report, furnishing himself with the

major role in the attack on Canrobert's Hill, and mentioning Crossman merely as 'the sergeant who formed up the invalids to assist in the assault'. A complaint went in to General Buller that Crossman had disobeyed a direct order. Buller asked if Dalton-James wished to have Sergeant Crossman disciplined in the proper manner.

After considering this carefully, and deciding that giving Crossman a chance to describe the events on the hill was not a good idea, the lieutenant replied, 'No, sir, but I would like my reprimand of Sergeant Crossman to go on record.'

'Very well,' said General Buller, but added severely, 'But mark this, Lieutenant. Crossman is our mongrel. We treat him as such because it suits our purpose. He goes into the enemy camp and brings us back scraps which often turn out to be highly valuable. You cannot expect a mongrel to behave as obediently as a good thoroughbred hunting hound. One thing or the other. An obedient bird-dog, or a mongrel.'

'Yes, sir,' replied Dalton-James, realizing that he was being rebuked. 'I see. In that case . . .'

'I shall treat this conversation as if it had never occurred.'

'Thank you, sir.'

Crossman went back to his bed. For him the great action of the day had been his stand with the 93rd. He had taken part in the battle, the battalion he had fought with – which just happened to be his father and brother's regiment – had been the victors. He felt supremely happy. Despite his hatred for his father he was glad to have fought with his brother. In later years perhaps he could reveal his secret to James, and the pair of them could bask in that warm glow of comradeship which is only felt by men who have fought the same action side by side, and are alive to recount their deeds.

Later, however, Major Lovelace came to him and told him the appalling tragedy of the Light Brigade's charge down the valley into the mouths of the Russian guns.

'Those poor devils,' Lovelace said. 'They were sent like sheep to the slaughter.'

'What a terrible thing,' said Crossman. 'What is happening now? Are the Russians overrunning our positions?'

'No, they've been halted, but it's a mess as usual. They still occupy the Causeway Heights, which as you know gives them control of the Woronzoff Road. You probably know the 4th Division finally arrived, after a tardy start, and a little later the Guards and another two Highland regiments, the 42nd and 78th. Some French troops joined in at the end too.'

'The French had little to do with it all?'

'They were not given a great deal of choice. However, the Chasseurs d'Afrique made a courageous charge on the Russian guns and cavalry in the North Valley. They fought well and deserve credit for allowing the Light Brigade a safer passage back to their lines after the charge.'

Crossman was desperately searching for some good out of all this mess.

'But the rest of the 4th Division? Cathcart engaged with the Russians successfully?'

'As I said, Cathcart's division came down over the col, after being ordered not to use the Woronzoff Road. They went along the Causeway Heights, with the Rifle Brigade skirmishing for them, to recapture the redoubts. The first two redoubts were empty, the guns either missing or spiked. This is after the Light Brigade's charge, of which at the time Cathcart knew nothing.

'No. 3 redoubt was still occupied, which P Battery and the 4th between them managed to recover. I'm told that Captain Ewart, one of the staff officers, was with the 4th Division and he went out to scout the ground and found dead a Captain Nolan, another staff officer. Near to him was Captain Morris, of the 17th Lancers, badly wounded but still alive, and also a trooper from the 5th Dragoon Guards, one of the Heavy Brigade, with his face smashed in. Ewart eventually had them all brought back.'

'This Morris, and the dragoon, will they live?'

'The surgeon is hopeful in both cases. The dead man, Nolan, is apparently the rider who took the message to Lord Lucan, ordering the charge.'

'You can't blame the messenger.'

Lovelace said, 'No, I suppose not. Anyway, we've reached a bit of a stalemate. The Russian advance has been halted, but they're staying put. And we've lost a third of the Light Brigade in one damn charge. It doesn't appear to be a victory for either side, but the 93rd put up a good show and the Heavy Brigade handled their part brilliantly.'

Crossman said proudly, 'I stood with the 93rd.'

Lovelace raised his eyebrows. 'Did you, by damn? I envy you, Sergeant.'

'I think I'm pretty pleased with myself,' said Crossman, smiling. 'The Rangers didn't get much of a go at Alma, so I'm glad to be of use to someone.'

'Of use?' exclaimed Lovelace. 'Man, you're one of my most important people. One of the first too. I'm hoping to build up quite a network of men like you, who go out and bring back useful information, do useful deeds. Of course you're of use, damn you. Just because you don't march in a straight line and shoot when you're told to, doesn't mean you're useless.'

Crossman said to his patron, not without feeling some discomfort, 'Yes, but it's all under the sheets, isn't it? It feels tainted somehow.'

'Not to me, it doesn't,' replied Lovelace, taking no offence whatsoever. 'This is the stuff of the future, if I'm not mistaken. Weapons are becoming too destructive for my liking. Look what we have with us here at the Crimea. Massive armaments: 24-pounders, 32-pounders, huge mortars, 8-inch howitzers. Each one capable of blowing a company of men sky high. Reduce a battalion to legs and arms in no time.

'Information. That's what's going to be important in the future. One will need to know when and where to strike, the enemy's exact strength, the disposition of his artillery, et cetera. The Lord Raglans have had their day. They should consider becoming vicars or deacons in some country parish, because that's their method of thinking. According to them we mustn't do anything sordid, like trying to discover who and what it is we're up against. We must go in blind.

'What rubbish. The enemy will certainly find out about us, so we need to find out about the enemy. We need to become more efficient at sabotage, at destroying him from within. War is no longer a deadly game, it's a serious business.'

He paused for thought, before adding, 'And I'll tell you another thing, Sergeant Crossman, ordinary soldiers will soon be demanding to know what they're fighting for.'

Crossman shook his head. 'You won't get men to fight any harder than these men have here. They fought magnificently at the Alma. And from what I've seen, and you've told me, they did so again today. How could you get a soldier to give more than he has here in the Crimea, living under appalling conditions, yet going out and giving his all? I can't see it.'

'Well, neither can I,' replied Lovelace, cheerfully, 'but I believe the time will come when questions will be asked by the common soldier — and will have to be answered.'

When Lovelace had left, Rupert Jarrard arrived to give his version of the events. He said the women were out on the battlefield now, sorting through the corpses, looking for dead husbands and useful clothing. The Light Brigade were moving camp, he said, to some other place in order to lick their wounds and try to recover.

'All in all,' said the American, 'I would say it's been a busy day for the cavalry.'

'The infantry played their part,' Crossman said, a little miffed.

'Yes, but even then the cavalry had a role. Not on the side of the allies, that's true, but it was Russian cavalry which charged the 93rd Highlanders. You forget I'm an impartial observer, a foreigner and a newspaper correspondent to boot. I just look on and congratulate the winner.'

'If you congratulate the Russians, Rupert, I'll call you out, so help me,' said Crossman.

'In your state?' laughed Jarrard. 'You couldn't call out a cross-eyed rabbit.'

'When I'm *not so ill*, I'll call you out.'

'You know full well where my sympathies really lie. I'm just giving you the official standpoint. Where's that nurse of yours, by the way? I hear she saw everything from the top of the ridge. She must have enjoyed the bloodbath.'

Crossman shook his head. 'She loves a battle and that's the truth . . .'

Rupert Jarrard became serious. 'You knew her before, didn't you – before all this.'

'I knew her very well, Rupert, in every sense.'

Jarrard looked thoughtful. 'I see. What happened?'

'Oh, bad timing I think you'd call it. Anyway, she's not the sort of woman who likes waiting around, no matter what the prize. I expect she married Durham for many reasons, one of them probably pique, but most of them good solid ones which men like you and I might respect if she ever let us know them.'

Lovelace came back into the room then, his expression showing he was deep in thought.

'More problems, sir?' asked Crossman.

'Not exactly, Sergeant,' replied Lovelace, more formal in front of a third person. 'We've discovered a Mr Upton, the son of a Colonel Upton, a gentleman who left England and was employed by the Czar. He's here now, having come out of Sebastopol with his wife and children – four pretty little urchins. They chatter away in English like sparrows.'

'Sparrows speak English?' said Jarrard.

Lovelace laughed. 'Anyway, this Upton fellow is offering us lots of information on the disposition of the troops and the defences of Sebastopol. As you are probably aware, the situation has not changed with regard to the city — we still have it under siege — there has been no push to penetrate its walls. Apparently this Upton is an engineer and built the greater part of those defences before Colonel Todleben took over the work.'

'So where's the problem?' asked Crossman.

'The problem, my dear sir, is whether to believe him or not. He may have more to gain by giving us false information.'

'How complicated this business of spying is,' said Crossman, settling back down on his bed. 'And you say it isn't sordid, sir? I think it's quite messy when you can't tell your friends from your enemies. For myself, I believe the man is genuine.'

'How so?' asked Lovelace, and Jarrard looked eager to know the answer to this one too.

'Because he brought his family out with him. If he were working for the Czar he would have left them under Russian protection. And anyway, it takes a lot for a man to go against the country of his birth, even if those whom he has much to be thankful for are his country's enemies.'

'You make a lot of sense, Sergeant, as usual.'

Perhaps, thought Lovelace, the civilian Upton could bring about the breakthrough in the siege where all the military strategists had failed.

21

Mrs Durham stayed on the ridge until evening, staring at the valley below. One of her followers brought her a shawl and entreated her to come down, but she would not. She could not leave those men on the plain, before they were safely gathered in, both Russian and British. Even as the corpses were being collected, the scavengers were creeping through the twilight, robbing the bodies. Occasionally a shot would ring out, when some infuriated soldier fired at these shadowy creatures, as they skulked across the blood-drenched valley.

Where these scavengers came from she had no idea, but it was the same at every battle. They seemed to manifest themselves out of rocks and stones, emerging perhaps from caves or forests. Dark, hunched, sexless beings. They took everything and anything which was lying loose, from weapons to wallets, even scraps of food from the pockets of the corpses. They would be there all night, working assiduously until the dawn's rays illuminated their grisly business and they had to slink back from whence they came. Dead horses would be stripped of their tack. Boots would be pulled from dead feet.

Supernatural creatures, they seemed; out of a nightmare.

The spoils of the battle, the armaments, were traditionally the property of the winner. In this case, however, there had been no winner, and the scavengers reaped much of the harvest. The two sides were more interested in rescuing their wounded and bringing in the dead than gathering weapons.

Injured horses had to be put out of their misery.

Finally, as darkness fell, Mrs Durham let herself be persuaded to go down. She went with some young officers to a tent where there was some food and wine. She could touch no food, but she drank a little of the wine. Finally, very late, she asked to be escorted to her quarters. She had been given a small house at the north end of Kadikoi village. When she arrived Durham was on duty and she found her own bed.

Unable to sleep, she slipped out again, and went to Crossman's hovel, hoping that Major Lovelace was not staying there that night. She sorely needed the comfort of Crossman's arms around her.

He was alone and awake, writing by the light of a guttering candle. He had been smoking his chibouque and the long, curved pipe lay across the top of the table.

'You'll ruin your eyes,' she said to him. 'What's so important at this time of night?'

'A letter to my mother,' he said. 'I wanted to tell her my father and brother are well. They will not think to write quickly and the battle will be reported in the newspapers very soon. That Russell is no sluggard.'

'What a thoughtful son you are,' she said smiling. 'Have you had any visitors?'

'Rupert Jarrard has been. I did not want to speak of the battle so soon afterwards. I'm sure he'll make a great deal of the Light Brigade's charge in his copy and I did not want to get into a quarrel about it. We talked of engineering instead.'

'Of course you did. And marvellous inventions.'

'Yes.'

'But not women.'

'Not really,' he said, peering at her in the dim light. 'Should we have done?'

'A lot of men might have done. I once knew a brigadier-

224

general who spoke of nothing else. Actually, he was really only a colonel.'

Crossman stared at this lady with a sad face, feeling a great fondness for her at that moment.

'Make up your mind,' he said smiling. 'General or colonel?'

'Both,' she replied. 'He was in the Guards. You know they often hold a double rank. His regimental rank was colonel, but his army rank was brigadier-general. One of these quirks of the military. They must have crises of identity, those Guards officers, not knowing who or what they are sometimes.'

'Yes, I must confess I don't ponder on such things, but I must remember to tell Rupert about that particular idiosyncrasy. It's the sort of thing he enjoys shaking his head over, when trying to understand us military men. He left early, but I'm afraid I could not sleep.'

'You too? Shall we go to bed? Not for anything. Just to hold each other for a while.'

He stared at her face. 'I knew you would not have liked it – that slaughter out there.'

'Others thought differently, did they?' she said, lifting her chin. 'They believed that terrible carnage would fire my lust? Oh, you need not deny it. I know what they think of me. Much of it is true, but certainly I could feel nothing but horror after watching those poor boys ride to their deaths. It was truly the most ghastly thing I've had to witness.'

She knew she was a strange being, for she had seen the Heavy Brigade lose men to the sword, and though she had felt sorrow she had accepted the losses. In reality one death should be as tragic as a thousand. Yet, the charge of the Light Brigade was something horrific. What had that French general said yesterday? *It is magnificent, but it is not war.* He had summed up her feelings about it all.

Crossman undressed and put his pistol by the straw mattress, within reach. Then the pair of them got beneath the blanket with his greatcoat on top for extra warmth. There she snuggled in his arms, allowing herself to be coddled. Her

225

thoughts still swam around in a disturbed way, but at least she had some arms about her for comfort.

He was soon slumbering, had probably been exhausted by the day's events, but she remained awake. The moon shone through the small mean window, throwing a bar of light across the floor. Her thoughts were tangled, like a jumble of brambles in her head, and their barbs would not allow her peace of mind.

At one point she began to slip away into a doze when a movement suddenly caught her eye. There was a flash of light from the doorway, as a dark shape stood there. Her mind immediately went to the scavengers on the battlefield. This figure looked like one of them. Slowly, ever so slowly, the shape entered the room. She saw now, as it crossed that bar of moonlight, that the figure was carrying an unsheathed sword, along which the moonbeam rippled.

Her eyes were transfixed by the wicked-looking point of the sword, as it drew ever closer to Crossman's throat. She was certain now that this was an assassin. Murder was about to be committed.

With a swiftness that astonished even herself, she reached across the sleeping form of her lover and snatched up his pistol. Cocking it, she pointed it at the advancing figure. It was on her mind to call a warning, but somehow she sensed that this would do no good, that the assassin would keep coming no matter what. He was tensed like a cat about to leap.

She squeezed the trigger of the pistol.

The sound of the shot was like thunder.

Crossman woke with the sound of the shot ringing in his ears and the smell of the gunpowder burning his nostrils.

'What is it?' he cried.

A man stood there before him, his form cut through by a

blade of moonlight. Something fell from his hand and clattered on the floor. A sword. Then with a final groan the figure fell into a heap and lay there, still illuminated.

Crossman jumped out of bed and inspected the body, then he turned to Mrs Durham.

'Are you all right, Lavinia?'

'I – I think so. Is it Bertie?'

'Who?' He looked down. 'The dead man, you mean?'

'I've killed him then?' she said in a faltering tone.

'Yes, but it isn't your Bertie. It's a Cossack. There'll be more somewhere around . . .'

He went to the window and looked out. There was no one to be seen. Perhaps the others, if there had been others, had slipped away as soon as they heard the sound of the shot. Bloody Cossacks. When would they leave him alone? His luck could not hold out for ever. If they kept coming at him like this, one of them would get him eventually.

He checked downstairs and discovered the door open but the room empty.

Going back up again, he found Mrs Durham sitting up on the mattress, shivering. She still had the pistol in her hands. He took it from her gently.

'I thought it was Bertie,' she said, 'come to kill you.'

'And you would have killed him to protect me?'

'It seems so.'

Crossman shook his head wearily. 'I thought you said Bertie didn't desire you. I thought you said you had an understanding with him.'

'Well, he's been feeling a little more possessive lately. I don't – I don't know why, I was certain it was him. He put his arm around me, you know, after the battle. I was crying and it upset him.'

'Lavinia,' Crossman said firmly, 'you know this has gone far enough now. We must stop this liaison. We've both been very foolish, indulging ourselves like this, blaming misfortune, using nostalgia and other such excuses to do what we felt we had a right to do. We had our chance and we lost it. You are a married woman.'

'Will we have to say goodbye?'

'You'll find compensations,' he said practically.

'Yes, I suppose I will. Women are good at that, you know. I shall forget you ever existed. Just as I did before, but then you had to pop up like a puppet right in front of my eyes and start it all up again.'

'Oh, so it's all my fault?'

She stared at him. 'It has to be, Alexander. You're the man. Men are always held responsible for everything. Women are foolish creatures with the minds of sparrows, easily led astray. I'm afraid you're the blackguard here, sir.'

She rose and dressed herself. Crossman dressed too and escorted her back to her house. She turned and kissed him on the cheek.

'Goodbye, Alex dear.'

'Goodbye, Lavinia.'

Then she was gone, into the blackness of the house, and he turned and made his way back to the hovel.

He wanted to go straight back to his bed, for he was feeling fatigued by the night's events but he could not leave that body on the floor of the room. When he got there he dragged the corpse down the stairs and left it lying in the doorway to the hovel, ready to take out when morning came. Perhaps he could get one of the marines to collect it?

In the morning the body was gone. Instead there was Major Lovelace, bent over a tin bowl, splashing water on his face. He looked up as Crossman descended the stairs, reaching for a rag to wipe off the soapy water.

'Ah, Sergeant, you're up.'

Crossman was still staring at the spot in front of the doorway, wondering if it had all been a dream.

'You're looking for the Cossack, I take it,' said the major, wiping his hands. 'I had the corpse removed quite early. That was a good shot. You got him right in the heart. I assume it was in a darkened room.'

'One patch of moonlight,' murmured Crossman.

'Excellent. Any more of the beggars?'

'Didn't see any.'

'Well, once again the doughty Sergeant Crossman defeats his traditional foes,' cried Major Lovelace, grinning.

Crossman went to the table and took a long draught of water from his bottle.

Afterwards he said, 'I'm not sure how it became traditional.'

'No one is ever sure of how these things come about. Suffice to say you will go down in Cossack legend as the evil anti-hero, to be eternally hunted by father and son. Mothers will use you to scare their young into obedience. Grandfathers will tell strange tales about you to their grandchildren in front of blazing log fires. You have slipped into myth in your own lifetime, Sergeant Crossman. You are a monster.'

'I feel like a monster today, sir. Are there any developments on yesterday's battle? Is there to be another today?'

'At the moment it looks as if the Russians are digging in, which leads me to another point. Are you fit enough yet to go out into the field again?'

'Alone, or with my men?'

'Does it make a difference?'

'I might be fit enough to do some work on my own, with Ali, but I'm not sure I could control Wynter at the moment.'

Major Lovelace made a gesture with his head.

'Unfortunately you will need Wynter and the others. We're thinking of sending you out for a good long time. The Russians will be using the road to Yalta for their supply lines. I want you and your men to sabotage as much traffic as possible. You will live wild for the foreseeable future. How does that sound to you, in your condition?'

Crossman thought it might be politic for him to be out of the way for a while, until Mrs Durham settled down to becoming a model wife. If he were here, showing his face, their resolve might weaken. He had had a taste of her fruits and his appetite was still not satiated. It would be easy to drink a little too much brandy and go seeking her favours, now that all the barriers were down between them. And perhaps she on her part had not really had enough of him? Better to be out of harm's way.

'It sounds all right. I should like to be back in action again. If I spend too long in that bed I'll grow old and die.'

'Good man. Will you go up to the lines and bring down the riffraff today?'

Crossman smiled. 'I'll fetch them at noon.'

'When you're all together, I'll brief you properly.'

22

Life in the trenches around Sebastopol was not good, especially in a wet autumn, with heavy dews and the cold morning mists. Wynter, Clancy and Devlin were obviously overjoyed to see Sergeant Crossman walking towards them. He might be taking them to certain death, but that would have been more pleasant than picquet duty or manning ditches with the guns crashing around them all day long.

Crossman had hitched a ride on an *araba* cart the five miles from Kadikoi to the trenches.

'Come on up, my boys,' he called to them cheerily. 'Let's see your smiling faces.'

Crossman was having to keep his head down at that point, for there was a constant exchange of guns firing between the trenches and the distant Sebastopol defences, with little protection from this fire, apart from shallow holes and hastily dug ditches with loose-earth dykes. The three soldiers joined him and they ran back to a safer point where they could talk, though the pounding of the guns still battered their ears. Wynter looked ecstatic.

'Oh, are we glad to see you, Sergeant. You know what it's like here? Three or four nights out of bed, and when you do get there it's just cold ground.'

'Poor old Wynter,' said Clancy. 'O' course he lives in the lap of luxury back home in England.'

The others laughed.

Crossman knew that even when back in Britain most of these hardy farm boys lived a life of privation and deprivation, spending most of their time out of doors because their parents' dwellings were often one-roomed hovels with a tiny floor space. The floor would be dirty and any fire would be an open one, throwing out sooty smoke. Life in the trenches could not have been so vastly different from normal life in Britain.

'Well, it might not have been luxury,' growled Wynter, 'but at least the inn wouldn't be far away.'

'You've got the canteen here,' replied Devlin, baiting Wynter further. 'What more could you want?'

'It's not like having four walls and a nice blazing log fire, now is it?' Wynter argued. 'When I drink my ale I like a bit of warmth and light and fine company.'

'That's enough now,' said Crossman. 'We've got company ourselves and it's not so fine.'

Lieutenants Parker and Howard, two Connaught Ranger officers, came striding across from the 88th's rest area wearing undress caps and the thick, warm, ample greatcoats that many officers wore. Before Parker could say anything Crossman handed him a note from Major Lovelace. The missive released Crossman's four soldiers from regimental siege duties, placing them under his command. Parker showed it to Howard, who lifted his head and stared disdainfully at the words.

'Sometimes,' said Howard, who moved in very high social circles, 'I'm inclined to think this Major Lovelace is overreaching himself.'

Crossman remained silent. He knew that any comment he had to make would only inflame the situation. Howard was a terrible snob and no doubt outranked Lovelace in civilian life. There was the possibility that at some time Howard would have the opportunity to cut senior officers like Lovelace dead in some social gathering. Parker on the other hand had come up from the ranks and while in the siege lines was permitted to be in Howard's company. Back in England Howard would not have deigned to wish Parker a good morning.

'Well,' said Parker, 'I have no choice but to obey the note. You may take your men, Sergeant Crossman, to carry out these clandestine duties of yours.'

Lieutenant Howard said, 'Is Lord Raglan aware of what is going on behind his back?'

Parker gave his friend a worried look.

Crossman stared Howard directly in the eyes. 'If you were thinking of telling him, sir, you would be well advised to speak to General Buller first.'

Howard looked down his nose. 'When I want the advice of a sergeant, which I cannot conceivably imagine happening in this lifetime, I shall order it forth from that individual. Now take your insolent eyes from my face, soldier, or you may find yourself in circumstances you will heartily regret.'

When Crossman remained unflinching before him, Howard looked as if he were about to explode. Parker took the lieutenant's arm and led him a few paces away. There was a short quiet conversation between the two, then Howard – with a final glare at Crossman – strode away.

Parker came back. 'You have my permission to leave now, Sergeant,' he said.

Crossman looked around him. 'Peterson,' he said. 'Where's Peterson?'

'He's with Captain Goodlake's sharpshooters,' said Parker. 'They're up near the Careenage Ravine.'

Crossman was a little mystified. 'Goodlake's sharpshooters? Has he joined the Guards then?'

A novel concept had recently come to fruition. The 1st Division had formed a band of sharpshooters, some sixty men who moved about in scattered order ahead of the picquet lines. It was their job to pick off enemy gunners and soldiers on the defences of Sebastopol, by using cover and their own initiative, often scraping out a hollow for themselves and remaining in position. Sometimes they would be out all night and day, in order to achieve an objective.

The Guards, under Captain Goodlake, had also raised such a force, but Goodlake's sharpshooters moved around in close order: a fighting unit that like Crossman's *peloton*, was free of any attachments to the main body of the brigade.

'The Guards borrowed a few of the 1st's sharpshooters this morning,' explained Lieutenant Parker. 'They were light-handed due to illness. Being a close order unit, they need to keep the numbers tight. Goodlake expects to find more sharpshooters from amongst his brigade today, but the patrol was due to go out at dawn.'

Devlin said, 'If they're using other regiments the Guards must be desperate for men, begging your pardon, sir.'

'I'm inclined to agree, Corporal Devlin,' replied Parker. 'Even Lieutenant Howard could not get into the Guards.'

Crossman noticed a twitch in the lieutenant's expression when he said this and the sergeant realized that this fact afforded Parker some amusement. He might be Howard's siege companion, but he knew what Howard really thought of him and his station. Parker obviously gained a certain satisfaction knowing that Howard, for all his pomp and circumstance, and his father being an earl, was not good enough to get into the Guards. It made Crossman wonder what Howard had done to blot his script. Perhaps even the Guards realized he was an idiot.

At that moment a company sergeant-major came riding on a mule towards the group. He looked excited. Dismounting he fought for breath.

'Sir,' cried the sergeant-major, 'they're engaging to the north-west, up beyond Mikriakoff Glen.'

Other off-duty officers and men began to gather around the small group, having heard the sergeant-major's remarks.

'Who's engaging?' asked Parker, quickly. 'General Codrington's main force?'

That the Division's 1st Brigade should be in a battle

without the 2nd Brigade, to which the 88th belonged, was clearly upsetting to Lieutenant Parker.

'Damn it,' he cried, before the other man could answer his question. 'Why do we always miss out?'

'No, sir, it's only the 1st Brigade's picquets at the moment. And the 2nd Division's picquets – Major Champion's lot. There's fierce fighting going on though. I were up in the Lancaster Battery visiting a pal of mine. There's about six battalions of Russian infantry come up from St George's Ravine.'

'Damn, damn, will they come down here, do you think?'

'Could well do, sir,' said the sergeant-major, his eyes shining with hope. 'The picquets is fell in, working in skirmishing order.'

Crossman and all those listening knew what that meant and the sergeant's heart began to beat a little faster. Perhaps this was a major attack. In which case surely the Connaught Rangers would see some real action at last. They were desperate to distinguish themselves. Many other regiments were already crowing over their victories, not least the 93rd, who *always* seemed to be in the thick of the fighting. If the picquet commander had formed his company in skirmishing order . . .

A company of picquets – now due to illness and death down to sixty men in most battalions – normally worked in pairs well out ahead of the main force, placed so they could see any enemy approach clearly on the horizon. Each pair would be positioned behind some natural or man-made cover.

One picquet would go out on reconnaissance occasionally to check visually and listen for any movement from the enemy. His partner would be in touch with the next pair along the picquet line, so there was constant contact down the whole line. Early warning would be given by rifle shots and the picquet commander would then form his men up in two ranks, in extended order, to try to delay the advance as long as possible so that the main force could organize.

'Was it just the picquets, sarn-major?' asked the 88th

captain. 'Do you think it'll come to something? Did the Russians have artillery with them?'

The sergeant-major was as eager as the rest of them that they should engage.

'Artillery, yes, sir. I saw the green guns.'

'Green guns, by Jove,' said the captain. 'That's them all right. I wondered what all those bells and the cheering was about this morning, coming from Sebastopol! They're making an assault, I'll lay a wager on it.'

Crossman knew what all the men were hoping, that this was not just a probing force, come out of Sebastopol to test their defences, but a major attack force. The boys were eager to settle the war here and now. Soldiers despise waiting around in thorough boredom for something to happen.

'It weren't just the picquets who engaged either,' continued the sergeant-major. 'From the Lancaster Battery I saw another battalion of Russians come up along Careenage Ravine. They was stopped by Goodlake's sixty sharpshooters.'

'Bloody Peterson,' cried Clancy, infuriated, 'he gets all the luck.'

The sergeant-major continued: 'My chum at the battery is working like a Chinaman to stop the Ruskies from getting through. They got a 68-pounder up there, under Midshipman Hewett's command. Just as I left they was ordered to spike the gun and leave it, but Hewett refused. He ordered the gabions to be knocked down so's he could turn the Lancaster on the enemy guns.'

At that moment the bugle sounded and every man jack of them dashed away to get rifle and kit. No man wanted to die, no man wanted to be wounded, each one had a cold clay feeling of fear in his gut, but almost without exception every man there wanted the 88th Connaught Rangers to be given the chance to distinguish themselves. They were fed up with other regiments fording it over them in the canteens, especially the Highlanders, calling them tardy and slow-witted Paddys.

Now at last the brigade was forming up. There was going to be a scrap.

The River Chernaya ran north-east from the Fedioukine Hills and widened to an inlet the shape of a half-open crocodile's mouth, before entering the sea. Sebastopol was situated on the lower jaw of the crocodile's mouth just below its nostrils. To the east of Sebastopol, on the far side of its harbour, towards the ruins of Inkerman, lay an area of rugged land some two miles wide incised with ravines and heavily ridged. One large ravine, called Careenage, ran obliquely across it from the north-west, brushing a ridge named after their queen by the invading British.

Here on this rough square of land, with its heights overlooking Sebastopol to the west, the British had established a number of posts from which picquets skirmished. A Russian force had come out of Sebastopol, keeping under cover inside the ravines, until they came upon the British picquets.

Beyond the Victoria Ridge sixty men of Lieutenant Conolly's 48th Hertfordshire picquets were facing an onslaught by six battalions of Russians – over four thousand men. At that point in the battle, however, only three hundred enemy skirmishers could bring fire to bear on Conolly's men. The Hertfordshire farm boys, spread wide across the ground, were gritting their teeth and crashing volley after volley into the Russian advance.

'A man with every shot,' cried Lieutenant Conolly, his sword waving. 'Bring 'em down, my boys. Don't give 'em a yard without they have to fight for it. Think of this ground as Hertfordshire countryside. Are we going to let 'em have it? By God, I think not.'

The roaring Miniés were doing devastating work for the Hertfordshires against Russian converted flintlocks, which merely spat out their balls, but there were monstrous odds against the British at over sixty to one. The air hummed with bullets and men were dropping on one side or the other. Wounded soldiers were receiving the support of their comrades. The sound ones were rapidly becoming exhausted by the intensity of the battle.

Foot by foot Conolly's men were forced back until the Russian battalions, bristling like giant porcupines with bayonets, were close enough to charge. Conolly could see the blank expressions of the square nameless enemy in their bulky, grey greatcoats. A thought suddenly occurred to him and he quickly removed his own grey overcoat, revealing his red uniform beneath, in case it should come to hand-to-hand combat. He did not want any of his men to mistake him for a Russian in the heat of the battle.

His sword flashing in the sunlight now, Conolly leaped forward, slashing and thrusting at the grey mass.

'Into 'em boys!' he yelled. 'Give 'em what for!'

'You heard the lieutenant,' shouted Sergeant Owens, following his commanding officer into the fray. 'Let's spike a few of these donkeys!'

At that moment, as his men let out a great cheer, and drove into the thick wedge of Russian soldiers, Conolly's sword snapped in half in a Russian's chest. The man fell forward, his mouth open in a silent scream, to drive the piece of sword even deeper into his chest as he hit the rocky ground. Conolly stared stupidly at the stump of blade for a moment, then flung it away in disgust.

With glee on their faces the grey soldiers facing him started to press him back. Reaching inside his coat Conolly laid his hand on an instrument which he began to use as a club, beating the heads of those who surrounded him.

'Take that, sir, and that!' cried Conolly, as if he were fighting some schoolboy bully behind the quad. 'And that! And that!'

Gradually, however, they overwhelmed him, drove bayonets and swords into him, struck him with their muskets.

Badly wounded, Conolly began to slip to the ground, but in a frenzied attack two of his own soldiers fought their way to those who encircled him. The two men grabbed their commanding officer by the arms and dragged him back to safety, where he lay bleeding profusely. Lieutenant Conolly still held his cudgel: an extended telescope with its glass and brass now smeared with Russian blood.

'Fall back,' whispered the lieutenant. 'Fall back, Sergeant – reinforcements are coming.'

'Are you bad hurt, sir?'

'Yes, it bloody hurts – but I don't believe badly enough to kill me, Sergeant. Do as I say, man.'

His sergeant organized the men to fall back to another skirmishing line of 2nd Brigade picquets, who had come up behind them. Sixty of the 30th's Cambridgeshire picquets were now advancing against the six battalions of Russians.

The British extended line was as wide as that of the enemy force, though of course not nearly as tightly packed. A party of the 30th broke away to attack the Russian gunners, harassing them in the hope of preventing their bringing their guns to bear. Grape shot and round shot would have tipped the scales too heavily in favour of the Russians at that moment.

Surprisingly the Russians were beginning to look beleaguered, despite their massive superiority. Not far away another battalion of Russians had come up the Careenage Ravine, hoping to outflank the British picquets. Goodlake's sharpshooters, another single company of men, were there to greet them with the most accurate withering fire the Russians had faced so far. They were cut down like stalks beneath a hailstorm and they swiftly went into retreat.

British batteries were now moving forward, their guns opening up. The 2nd Division had mobilized under General de Lacy Evans, with the 95th Derbyshire driving the enemy back towards Sebastopol. The 95th battalion halted out of range of Sebastopol's batteries, but their Light Company followed the Russians as skirmishers until the enemy ran back into the town under the cover of their guns.

Whoops of joy could be heard along the British front as they realized the Russians were in full retreat. Skirmishers on both sides picked a last man or two, then let their hot weapons cool in the morning air. Prisoners were gathered up by the dozen, mostly by the 30th, who were out in front. The Russian Bear had probed the British defences, had not found the soldiers there wanting, and had retired back to his den.

Unfortunately once again expectation came to nothing for the 88th. There was a big fight up near the Inkerman ruins, but the Connaught Rangers had no part in it. Peterson came down later, to the hovel, where the others were changing into their sheepskin coats and baggy Turkish trousers. She was full of it all, much to the chagrin of the rest of the group.

'It was mean stuff,' she said. 'We had a whole battalion coming at us. We just had to keep firing, one man loading while the other discharged. They were swarming after us, but we just laid into them, slating them something bad.'

Envious as the others were, they could see Peterson had been through a hellish time. She was filthy dirty, from kneeling and lying on the ground. Her Minié was smeared with mud. Clearly the fighting had been heavy, for most of her ammunition was gone from her pouch.

'Captain Goodlake and Sergeant Ashton were in a cave when the Russian column first came into view,' said Peterson. 'The Russians were so quick they rushed past them and cut them off from us. But it was like a miracle. The pair of them came running out of the cave bashing and shooting their way through the Russian stragglers to their main column. Then they just charged through their ranks.'

'Didn't no one stop them, or shoot at them?' Wynter asked sceptically. 'I mean, they just strolled through a whole column of Russians?'

'The column was in rather loose order in heavy brush,' Peterson said, 'and Goodlake and Ashton had their greatcoats on, covering their red coatees, so they weren't recognized. The captain and the sergeant both made it back to us. We all cheered like mad and then stood and poured fire into the Russians till they lost heart. Every minute we expected them to charge, for they outnumbered us ten to one, but then the Lancaster gun opened up on them . . .'

'The 68-pounder with the midshipman behind it?' scowled Clancy.

'Yes,' replied Peterson, her eyes opening wide. 'How did you know? Were you there, Clancy?'

'No I wasn't and I'm glad I wasn't,' sniffed Clancy, 'for it sounds to me like a piddling little action, of no account at all.'

'You're just jealous,' crowed Peterson.

'Why would I be jealous?' said Clancy, darkly. 'I've throttled more Russians with a piece of knotted cord than you've shot with that precious rifle of yours.'

'All right, all right,' Crossman intervened wearily. 'Settle down now. Save your arguments for later. We're off into the hills again, my boys, to give the Russians a hard time with their supply lines. Jump to it! Where's Ali?'

'Round back,' replied Clancy.

The men did as they were told, soon forgetting how envious they were of Peterson, and a short while later the Bashi-Bazouk was with them, taking and returning their individual greetings with a smile on his broad Turkish face.

Just before they left for the hills, a large Tartar woman brought Crossman a message. She wore a big grin as she handed it over. The men stood around, waiting for him to read it. He opened the small envelope, which was unsealed, and extracted a billet written on stiff white card.

'The fox hunt an't cancelled, is it?' asked Wynter, in his usual aggrieved tone.

Crossman stared at the words on the card: *Please meet me down by the harbour at seven o'clock this evening.*

As was the custom with her, she had used no names, nor anything personal in case the billet went astray. So, she could not keep to their bargain? Or perhaps she had one last word to say to him before they kept to their own sides of the fence? It was difficult to tell what was going on with Lavinia Durham, who thrived on a little intrigue. Perhaps she was even testing *him* and would fail to turn up, but send some little Turkish child to watch out for him and make sure that *he* did? It was all in the game with such a woman as Mrs Durham.

'No, it's not a cancellation,' said Crossman, putting the card carefully back into the envelope and then slipping it into his pocket. 'You can rest assured that we will be out in the wilderness soon, Wynter.'

The others heaved sighs of relief, but Wynter still managed to grumble.

On their way out of Kadikoi they happened to bump into Lieutenant Dalton-James.

'Don't let me down, Sergeant,' said Dalton-James. 'I want your best work, mind you – your very best.'

Crossman was slightly nettled by this remark. He felt he always gave his best, whether Dalton-James desired it or not. Then, just as he was about to walk away from the lieutenant, he remembered the note. He reached into his pocket.

'A Tartar woman brought this, sir. I believe she said it was from Mrs Durham, but I can't confirm that because I did not read it. I didn't feel it was my place. The woman expressly said to put the envelope in your hands alone. I understood that you were not to mention the existence of the note again, not even to Mrs Durham herself.'

'A Tartar woman told you all that?' said Dalton-James, looking mystified.

Crossman realized he was overdoing it.

'Not as such, but I inferred as much.'

He handed over the little white envelope and walked away, leaving Dalton-James to open and read it.

Glancing back, Crossman was amused to see a look of bewilderment pass over the lieutenant's face, swiftly followed by something that might have been a faint smile of self-satisfaction. The officer put the billet in his pocket and then, looking around him quickly as though he had some secret to hide, he strode away towards Kadikoi village. There was a bounce in his step, as if the season of spring had unexpectedly decided to replace autumn.

Crossman imagined Dalton-James going down to the harbour and approaching Mrs Durham as if they had met by accident, then becoming increasingly agitated when she did not respond to his gentle advances, while she in turn – Crossman knew her so well – would become irritated and waspish with this silly officer who was obviously keeping her ex-lover at bay by his presence.

'I promised to fix you, Mr Dalton-James,' said Crossman in satisfaction. 'And so I have.'

'What's that, Sergeant?' asked Clancy. 'You said something?'

'Nothing worth repeating,' Crossman replied. 'Look to the path, Clancy. We're going into the wilds.'

The party went single file into the hills.

23

The craving for laudanum had of course not gone from Sergeant Crossman's body or mind. Since the stand with the 93rd against the Russian cavalry, Crossman bit the bullet, fighting against the urge. When he had been lying on his back at the mercy of Mrs Durham, the gnawing need had seemed uncontrollable, but he was stronger physically now. Out here in the hills of the Crimea he could not obtain it even if his will collapsed under the battering it was receiving. However, that did not make the craving go away.

'Keep up, Wynter, you're always lagging behind,' he said irritably.

'I'm keepin' up,' grumbled Wynter, indignantly. 'What's the matter with you then, Sergeant? Feelin' out of sorts?'

'My medical condition has nothing whatsoever to do with you, Lance Corporal, and I'll be obliged if you will keep your mind on the trail.'

He knew he was being unreasonably snappy, but he could not help it. Instead, he tried to concentrate on his surroundings. The year was moving inevitably towards winter. There were still many birds to be seen, some of them game birds suitable for the pot. The plant life looked a bit drab though, with the wayside herbs and weeds hanging limply on their stalks, many of them turning a dirty yellow colour.

It was pleasant enough out here on an expedition, rather than being stuck in the mud and squalor of Kadikoi and its surrounds. Despite that, Crossman began to wonder why he was taking part in all this subterfuge. True, they had given him little choice, but he might have put up more resistance than he had done. It was certainly not the way to quick promotion. He might be doing this thing as well as anyone could, but quite different skills were required of sergeant-majors.

Sergeant-majors were men whose personalities were stronger and more wilful than those of most men. They were men who could bond groups of males together by the power of their character, yet still remain aloof and in control. They had to be admired and held in awe, even though they were hated. The men had to be able to say, 'There goes Company Sergeant-Major Robert McKay, whose guts I hate for making me drill like a Roman when I don't want to, who makes me charge the enemy when the position is hopeless, who makes me clean my kit even before a battle, yet I'd follow the bastard into hell and back, if he told me to.'

When you looked into a sergeant-major's eyes, they were usually surprisingly true and honest, for men would not give their all for an unfair leader no matter how much they were bullied. But those eyes were also firm and uncompromising. The regiment came first, the individual second. Discipline. Unbiased discipline. The sergeant-major was the bridge between officer and ranker and a good one favoured neither. He made stupid orders from above work and stupid soldiers below give their best and surpass themselves.

Many is the man who promised himself to give the sergeant-major a facer if he ever ran into him in civilian life, yet found himself talking softly and with respect to that man when such a thing occurred, recalling old times, finding that the sergeant-major was as quietly awesome out of uniform, as he had been in it.

Crossman did not believe he was made of that kind of material. He had much of his surrogate mother in him and she was a gentle soul with an enquiring mind and spirit. Crossman asked too many questions of himself for a sergeant-major, who needed to believe in only one thing: that the regiment's honour was priceless, and the rest of the world, humanity and spiritual well-being were nothing beside it.

'Right, we'll set up camp here,' he told his men. 'Yusuf Ali, can you climb up higher and check on our position, just to make sure we're not situated on some faint trail that we can't see for looking at it?'

'Yes, Sergeant,' said the Bashi-Bazouk, his stocky, barrel-shaped form disappearing into the brush.

'Corporal Devlin, organize the camp, if you please. I'm going to scout ahead.'

'Yes, Sergeant. All right, you three, you heard the sergeant, get to it. Clancy, make a ground oven. I don't want to see any smoke that'll bring the Russians running up here. Peterson, you take first sentry. Find a suitable high spot, but not on the skyline. Wynter, look for water. Good, clear *running* water, not stagnant puddles.'

Predictably, Wynter whined, 'Why me for the water?'

'None of your backchat, Wynter; do it. And when you've found it, fill the water bottles. You'll get your chance at making fires and doing sentry duty sooner than you'd wish.'

Corporal Devlin was good at managing the men. They grumbled less at him than they would have done at Crossman for the same orders. Corporal Devlin, unlike Crossman, would one day make a good sergeant-major. He knew what had to be done and he saw that it was done. He did not stand there thinking: Am I being unreasonable to expect this of exhausted men?

Crossman made his way through the bushes and trees, towards the road he knew lay below. He wanted to see if he had a useful spot for an ambush. It was no good if the brush did not go right up to the edge of the road. If there was open country to cross they would lose precious seconds of surprise. When their numbers were so few, and the enemy's so many, they needed every element of shock and the unexpected.

He found the surroundings ideal for attacking supply wagons and mentally studied the landscape for an escape route, one which would hamper heavily-armed troops but allow the *peloton* to slip through. There were some narrow craggy passes that would be suitable for such an exit, plus some slopes with loose scree, which would hamper a larger force of men. There were also numerous thorny shrubs, rocky outcrops, and various other obstacles that would slow down pursuit.

Satisfied with the location, Crossman went back to the camp site. On reaching there he sent down Devlin and Wynter, posting them by the road to watch for any signs of company. They were not to attack anything yet, but were simply there to record any activity. Peterson came down from sentry duty, handing it over to Yusuf Ali for a while.

Clancy tended the fire and made a bush kitchen. He loved outdoor craft, which the others were pleased to let him do. He would build a rack for their camp kettle, make pegs from which to hang their water bottles, a wooden spit for roasting birds when they were able to use an open fire. He made an art of it, impressing even the jaded Bashi-Bazouk with his efforts.

Clancy had learned how to make earth-ovens in India, so that the smoke was contained by loose soil or chambers dug parallel to the fire. In these ovens he would cook pigeons and small mammals to supplement their meat ration, or roast vegetables until they were soft and succulent in their own juices. Peterson was enthralled by the backwoodsmanship of Clancy and her eyes would watch every splice of a rope. He taught her various knots and lashings, showed her how to make a bivouac out of branches and leaves, taught her how to measure vertical heights by the shadows they cast, and tell the time from the stars.

Crossman was sitting on a log making notes in a small

pocket-book which he kept for the purpose, just in case he was asked at a later date where he had been, what he had been doing and for what purpose he had been doing it. Suddenly, in the late afternoon's sunlight slanting through the trees, a set of shadows fell on him. He shivered and looked up, hearing a noise.

It was Wynter and Devlin coming back to report that they had seen travellers on the road. A squadron of Cossacks had gone through, an army detachment of sorts with wagonloads of fuel, food and ammunition: a group of young officers with an Orthodox priest, and a company of marching infantry.

'Well done,' said Crossman. 'We'll have to choose our first target carefully, strike, then move on to another part of the trail. Now, Clancy has made us some bread in that underground oven of his. We'll need to maintain our strength for the action ahead.'

Crossman chose an easy target for his first attack on a Russian caravan, probably coming from Yalta in the east, heading towards Sebastopol. The escort amounted to only six men – Cossacks – and the booty itself was in large crates stacked on an *araba* drawn by four hefty oxen. Wynter was convinced it was gold. He saw himself becoming rich in prize money. Already he had taken a sword from one of the previous Cossacks he had killed and sold it to the regiment's paymaster for a healthy sum.

It was mid-morning, with a weak sun scattering its light amongst the trees. Crossman and his men had been waiting since dawn. They were all impatient for some action.

'What, *gold*? With only six cavalrymen to guard it?' said Peterson, sceptically.

Wynter argued, 'But that's only to fool us, don't you see? It's to make us think the load is not worth very much. I reckon it is, though. I know what I'm going to spend my money on. There's some of the women camp-followers who give out their favours for a coin or two. I haven't had a good shag since I left home.'

'You had several in Turkey, you liar,' said Peterson. 'I'm surprised you didn't get the pox.'

'I don't know as I didn't,' replied Wynter with a worried look, 'but there an't much I can do about it at the minute. I know it hurts when I piss. I'll have to see the surgeon for some powders.'

They had no further time for discussion, because Crossman was signalling to them that the wagon was coming.

Four of the Cossacks were cut down in the first volley. Peterson got one of them through the head. Crossman and Devlin got theirs. Wynter's target was only wounded. This man started to ride off, back along the road. Peterson tried to finish that one off too, after reloading, over a distance of about seven hundred yards. The man appeared to be hit again, but the horse carried on with the figure on its back. If he were still alive the *peloton* was in a little trouble. Others would be back to hunt them down.

The other two Cossacks died in the hands of Yusuf Ali, who had positioned himself behind the caravan, at the mouth of the gorge. He stood by a rock with two pistols in his hands and blazed away as the Cossacks tried to retreat into the woods. Ali caught their horses and hobbled them before joining the others at the *araba*.

There were two men up on the wagon, one of them a Tartar, the other a Russian soldier. The Russian was on his knees, ready to die. He had carefully placed his rifle beside him and was waiting with head bowed for the shot that would blow out his brains. The Tartar was glaring at his captors, chewing steadily on some weed or other. Staring at the bulge in the man's cheek, Crossman guessed he was ruminating on qat, a grass drug which would have come up from one of the Arab countries.

'Strip the Russian of his weapons and send him on his way – we can't take prisoners,' Crossman said.

'I'll have his purse,' said Wynter, reaching into the kneeling man's greatcoat pocket. 'I saw him first.'

'The sergeant said weapons,' growled Corporal Devlin. 'Leave the man's personal belongings where they are, Wynter. You should be ashamed of yourself, man.'

'Well I an't, and that's a fact,' Wynter replied.

'I'll have your name posted up in your parish church one of these days, so help me,' said Crossman. 'There'll be no looting a soldier's private property. You may take his weapons and horse only, not his purse.'

'Finicky,' muttered Wynter, giving the Russian a prod with his Victoria carbine. 'Go on, imshi. Get running.'

The man got to his feet, clearly unsure whether he should go or not. But then he saw the Tartar walking away, scowling over his shoulder, and he ran off and joined the man. The pair of them left through the end of the gorge.

'Come on then,' Crossman ordered, 'get these crates opened. We need to be gone before those two bring back a whole regiment of infantry.'

Clancy and Wynter jumped up on the *araba* and began to prise open the lids to the crates. They were bitterly disappointed with the outcome. Jars and jars of pickled food.

'Bloody red cabbage,' snarled Wynter. 'What good is that to a man?'

Crossman had to admit that he himself was a little disappointed. Here was an opportunity for some prize money, yet the one wagon they had to choose to stop was full of pickled red cabbage.

'All right,' he told them. 'Take a few jars for ourselves, then smash the others. Turn the oxen loose. We've got six horses now. Who can ride?'

Wynter grinned. 'We're farm boys, Sergeant, all except Clancy. O' course we can ride.'

'You've been on plough horses, no doubt, but can you ride a Cossack charger?'

'I can damn well try,' Wynter grunted.

Devlin and Peterson agreed. They had been on a variety of horses, back on the farms they worked in their shires. The pair of them mounted their horses, who immediately became frisky feeling unfamiliar riders. The soldiers struggled with them, Devlin being unseated once, but after a while the horses grew calmer and began to obey commands. Wynter leaped on his chosen steed and fought it until it was under control. Ali and Crossman, both of whom could ride to an inch, subdued their mounts in a very short time.

Clancy stood and held the reins of his little charger. It shuffled and shied away from him, showing the whites of its eyes. He stared at the beast in horror. Like the others it was a small animal, almost a pony, but it frightened the wits out of him. He was obviously trying not to show his fear in front of his comrades.

Wynter crowed, 'What's the matter, an't they got no horses in India then, eh? Good at riding a desk, I'll be bound, but never had flesh between your thighs, Clancy. You ought to just get on quick and show him who's master.'

Clancy bit his lip and attempted to mount, finding that the horse kicked and shied away from him.

'Mount on the *left*,' Peterson screamed at him, making him more nervous than ever. 'Don't ever get on a horse from the right side.'

'I know that,' Clancy replied desperately. 'I was just testing him.'

Sergeant Crossman knew that Clancy had to learn how to ride very quickly. They all had horses and they were going to leave the area immediately. Clancy could not possibly stay on foot.

'Here, I'll hold him,' said Crossman, feeling sorry for the man. 'You stand on that rock over there.'

Clancy, his legs shaking violently, did as he was told. Crossman, himself on horseback, led the mount to the rock. There he stroked its nose, calming it down, while Clancy clambered awkwardly into the saddle. There he sat, bolt

251

upright, while the horse fidgeted below him. Crossman handed him the reins.

'Now just give him a little kick in the ribs with your heels,' cried Wynter, delighting at Clancy's nightmare. 'Just a bit of a nudge . . .'

Clancy did as Wynter suggested. Immediately the stocky little horse bolted, with Clancy bouncing up and down on its back. It galloped full speed down the gorge. Clancy was white with fear, the reins loose in his hands, his legs wide apart.

'Rein him in, rein him in,' cried Peterson.

But her advice fell on deaf ears, for Clancy was in no mood to listen to more counsel. All the wisdom in the world would have gone in one ear and out of the other. Finally the horse bucked, sending Clancy flying through the air. His carbine went one way, and he the other. Luckily he landed on some gorse bushes, which broke his fall. He lay there amongst the prickles, stunned and unhappy, while the horse charged on out of the gorge, to some unknown destination.

Crossman rode over and looked down on the private.

'Get up,' he said. 'Go and fetch your carbine and then climb up behind Peterson.'

'I'm not going on another horse,' said Clancy, pathetically. 'I'm never going on another horse.'

'Get up behind Peterson, and that's an order,' said Crossman. 'He's the lightest. If we leave you behind the Cossacks will cut off your testicles and put them on a lance to dry like nuts.'

'I don't think they're good for much, anyway,' Clancy moaned, feeling himself. 'They got crushed by that horse, then punctured on a thorn bush.'

'They'll also cut out your tongue, prise out your eyes, and cut off your nose – then sew the lot inside your mouth. Up, up, lad, unless you want to die a very slow death. Get behind Peterson.'

Clancy collected his rifle. He looked a scruffy sight. His sheepskin coat was covered in gorse thorns and bits of twig.

Since he was bareheaded his hair was full of dust and grit. Nevertheless he managed to find a suitable rock and was able to climb up behind his comrade. Sitting on the horse's rump, he was as stiff as a board. There was still terror registering on his face. He gripped her around the waist, holding on painfully hard.

'Not so tight,' she told him angrily.

'I'm just trying to hold on,' complained Clancy, in a tone of exasperation. 'That's all I'm trying to do. God never intended us to ride beasts, of that I'm certain. They're the devil's own creatures.'

'Since we're the Devil's Own,' said Wynter, 'that's what you might call . . . somethin',' he ended, weakly.

'Appropriate is the word you're looking for, Wynter,' said Crossman. 'Now lead off, Ali. Take us up into the high country. They'll be after us as soon as those two men we released find their way back to friends.'

'We should've killed 'em,' said Wynter. 'Major Lovelace would've done.'

'Do not threaten me with Major Lovelace. He is not in command, I am,' Crossman told him. 'Anyway, I'm not so sure even the major would kill helpless prisoners. Who would I get to blow out their brains in cold blood, eh, Wynter? You, man? Would you do it?'

'I'd do it all right,' Wynter replied. 'You just watch.'

Crossman believed him. Wynter was probably capable of doing away with a Russian as he might a chicken or a wild rabbit. The Wynters of the world had a way of viewing men as animals when there was slaughter to be done.

The group made their way to a safe place that had an escape route to the rear, yet the approaches could all be seen without the watchers being observed. They hobbled the five horses and made camp for the night. Yusuf Ali ate a whole jar of pickled cabbage by himself, but the others had smaller, varying amounts, mostly just enough to stave off their hunger.

The horses had to be fed and watered. Peterson seemed

quite happy to be made responsible for their well-being. Clancy offered to help her but she declined, saying that he had enough to do with his cooking and making contraptions.

All knew that she did not want to let Clancy near the creatures, for fear they would lose every mount before morning due to some act of stupidity on his part. Crossman did not blame the man. Cossack horses were almost wild animals and to start a man's riding lessons on one of them was tantamount to committing murder.

The evening came on and the low distant sun dipped down between the peaks. Lanes of shadow developed on the valleys below. Crossman ordered that no fires should be lit, not even one of Clancy's earth-ovens. There would be search parties out for them soon and the Cossacks had one more excuse to hunt down their hated enemies, Sergeant Crossman's *peloton*.

24

The rangers managed to avoid the Russians who were out scouring the countryside for the perpetrators of the ambush. Eventually the Russians must have thought the cabbage thieves had headed back to Balaclava. After two days the search parties ceased and the road was once more usable.

Crossman felt his men were beginning to settle in a little too comfortably. He guessed it was time to move on.

Wynter and Devlin had laid snares for rabbits, hares and game birds, and because they were reasonably successful were quite willing to remain there until they had cleared the area of wildlife. These two men were old hands at poaching. In their time they had been the bane of gamekeepers and their lords, and might well have been hanged by now had they not joined the army. Crossman sent them out on patrol together to wean them away from their preoccupation with making animal traps.

Clancy, as a member of the Thugs, had throttled men with knotted cords, but was no good at strangling rabbits by the same method. A grown man with a loud mouth and skin on his back was one thing, but little furry animals were another.

Clancy's idea of settling in was to make himself comfortable. He had constructed a pillow of dried grass wrapped in a large kerchief, which he laid at the head of his blanket. He had sticks to keep his boots in shape, a drying rack for his socks and shirt, a hook on which to hang his knapsack, and various other contrivances.

On the third evening, Devlin did not return from a two-man patrol consisting of himself and Wynter. Wynter arrived back at the cave where they had made their hideout to inform Crossman that he had last seen Devlin near an orchard.

'He went into the orchard, while I scouted around on the outside. I thought I heard him yell, but it could have been a magpie or jay or some such bird. You know how them crow birds screech. I went back to look, but Devlin never came out. I tried callin', not too loud though, but he never answered.'

Crossman asked, 'You didn't go in after him?'

'I thought, if he's been took by the Russians I don't want to be took too. There'd be no one to come back here. I decided it's best I tell you and more of us go down.'

'Very sensible, Wynter,' replied Crossman. 'No point in two of you being taken, is there? Right, let's get organized. We'll all go. It's time we moved camp anyway. Peterson, Clancy, get your knapsacks together. Wynter, go and fetch Ali, he's doing sentry duty . . .'

They covered any traces of their having been at the cave as best they could, then struck out on the trail. Crossman handed out biscuits to everyone. Wynter took his and stuffed them in his knapsack when he thought no one was looking.

'Not hungry, Wynter?' asked Peterson, causing Crossman to glance at the soldier being questioned.

'No, not just yet,' mumbled Wynter, 'I'll eat 'em in a bit.'

However, Crossman observed that Wynter did not eat the biscuits, which made the sergeant a little suspicious. Wynter was never one to pass up food. He wondered whether the lance corporal was feeling sick, but was afraid to say so. The men were terrified of being sent to the hospital. Most soldiers who went there died. He decided to keep an eye on Wynter to watch for signs of exhaustion.

They reached the orchard after dark and could do nothing until light. If they lit torches they might be seen. Crossman told his men to get some sleep. They curled up in ditches and hollows, keeping out of the wind. Luckily the night was dry and they did not have to suffer lying in pools of water.

At first light, Crossman roused them. He noticed that Wynter now ate his biscuits and was relieved that he had not got a sick man on his hands. Ali immediately went into the orchard to see what he could find. The Bashi-Bazouk came out a short while later, having found a patch of dried blood.

'Is it human blood?' asked Crossman. 'Could be a fox got something.'

Ali shrugged his shoulders. 'I do not know for sure, Sergeant, but if it was fox with rabbit or bird, maybe some feather or piece of fur left too, yes? I see no such telltales. Only flat grass and patch of blood.'

'If it is Devlin's blood, we must assume he has been wounded. But with what? Wynter did not mention a shot. You heard no rifle fire, Wynter?'

The soldier shook his head emphatically.

'Only a sort of cry, like I said, Sergeant.'

'Then he must have been stabbed or struck over the head with something. We must assume he is still alive for the moment. It may be a trap. You three stay here,' he told Peterson, Wynter and Clancy. 'Ali and I will go into the orchard further and see what we can discover. If you hear shooting, come to our assistance. If we do not return, then make your way back to Balaclava and report to Major Lovelace.'

'Don't we come in after you?' asked Peterson.

'If the orchard has swallowed up Devlin and then us, you can be sure it will swallow you too, should you be foolish enough to tread in our footsteps. You're in charge, Lance Corporal Peterson.'

'Aw, what?' cried Wynter, predictably. 'I'm a lance corporal too! Peterson's nothin' more than — than a sprat.'

'He's proved himself more reliable than you in the past, Wynter, despite your success in Sebastopol.'

'Didn't I do well this time? Comin' back for you?'

'Yes, but there's more to that than meets the eye, Wynter, and well you know it. I'll find out what it is when we get Devlin back. You can give me those sly looks as much as you like, I'll get to the bottom of it.'

Wynter said nothing to this, which confirmed Crossman's opinions that the soldier had been up to something.

Crossman and Ali entered the orchard and made their way silently through the trees. There was a heavy dew on the grass, which helped to soften their footfalls, but in fact there was no one in the orchard. The pungent scent of rotting fruit wafted up from the short grasses.

On the other side of the orchard a tinge of hoarfrost decorated the sides of a goat track, which wound its way lower in the shade of a rugged cliff. After a while they could hear the clanking of copper bells coming from the east.

They followed this sound.

A short way east of the orchard, where no doubt the goats had been eating the windfall apples and plums, was a hidden gully which dropped sharply down to a running stream. At the bottom of the gully stood a goatherd's stone croft. It was built partly into one side of the gully itself, so that its back wall was formed of natural rock. Smoke was coming from a hole in the surfed roof winding slowly up to the heavens.

There were goats in makeshift pens out in the yard, shuffling and bleating softly, their bells making a muffled donging sound in the heavy air.

Ali put a finger to his lips and indicated that the pair of them should squat down and wait. Crossman was impatient to find Devlin, but he did as the Turk suggested. They had not been there more than half an hour when a wooden door fell open with a thud against the stone wall.

A man stepped through the doorway. Going by the smell which drifted up to the two soldiers, he was dressed in multiple layers of half-cured goatskins. There were knee-length home-made boots on his feet. On his head was something which resembled a dead cat, but was no doubt intended to be a hat. A weapon like a bent and battered musical instrument was hanging by a frayed cord on his back. Its stock was so worn it was merely a rounded stub of wood about three inches long.

The strange figure went down to the bank with a hide bucket, which he filled from the rushy beck. While he was there he drank deeply of the clear running water. He smacked his lips as he did so and stared towards the croft. Crossman was in no doubt he was tormenting someone who was thirsty. There was a very smug-turned-ugly look on the man's dirty face, as if he were enjoying a morning's illicit entertainment.

'For mercy's sakes,' came a croaking voice from the croft, 'give me a drink, will you, man? I'm as parched as a bloody desert snake.'

'Devlin,' whispered Crossman.

He had misjudged the goatherd's hearing though, for the man looked up sharply towards the escarpment. At the same time he dropped his bucket, which collapsed on impact, shedding its load of water. With one easy movement he unslung a blunderbuss and fired a blast in the general direction of the cliff.

Crossman and Ali dropped quickly to the ground.

Pieces of metal showered a scraggy tree clinging to a crevice in the rock above the two men.

Seconds later when Crossman jumped up, bent rusty nails, shards of pottery and other bits dropped from his sheepskin coat. He rushed down the steep track with Ali close on his heels, oblivious of the fact that there might be more armed men in the croft. The goatherd himself ran full pelt for the door which was hanging on its leather hinges, and slammed it shut.

Overtaking Crossman, Ali reached the door first. He kicked it down in one motion without pausing in his stride. Crossman was right behind him. In the dimly lit room beyond, the goatherd was desperately trying to reload his weapon, pouring gunpowder down the bugle-shaped barrel from a cracked old powder horn. He looked up as Ali bore down on him, then tried urgently to use the weapon as a club.

Ali knocked it from his grasp and pressed the muzzle of his Ferguson breech-loader against the man's temple. The goatherd dropped to his knees with a frantic cry and assumed the genuflective position of a man at prayer. His wild eyes showed their whites as he stared up at Ali, expecting to have his head blown off.

'Thank God you've come,' whispered Devlin hoarsely. 'Can I have some water, please?'

Crossman looked to where the sound was coming from and saw his corporal trussed like a chicken ready for market, lying in the corner of the dirt-flooded room. He took out his German hunting knife and cut Devlin's cords. The Irishman sat up and rubbed his wrists, but then pointed to his foot.

'I'm not able to walk, Sergeant. This heathen bastard caught me with a mantrap in yon orchard.'

Crossman gave Devlin some water from his bottle.

'A mantrap?'

Devlin pointed to some rusty devices in the far corner of the room. As Crossman's eyes became used to the gloom he saw that they were gin traps, with chains and securing spikes. They appeared too small for mantraps though. He guessed the goatherd laid them for predators which might attack his goats.

'Let's see that foot out in the light,' Crossman said. 'Ali, take that man outside.'

'Shall I shoot him, Sergeant?' asked the Bashi-Bazouk, matter-of-factly.

'No, don't do that. I want to speak to him in a minute. I suspect he was only trying to protect his property, although he was having a fine time with my corporal here. Just get him out of my way while I attend to Devlin's wound, please.'

The goatherd was gibbering now and shaking in fear. Ali

nudged him with the toe of his boot. The man understood that he was to go outside and indeed he believed he was going to be shot. His gibbering turned to whimpering, which Ali steadfastly ignored, lighting up an evil-looking cheroot and blowing out the smoke in a bored fashion.

Crossman helped Devlin to hobble outside, where the sergeant saw that the Irishman's foot was crushed at the ankle, his boot pierced on both sides by the iron teeth of the gin.

'Is it broken, do you think?' asked Devlin. 'I'm not sure myself.'

Crossman eased off the corporal's boot and they inspected an ugly wound, which was already beginning to fester. It did not seem as if the ankle had snapped, but there might be chips of bone loose amongst the mangled flesh. Devlin would need treatment for the injury fairly quickly.

'I'll wash and dress it for now,' said Crossman. 'Then we'll see if we can get you back to the lines.'

The goatherd, now sitting on a rock not far away, was gabbling animatedly to Yusuf Ali, who still looked rather bored as he puffed on what Wynter called one of his pieces of 'tarred hemp'. He nodded occasionally.

Crossman fetched the discarded bucket and filled it with cold, clear water from the beck. He carried it back and swabbed Devlin's ankle with it, until the dried blood and pus were gone. Then he took out a clean kerchief and, making a pad of a piece of shirt torn from Devlin's tails, effected a bandage and moss poultice.

'There, that'll draw the wound. Can you walk, do you think? Try it?'

Devlin climbed unsteadily to his feet and tried to put weight on the ankle. He winced and shook his head. Crossman then went to the goat corral and found a piece of fencing with a fork at the top. He cut it to size with his knife and handed it to Devlin to use as a crutch.

'That'll be fine, Sergeant – but I'll be very slow.'

'We'll worry about that later. Hey,' he called the Bashi-

Bazouk, 'what's Mr Raw-and-reeking chattering on about there, Ali? Sounds as if he's telling you his life story.'

'He tries to buy his life with information, Sergeant,' smiled Ali. 'He is telling me that there is another road further down, an old one, where we can rob Russians on their way to Sebastopol. He thinks we are brigands from the steppes. Says they use this old road for valuable cargo, only using the top road for not so important freight. He heard we stole the pickled cabbage. Tells me we will get far better pickings on the old road.'

'How does he know this?'

'Some brigands came down from the north and robbed a Russian caravan of gold. There was a battle but Russian soldiers caught and hanged the thieves. Only one got away. He told his story to the goatherd, saying the road was much used by the Russian military for carrying ammunition and precious payloads. This is interesting, eh, Sergeant?'

This was a most fortunate and unexpected discovery.

'Very interesting, Ali. Keep him talking.' He turned to Corporal Devlin. 'What happened to your carbine?'

'It's in the orchard. I threw it into the long grass when I got caught in the trap. I didn't want whoever set the trap to take it from me.'

'All right, we'll send someone back for it.'

There was a commotion from above now and Wynter appeared, followed by Peterson and Clancy. They had obviously heard the shot from the blunderbuss and had followed orders. Wynter seemed very agitated as he raced down the goat track.

'It was Corporal Devlin made me do it, Sergeant,' he cried. 'I told him you wouldn't like it, but he surely didn't listen to me, so I had to go along with it.'

'Made you do what, Wynter? Devlin, what's he talking about? What have you done, the pair of you? Speak up, man!'

It emerged that the goatherd had taken Devlin prisoner, not for devious reasons of his own, but because the Irish corporal and his lance corporal sidekick had eaten the man's pet duck. Wynter explained in halting tones that they had set snares for rabbits in the orchard. After two hours, however, they heard a commotion and went to find they had snared a duck.

'I put it out of its misery quick and easy,' explained Wynter. 'We was congratulating ourselves on our luck, as anyone would. How was we to know it was a *tame* duck? We thought it had got separated from the rest of its tribe and had wandered into the orchard.'

'So, you cooked and ate it?' Crossman said.

'That we did,' said Wynter, with a hard look at the goatherd, 'and delicious it was too.'

The goatherd seemed to understand what was being said, from the way Wynter smacked his lips. He flew at Wynter with remarkable alacrity, screaming in his Tartar tongue. Clancy ran forward and with Crossman managed to keep the two men apart. When the goatherd had been calmed and was left muttering to himself, casting dark glances at Wynter, and appealing to some deity in the heavens to witness his persecution, Crossman went back to Wynter.

'How did you cook the bird? I expressly ordered you were not to light fires.'

'We didn't,' said Devlin. 'We used the old gypsy way.'

'Which is?'

'We stuck it in the heart of a haystack – you know it gets as hot as an oven in there when the hay's damp.'

Clancy nodded excitedly. 'Yes, that's right – we used to do it that way in India too.'

'Cooks a bird nice and tender, you just leave it there a few hours,' nodded Wynter.

Crossman was satisfied he had heard the truth now, but he felt the goatherd was owed reparations. He ordered Devlin and Wynter to pay the man a shilling. Wynter started to put up a fierce argument but when he looked at Crossman's face, he shut up. Devlin said he would pay the man the shilling and

Wynter could give him sixpence later. The deed was done but the goatherd seemed far from mollified.

He looked at the shilling in his hand in disgust and gabbled like mad at the circle of men around him, then flung the coin from him into some bushes.

'Bloody hell!' cried Wynter, diving after the coin. 'See what you get for being kind to the old coot.'

Crossman guessed that the man did not know what a shilling was worth. The sergeant shrugged his shoulders. Having done his best, he could do no more. The filthy old goatherd would have to sing to the moon for his lost duck. However, Clancy came forward and took some salt-pork out of his knapsack. He gave it to the goatherd, whose face brightened. He smiled up at Clancy and said something in a softer tone.

Ali said, 'He accepts your gift with thanks.'

Clancy nodded at Wynter, who had retrieved the shilling and given it back to Devlin.

'You owe me,' Clancy said.

'Right,' said Crossman, 'let's forget it now. Keep that man under surveillance at all times, Lance Corporal Wynter. He's your responsibility. But I don't want to see him mistreated in any way – just prevented from running away.'

'What if he runs and I can't stop him?'

'Shoot him dead,' said Crossman, aware that kindness could be taken too far. He was after all responsible for the safety of the whole group. If it meant endangering his fox hunt or his men, he had no hesitation in ordering the execution of the grubby individual. 'Just make sure you can justify it to me afterwards.'

Crossman made sure Clancy took first watch on sentry duty, then asked Peterson to see him alone in the croft.

'What is it, Sergeant?' asked Peterson.

'I just wanted to congratulate you on your success with Goodlake's sharpshooters.'

Peterson's brow was ridged with a frown. She stared at

Crossman as the sergeant took his chibouque out of his pack and began to stuff the bowl with tobacco. She too then took out a clay pipe, stained brown with nicotine juice and tar. Crossman offered her a quid of his tobacco.

'Here,' he said, 'take a plug. I've got plenty.'

'Thank you, Sergeant,' she said, filling her own pipe and accepting a light from him.

She sat down opposite Crossman on the dirt floor. Outside the goats were bleating, their bells donging dully. The pair of them puffed away together, making quite a comfortable fug in the croft. They could have been a pair of goatherds themselves, in their sheepskins and leggings. Both were aware that the time for relaxation might be all too brief.

25

The Turk came to Crossman in the early hours of the morning.

'A wagon comes, with lancers,' said Ali, shaking him gently. 'I speak with the goatherd.'

Instantly Crossman was wide awake.

'The goatherd told the truth?'

Yusuf Ali nodded. 'I give him money,' said Ali.

Crossman got up and woke the rest of the *peloton*. Clancy was on sentry duty, but he too was called in.

'We've got another convoy,' said Crossman to his attentive soldiers. 'Let's hope this one is more lucrative than the last. We must separate the lancers from the wagon somehow. Any suggestions?'

'Kill the officers, the rest will run away,' said Wynter, sneeringly.

'These Russians have more backbone than you give them credit for, Wynter,' Crossman said. 'I don't think one should ever lay down plans for an assault, the success of which assumes and indeed relies upon cowardice amongst the enemy.'

Clancy said, 'Where are the lancers, Sergeant? I mean, in front of the wagon, or following behind?'

'Ali?' asked Crossman, deferring to the Bashi-Bazouk.

'Most of them behind, some in front – maybe . . .' he

showed them ten fingers. 'Altogether, one squadron. Maybe five miles down track now.'

'A hundred of 'em?' Peterson gasped.

Clancy said, 'Wait. When I was out patrolling with Wynter, we saw a gorge back there, two miles away. You remember, Wynter? It's quite narrow. If we could cause a rock slide while the main part of the squadron's going through, we'd split them away from the wagon.'

'That's the kind of thinking I like in a man,' said Crossman, excitedly. 'Well done, Private Clancy.'

Wynter sneered and Peterson sniffed.

They worked out the details of the plan.

Ali and Wynter would lay charges on either side of the gorge, using gunpowder which Ali carried for the purpose. It should not take a great amount to shift the initial boulders in order to begin the landslide. Once the lancers were cut off from the wagon, the two soldiers would attempt to keep them pinned down with rifle fire from either side of the gorge. They would have the advantage, firing down on their opponents, who hopefully would be fighting a panic in their horses and unable to organize quickly enough to climb.

In the meantime, Crossman, Clancy and Peterson would cut down those around the wagon and attempt to wrest it from the remaining lancers. The surprise element, as always, would be most important. Even if they did not get the wagon, the supply line would have been seriously hit. Crossman and his men were there to disrupt communications more than anything.

'What about me?' asked Devlin, pointing to his foot.

'You'll have to stay here, Corporal.'

'With that devil?' He nodded at the scowling goatherd, who had been allowed to tend to his stock under guard, but was still restrained at all other times. 'He'll slit my throat, first chance he gets.'

'We'll tie him, don't worry,' Crossman replied.

They left Devlin with his rifle, recovered from the orchard

grasses, and the goatherd bound to a stake nearby. The Irishman said he would watch him like a hawk. The rest of the group then set off to arrange the ambush.

'I wish we had a small cannon,' said Wynter. 'We'd really set 'em alight with one of them.'

'Perhaps you would like to be the one to drag it over the hills?' enquired Crossman, knowing the answer.

The gunpowder charges were laid and the men were placed in position. Further up the dirt road a tree had been felled in case the horses drawing the wagon bolted. Ali scouted back on the trail and returned later to inform them that the wagon and its escort were close at hand. Soon they could hear the clinking of bridles and swords, the clatter of hooves on the rocks, the occasional snorts of horses. Then came the lower sound of chatter and the rumble of cart wheels on hard earth and stone.

'Here they come,' whispered Peterson.

There were a dozen lancers leading the wagon. Crossman suspected they were mainly there to help in case the vehicle became bogged down. They wore helmets in the Prussian style, whose spikes glinted in the sunlight. Apart from lances with fluttering pennons, the lancers had horse pistols and heavy straight-bladed swords.

On the battlefield the lancers would have been formidable, but here in rough country, with bush and rocky outcrops, they were awkward and overencumbered. Crossman knew that if they met their adversaries on the flat track they would lose. But since he had no intention of meeting them on the road, the lancers were at a definite disadvantage, *especially* since they were on horseback.

The wagon lumbered through the pass. Behind it the squadron were in loose order, their discipline lax. They were chatting away to one another, clearly not expecting any sort of trouble. One or two had their helmets off and had hung them from their saddles by the chinstraps.

The explosions startled even the waiting members of the

88th Foot, Connaught Rangers. Immediately after the rocks began falling on the unfortunate horsemen in the gorge, Crossman and his two soldiers shot three of the twelve leading escort. Two of the remaining lancers panicked and charged off ahead, galloping their horses away from the ambush. The others drew their horse pistols. One or two had clearly not loaded them, but wild shots zinging amongst the rocks confirmed that there were those amongst the Russian cavalry who had been prepared.

Within a quarter of a minute Peterson had felled her second Russian, Crossman missed with his shot as a horse shied, and Clancy actually hit the wagoner in the arm.

Noting now where the shots were coming from, the remaining half-dozen lancers charged their horses up the steep slopes of the valley towards Peterson and Clancy. Their horses' hooves slipped and slid on the scree, causing at least one of the mounts to fall. Consequently his heavily accoutred rider crashed to the ground and rolled down the slope.

Crossman shot another man from his saddle. A further rider toppled on reaching a small ridge, when his horse lost its footing. Clancy rushed out and bayoneted this man as he lay helpless on the ground. Three of the riders, realizing now that they were being shot at from both sides of the pass, turned their mounts and awkwardly descended to the road below.

Peterson shot the last rider in the hip, the only section of him visible to her as he passed across a window between two rocks, and he groaned and slumped forward, letting his mount find its own path thereafter in the bush at the top of the rise.

When the three remaining lancers reached the wagon, one of them grabbed the reins of the leading carthorse and urged it forward. By this time the two who had at first run had returned. Between them the five cavalry troopers got the wagon on the move, with the wounded wagoner still clinging white-faced to his high seat. They went trundling off along the track, with the wagoner bouncing awkwardly in his seat.

This whole attack from start to finish had taken about two minutes.

In the gorge the lancers were fighting for control of their horses, while Ali and Wynter picked them off. Five men were already dead or wounded. The officer in charge was screaming at his men to go forward to protect the wagon, but since the road through the gorge was now strewn with large boulders, the way was if not blocked, extremely hazardous.

To the rear of the squadron some wise NCOs were leading their troopers back along the trail and out into the clear. Some were attempting to circumnavigate the gorge by riding up the slopes before the gorge became steep, to the ridges above, but it was a slow business.

On hearing a whistle from Crossman, Wynter and Ali slipped away, and ran through the bush to join their comrades. They knew that it was a race now to reach the spot where they had felled the tree, before the horsemen could remove the barrier and gallop the wagon further out of reach. It was one of the drawbacks of being on foot. If they did not strike the enemy hard enough the first time, there was the danger that the mounted men would escape with the goods.

The Rangers reloaded their carbines as they ran, which was a curious business involving teeth, hands and armpits. When they arrived at the place where the wagon had been halted by the felled tree, they saw that three of the lancers had managed to heave the log aside and were leading the vehicle through the gap. Giving his men a second to recover their breath, Crossman then gave the order to fire a volley. All three dismounted cavalrymen were cut down. The other two, still in their saddles out in front of the wagon, returned fire with their pistols.

Ali slung his rifle over his shoulder, whipped two small revolvers out of the voluminous folds of his clothing, and rushed along the track blazing at the troopers. Crossman drew his five-shot Tranter and joined in the fusillade. One of the lancers fell under this less accurate but denser hail of fire, while the other wisely turned and fled along the now open road, leaving the wounded wagoner to fend for himself.

Clancy lifted a canvas sheet on the back of the wagon.

'Two boxes like sea chests,' he called to Crossman. 'One bigger than the other. Brass reinforced on the corners and edges. Locks on both.'

Crossman looked for himself. The boxes were of strong, solid oak with fleur-de-lis brass corners and hinges. They were studded with pyramid-headed brass nails all over. The fasteners were massive steel padlocks holding heavy bolts in place. There would be no red cabbage in these crates, unless it were pickled in the finest beluga caviar.

'Right, unhitch the horses and tie a box behind each. We'll drag them both to the croft. Use the reins as ropes.'

The soldiers applied themselves to the task while the dour wagoner still sat up on his seat, his right hand resting on the iron brake. He glowered at the foreigners in their rag-tag clothes. His grim expression told Crossman he was not only wounded but unhappy to be put to such inconvenience. For their part the soldiers ignored him, working round him, treating him as if he were not there. Finally, once the carthorses had been removed, the wagoner was left alone on his perch, looking like a man stranded on an island of boxwood.

Crossman and his soldiers led the horses into the dense brush on the slope that ran down to the road. They travelled quickly, knowing that the Russian cavalry were not far behind them. One of the boxes was tremendously heavy and left a deep groove in the earth. When they had gone about a mile, Crossman ordered his men to unhitch the boxes and to tie angular rocks in their places. With a slap on each rump, the carthorses were sent on their way in the opposite direction to the goatherd's croft, the rocks making similar marks on the earth to the boxes.

Poles were cut and the boxes slung between them, but the smaller box was impossible for just two men to carry. Four might have managed it, but that would have left only one man for the bigger, lighter chest. Crossman found a hiding place, a crevice, where they could hide the smaller box. They continued their journey back to the croft with the other one slung between two poles, one man at each corner.

When they reached their destination, Devlin was there to greet them.

'Well done, lads,' he said cheerfully. 'So you did it, did you?'

'Indeed begorra, it's certain sure we did,' cried an elated Wynter, mimicking the corporal's accent. 'Oh yes, indeed we did, sor.'

Devlin grimaced at Wynter's efforts. 'You'll never make an Irishman, Wynter,' he said. 'You haven't the musical cadence in your tones.'

Crossman untied the goatherd and gave the man some water. He seemed anything but grateful. Then the sergeant ordered the opening of the chest they had managed to haul up to their hideout. Ali and Wynter smashed open the locks with rifle butts, though it was a difficult task. Rifle shots, however, might have brought the lancers to the hideout, since the Russians would now be scouring the slopes below.

Finally the lid to the box was thrown back, to reveal its contents.

'Paper money!' whispered Wynter, reverently. 'We're rich!'

He grabbed a handful of the bills and smelled them.

'Old money too,' he said. 'And it's all ours — an't it, Sergeant? Spoils of war?'

'Yes it is, lads,' Crossman said in a low voice, as they all stared at the wads of printed cash with wide disbelieving eyes. 'What Wynter says is true — this money belongs to us and we can divide it among ourselves.'

26

Crossman had smelled the interior of crofts before, when he had run away from home as a young man. Living in this croft, smelling the turf roof and the other odours associated with such a dwelling, returned memories he would rather be without. In this state of mind he fell asleep one night, failing to check on the Tartar before he did so.

Peterson woke Crossman early in the morning, just as the shooting started.

'What? What is it?' cried Crossman, leaping up from his bed on the ground.

'The Tartar slipped away in the night,' said Peterson, grimly. 'He's brought the Russians. They're covering all our escape routes. They have us trapped, Sergeant.'

Shots were whining through the air outside. Crossman knew, however, that if the two sentries were in place, one in the rocks above the croft, and one down below, it would be difficult for the Russians to attack in force. There were only two narrow paths to the rock shelf on which the croft was perched, one from above and one from below. Both these paths were little more than goat tracks. The Russians would have to come single file down from above, or up from below.

This they had already tried, hoping to surprise the group

in the early dawn, but Yusuf Ali had already blocked the path from above with two Russian dead. Wynter had wounded another man from the party coming up. Both Ali and Wynter had been wide awake and alert, having just taken over sentry duty from Crossman and Clancy.

Time favoured neither the Russians nor the British. The Russians had their quarry pinned down. But the British had a large food supply in the goats, and the beck ran almost through their camp. They were fairly secure, their position protected by rocky outcrops. The Russians could only fire in their direction at will, hoping a lucky aim would find its way into a British or Turkish heart. Shots zinged from the rocks all through the morning, so that it was necessary for the whole *peloton* to keep their heads down.

For their part, Crossman's men could not get a good shot at the Russians either. The enemy hid themselves behind the same rocks that were protecting the British group. It was going to be a waiting game. While the allied armies were laying siege to Sebastopol, the Russians were doing the same with a small party of allied soldiers up in the hills.

It was stalemate for the time being.

Devlin said to Crossman, 'You'll have to leave me here.'

'I'm leaving no one,' said Crossman in a determined voice. 'If we go, we all go together. Besides, they have us locked in here. It would take a fox to get through that lot without being seen.' He paused and collected his thoughts. 'Fortunately we have two foxes in our group and I'm going to send one of them out for help.'

'Well, I know Ali is one of those you're talking about, Sergeant. Who's the other one?'

'Clancy. In fact I think he's nearer a fox than our Bashi-Bazouk, who's more like a wolf. Have you ever heard that Irish-Indian come up behind you? He has no footfall. Silent. And like Ali, he's not afraid to kill with his bare hands. If anyone can get through, it's Private Clancy. Also, Ali is more use to us here. He scares the Russians.'

That evening, with Clancy and Ali guarding the paths, Crossman made one of two decisions. He, Peterson and Wynter gathered around Devlin in the croft. They had a fire there now, since it no longer mattered whether the Russians saw the smoke or not. Wynter looked a bit jumpy, probably thinking he was going to be asked to do something dangerous. Not that Wynter was a coward, but the group were in a bad position.

'I've decided to send Clancy back to Major Lovelace, to get some help. Whether the major will think it worth sending it or not is up to him.'

'Why shouldn't he?' exclaimed Wynter, sounding indignant. 'We're as important as anyone, an't we?'

'You may think so, Wynter, but perhaps the major will decide not to risk other lives in saving ours.'

'Tell him about the money, then,' Wynter said. 'Tell him he can have a share . . .'

Devlin and Peterson exchanged sour looks.

Crossman said, 'I can't do that, Wynter, because we're going to burn the money tonight.'

Wynter actually jumped to his feet, his eyes wide with surprise.

'You can't do that. That's our money. I was going to be rich. I was set for life.'

Crossman shook his head. 'I'm sorry, I know how you feel – I know how you all feel. I'm human too. I had the same idea as the rest of you. Once the war was over I was going to use my prize money to buy a small farm in Scotland.' He paused to stare into the flames of the fire. 'But we have to destroy it. If it falls back into Russian hands this raid will have been for nothing. We will be captured or die for nothing. I can't risk it, I'm afraid. I'm sorry, men.'

'Oh no – oh, no, no, no,' wailed Wynter.

Devlin said grimly, 'Shut up, man. You're making it worse. As the sergeant said, we none of us likes it. We all wanted to go back kings from this war. It cannot be. We must take it on the chin like men.'

There were tears rolling down Wynter's cheeks as Crossman got up and dragged the chest near to the fire.

'Please, Sergeant. Let me hide a wad in me sock. Yes, yes, we can all do that, eh? Just a few notes in me sock . . .'

'It's going to be burned, Wynter, so get that through your thick head now.'

'I never saw you cry for a dead soldier,' said Peterson in disgust, 'but you cry for *money*.'

'Too damn right I do,' cried Wynter, angrily rounding on her. 'Money's the only thing you can trust in this world. You can't trust bloody people, that's for sure. Oh God, I don't want to watch this. It's sacrilege.'

Crossman began taking out wads of bills from the chest and putting them on the fire. They were surprisingly difficult to burn, but when they did so their flames were colourful. Wynter sat in mourning, as if before the funeral pyre of his own father, moaning softly occasionally, sometimes staring at the conflagration, at other times wrenching his eyes away to look out of the doorway into the darkness beyond.

'It's a cryin' shame,' he kept saying to himself. 'It's a bloody sacrifice, that's what it is.'

It took about two hours to burn the money and even then there were small pieces of banknotes left in the ashes. Wynter took his sorrow and went out to relieve Clancy, who came back in to be told what had happened. The Irish-Indian shrugged.

'Easy come, easy go,' he said.

Crossman said to Peterson, 'Would you relieve Ali from sentry duty? I need to talk to him.'

Once Ali had been relieved and came to sit by the fire, Crossman informed him of a new plan.

'I want you, Clancy, to try to get through the Russians tonight. You're to get hold of Major Lovelace and tell him of our difficulties. If he doesn't feel he can come, we'll understand. Tell him we have wounded we can't leave, but say he's under no obligation. Can you do it?'

Clancy looked at Sergeant Crossman with those dark, cryptic eyes of his.

'You want me to sneak through the Russian lines? I may have to kill one or two on the way out. If I do that, in the way I know best, you realize they'll execute you all when they eventually overrun this place?'

Crossman knew that fact. If Clancy had to throttle any of the Russians, they would be so incensed they would probably hang any survivors of an attack. It was not a pleasant prospect, but Crossman had made his decision.

'You must do whatever is necessary, Clancy, to get to our lines. Use your discretion, but get through at all costs.'

'I'll do my best, Sergeant.'

While Clancy was preparing himself, Ali came up to Crossman quietly. He looked a little hurt.

'You no want Ali to go for the major, Sergeant? I do good job – better than this man. He is very good for an English soldier, but not like Turk.'

'I agree with you, Ali,' said Crossman, diplomatically. 'You are the best man for the job – but I need you here much more than I need Clancy.'

'Is this true, or you tell me this for make me feel better?'

'Ali, you and I have been through much in the short time we have known each other – do you think I would lie to you?'

The Turk shook his head slowly. 'No, you would not lie, Sergeant. You think I more important here?'

'I believe so.'

'Then I stay,' the Bashi-Bazouk said in a firm voice, as if it were his decision in the first place. 'We fight the damn Russians together and we die together if we have to.'

Crossman put a hand on Yusuf Ali's shoulder. 'Good,' he said. 'You are the last man I would wish to upset . . .'

'I'm ready,' said Clancy, suddenly at his elbow. 'Wish me luck, Sergeant.'

Crossman turned. Clancy had blackened his face with soot from the burned money. He had also taken off the bulky sheepskin and was now dressed only in a blackened shirt, Oxford trousers and bare feet. In his belt was a bayonet. From his pocket dangled a knotted cord.

Crossman said, 'I've sent Ali to warn Wynter and Peterson that you're coming through.'

Clancy shook his head with a white, toothy smile.

'If I can't slip past those two, I'll never get through the Russians, will I?'

'All right. Do you want my revolver, Clancy?' asked Crossman. 'You can have it if you wish.'

'No, Sergeant – if I use a firearm, I'm done for.'

'Then good luck, Private.'

'Thank you, Sergeant,' Clancy said, and slipped out into the night.

Clancy had felt nervous as Crossman briefed him. So much – the lives of his brothers-in-arms – depended on the success of his mission. However, now that he was in a familiar darkness, as much a part of the night as a bat, he felt reassured, certain that once again his talents as an assassin would see him through. His shape melded with the deeper shadows and shades of the dark hours. A watcher might think a fox was sweeping by, rather than a man.

He reflected, as he drifted silently down between rocks and trees, that there was another man inside him who was a killer of British soldiers.

This certain *other* Clancy had assassinated three British soldiers once upon a time when he was a member of the Thugs in India. But that had been war too. In those days he had been an Indian. Now he was an Irishman. A man of two halves, he kept one side of himself completely separate from the other. The Indian did some things, the Irishman others, and though the twain were like twin brothers they were definitely two completely different men sharing the same body.

This state of mind was not difficult for a man who had

been with the mystics of India, steeped in oriental sorcery, a man who could put himself in a trance simply by staring at a lamp flame, a man whose mind was flexible and pliable, not rigid like that of most British soldiers.

In any case he did not consider himself a murderer. You did what was necessary in war and then you put it to one side. Uncomplicated justification.

There was a glow in the sky at the bottom of the slopes. The Russians had lit small fires behind their natural rock fortress walls, which would make it more difficult for him to pass through their ranks. Clancy began to move more slowly, in an exaggerated gliding motion, knowing that he had hours of darkness around him. Patience was his friend, impetuosity his enemy.

Some of the men were asleep, curled up beneath rocks in their greatcoats. One or two sat around the fires, tending them with sticks. There was the smell of cooking vegetables in the air. An officer's tent stood some way off, under a clutch of trees, a lamp or candle glowing from within.

Clancy drifted along the line, found a fire where a single soldier had his back to him. Clancy then moved out and through the sleeping bodies, stepping quietly between them. In a short while he was through to the other side. There he ran up against his first real obstacle, two sentries guarding the narrow exit down to the road far below. He slipped his knotted cord from his pocket and eased himself closer to his targets.

One of the men was talking softly but animatedly to the other, using his free hand to emphasize a point. His other hand held his musket at the balance point in the centre. He kept looking at his companion, who nodded and grunted occasionally, as if he wanted agreement for all he said. Clancy waited in patient silence for the right moment.

Finally, there came a point when the two men were about three yards apart and the talkative one stood just in front and to the right of the listener. The front one was still jabbering away, staring out into the night now, speaking no doubt of domestic problems for which he required the other's sympathy and support. The listening soldier actually looked very bored and lit a pipe while the other prattled on and on.

Clancy drifted up behind the one with the pipe, whose right hand was on the bowl of his pipe. While he was in that position Clancy could do nothing. The Irish-Indian waited, waited, waited, his forearms crossed and the knotted loop at the ready. Finally the man's hand dropped down to his side. Immediately Clancy's cord was round his throat and his knee pressed in the soldier's back to get leverage.

The man's larynx was instantly crushed as he arched backwards and he let out the faintest of coughs. The talking soldier did not even pause in his chatter, no doubt taking the sound as one of those grunts of agreement. A split second after the cord was twisted on tight like a tourniquet, Clancy let go one hand and caught the musket before it hit the ground. A few moments after this the man was in a coma, on his way to death, the blood supply to his brain having been arrested. Clancy lowered him to the earth and laid his musket across his breast.

The Russian's glowing pipe was still gripped between his teeth, his jaw locked hard as if to try to keep his life spirit from escaping through his mouth.

Clancy then went up behind the talkative one, who had turned to look over his left shoulder. Clancy slipped downwards to the man's right. The soldier now paused in his speech, a puzzled expression forming on his face, when with a double-handed sweeping movement Clancy drove his bayonet sideways through the soldier's neck.

Again Clancy caught the musket before it hit the ground. The man gargled, staggered two or three paces, and then fell thrashing on the floor. Clancy brained him behind the right ear with one blow from the butt of the musket.

It was all over with the minimum of fuss in less than two minutes.

Clancy retrieved his weapons and then set off down towards

the road. On the way he still ran into small units of Russians but it was now open country and he was able to circumnavigate any trouble. Soon he was on the track and heading back towards Sebastopol.

All went fairly smoothly until he turned a corner, not expecting any company, to find a unit of infantry camped in the middle of the road. Why they were there, he had no idea, but he was seen and challenged by a sentry standing not two yards away from him. One or two men at the fire turned their heads and then looked expectantly at the sentry.

Clancy's boyish face broke into a charming smile and he blinked in the firelight.

'Hello,' he said to the grim soldier. 'Sorry . . .'

Clancy drove his bayonet deep into the chest of the soldier, then slipped into the bushes at the side of the road. A minute later muskets crashed and shots snicked through the shrubs and trees and whined off rocks. A hot ball seared Clancy's arm, causing tears to start to his eyes. He blinked and bit his lip to stop himself from crying out, for though the pain was minimal Clancy had a very low pain tolerance threshold.

He licked the wound, tasting his own blood, to feel how deep it was. Once he knew it was only a small gouge, he began running, putting distance between himself and the Russian soldiers. He saw lamps floating from the road into the bushy area and knew they were searching for him, but he was soon out of their reach and on his way back to his own lines.

It took him most of the night to reach the gorge which led down to Balaclava harbour. As he approached he deliberately made a noise about it and was challenged by a Scottish picquet. He emerged dark and almost invisible in front of the sergeant who had issued the challenge. The Scot jumped nervously.

'It's me, Scotchman – Private Clancy of the 88th Foot.'

'Where have you been, mon, dressed and painted like a damn phantom of the night?' said the Scot, testily, as Clancy was allowed past the picquets. 'Out for a wee stroll?'

'Mind your own bloody business,' said Clancy, hurrying past. 'You want to get a lady into trouble?'

The 83rd picquets laughed at this.

On reaching the hovel Clancy found to his relief that Major Lovelace's batman was there.

'Wake the major, quickly, Private,' said Clancy. 'I've got something to tell him.'

Having been roused himself by this strange black-faced creature coming out of the darkness, the batman protested.

'I certainly ain't goin' to disturb the major for no piccaninny, that's for sure . . .'

Clancy grabbed the man by the collar and hauled his face close.

'You insult me, you insult my father,' said Clancy, quietly. 'I've killed three men tonight, don't make me do it a fourth time because it might get to be a habit.' He ran a finger across his throat, taking some of the fire ash with it and leaving a pale mark like a slash.

'The major won't be happy,' gargled the private, unimpressed. 'He'll 'ave my eyes and liver.'

'What's going on down here?' asked a voice from the stairs. 'What's all this commotion? Is that you, Private Clancy, under all that soot?'

The batman looked smugly at Clancy, as if to say: I told you so.

Major Lovelace emerged, dressed in vest and Oxfords. He had a pistol in his hand. Clancy saluted.

'Major, Sergeant Crossman and the rest are trapped by a regiment of Russian soldiers. They sent me to find you and ask can you get them away? We attacked a wagon carrying money to Sebastopol – pay for the troops the sergeant thinks – and the Russians want it back.'

'I expect they do,' said Lovelace, a smile twitching in the corners of his mouth. 'Where is the sergeant?'

'Few miles north-east of here. I can take you there, sir.'

'And the money?'

'Ah, well, we were all going to be rich, but that was when we thought we'd got away with it. A goatherd led the Russians to us and the sergeant made us burn the money. Said he didn't want it to fall back into enemy hands. The Russians are going to be very angry when they find out what he's done.'

'I expect Wynter's none too pleased either,' said Major Lovelace.

Clancy's eyes opened wide at this remark. Here was an officer who not only knew the names of the men, but knew their dispositions and character as well. It gave Clancy heart for the British army.

'Wynter's hopping mad,' he said, smiling. 'He's crying in his soup.'

'I thought he would be. Well, young Clancy, let us get some men together and go and rescue your brave sergeant and his merry men. Wilson,' he said to his batman, 'my sheepskin, if you please.'

'Yes, sir,' said the crestfallen Wilson. 'At once, sir.'

27

Crossman and his men had a weary time of it now that they were two men short. Sentry duty had always cut deeply into their resources of strength and stamina, even when there had been six of them. Now the sergeant was down to four men including himself. It was necessary to have at least two guards posted at all times and for the remainder to keep watchful. On occasions the sentries would call the off-duty men from their beds or work, to help thwart an attempted attack.

Luckily with only two narrow access points to the rock shelf the Russians were easily held at bay. Their attempts at storming the British *peloton* were not very serious. They seemed content to wait until morale broke down or the British were starved into submission.

Crossman guessed that the commander of the Russian forces besieging them had discovered that someone had escaped from the croft. A bugle had sounded in the middle of the night and men are not roused from their sleep for trivialities, even in a Russian army on active service. The commander was obviously deeply unhappy about something.

A quick reconnoitre by Crossman revealed that the enemy had posted many more sentries than they had previously, some of them facing the trail. They were obviously expecting an attack from behind them. Clancy had left a calling card, or they would not have known he had been through them. Either that, or they had caught him, and wanted to display him.

For their part, Crossman's little band kept up their vigilance.

The morning after Clancy's run Crossman spoke with Ali concerning the success or failure of this move.

'Do you think he made it, Ali?' asked the sergeant. 'I'm wondering about that commotion in the early hours.'

'I think he get through, Sergeant. If not we hear shots. They not bother too much saying "Hello" to Private Clancy. They just shoot him.'

'Maybe they're holding him as a hostage?'

'Why they need hostage? They have us all?'

Crossman nodded. 'You're right. I'm sure they realize we would not vacate our stronghold for a hostage. So you think he got through?'

'Yes, Sergeant — but he still have to find his way back to Kadikoi in dark. Maybe he get lost? Who can tell? Or maybe he meet more Russians and get shot? We just have to wait and see.'

'Well, if no one comes within a couple of days, I think we're going to have to try and break through ourselves. We can't keep doing four hours on watch, four hours off, and remain alert and sane. Perhaps Clancy's efforts have given them ideas too? Maybe we should keep a watch out for assassins in the dark?'

The Turk shrugged. 'Possible, yes.'

It was a chilling thought.

Crossman was anxious about Corporal Devlin's injury.

'How are you, Corporal? Is that wound hurting?'

'The poultice seems to have done a lot of good, Sergeant. I can't walk on my ankle yet, but the swelling's gone down and there's no nasty red line going up my leg.'

The Irishman always made light of any problems. Crossman knew that he was probably concerned, since any wound in the Crimea, no matter how shallow, was always dangerous. Men had died from being hit in the arm by a ball. Wounds just seemed to go bad, then from bad to worse, many of them carrying away the life of the injured man through gangrene or blood poisoning.

'That's good,' said Crossman, inspecting the injury. 'We don't want blood poisoning to add to your problems. No,' he said, peering under the pad of moss, 'it looks quite clean to me. There's a bit of pus and black blood, but that's to be expected.'

'Would you like me to take a turn at sentry duty, Sergeant? You could prop me up with some logs or something. I feel a little useless lying here doing nothing. It'd do my spirit good.'

'We'll see. If one of the others becomes too exhausted, we may have to use you. In the meantime, just get plenty of rest. There's nothing any of us can do really except wait.'

They waited all that day, growing more and more anxious with the passing of time. Towards evening Crossman was fairly certain that Clancy had not made it through to the British lines. Of course, Major Lovelace might not have been available if Clancy had got to Kadikoi, and Crossman did not trust Lieutenant Dalton-James to answer his call for help. No one else, save Parker, would have the faintest idea what Clancy was talking about. That was the trouble with these clandestine operations.

Crossman was just wishing that he had given Clancy instructions to go to Lieutenant Parker, in the case of Major Lovelace being absent and Lieutenant Dalton-James refusing to take action in his stead, when shooting started above and below the position of the croft.

Wynter, watching the lower path, called out, 'Are they attacking, Sergeant? I can't see them.'

Ali was on the path above.

Crossman called to the Bashi-Bazouk, 'What's happening, Ali? Are you firing?'

'No, Sergeant,' came the unperturbed reply. 'I think maybe Major Lovelace come.'

Crossman felt elated.

'Good – good man. Come on then, Rangers, assist the rescue party. Don't let 'em find us waiting here pathetically for their help. Show them we've still got some fighting spirit left in us!'

Wynter let out a whoop of delight and began shooting at shadows down amongst the rocks below. Peterson found a suitable spot and began firing alongside Wynter. Ali and Crossman sent lead flying up into the hills. None of them could see the enemy, but it felt good to let off a few rounds in their direction. It would also help to confuse the Russians, make them believe they were being seriously assaulted from behind too.

The battle raged for about twenty minutes, at the end of which the Russians began to retire. Major Lovelace had wisely left the enemy commander an escape route. It was not his policy to trap them like animals so that they were forced to put up a do-or-die resistance, rather than retreat. He believed it was better to leave the back door open and allow them access to it.

Peterson and Wynter gave chase, the two soldiers following the Russians, picking some of them off as they tried to regroup. The rocks and trees rang with shots for a while, as the Rangers were covered by Lovelace's men, themselves not experienced enough with this rough hinterland to join Crossman's men. Peterson and Wynter were able to use their knowledge of the area to make sneak attacks on the Russian rearguard and harass them deep into the countryside. They employed the gullies and rocky outcrops, frustrating the Russian retreat. When they felt they had gone far enough they returned to Crossman having satisfied a little of the anger that had built up in them during the siege.

Once the Russians had melted into the hinterland the major came down to the croft, escorted by Lieutenant Dalton-James, Private Clancy and a smiling Rupert Jarrard. Jarrard's navy Colt revolver was smoking in his hand. The American correspondent, ever spoiling for a fight, had obviously been allowed to take part in the battle.

Crossman almost leaped up and shook everyone's hands. Instead he remembered his position as an NCO of the 88th Foot and saluted the officers instead. The gravity of Dalton-James's expression told him he had done the right thing.

Crossman said to Major Lovelace, 'Thank you for coming, sir – good to see you.'

Major Lovelace gave him a faint smile.

'Thank *you* for the invitation, Sergeant. All alive and well then?' He then noticed Devlin, lying in the dimness of the croft. 'Some not so well, eh? Will he live?'

'I'll live, sir,' called Devlin. 'Don't you worry about that.'

'Oh, we weren't *worried* about it, Corporal,' sniffed Lieutenant Dalton-James. 'We were merely enquiring out of idle curiosity.'

Major Lovelace gave the lieutenant an old-fashioned look, then turned to Crossman again.

'What about this money?'

Crossman grimaced. 'Quite a lot of it. Unfortunately we had to burn it all in case it fell into Russian hands again.'

'So I understood from Private Clancy. It was probably pay for their troops in Sebastopol. Well done. You were sent out to disrupt their communication and supply lines and you seem to have done that. They'll be wary about using this hidden trail again. I understand you attacked the top road as well with fair results?'

Crossman coughed. 'We – er – we captured a quantity of pickled cabbage.'

Wynter, Peterson, Clancy and Devlin all looked away in embarrassment.

Dalton-James, who had been standing stiffly alongside Major Lovelace, snorted.

'That will seriously disturb the Russian war effort, I'm sure.'

Lovelace whirled on Dalton-James.

'Do not underestimate the importance of pickled cabbage to the Russian troops, Lieutenant. There are three things which are significant to your Russian soldier – vodka, pickled cabbage and religion, in that order. When he cannot get supplies of the former, he turns to the latter, but his solace is that central ingredient and mainstay of his diet – pickled cabbage.'

Yusuf Ali nodded vigorously.

'Cabbage very good. Make iron for the blood. Russian soldier lose all strength with no cabbage to eat.'

By this time Dalton-James was aware that he was being made fun of and he walked away wearing a sulky expression.

'By the way, sir, there is another chest,' said Crossman to Major Lovelace. 'We hid it in some rocks. It was too heavy to drag up here, but it might be worth a look at it sometime.'

'I'll send someone, or come myself, when things have calmed down a little. Unless I miss my guess the Russians will be back in force soon. Their answer to being attacked by a larger force than themselves is to go and get an even larger one and counter-attack. Let's be on our way for now. You can give me the location of this heavy box later.'

'Yes, sir.'

Major Lovelace began to walk towards where Lieutenant Dalton-James was standing smouldering by himself. However, the major turned after going a few steps. He looked Crossman in the eye.

'That's a rather unusual firearm your Bashi-Bazouk has in his possession, Sergeant. I should tell him to keep it out of the way if I were you. There are those amongst us who would have it off him.'

Crossman nodded in mortification. 'I'll do that, sir.'

'Good. And for my part, I'll pretend I haven't seen it.'

'Thank you, sir.'

'No, thank you, Sergeant. You're making this war pretty exciting. We do a rather underhand, unpleasant but necessary service for our cause. I think General Buller did well to bring us all together, don't you?'

'With the exception of a certain lieutenant, yes, sir, I do.'

'Well, the world's not perfect, Sergeant,' smiled the major, 'and he too makes it interesting, in his way.'

With that Major Lovelace strode off, to join the man they had been talking about.

Crossman put an arm around the waiting Clancy's shoulders.

'Private Clancy, you're an excellent mischief-maker and saboteur. You're an even better assassin, but I'm not sure we should become too proud of that part of you. That ingredient of your character is a little unsavoury I imagine even for the indelicate taste of Major Lovelace, who is not renowned for being fastidious. Anyway, I'm mightily pleased with your efforts. You did extremely well. You did exactly what was required of you with the minimum of fuss.'

'I would've done the same,' said Wynter, sidling up. 'I would've got help if you'd sent me instead.'

'Yes you would, Wynter, but with the *maximum* of fuss,' replied Crossman. 'You court praise, Wynter, and that doesn't sit well on a man.'

Wynter nodded. He looked unusually serious, but without that pathetic expression which irritated Crossman so much. For some reason he commanded Crossman's attention, and that of the others, in a strong way.

'Yes, that's true,' Wynter said with quiet dignity. 'You can say that from the comfort of your cosy upbringing, Sergeant Crossman. But it an't easy, bein' born of the low classes and having to make your way in the world. You'll never know it, because you didn't have to do it, but making the most of what you've done gets to be a habit. If you don't, nobody so much as notices you. When you're wearin' these boots, you yell your victories from the rooftops, or nobody hears.'

Crossman stood, uncomfortable under the steady gaze of Private Wynter, not knowing how to answer him.

But Rupert Jarrard said, 'A boaster's a boaster, whether high or low, Wynter, and well you know it.'

'I didn't say you should admire such a thing,' answered Wynter. 'I said it gets to be a habit.'

'You're right, Wynter,' said Crossman, 'I should make allowances.'

Peterson introduced a little levity into the conversation, since she felt they were becoming far too serious.

'What are you saying, Wynter?' she cried. 'You've been gentry in your time.'

Wynter whirled on her. 'Me? How so?'

'Why, for a short while you were one of the wealthiest men in the Crimea – you had a share in a chest full of money. Surely you can't have forgotten so quickly? You were rich.'

He grimaced at her joke. 'Till it was all burned.'

'Still, you had your hour.'

He found it in himself to grin at the ring of faces around him.

'Why so I was,' he said. 'As rich as Croesus for a while – I wisht I'd had the chance to spend some, though.'

'Don't we all, Wynter,' said Crossman. 'Don't we all.'

28

___

Back in the hotel at Kadikoi Crossman was sitting sewing a tear in his uniform. He was working by the light of a candle stub, the oil for the lamp having run out. There was no more oil available for the moment. Someone said there were bottles of lamp oil to be had by the plenty, but these were buried in the hold of some ship either now on the high seas or bobbing with fifty others in Balaclava harbour.

He had just finished the last stitch and was biting the cotton, when Rupert Jarrard came in through the doorway.

'Hello, all on your own, Jack?'

'Come in, Rupert, take a seat. I thought the men would enjoy a night at the canteen after their fox hunt. Even Devlin has gone – carried between Wynter and Clancy. God knows how they'll get him home again afterwards, for they're certain to be in a drunken state.'

Jarrard sat down and took out a cigar case, offering one to Crossman.

'No thanks, Rupert – I'll smoke my pipe.'

The two men eventually lit up after Crossman had filled the bowl of his chibouque, and they sat in the peace of the quiet evening, comfortable enough in one another's company, not always needing polite talk to fill in the gaps.

Inevitably, when they did speak, it was to discuss some new invention.

'I have heard,' said Jarrard, 'that a Belgian musician by the name of Adolphe Sax has invented a new wind instrument.'

'Old hat, Rupert. It was introduced to military bands nearly a decade ago.'

'Well, it's new to me,' Jarrard said. 'What is it exactly, Jack? I understand it uses a reed, like an oboe.'

'It is neither fish nor fowl, Rupert,' said Crossman, emphatically. 'It is Cornucopia-shaped. It is made of brass, like a trumpet, yet to all intents and purposes it is as you say, a woodwind instrument. My opinion is that the *saxophone* – the very name of the object is decidedly vulgar – is not a musical instrument at all in the true sense of the word. There are too many valves and fiddly bits on the stem and the sound is reminiscent of cattle being castrated.'

'You don't like this saxophone,' Jarrard said, stating the obvious.

'I abhor the instrument. I think it is the epitome of all that is bad taste in modern music. It has the dirty-sounding blare of a fallen woman; it has a form which recalls the sinuous shape of the serpent in the garden of Eden, responsible for original sin; its player becomes far too intimate with it during performances and there is something in the manner of its glitter which reminds me of worthless decorative tinsel at a masquerade.'

Jarrard grinned and took the cigar from his mouth. He said, 'I *like* this instrument.'

'That is because you are from the ex-colonies, Rupert, and cannot discern between the refined and the uncouth.'

Jarrard stuck the cigar back in his mouth in a belligerent fashion. 'By God, if I thought you were serious, Jack, I'd take you outside and show you the difference between a refined fist and an uncouth one,' he said, out of the side of his mouth.

'Before you do that I have to warn you I am an accomplished pugilist, Rupert, in the style of the champion John

Broughton, who when he was alive taught my grandfather the art of fisticuffs – and of course my grandfather passed on his learning to me.'

'Well I don't have a style, Jack, I just knock people down like I knocked down that grizzly bear out west – struck him on the nose with my bare fist and laid him out cold.'

'That sounds like a tall story, Rupert.'

Fortunately for both men at that moment the doorway was darkened by a figure. Crossman looked up to see Lieutenant Dalton-James standing there, looking very stiff and formal in his rifle green. The lieutenant seemed agitated as he stared at Crossman, who got to his feet.

'Sir? Can I help you?'

The thought went through Crossman's mind that the lieutenant had come to settle a score with him. Crossman had suddenly remembered he had sent Dalton-James on a fool's errand the night the sergeant had left for the hills. He wondered if Lavinia Durham had given the lieutenant short shrift and then told him that it was probably Sergeant Crossman who had set him up. No doubt Dalton-James wanted revenge.

'I – er – I rather wanted to speak to Mr Jarrard, if I may?' answered an unusually subdued Dalton-James. 'Could we speak outside in private, sir?'

Jarrard looked at Crossman and then said to Dalton-James, 'By all means. Outside, you say?'

'If it is convenient.'

Jarrard followed the lieutenant through the doorway and they stood some ten yards from the hovel. They could not move further because the mud-surfaced track to and from Balaclava was still heavy with traffic. In fact Dalton-James had to move out of the way of an ox-drawn *araba* while speaking in a low and serious voice to the American correspondent. Crossman wondered if he himself were the subject of the conversation, since Dalton-James had been so anxious not to let him hear. Crossman stared through the doorway at the silhouettes of the two men, as the sun went down to leave a red balanced sky in its wake.

Finally, after a brief nod from Jarrard, Dalton-James strode off in the direction of Balaclava harbour.

Jarrard came back and resumed his position at the table.

Crossman made them both a drink of field coffee.

'Well, Rupert,' he said, 'aren't you going to tell me?'

Jarrard sipped the foul coffee and made a face, before saying, 'It was in confidence, you understand. I promised him I wouldn't tell anyone.'

'Yes, but you can tell *me*,' protested Crossman. 'I am the soul of discretion.'

'No,' Jarrard said, sighing heavily, 'you misunderstand me. I mean it's an affair of honour. A duel. Pistols for two, coffee for one . . .'

Crossman's eyes opened very wide.

'He's asked you to be his second?'

'Yes. Said he needed me because I'm a civilian. Anyone in the army would get into trouble from Lord Raglan.'

'*He's* in the army, damn it.'

'So's his opponent and his opponent's second. However, Dalton-James does not want to get anyone else involved. He says although I'm an American I have the bearing and trappings of a gentleman . . .'

'How condescending of him.'

'. . . and as such I qualify for the position of an officer and gentleman's second. He begged me to assist him in this matter. Pistols at dawn tomorrow – six o'clock on the dot. What an unearthly hour! Sundown is when we American westerners favour a shoot-out. Sundown is a warm, mellow time, just right for such chivalric activities as single combat. I would not be able to shoot straight for yawning before breakfast. And conditions so cold and misty for a gunfight!

'Actually, you Europeans don't have a monopoly on early

morning duels. Our southern gentlemen enjoy the same pastime. They use it as a means to cull the poor shots, should they ever need to go to war with the north.'

'Rupert, this is very serious. Who is the other man? We must put a stop to this.'

'You see, I knew I couldn't trust you, Jack.'

'Yes, but—

'There are no buts, Jack – I have given my word to Dalton-James, just as you have given your word to me. We must say nothing and carry out the affair.'

'Damn it, Rupert, at least tell me who is the other man. I insist on knowing that much at least.'

Jarrard sighed, going to the doorway and looking out. The stub of his cigar glowed very red against the darkening sky beyond. He threw the butt out into the roadway, causing a shower of sparks to tumble along the road. Then he turned and faced Crossman.

'All right,' he said, 'you asked for it. I didn't want to have to tell you this, Jack, because it will hurt. The man Dalton-James is to fight is Captain Durham. The captain had an argument over the amount of time Dalton-James was spending with his wife. It became heated and resulted in a challenge. Now I know you and Mrs Durham—'

'This is ridiculous,' interrupted Crossman, feeling the blood drain from his face.

'Well it may be, but it's certainly going to happen.'

'No, I mean, Lavinia – that is, Mrs Durham – couldn't possibly – good Lord, not Dalton-James.'

Jarrard put a steadying hand on his friend's shoulder.

'I know, Jack, but whatever you and I think of the man, he is handsome, in those tight trousers and his rifle greens.'

'I still cannot believe that she has been with Dalton-James. I was certain she would find him an obnoxious bore . . .'

Jarrard looked sharply at Crossman, who turned away in embarrassment.

'Jack? You're withholding something. What did you mean by that remark? You were *certain*?'

Crossman sighed. 'I played a trick on Dalton-James in a moment of rashness. I was summoned to meet the lady and I gave Dalton-James the note, told him it was addressed to him. He went along thinking she had asked to see him. I never dreamed it would come to this. It was just a joke.'

'Someone will die laughing.'

'Oh God, Rupert. I have to stop this affair. Please release me from my promise.'

Jarrard shook his head. 'No can do, Jack. You'll have to live with the consequences, I'm afraid. You should have thought before you played your little trick. Now I have to go and see Captain Durham to make the final arrangements.'

Crossman grabbed the sleeve of his friend's jacket.

'Rupert, listen to me. I have no doubt that Captain Durham is a poor shot and will probably miss his opponent. Dalton-James, however, is a crackshot. It will be murder.'

Jarrard looked uncomfortable. 'What do you propose?' he asked.

'You're one of the seconds. Fix the pistols. Load them with gunpowder and wadding only. Leave out the ball.'

'You honestly think that a man with Dalton-James's experience of firearms will not know the difference when he fires his pistol? They will accuse me of mishandling the affair. I'm sorry. Now good night, Jack.'

Crossman turned away. 'Good night, Rupert.'

Once Jarrard was gone, Crossman slumped into a rickety chair. What was he going to do? Dalton-James and Lavinia? He did not like the picture in his head. What on earth made her go for a man like him? Crossman still could not believe it. The man was a revolting snob. One of those old Harrovian boys who used to lisp just for the effect. Crossman decided he had to talk to Lavinia just one more time.

Risking a confrontation with Captain Durham himself,

Crossman went to Lavinia Durham's lodgings. Investigating the premises before entering, Crossman found to his good luck that she was alone. Looking through the back window he could see her brushing her long hair in front of a cracked shaving mirror. She was a very attractive woman, especially with her locks falling over her shoulders, tumbling down between her breasts.

Once he knew she had no one with her, he quickly went round the front of the dwelling, mortified that he would be caught peeking into a lady's bedroom window. Such an offence would have been the death of him, if not from firing squad from his own embarrassment. He went into the house without knocking, but called her name softly before entering her room.

She turned as he stepped through the doorway.

'Alex, is that you? Oh, I thought you had been killed. You're all right?'

When he was by her side she got up and linked her arms around his neck and kissed his lips.

Gently he unlocked her hands and stood back from her.

'Lavinia, I didn't want to come here tonight to revive something which should never have taken place in the first instance. There's a much more serious matter to deal with. What about this duel between Durham and Dalton-James?'

29

The duel was due to take place in an orchard just east of Kadikoi. Mist lay in a thick layer over the whole surface of the ground, so that if a body fell it would lie unseen below the surface of this white, mysterious mantle until retrieved. A weak, waxy sun tried to stir the mist into leaving, but the vapour remained obstinate and clung to the turf with tiny claws, refusing to budge.

Two men, stripped to their shirts in the cold air, selected a pistol each from the velvet-lined box proffered by Ensign Chauncy, Captain Durham's second. Rupert Jarrard had already inspected the weapons and found them both to be loaded and primed, ready to kill or wound.

Jarrard stood a little off now, by the referee, a French lieutenant by the name of Lehmann. The lieutenant was also a surgeon of sorts, though without paper qualifications. He had told Jarrard he had been through medical training, but had spent too much time chasing ladies and drinking wine with his friends, so never actually managed to become a doctor.

Lieutenant Lehmann had his own pistol, ready to shoot either of the combatants should they dishonour themselves by breaking the code of practice. If a man turned and fired before the requisite ten paces, then that man would fall foul of the referee's weapon. The French lieutenant, a Zouave in his embroidered blue coatee and red pantaloons, had been the referee of many duels and knew his business.

'Are you ready, gentlemen?' he asked in his heavy accent. 'Please be on your marks.'

Dalton-James and Durham stood back to back, their pistols cocked. The former's brow had only a slight frown marring its otherwise smooth features, but the latter was deathly white and perspiring a little. For his part Dalton-James gave the impression of having been told he could not go hunting deer this morning after all, but would have to accompany his younger sisters to the milliners. Durham looked as if someone had told him he was going to die within the next few minutes.

'Gentlemen, start walking *now*,' said the Zouave.

Both men had taken but one pace when two riders came out of the mist, galloping up to the tree line.

'Halt!' screamed the Frenchman. 'Please desist from the duel for one moment, gentlemen.'

All five men – the two combatants, the two seconds and the referee – turned to see who it was who had the temerity to interrupt their early morning business.

'Jack?' cried Jarrard, seeing Crossman on one of the horses. 'What are you doing here?'

'Lavinia!' said Durham, in a dull tone.

'Mrs Durham!' Dalton-James exclaimed.

The other two gentlemen said nothing, though the Frenchman shrugged and the ensign shook his head in bewilderment.

Dalton-James was the first to recover from the shock.

'Sergeant Crossman,' he said sternly. 'You will oblige me by taking Mrs Durham back to her quarters.'

'No, sir,' replied Crossman, 'I will not. Mrs Durham is free to go where she chooses. We happen to be out on a recreational ride together.' He dismounted, saying to the lady in question, 'I think we'll rest the horses here, ma'am. There's plenty of lush green grass on the edge of the orchard. We don't want to take them back blown.'

'Sergeant Crossman,' screeched Dalton-James, red in the face, 'I gave you an order.'

'I'm afraid you're outranked, Lieutenant,' said Mrs Durham, dismounting, her highly polished brown boots disappearing down into the mist along with the hem of her riding habit, 'I asked General Buller to provide me with an escort and he ordered Sergeant Crossman to remain with me wherever I wished to go. I chose to come here, to this pretty little orchard.'

'Strict instructions, sir,' Crossman said. 'There would be hell to pay with the general if I were to assert myself with Mrs Durham – I'm only a lowly sergeant, after all.'

Jarrard snorted in merriment, while Dalton-James continued to look thunderous.

The lieutenant said, 'Captain Durham, please order your wife to return to her quarters.'

Durham said weakly, 'Lavinia, dear—'

'Bertie,' she interrupted, 'you may save your words. I am staying here. If Lieutenant Dalton-James is to kill you, then I must be here to watch it. I am your wife, after all. You are going to kill my husband, Lieutenant, are you not?'

Dalton-James looked embarrassed. 'He has an equal opportunity of shooting me also, Mrs Durham.'

'Don't be ridiculous, Lieutenant,' she said, 'you know he can't shoot for toffee. Bertie couldn't hit his own horse if he were sitting in the saddle at the time. So, make no mistake about it, sir – you will be shooting a man in cold blood.'

'He called me a liar, ma'am.'

'Then of course he must die for it, because he will not retract what he believes to be the truth.'

Dalton-James bristled. 'This is rather indelicate, ma'am. You realize what he has accused me of? It would be indiscreet of me to state it here in front of witnesses – quite impossible.'

'Lieutenant,' she said in a low husky voice, 'if my husband accused you of something, he did so because he believed it to be true. We have been much in each other's company of late, you and I, but of course Captain Durham is mistaken in the idea that you forced yourself upon me, or that we talked of improper subjects. I have told Durham we remained within all the rules of propriety, but by that time you had challenged him. He has his code of honour too, you know. Like a good, watchful husband Captain Durham feels it is his duty to protect the innocence of his wife. He is wrong, of course, in thinking that you did not have my welfare at heart, and that you behaved in any way but what was appropriate. Captain Durham has always been a little strongheaded when it comes to defending me – he is rather overfond of me, you understand. Would you kill one of your brother officers for being overzealous in his protection of a lady – the wife he holds dear?'

Dalton-James stared at Mrs Durham, next at Crossman, and finally at Captain Durham. Then without a word he fired his pistol into the ground, disturbing the mist. The sound of the shot rang through the orchard. The lieutenant then bowed to Mrs Durham, saying, 'By your leave, ma'am,' made his apologies to the French Zouave, before striding off towards Jarrard who was holding his coatee.

Durham, not to be outdone by this wonderfully dramatic exit, also fired his pistol into the turf. Unfortunately the bullet hit a flint and ricocheted away into the branches of the trees, making one or two of the observers – including Captain Durham himself – flinch and duck their heads. After that it was difficult for him to stride off in a similar manner to Dalton-James.

Instead he took his wife aside and spoke to her quietly, before retrieving his coatee from the patient ensign.

The ensign's expression showed how relieved he was that the duel had been called off. He was a young lad, newly commissioned, and the whole thing was a bit of a nightmare for him. Durham had requested his aid, he had given it rather unwillingly, and now he was quite glad that there was not a body lying on the orchard floor, seeping blood into fallen leaves and rotten fruit. Had there been so, he might have been sent home in disgrace.

A week later, Sergeant Crossman and his men – including Devlin, who was now on the mend – were in the hovel they called their quarters when Major Lovelace came to the doorway beaming.

'What is it, sir?' cried Wynter. 'Is the war over?'

The major shook his head. 'I'm afraid not, Wynter, but news almost as good. You remember the second strong box you hid in the rocks. We have retrieved it.'

'Yes, sir,' said Crossman, with bated breath. 'Did it contain anything valuable?'

'Only ten thousand pounds in silver – Maria Theresa dollars, minted in Austria.'

He tossed a coin to Crossman, who inspected the large silver piece. On one side was an Imperial double-headed eagle, and on the other a profile of a lady.

'Ten thousand pounds?' he repeated for the benefit of his men. 'Shared between us?'

'Two thousand for me, two thousand for Lieutenant Dalton-James, two thousand for you as commander of the fox hunt, Sergeant Crossman, and a thousand for each of the men.'

Wynter's eyes bulged. 'A thousand pounds – I'm rich,' he said.

Lovelace laughed. 'Hardly rich, Lance Corporal Wynter, but more money than you've seen in your life before, I expect.'

'When do we get it?' asked Clancy. 'Can I have mine now?'

'I'm afraid it'll have to wait until after the war is over, Private Clancy,' said Major Lovelace. 'The box is being transported back to England. You – or in the event of something happening to you, your nearest relative – will receive the money once the Army of the East returns to Britain.'

There was a momentary look of disappointment on the

faces of the soldiers, but they soon cheered up again, chattering amongst themselves, telling each other how they were going to spend their money once they had it in their hands.

Major Lovelace took Sergeant Crossman aside.

'Well done, Sergeant,' he said. 'You deserve your prize money. I don't think the lieutenant and I actually earned ours – the rescue was rather easier than your part of the action – but we're not going to pass our share over. We have expenses in life too.'

'Of course, sir,' grinned Crossman. 'I'm not greedy – and the men are happy with their share.' He became serious again. 'There's just one thing that puzzles me, sir. Why paper money for the troops in Sebastopol – and then this chest of silver coin? Who was the coin intended for?'

Lovelace looked grim. 'I've thought about that too. There's a conclusion I've come to, which I do not like. The money was intended for a non-Russian, a foreigner, who insisted on currency that was instantly redeemable.'

'A foreigner?'

'A traitor, Sergeant. I believe that money was destined to come here, to someone on our side. Payment for services rendered, or to be rendered. I think we have a traitor in our ranks somewhere – not just some Greek or Bulgarian servant – someone of high rank.

Crossman's mind ran over the possibilities.

'Mr Upton? The Englishman who came out of Sebastopol?'

'No – too obvious. We've had him thoroughly investigated. I think it goes deeper into us than that. I really think the traitor is someone very close to us, one of us.'

'Have you any ideas, sir?'

'Not yet – but I will have. Keep your eyes and ears open, Sergeant – and your mind. We'll get him, eventually. Until then, let me shake your hand, sir. You have put two thousand pounds into mine – it is the least I can do.'

Crossman grinned and took the proffered hand, shaking it firmly.

Other titles available from Robinson Publishing

The Devil's Own   Garry Douglas Kilworth   £6.99 ☐
Sergeant Jack Crossman is a tough, shrewd and skilful soldier, a member of the proud 88th regiment also known as The Devil's Own. He is nicknamed 'Fancy Jack' by his comrades because although an aristocrat by birth, he has chosen to join the ranks instead of buying a commission. The military scene is set in the Crimean War, notoriously one of the most brutal and bloody conflicts of the 19th century. Within the regiment, Crossman is picked out to lead a covert operation, knowing that the outcome could alter the course of the war.

The Sea Warriors   Richard Woodman   £7.99 ☐
Maritime heroes of the late 18th and early 19th centuries stride across these pages – some like Warren, Pellew, Cochrane and Collingwood are still renowned; others are almost unknown today, yet their brilliant exploits deserve to be pulled from under the long shadow of the greatest naval figure of all, Horatio Nelson. The Royal Navy's struggle is set against the political backdrop of the Napoleonic Wars and the sea war with America.

The Escape of Charles II   Richard Ollard   £7.99 ☐
Charles II's escape after the Battle of Worcester in 1651 is an extraordinary tale of adventure and suspense. This new edition of Ollard's classic book vividly reconstructs the six weeks during which the King was on the run. His great determination and good humour through it all won the admiration of many who risked their lives to aid him. This is a fascinating view of life in 17th century England.

Robinson books are available from all good bookshops or can be ordered direct from the publisher. Just tick the title you want and fill in the form below.

TBS Direct, Colchester Road, Frating Green, Colchester, Essex CO7 7DW
Tel: +44 (0) 1206 255777   Fax: +44 (0) 1206 255914   Email: sales@tbs-ltd.co.uk

UK/BFPO customers please allow £1.00 for p&p for the first book, plus 50p for the second, plus 30p for each additional book up to a maximum charge of £3.00.

Overseas customers (inc. Ireland), please allow £2.00 for the first book, plus £1.00 for the second, plus 50p for each additional book.

Please send me the titles ticked above.

NAME (block letters) ....

ADDRESS ....

....

POSTCODE ....

I enclose a cheque/PO (payable to TBS Direct) for ....

I wish to pay by Switch/Credit card

Number ....

Card Expiry Date ....   Switch Issue Number ....